FOREVER
LARGE
PRINT

Praise for *Axes & O's*

"Everything I crave in a good MMF: blazing hot spice, beautifully complex characters, and kink that's both hot and heartfelt. And can't forget that broody lumberjack."

—Sara Cate, *USA Today* bestselling author

"Sweet, seductive, and hella kinky. Kayla knows exactly how to make readers swoon endlessly and blush profusely. An adventure in the woods not to be missed."

—Elliott Rose, author of *Chasing the Wild*

"Steamy, snowed-in, and deeply tender. Kayla has a way of blending raw emotion with irresistible spice, and this one is no exception."

—Bailey Hannah, *USA Today* bestselling author

Also by Kayla Grosse

Starlight Haven Lumbersnacks

Axes & O's

Brother Puckers

Trick Shot

Puck Shy

The Cowboys of Night Hawk

Rein Me In

Rope Me In

Standalones

Scrooged for the Holidays

Stuffed with Cole

Struck by Eros

Silver Foxed

Whirlwind

Change of Pace

I Like You Like That

AXE MARKS THE SPOT

KAYLA GROSSE

FOREVER
LARGE PRINT

Forever
Hachette Book Group
1290 Avenue of the Americas, New York, NY 10104
read-forever.com
@readforeverpub

First Forever Trade Paperback Edition: July 2026

Forever is an imprint of Grand Central Publishing. The Forever name and logo are registered trademarks of Hachette Book Group, Inc.

Print book interior design by Jeff Stiefel.

Library of Congress Cataloging-in-Publication Data has been applied for.

ISBNs: 9781538780602 (Trade paperback);
9781538783009 (Trade paperback—Large print);
9781538780619 (Ebook)

Axe Marks the Spot Vibes Playlist

AXE MARKS THE SPOT

@DomInTheWoods
New Upload From @DomInTheWoods

[IMAGE ALT TEXT]: Dom is sitting in a chair close to the camera. Only his jaw and lips are visible. He's wearing a black button-up shirt with the sleeves rolled up to expose his forearms, and a few buttons are undone to show off his muscular chest.

Auto Captions:

Did you drink your water today, baby?

I'll take your silence as a no.

Such a defiant woman you are.

I know you're sorry, but a sorry doesn't keep you hydrated. I'm only looking out for your well-being, you know that, right?

Hmm, well, I think you want to be punished, don't you?

What privilege should I take away from you for disobeying me?

You don't know?

*I'm thinking no underwear for a week, your bare p*ssy brushing against your clothes while you work, the rough fabric of your jeans the only touch you'll receive until you can't take it anymore. Until you're begging me to let you touch yourself.*

Hmm...No, no, that won't do. You'd like that too much, wouldn't you?

*You're such a beautiful and naughty little sl*t.* [End video]

100,222 Views
Username @DomInTheWoods
view all 100 comments
1 HOUR AGO

1
Lindsey

You know that limbo between exhausted and horny? That state of being where you want to face-plant into bed, but you could really go for a good orgasm . . . or two?

No? Just me?

"Mom!" Kas yells, scaring the shit out of me to the point where I jump, hand flying over my chest as my heart beats rapidly.

"Goodness, Kasandra. I'm right here."

My eight-year-old rolls her eyes at me from across the picnic table. It's her new favorite way to express her annoyance, one I've tried and failed to nip in the bud.

"I've been calling you for five minutes," she chides.

"You have not been," I assure her.

"She yelled it five times."

I flick my gaze to my brother, Nathan, who's sitting next to Kas. His scruffy face is lit with a smile, but there's concern in his earthy brown eyes as he takes a bite of his funnel cake.

I hold back a sigh and give my attention to Kas, who's shifting on her butt excitedly as if she's ready to take off and run somewhere. Which is odd to me because she hates running.

"I'm sorry." I exhale and put a smile on. "What do you need, honey?"

"Uncle Nate said there's a kids' obstacle course. I was asking if I could go."

"I thought you wanted to watch the speed pole climbing." I check the time on my phone. "It starts in thirty minutes."

"*You* want to watch that, Mom."

Nathan chuckles, and I bite the inside of my cheek. My kid is becoming sassier every day, a trait I fear she inherited from both me and my smart-ass brother.

"I'll take her. You can go watch loggers climb poles." He waggles his dark eyebrows at me, and I glare at him.

"Yeah, Mom," Kas adds, Nathan's innuendo thankfully going over her head.

I take a sip of my sweating lemonade, the cold

condensation on the cup feeling good against the heated skin of my hand. It's July, and while it's fairly cool in our little mountain town of Starlight Haven during the summers, it's still hot enough that I'm sweating even while wearing a tank and shorts.

I look from my bouncing kid, who's had too much sugar today, to my younger brother, who's observing me with interest. I'm still getting used to the fact that he looks like a logger now. The once clean-shaven, ex-corporate businessman used to wear button-up shirts, slacks, and loafers. Now, he's in a T-shirt that sports the logo of the logging company that Morgan and Fox, his partners and soon-to-be husband and wife, own and a pair of jeans with red suspenders. His tapered brown hair is still neatly styled, but the beard and laid-back look throw me every time. It's been a year and a half since he met them, and yet it feels like he's transformed overnight.

"Okay, but you have to promise to stay in your Uncle Nate's line of sight."

"I'm eight," she groans.

Nathan holds in his chuckle, but a bit of a snort breaks through. God, this kid. I should be grateful she inherited my and my brother's cheek over the stick-up-his-ass personality of my ex-husband, Jeremy, but sometimes it's a lot. Especially when I'm tired, overworked, and in desperate need of...well, release.

It's been years now since I've had sex that wasn't with a silicone dick. Two years, to be exact. I feel as if my pussy is gnawing at the bars of my self-imposed chastity.

God, Nathan is right. I do want to watch loggers climb poles. And it would be nice if I was climbing one of their poles, too.

"Sis?"

I flush, and I snap my eyes to his. I should not be thinking about that right now. What the hell is wrong with me?

You're exhausted and horny, remember?

I push back the thought and shoot Kas the classic mom-eyebrow, head tilted just enough in question. "And you won't try to ditch your uncle?"

She sighs. "I won't, but Starlight Haven is safe. Lowest crime rate in California, remember?"

Nathan tugs on Kas's ponytail and chuckles. "She is right about that."

"Regardless, you stay in sight of your uncle, or you'll lose your video game privileges. Got it, Kas?"

"You wouldn't!"

She's right, I probably wouldn't enforce it with how things have been going for me lately, but I nod and keep my features stern. "I would."

Kas presses her lips together. It's no secret she loves her video games and would dramatically "die" without them. Or so she's said before. I often think it makes me a bad mom, letting her play them so young, but I'm doing the best I can. After a long day of working in the ER, I don't have the energy to force her to go outside all the time. I guess I should be glad she wants to go to the obstacle course now.

"Okay," she says finally.

"Alright, then, have fun."

Kas jumps up. "Let's go, Uncle Nate!"

"Go wash your hands and face and use the bathrooms first—there aren't any over by the course. The portable bathrooms and sinks are right there," Nathan says, pointing to an area behind me in his line of sight.

Kas takes off without complaint, and I sigh. "I'm glad she listens to you, at least."

"She listens to you, too." He smiles softly, polishing off the last bite of his funnel cake and brushing the powdered sugar from his hands.

"Only after arguing with me."

I take another sip of my lemonade as Nathan stares at me. "You okay, Linds?"

"Yep, I'm fine."

"Liar. Tell you what—why don't I watch Kas for the rest of the afternoon? I bet you can finally meet a lumbersnack to throw you around." He waggles his eyebrows at me teasingly.

I laugh. "I forgot I told you that."

"You've only been talking about it since you moved here. Truthfully, I think you wanted to come to the games today more than Kas did."

Nathan's right. Kas didn't really want to come to this event at all. I convinced her with the promise of funnel cake and other sugary items. Plus, Fox and Morgan's company, Starlight Lumber & Logging, hosts the games. The couple doesn't participate in it anymore, but they are a huge part of setting it up and getting sponsors for it.

"Linds? Are you really fine?"

I look into my younger brother's eyes. We've always been close—even more so after the death of our dad three years ago from a stroke and then my divorce from Jeremy. In many ways, he's become more than just a brother. He's a friend and a solid male presence in Kas's life.

But though we're close, I'm not going to share with him that I'm not only exhausted but in need of a good lay, too. I'm also not going to tell him that the reason I haven't put myself out there in the past two years is because I'm still dealing with hang-ups from my ex. That's not stuff I want to talk about with Nathan, especially when he has such an amazing relationship with not one but two people. A relationship I can't help but feel jealous of sometimes.

"I really am," I assure him. "I'm just tired."

He taps his fingers on the table. "I don't believe you, but maybe if I get you liquored up tonight, you'll spill the beans."

"Tonight?"

"Okay, yeah. Definitely not fine if you forgot."

"What's tonight?"

"Kas has that birthday sleepover at Moira's, and you're going out to Moose's Bar with Fox, Morgan, and me. No backing out."

I want to smack my forehead. "I totally forgot."

"Obviously." He chuckles.

"Maybe instead of watching the speed climbing, I'll just go home and nap. I could use the sleep instead. I can pick up Kas's room, too, while she's with you."

"Nope. Not happening. And why are you cleaning Kas's room? She's old enough to do that on her own."

My stomach sours and gurgles, the acidic lemonade turning into heartburn. Nathan's question is valid, and I know it's not meant to be mean, but it only reinforces this idea I have of myself: I'm not a great mom. I probably let Kas get away with too much, but she's been through a lot between her dad and me breaking up and then moving to a small town. I think it also hurt when her grandma left. The two of them had become close. My mom tried her best but deemed small-town life not for her. She moved back to our home city, Santa Solana, at the beginning of the year.

"I—wait, where is Kas? She should be done by now."

Nathan points up ahead. "I've got eyes on her. She's talking to some kids."

I peer in that direction and see she's chatting with a boy and girl her age. My heart warms at seeing it, and a bit of my stomachache eases. Besides her best friend, Moira, whose birthday I forgot about—which reminds me, I need to get the kid a gift—she doesn't have many friends. She's like me in that way, too.

I turn back to Nathan to find him still staring at me. But I don't want to get into why I clean my kid's room, so I divert. "Okay, fine. I'll go to the speed climbing event now, and still meet you all at Moose's later. But only if you stop asking if I'm okay."

Nathan looks hesitant at first but eventually nods. "Fine."

"Uncle Nate!" Kas runs up to the side of the picnic table. Her short auburn hair swishes around her cherubic face. "Tyler and Sara are here for the course, too. Can we go now?"

He glances at the two kids behind me with a smile and stands. "Of course we can."

I stand, too, and move from the table over to Kas, who's bouncing on her feet and looks more than happy about her new afternoon plans. I thought Kas only wanted to play video games and hang with Moira, but maybe that's because I don't get her out enough to be with more kids. I'm just so busy and tired from working three twelve-hour shifts a week and picking up extras.

I wipe off a bit of powdered sugar still on her cheek. "Have fun, and don't get hurt."

"If I do, you'll fix me. You're a nurse."

My heart clenches, and I pull Kas in for a

hug. She goes willingly, and I'm glad she hasn't hit that phase yet where she finds me embarrassing. "I'd rather not have to fix you. Now go, have fun." She lets out a little excited noise and runs toward her friends.

Kas yells for Nathan, and he bumps my shoulder with his. "Go have fun, Linds. You deserve it. And you'd better not go home!"

I watch them leave while debating if I should defy my brother or stay. I could get some cleaning done, maybe even take a bath instead of having a nap.

But then I remember I need to get a gift for Moira. Ugh, Mom life.

I walk out of the open-sided tent and head toward the parking lot instead of the speed climbing event. There's a toy store not far from here, but I'm not sure they're open today—the downside of living in a small town is the stores are all closed on random days and times, even on Saturdays.

I pull my phone from my purse to look it up and get only two steps before I run into something hard.

A startled yelp escapes me as a solid weight slams into my body, knocking me off-balance.

Gravity yanks at my spine, the ground tilting away beneath me. But before I can fall, strong hands clamp around my biceps. Air rushes past my ears, my stomach flipping with the sudden shift in direction.

In a split second, I'm upright again, feet planted, chest flush against a sturdy and warm chest. I squeeze my eyes shut and inhale a breath, the scent of cedar and spicy vanilla wafting into my nose.

"Are you okay?"

The deep male voice thrums through my body like the vibrations of a guitar string. If my pussy could meow, I think she'd be doing it. I was horny before, but that voice mixed with his warm body and touch has clicked the lock of my self-imposed chastity belt wide open. I don't even know what he looks like, but in a way, I don't think I even need to.

"Miss?"

Did he just call me *miss*? I think I love him already. People usually call me *ma'am* now that I'm over thirty.

I take in another breath and open my eyes, but part of me wishes I hadn't. If I didn't have thick thighs and he wasn't looking at my face, he'd have seen me squeeze my legs together because *holy lumbersnack*.

Determined hazel eyes stare into mine. They're a mix of blue and green with flecks of golden brown and a dark-brown ring around the iris. The midday sun above us only adds to their power, drawing me in and making me forget my own name and the fact that I'm pressed against a strange man who I'm staring at like a cut of Wagyu beef.

"Do you need help?" His light-pink lips, framed by a well-trimmed dark-brown, nearly black beard mixed with silver hairs, say the magic words that finally break me from my spell.

"No, no. I'm fine."

He makes no move to pull away, but I don't, either. His hands on my biceps squeeze gently as he studies me with those beautiful eyes of his. My nipples, which, like my vagina, have a mind of their own all of a sudden, harden against what feels like a very muscular chest. Heat rises to my cheeks, and I step back, forcing him to drop his grip.

"You sure?" his velvet voice rumbles.

"Yeah, I'm sorry. I wasn't looking where I was going." I cross my arms over my tank-top-clad chest and look down at the ground. While

I'm curvy everywhere else, my boobs are small, so I only wore a thin bralette under my shirt. If I leave my hands down, this insanely attractive man will see my headlights.

"It's okay. I wasn't, either. I'm glad you're okay."

He clears his throat with a sound almost like authority. The tone of it has my gaze snapping to his without thinking. His eyes are partially closed now to block out some of the sun, and to avoid looking at the rest of him or falling into a trance staring at his eyes, I focus on his nose. It's a nice nose. A *perfect* nose. Is having a nose fetish a thing?

"Miss?"

"Uh, yeah?" My voice comes out in a weird and squeaky tone that has him chuckling.

"Are you sure you're good?"

I dare a glance at his eyes once more but force myself not to look anywhere else. I think I'm going to find every single body part, down to this man's ankles, attractive. At least I've already seen his eyes, right?

"I'm good. Just tired." I don't know why I told him that—I felt like I had to justify my weird behavior, I guess.

The stranger's hazel pools study me, and after

a second, it's almost as if he's staring at me with disapproval. I dip my chin to the ground and drop my arms from my chest, hiking my purse up my shoulder and slipping the phone I'd managed to hold on to into the main pocket.

"Sorry I ran into you again," I mutter. "Have a nice day."

I hear a sound slip from his mouth as if he's about to say something, but I don't wait to hear what it is. I walk off, not looking back. And while I'm not positive he's watching me walk away, I swear I feel the weight of his stare on my back. My skin prickles, and my nipples, which haven't gotten the memo to chill, become so stiff they hurt. I cross my arms over my chest again, weaving my way through people.

When I get to my car, I pull out my keys then stop and look at my reflection in the driver's side window. My medium-length brown hair mixed with blond highlights is ruffled and a bit frizzy from the summer heat and my run-in with Mr. Perfect Nose. My chest is heaving from the mad dash I made to get away, and despite the light makeup I put on this morning and the flush on my cheeks, I do look tired.

There are imprints under my eyes from lack of

sleep, and the spark my brown pools once held is long gone. Not only from being exhausted, but from the last several years of my life, too.

I could listen to Nathan, stay here, and... hell, maybe Mr. Perfect Nose/Pretty Eyes is single. I *did* want a lumbersnack to throw me around. And that man... just by the strength of his hands and chest, I know he could throw even my plus-size frame around. That voice, too...

Shivers run up my spine, and I close my eyes to collect myself. I should turn around and go watch the games. I should listen to my brother and take advantage of the time I'm child-free. But that nagging voice in my head drowns out my needs and desires. I'm a mom first, and I've been slacking. I forgot about this slumber party, and Kas can't show up empty-handed.

I also can't forget my little A-frame cabin is a mess. It's gotten bad this week after I worked a couple of extra shifts to help pay off the lawyer fees I accumulated fighting dumbass Jeremy for primary physical custody and child support.

I nibble on the inside of my cheek. It's something I tend to do—biting my nails is another—when I'm stressed. However, there are no nails left to bite at this point.

My phone pings, snatching me from my thoughts, so I fish it out of my purse. It's a text from work asking if I can take a morning shift next week. I quickly respond that I can, grateful for the extra money, then decide it's a sign I need to tackle my responsibilities—no lumbersnacks or sex for me. I have shit to take care of that's more important.

2
Dane

"DANE, MY MAN. THERE you are!" Levi says, stretching his long-ass arms over his dark-blond head. He's one of those guys who's tall and gangly and looks like he's probably not that strong. But I've seen him split an eighteen-inch oak log with no problem.

He bends over and stretches some more before standing back to his full height. "I was beginning to think we'd lost you to the woods forever." He chuckles.

"Funny." I grin dryly. I throw my duffel with all my gear onto a folding table they've set up in a tent for competitors that's mostly empty now except for two other guys and Levi. "I ran into someone." *Literally.*

"A hot someone?"

I think of the woman I ran into—body made

of curves and soft lines with hard nipples pressed against my overheated chest. Her eyes reminded me of rich cognac, and I'd happily drink her in all damn day. My dick comes to life in my shorts at the thought, so I try to think of something else, like the speed pole competition I'm about to take part in.

My gaze meets Levi's as I open the zipper of my bag. The way he's grinning has me thinking I said my thoughts out loud, though I know I didn't.

"How'd you know?" I ask.

He bends down and tightens his knee brace. "I have a sixth sense for these things. Don't ask further questions."

I take out some of my gear, including my high-grip boots and climbing spurs. "You're a weird man, Levi. Sure you're not the one spending too much time in the woods?"

He chuckles again. "I do spend a lot of time there, but unlike you, I hang out with people in the real world, too."

"And you think I don't?"

"Says the man I see only a handful of times a year."

I could argue with him, remind Levi that I

don't work full-time for Starlight Lumber & Logging like he does, especially during the summer season when work is sparse. He also doesn't call Starlight Haven home like I do, choosing to find work as a logger in different parts of the country during the year. He has, however, been spending more time here lately, and many consider him a local.

What's more, I could remind him that I'm not a partier like many of the guys that drift through town for work are, but we've had this conversation before, every time he tries to get me to hang out with him. I don't mind Levi, even though he can be annoying, but I'm not a man who has meaningless hookups at bars or enjoys getting hammered. I haven't been since I was in my early twenties.

"I'm here now, aren't I?" I answer, choosing to keep things simple.

"You are, but only because the prize money is good. And you want to keep your Speed Pole Climbing Champion title five years in a row."

The corner of my lips tips up. "Do I need more of a reason?"

"Yeah, to hang out with people who aren't virtual."

My jaw ticks. This is one of those moments I'm finding Levi highly annoying. This line of questioning isn't new for him, and I know he's baiting me to get what he wants. It's his way of digging around in my personal life and an attempt to take a stab at my preferred line of work outside of logging, a line of work he doesn't understand or try to.

I swallow down my annoyance and give him the same dry smile from before. "That would mean I would have to hang out with you."

He clicks his tongue. "Yeah, and you'd have fun. Something you should try."

"And you think I don't have fun?"

"I mean, maybe. But I think in-person sex is better than virtual."

I look around the tent, glad the few competitors that were here before have gone, leaving us alone. I'm positive a volunteer will come get us so they can start the competition, though—I was late getting here, and I know our event is set to begin soon.

I sit down on a nearby chair and take off my hiking boots to put on my climbing ones. "Levi, you don't have to have sex to have fun. And need I remind you, what I do is not virtual sex."

"So you've told me, but that's hard to believe. Who plays virtual Dom to people online but doesn't have sex with them, even the virtual kind?"

I tie the laces of my shoes before I look back up at Levi. His arms are crossed over his chest, and there are questions mixed with judgment in his blue eyes. The look reminds me why I prefer my work as a Pro Dom online to be anonymous. Levi only knows because he came across my DomInTheWoods videos on the popular app I use called Loopr and recognized my neck tattoos and voice. He agreed to keep it close to the vest, which is something I appreciate about him.

But I'm pissed he brought it up. Nobody in town knows about said persona and line of work except my friends and the owners of Starlight Lumber & Logging, Fox and Morgan.

I lower my voice despite it only being us here. "You can think what you want, Levi, but that's not the kind of intimacy we share. Take my word for it or not, but keep your opinion to yourself." I lace my voice with the tone I use on my clients when they're being brats. It's lower in my register and has a darker edge to it.

I don't miss how the tone makes him automatically straighten.

Levi stares me down for a moment, attempting to retain whatever control he thinks he has over the conversation. But then, like a dog to his master, I see the moment he heels. His eyes soften, and his lips quirk into a smile.

"Damn, man, I won't say anything. But fuck, I see why people pay you the big bucks."

I stand and grab the rest of my gear from my bag. "If you want more examples, I'll send you my price list."

Levi, clearly still thinking I mean sex despite my declaration and warning, looks me up and down. "I don't have a thing for men. But maybe I can make an exception for you, Daney-boy."

It doesn't get past me that he's trying to regain some semblance of dominance over me. When he meets my gaze once more, I hold eye contact with him. I don't say anything, nor do I blink.

Eventually, he shifts on his feet and sticks his hands in his pockets. "Look, man, I'm sorry. I didn't mean to ruffle your feathers. I only wanted to hang out with you and have some fun. I bet you can find that hottie you ran into and invite her out if you want."

The woman's image enters my mind again. While she's exactly my type and obviously had a reaction to me, she ran away faster than a rabbit with a coyote on its tail. Besides that, I've got my hands full with work and am not looking for a relationship or a one-night stand. My Loopr account has gone viral more than once, and I've got a waiting list for my Pro Dom services.

"I'll think about it." I'm being honest, too. I *will* think about it, but I already know what my answer will be. I'm only throwing him a bone to ease the tension of our conversation and get out of the tent.

Levi turns and picks up his gloves and climbing belt from the folding table as I put my belt around my waist.

"I guess that's better than a no," he says.

"Are you both ready?"

Levi and I turn toward the voice of a volunteer, Cheryl, a blond local that normally works at the diner.

"That we are, Cheryl-baby," Levi says. "Think I can beat Dane here this year?"

Cheryl blushes when she looks at me. "Maybe, but probably not."

The skin around my eyes crinkles in amusement, and I nod at Cheryl in thanks while Levi groans and pats his hand over his heart.

"You wound me."

"He *is* the champion four years running," Cheryl reminds him.

"Five," I say confidently.

"Hey! You haven't won yet," Levi says. "I've been practicing. I've also put in way more logging hours than you have this year."

Levi's words are true, but I'm good at logging games, especially speed pole climbing. I know I'm going to win; there's no doubt in my mind.

I pat Levi on the back and then grab the rest of my gear. "You can try."

"Oh, Dane. I'm going to do more than try."

"You're going down, Dane!" Levi calls from the pole next to mine. On my other side is a man I don't know, probably an out-of-towner who came to try to win the prize money. All some of the guys here do is compete in competitions like this and even participate in world championships. But the ninety-foot speed pole climb is the only event I compete in, and I only do it here in Starlight Haven.

I'm sure these guys know it, too. A lot of them

might even have come here specifically to beat me and my record of four-point-seven-three seconds. Which I set last year and intend to beat by at least a half a second this year.

I think the man next to me says good luck, but I don't acknowledge him or Levi, who's talking to the man next to him. I inhale a calming breath as the announcer comes over the PA system to give us a ninety-second warning. I do a quick triple check of all my gear, making sure my fall-arrest harness is good for my descent after I win.

I secure my flipline, a rope to stabilize and assist my climb in my gloved hands, wrapping it securely around the pole. The buzz of the crowd cheering around the perimeter spikes my adrenaline, and a thirty-second warning is given. I hear grunts of the men around me, near battle cries, but I remain focused. Lifting my right leg, I secure my foot on the pole with my climbing spur.

Ba-boom. Ba-boom. Ba-boom. My heart accelerates in my chest, and I feel my pulse in my throat. It's easy to forget how much this competition excites me since it only happens once a year, but it returns to me quickly, lighting every nerve ending in me from the soles of my feet to the roots of my hair. I inhale again, and my muscles tense, ready and waiting for the final countdown.

"Competitors ready?" the announcer asks rhetorically. "Three—"

My hands grip my flipline, and everything in me screams *Win!*

"Two—"

My calves tighten, and I relax my jaw so I don't grind my teeth.

"One—"

I fill my lungs with air and focus my eyes on the wood grain of the pole.

"Go!"

My muscles bunch and release as I explode upward off the safety cushion beneath the pole. I drive my left foot up, sticking the spike on my high-grip boot into the wood. My right leg follows, and I repeat the process, my mind almost going blank as I climb upward, eating up each foot of the pole in seconds.

I breathe hard as I exert myself, loving how the dry mountain air burns my lungs. I feel alive, blood pumping through my veins, and sweat prickling at my brow. My arms and legs strain as I push my body upward and upward until I've hit the finish at the top of the pole.

The whole thing is over in a matter of seconds. I exhale and release the grip of my spikes on the pole, falling ninety feet toward the ground in the safe way I was trained, taught by my late dad many years ago.

The moment my feet hit the cushion at the bottom, the sound of the excited crowd is deafening. I don't even need to hear the announcer say that I broke my own record to know that I did it. I knew I would before the competition began. When I set my mind to something, it will always happen.

I wipe the sweat off my forehead and take in several breaths to calm my burning lungs. As the world comes back to me and reality fills my ears, I realize the crowd has gone quiet, and the announcer is calling for medical attention.

Turning toward the commotion, I see Levi in a crumpled heap on the mat by his pole.

3
Lindsey

MOOSE'S IS CROWDED, NOT that I should've expected anything less. Not only is it a Saturday during the summer, but with the annual Lumberjack Games and the axe throwing tonight, it's even busier than usual.

"You showed!"

I hear Nathan's voice over the thrum of the crowd that's well on their way to being drunk—if not drunk already—and country music playing from the old jukebox in the far corner of the bar.

I tuck a piece of hair I straightened for my rare night out behind my ear and plaster the biggest smile on my face I can muster. I'm already itching to go home and rest. I never did get to take that bath I wanted.

By the time I was done getting a gift for Moira then picking up the house, I had to run back to the games to meet Nathan and get Kas. Both were none the wiser that I ever left in the first place, though Nathan did look suspicious.

Kas was so hopped up on sugar and excitement that she didn't stop talking about it until I dropped her off at Moira's. She even mentioned a summer obstacle course program that one of the loggers is running, which starts on Friday. The kids she was hanging out with are doing it, and she wants to sign up too. Count that as another surprise for the day—one that I'm happy about.

"I showed," I reply, stepping up to the booth where Fox and Morgan are sitting. Nathan hugs me, the rough stubble of his facial hair scratching my cheek. When I pull back, Fox is standing. He towers over my five-foot-eight frame, and I won't lie, he still scares me a bit. He's not only tall but also covered in tattoos. His long blond hair is up in a bun at the top of his head, showing off the geometric shapes spanning the skin of his throat and up to his ears. I've learned his gruff and grumpy demeanor is simply part of who he is, though the more I get to know him, the more I see it's a mask for the sweet man he is underneath.

That part of him shines through most when he

looks at his wife, Morgan, and now my brother, something I also had to get used to. I love that Nathan found love, and I'm fully supportive of him coming out as bisexual, but it took me a bit of getting used to having him date then get engaged to a married couple. Especially after Jeremy cheated on me while we were married.

But their relationship and how they started is completely different from what happened to me. It's not even in the same ballpark. There was no cheating involved. The love between this polyamorous throuple is truly beautiful.

"Nice to see you, Lindsey." Fox hugs me briefly after I greet him back. He's roughly pushed aside when Morgan slides out from the booth and pulls me in for a tight hug. Her warm body wraps around me, and the scent of her shampoo tickles my nose, a scent that reminds me of sunshine—a good descriptor for Morgan.

When I first met her, I told Nathan she was sunshine personified, the exact opposite of her husband. She's open and friendly, someone that I've come to consider a friend. She's even come over for girls' nights with me and Kas. This summer, she's also taken Kas to work with her on days I needed unexpected childcare and bought a video game console for their cabin so Kas could teach her and Fox how to play with her and Nathan.

The loggers have really become part of our family in the last year, and Kas loves her aunt and uncle. Or so she's started calling them already. The first time it happened, I swear I saw Fox tear up, but he quickly masked it with his usual half smirk.

"Thank god you're here!" Morgan says, squeezing me even tighter. "I needed more femme energy in this bar. It's full of burly dudes who smell."

"Hey! I smell good," Nathan chides from next to me.

"Only sometimes," Morgan says quietly in my ear so Nathan doesn't hear. I chuckle and squeeze her back, feeling better about coming to the bar already. Maybe I did need to get out of the house and see them.

Morgan leans back from the hug and checks me out. "Hot as usual. Love that dress."

"Thanks." Truthfully, the dress is nothing special. It's a simple rose-colored sundress, but the bell sleeves are cute, and the short-cut hem shows off my legs and very round ass.

"Come sit next to me, Linds. Fox, you be a good boy and sit next to Nathan."

Fox stares at Morgan, and they share a look that's almost like Fox scolding a child who's being bratty. Nathan says something that sounds like "you're asking for it" under his breath, but I ignore it. I've learned that the three of them have their own language and inside jokes. It can be a little annoying sometimes but only because I can get envious of what they have.

Fox maintains stern eye contact with Morgan for another moment, but then Nathan slides in the right side of the booth, tugging Fox with him. The two of them settle in next to each other, and Fox doesn't waste time draping an arm around Nathan's shoulders, pulling him into his side and laying a kiss on the top of his head. My heart squeezes, and I decide that I need a drink. Stat.

Morgan takes my hand and gestures to the table. "We got a pitcher of beer. That work for you, or do you want to get a shot?"

I meet her hazel gaze and wonder if I looked that obvious. I'll have to do better at schooling my facial features.

"Beer is fine."

"You sure?" She squeezes my hand. "Or we

can have Moose crack out a bottle of wine—I know you like a good dry red."

I snort thinking about the owner of this place—who is, in fact, named Moose—having a bottle of wine in this dive bar. He's a big man with a round belly who wears shorts all year, even in blizzards.

I shake my head and slide into the booth so Nathan is across from me. "Beer is good."

Morgan accepts that answer and sits beside me, taking the empty glass they had waiting for me and filling it with the bubbling yellow-colored beer.

"I was about to text you when you didn't show up on time," Nathan says.

I meet his eyes and take a sip of the hoppy liquid. "Sorry, my dress was in the dryer." It's true that it was, but I was also waffling between playing sick and following through on my promise to come.

"I'm glad you came." He smiles while leaning into Fox.

"I am, too!" Morgan chirps. "It feels like we haven't seen you in a while."

"Sorry, work has been so crazy. Especially with the games in town."

"Big baby-men coming to get splinters removed from their fingers?" she asks.

I laugh. "Funnily enough, yes. A guy came in last night complaining that he was in so much pain he needed to be seen right away. When I removed the splinter, you would have thought I was cutting off his finger."

Nathan and Morgan laugh along with me while Fox's chest shakes.

Morgan clears her throat. "Speaking of overreacting men, I'm surprised you didn't get called in to help with Levi. He can be a bit of a handful."

"You can say that again," Fox grumbles.

"Levi?" I ask.

"Yeah, the competitor who broke his leg today at the speed pole competition. It's the first time we've ever had an injury like that while hosting the games, but I can't say I'm shocked. He works for us as a logger. I told him he wasn't ready to go up against men like Dane. He should have done the forty-foot climb instead of the ninety."

My stomach flips, and my eyes skirt to Nathan's. He's watching me carefully, and I know I do a crap job of hiding the fear on my face. Fear because I know I'm caught.

"You went home after Kas and I went to the obstacle course, didn't you?" Nathan asks.

I'm busted.

I pull the pitcher of beer toward me and refill my glass, taking a sip.

"Linds—"

"Don't be mad," I cut Nathan off. "I got a lot done and did exactly what you told me to do. I had an afternoon to myself."

"Did you rest at least?"

"Define *rest*."

Nathan sighs, his face visibly tense with disappointment. It reminds me of Dad, even though I know he doesn't mean it in the way Dad did. Nathan loves me, and I know he's not disappointed *in* me, just that I didn't do what he hoped I would do.

"You know what, I think we need that shot," Morgan says.

"I'll get them," Fox adds, standing.

"I'll come with you, baby." She scoots out of the booth but not before shooting a "behave" look at Nathan.

With the couple gone, Nathan and I are left alone. I take another sip of my beer before I meet my brother's eyes. They're the same earthy-brown color as mine and Kas's.

"You lied to me."

I stare down at the wood grain of the table we're sitting at, tracing one of the knots with my finger. "I didn't want you to get angry that I left."

Nathan reaches across the table and tugs my hand into his. "I'm not angry. I just—you're starting to freak me out."

I pull my hand back and sit straighter in the booth. "Freak you out?"

"You're different. Not just tired, sadder. Is something going on with Jeremy that you're not telling me?"

The name of my ex-husband makes me flinch. "Nothing he isn't known for doing already."

"Does he want Kas to come down for the summer?"

I shake my head. "He's too busy with his girlfriend and some new deal he landed for a fancy NBA player. She'll continue to visit him one weekend a month—that's the agreement as of now."

"Too much, if you ask me," Nathan says.

I nod, agreeing. But while I hate Jeremy and the woman he cheated on me with, I'm not going to deprive Kas of her dad. He may be a dick to me, but he loves his daughter, and Kas likes the one weekend a month she spends there.

"Then what's going on?"

The truth is on the tip of my tongue. I should tell him that it's more than being overworked and overtired—I feel as if my life has gotten away from me.

And while I'm sure Nathan knows, Mom leaving us hurt. I understand why she moved back to Santa Solana, but it really messed up the pattern we'd fallen into and brought up some abandonment issues I've never addressed after Jeremy cheated. Not to mention, with it being summer and Kas not being in school, I've had to find childcare for her, which has taken more money from my paycheck. Between that and the lawyer bills I'm paying, I'm drowning.

The house is often a mess, and I feed Kas cereal or Pop-Tarts for breakfast and frozen food for dinner instead of home-cooked meals like Mom used to.

On top of that, I'm so goddamn lonely. I miss being touched, held, kissed.

I take a breath through my nose and force a smile for my younger brother. Since he was a kid,

I've always tried to be strong for him, show him that I've got it all together. With age, that hasn't changed.

"Like I said, just tired." He cocks his head at me, the "really" look now plastered on his face. I sigh.

"The summer is just a little rough is all. Kas not being in school puts pressure on me financially since I need childcare without Mom here. I've been paying Rina's daughter, JoJo, from next door to help out. It's been difficult, and I know that sounds selfish because I'm not entitled to Mom's help."

"That's not selfish, Linds. Not at all. And I hope you don't think Mom left because she felt like you were taking advantage."

A nagging voice in my head that's been saying that since she left comes to the surface. "I wouldn't blame her if that *is* why she left. She already raised us and took care of Dad when he was alive. She deserves to have time to herself now."

"That may be true, but you know it's because she didn't like the small-town life here. She missed her friends and the ocean. You know she probably would have stayed if you were honest about needing help. You told us you were fine."

"I'll be okay. I just need to make it till the start of the school year at the end of August."

"Until then, let me know what days you need help. I'll take Kas as much as I can."

"You already take care of her when I pick up extra shifts and helped so much last school year."

"Make a calendar, and tell me what days," Nathan insists. "You know Fox and Morgan love Kas, and I can do my marketing work for Morgan and Fox while I watch her."

"Are you sure?" I exhale.

"Positive. Make the calendar tomorrow and email it to me."

Fox and Morgan return with two rounds of shots collected in their hands. Morgan slides in next to me and throws an arm around my shoulders, using her free hand to push a shot toward me.

I stare at the layered brown-and-white shot. "What the heck is this?"

Morgan shakes me playfully. "I went safe and got some slippery nipples since Moose and his bartenders didn't know how to make a lemon drop. The weirdos."

The name of the shot is ridiculous, and I find myself smiling again, my conversation with Nathan and my problems starting to slip away.

Morgan's infectious energy also helps, and I'll admit having my brother's help more during the next month and a half will ease the pressure I've been feeling.

"Couldn't have just gotten us vodka?" Nathan asks, picking up the shot and staring at it.

"Where's the fun in that, Wolfie?" Morgan sing-songs.

Fox picks up a shot and, without a word, downs it. All of us watch him as he swallows then slams the empty glass on the table.

"That tastes like shit."

There's a pause before we all break out in laughter and quickly follow his lead, drinking down the concoction.

@DomInTheWoods
New Upload From @DomInTheWoods

[IMAGE ALT TEXT]: Dom is standing close to the camera, only his bare chest visible. The image is in black and white, and his muscles are taut and flex as he speaks.

Auto Captions:
Did you get your steps in today, baby?
No? That's alright. Life happens. But you and I both know your goals matter, and I know how badly you want to meet them. So let me ask you: What are you going to do differently tomorrow?
Waking up earlier? Mm, I like that. That shows commitment. And you know what? That pleases me. But forget about me for a second; how does that sound to you? Does waking up early tomorrow feel like something you can actually stick to?
You think…or you know?
You know. That's what I thought. Good girl. [End video]

850,000 Views
Username @DomInTheWoods
view all 999 comments
1 DAY AGO

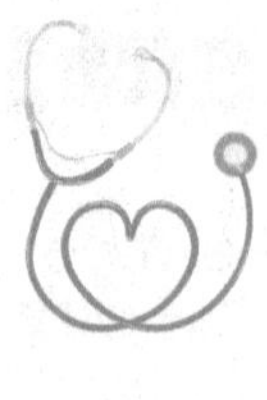

4
Lindsey

My body buzzes with laughter and alcohol. I don't think I've been this drunk or had this much fun in years. The last two hours have been filled with jokes, stories of Morgan and Fox's interesting life, and even me blabbing a bit about my asshole ex.

Maybe I should let people in more often. I might regret opening up tomorrow when I'm hungover and looping what I said on repeat, but for now, I'm enjoying the moment. The moment that is currently occupied by Morgan sharing a recent obsession: people who don't show their faces online but use their voices and bodies to make the internet go wild.

Right now, she's showing me a masked man—a shirtless masked man, I might add—in a *Scream* mask on her phone. He's ripped and leaning back on a couch, eight-pack glistening with what looks like baby oil.

"I didn't know you had a thing for men in masks," Nathan says curiously, eyes moving from her phone to his fiancée's glassy eyes. He's sitting next to me after getting another pitcher of beer, and Fox and Morgan are sitting with each other, Morgan leaning against his broad shoulder. She's drunk, like me, and so is Nathan. The only one who isn't is Fox. He stopped a while ago so he can drive us all home later.

She waggles her eyebrows. "You know I don't go online much, but a friend of ours asked me for an opinion on a video of his, and I went down a rabbit hole."

"Wait, wait, wait. Is *that* your friend?" Nathan points at the man in the mask, his short video looping on Morgan's phone.

Morgan shakes her head. "He doesn't do the mask thing. He films videos from the mouth down, and, on a rare occasion, from the back. He's a professional Dominant who offers online services like helping people develop routines and discipline through consensual control. His Loopr videos get him a ton of clients."

"What?" Nathan sits up straighter. "That's a thing?"

I sit up straighter, too, because I didn't know

it was a thing, either, and now I'm curious. I do know a bit about kink and BDSM. I'm an avid reader if I can find the time, and it's a common theme in romance novels.

"I don't know how many people have set up his type of business model, but yes. Pro Domming is a thing," Fox says.

"Fox and I have known him awhile," Morgan adds. "He worked for us, and now he's a friend."

"Does that mean he lives here?" Nathan asks, his tone curious.

Morgan goes to answer, but Fox cuts her off. "He likes to keep his privacy as much as possible, so we won't be answering that."

Morgan's cheeks flush as she makes a motion of zipping her lips before turning her gaze to me. "You're quiet over there, Linds. What about you, do you like men in masks?"

Nathan groans. "Fox, baby, I'm going to the bathroom. Come with me so they can chat. I don't need to hear this."

A second later, Nathan and Fox are walking off, leaving Morgan alone with me.

She moves to my side of the booth and bumps my shoulder. "So do you have a thing for men in masks?"

I shrug. "I've never thought about it. I'm not really on social media much."

"Me, either, but I see the appeal. Especially with these faceless videos. Not knowing who someone is, especially if you imagine them chasing you. There's something fun about anonymity, you know?" she says. "I think that's why my friend's business does so well. While it sounds counterintuitive to trust a Dominant you've never seen or met, sometimes that makes it easier to be yourself."

I think about what she's saying. "I guess I could see that."

Morgan scrolls away from the masked man, and the next video is of a man chopping wood. The shot is close, so I can only see his body and not his face. He's shirtless, sweat glistening from his muscles as he effortlessly slices through a massive log as if it's butter.

I shift in my seat and lick my lips.

"Hot, right?" Morgan says.

I focus on the man on the screen. His corded muscles bunch and release as he hacks another piece of wood effortlessly. Morgan is right—it *is* hot. More than hot.

Morgan scrolls through his videos and stops

on one where he's close to the camera with his shirt on, though some of the buttons are undone so a smattering of dark chest hair is visible over his muscled pecs. He runs his fingers sensually over his bearded jaw. The video is in black and white, so it's obvious there are silver threads in the coarse hair and that tattoos mark his neck. I trail down his chest to note the name of the account. *DomInTheWoods*.

Then it clicks—this must be the friend Morgan spoke of, the Pro Dom. She scrolls to another video, and this time, he has a belt in his hands. He's bending and tugging on it. I imagine if I could hear the sound, it would be snapping. Across the screen, captions scroll:

You want to be my good girl, don't you?

You want to please me?

Surrender to me?

I shift in my seat, the hairs on the back of my neck standing on end. I do not want to get turned on right now in a bar sitting next to Morgan, especially over something I didn't even know turned me on. He's snapping a belt, for goodness sake.

Sure, I read my romance novels, and I know Nathan has started to walk on the wild side now—evident from things I've accidentally overheard when I came to their cabin earlier than I was supposed to once. I've never made that mistake again. But I've never felt like this before thinking about…I look at the video of him snapping the belt again. Well, that.

I bring my attention to Morgan. She's watching me instead of the video with a tiny smile playing on her red-painted lips. "Would you ever be interested in exploring submission with someone like DomInTheWoods?"

My eyes saucer at her question, and the heat in my body increases a few degrees. "I um… well, I—I've, um—"

"Oh, have you already dabbled in kink?"

I shake my head. "I know about it from reading, but that's it. But there is something appealing about surrender," I say before I can think it through. "It would be nice to not have to always think so hard about everything and everyone." Admitting that out loud is freeing, but I also feel as if I'm going to throw up.

"Lindsey," Morgan says, and my eyes meet hers. "I can understand that feeling. I think a lot of women can. I can only imagine what that must be like as a single mom and ER nurse. You do a lot for not only your family and friends but for the community as well."

I find myself blushing at her praise but push it away. For some reason, the idea of a hot stranger online praising me is easier than Morgan doing so in real life over things I should accept praise for.

I clear my throat. "I enjoy doing it."

"I know that." She pushes back against my defenses. "But it doesn't mean you can't surrender some of the weight sometimes."

I run my finger along the rim of my beer glass. This is essentially what Nathan was saying to me earlier when he offered to help with Kas. I know she's right, but why is it so hard to accept help and let go?

Morgan's hand lands on my shoulder, and I meet her soft hazel gaze. "Not saying you should jump into anything—experimenting with kink isn't for everyone—but this is just my friendly little nudge to maybe check out Dom's page on your own time. If anything, he's hot to watch." She waggles her eyebrows playfully, and a laugh loosens from my chest.

Morgan shows me another video of him. In this one, the camera is focused on his spread legs. He points to the ground and snaps his fingers, the caption reading: *Be my best little sl*t and kneel for me.*

My breath catches in my throat as the video loops. This time, my eyes focus on the way the veins in his hand pulse when he snaps his fingers. Would I like kneeling like that? Getting turned on by the degrading language is new, too.

"If you do end up interested in his services, tell him I sent you. I think he's got a waiting list, but he'll do anything for a friend of mine, and he owes me a favor."

Morgan's words break through my lust-filled haze. I look up at her to see a knowing half smile on her face. I realize, too, that I have my hand clutched to my chest as if I'm about to jump inside the phone and ravish the man.

"Thanks." My voice sounds squeaky when I talk, so I clear my throat. "I don't think that's going to happen, but I appreciate it."

Morgan moves to speak, but Fox's tattooed hand that reads M I N E lands on her shoulder. She closes her mouth and turns her head to look up at him, and I give my focus to him and Nathan, who looks a bit flushed.

"You two ready to call it?" Morgan asks Fox.

He nods then looks at me. "If you're ready, Lindsey. I don't want to rush you."

"Nope, I was just thinking it was time for me to go home."

We all make our way from the bar, a drunk Nathan and Morgan telling jokes as Fox drives. But I'm only half paying attention, because the entire way home, I can't stop thinking about DomInTheWoods.

5
Dane

To: info@dominthewoods.com
From: morgan@starlightlogging.com
Date: July 16, 12:46AM
Subject: Possible new client

Dane, I'm drunk, so if this doesn't make sense, call me tomorrow.

I don't know if she'll email you, but if you get a message in the next twenty-four hours from a woman, please take her on. She's someone close to me. Don't worry, I didn't reveal who you are or that you work for us sometimes, but she does know that I know you and that you probably live around here. But I kept your identity a secret! Anyhoo . . .

This can be that favor you said you owe me for helping you set up your website and giving you a job when you first moved here. She's the best, and I think she needs your guidance and support. I won't say her name in case she gives you a fake one, but she'll probably say she doesn't know why she's emailing you (just a guess 😉). I also told her to tell you that I sent her.

HOPE TO SEE YOU SOON, YOU HOT LUMBERSNACK!

P.S. I know you're busy, but don't be a stranger. I like your face, and I want you to meet me and the grumpy man's new soon-to-be-husband. Okay, g2g, Fox wants to spank me for calling him grumpy and taking forever to send this email that he said I could have texted.

Bye bye bye (Sung like that boy band song) xoxoxoooooooooXooooooooooooooo

Morgan

My lips tug into a smile as I read Morgan's email. I will say that after the day I had, it made my night. Or I guess morning, considering it's nearing one AM.

I spent the afternoon at the hospital, waiting to make sure Levi was good. He fractured his tibia, but thankfully, it was non-displaced, so he won't need surgery. He'll be staying in the hospital on painkillers until tomorrow.

After I left, I spent the day catching up on work and filming simple content I'll post over the next couple of days. With the eventful day I had, I feel almost as if I didn't even win the speed pole competition—or that it even happened. When I remembered, I poured myself some expensive cognac a client sent me as a thank-you gift and set myself up by the fireplace, responding to comments I've been neglecting on my socials.

I start typing back a quick response to Morgan's email. It will be difficult to take on a client with the ones I already have, but I do owe Morgan.

When I first came to Starlight Haven, she and Fox gave me a job. I had prior experience in logging since my late dad was a logger, but they hired me, no questions asked. Even if I didn't have experience, they would've given me the job because I needed it. That's the kind of people they are.

Then there's the website Morgan mentioned.

When my DomInTheWoods persona took

off, and I decided to become a full-time Pro Dom—not just to help people reach their goals when they're struggling on their own but to fulfill my need to lead, to take control, and to give people the structure they crave in submission—she came to the rescue. My website, which looked like it hadn't been touched in ages, got a full overhaul that would have cost me thousands if I had hired someone, thanks to her.

I'm guessing she won't see it until late in the morning, but I shoot off the quick message to her. I thank her for the entertaining email and let her know I'll take on her friend if she contacts me. I also can't resist reminding her to drink water with an electrolyte packet and take painkillers. Fox is not only her husband but also her Dom, and an incredible one at that, but she's a friend I care about, so I type it out anyway.

I sip my cognac, the oak and black pepper taste popping on my tongue. My shoulders relax as I fill my lungs with the dry air of my cabin and stare at my unlit fireplace. I was tempted to light a fire, but while it's cooler at night in the mountains, it's not cool enough for one.

Imagining the flames flickering and heating

my face, I sink into the cushions of my recliner and revel in the silence, a silence that comforts me and provides a level of peace I crave and have continued to crave since I was young.

Before the memories of my childhood can fill my mind, I take another sip of my drink and open my DomInTheWoods account. I posted a late-night video about two hours ago, and there are already over two hundred comments. While I don't respond to every comment made, I try to respond to a few on each post. It makes my followers feel good and appreciated, and I like to connect with people all over the world who find comfort in my content and what I offer.

I scroll through my notifications and stop when I see several comments from a user with no picture and the handle @WhyAmIHere33. While profiles with no picture and funny names are common, what has me pausing is that they're commenting on old videos from when I first started my account years ago. It also appears that they're making their way through every video in order.

I read each comment, a smile teasing my lips as they get progressively more interesting.

@WhyAmIHere33: Do all Doms look like you?

@WhyAmIHere33: Is wood chopping part of being a Dom?

@WhyAmIHere33: WOW, they allow this on the internet?!

@WhyAmIHere33: I never thought I'd be into this but... here I am.

@WhyAmIHere33: How do you give up control but have control?

@WhyAmIHere33: What makes someone qualified to be a Pro Dom?

@WhyAmIHere33: How do you know if you're in need of a Pro Dom? Or that you're a submissive, for that matter?

I'm about to respond to their last few notifications—ready to explain that their question is nuanced and depends on the individual but I'd be happy to elaborate over email—when a new comment notification pops up.

@WhyAmIHere33: I swear I've seen your nose before!

I laugh as I read her comments. My old videos do show me from my nose down, where my new videos are shot from my mouth down. I read the comment again and sit straighter in my chair when the pieces click together. This commenter must be Morgan's friend she emailed me about. It aligns with the timing and what she said about her friend, how if said friend *did* email me, she'd say she's not sure why she's emailing. It also makes sense with what she chose for her username.

Does WhyAmIHere33 live in Starlight Haven? Or maybe she was out with Morgan tonight and visited for the games? If she does live here, have we met before? If we have, she's not putting the pieces together, so maybe I just have a familiar nose. It's not like my nose is special—it's an average nose.

I haven't been into town enough beyond my weekly grocery run and stop at the diner to know if someone new has moved here in the last few months, let alone the last year or more. If I don't run into them at the General Store, I don't know them.

Fuck, maybe Levi is right. I should get out more.

Pushing that thought away for now, I respond to her comment.

@DomInTheWoods: Maybe you've seen my videos before?

I stare at the fireplace devoid of flame, and a second later, I see she's already responded.

@WhyAmIHere33: Oh my god, you responded. I think I'll go die now.

I chuckle to myself and comment back.

@DomInTheWoods: If you do that, you'll never get the answers to your questions.

Her response is so fast, I know she must be waiting for my replies like I'm waiting for hers.

@WhyAmIHere33: I don't know if I want the answers.

I pause, considering how to respond. It's clear

she wants answers and is genuinely interested in my page and what I have to offer. Morgan wouldn't have emailed me if she wasn't certain her friend—I'm almost certain that's who this person is—would reach out to me in some way.

I tap out my answer with this thought in mind, wanting to be as gentle as possible since she's obviously skittish.

> **@DomInTheWoods:** Take your time to decide, but I wonder: Don't you want to find out why you're here, replying to me in the early hours of the morning when you should be getting rest?

I read it over twice before I hit enter, my comment popping up under hers. I read over the conversation again while I wait for her to respond. Another minute passes by, and another. My eyes start to drift closed, the events of the day and the alcohol catching up to me.

I sleepily refresh my phone, wondering why I care so much about her responding. More time passes, and right before I fall asleep, a new notification comes through. A ghost of a smile appears on my lips as my bleary eyes read her reply.

@WhyAmIHere33: Yes, I do.

I wake myself up enough to type out a response.

@DomInTheWoods: Then email me, WhyAmIHere33. I look forward to giving you the answers.

6

Lindsey

SOMEONE IS CHOPPING WOOD in my head. That's the only explanation for why my skull feels the way it does right now. I groan and bury my face in my pillow to hide from the horrible sunlight attempting to blind me.

When the cobwebs of sleep and alcohol clear from my brain a bit, I sit up. A wave of vertigo and nausea hits me like a twenty-foot wave. I clasp my hand over my mouth and breathe slowly through my nose.

After another minute of collecting myself, I check the time, and my eyes bug out of my head. It's nearing ten in the morning. I never sleep this late and wouldn't have if Kas wasn't at her friends', then being picked up by Nathan later to spend the night at their place while I work—something he insisted on before the trio dropped me off last night.

Pushing back another bout of nausea, I get out of bed only to discover I'm naked.

What the fuck did I do last night when I got home?

I ignore my headache and stomach roiling obnoxiously, walking to the bathroom that's thankfully connected to my room. I turn on the faucet, cupping my hand under the water and bringing it to my lips. I would have never drunk from a sink in the city when we lived there, but the water here is from a well and tastes crisp on my tongue.

Feeling a little more like myself already, I splash water on my face then brace myself enough to look in the mirror. I'm happy to see that before I passed out, I at least took my makeup off.

My haggard reflection glares back at me. My hair is a mess and knotted, a bit of mascara I missed smudged under my eyes.

I ignore looking at my naked body, knowing that I'll focus on the way my apple-shaped stomach got rounder in the last couple of years while my boobs stayed small. And how my C-section scar didn't fade the way I hoped—the scar under my belly near my bikini line is jagged and pink.

I once loved my body, felt confident in it, but

not so much anymore. It's why I avoid looking at it most of the time.

My gaze falls away from my reflection, and I open the medicine cabinet mirror, taking out a couple of painkillers. I down them with another gulp of sink water, then make my way to the bathtub.

While the A-frame cabin I bought upon moving to Starlight Haven was built in the eighties and needs renovations, one of the reasons I fell in love with it was the large tub with jets the last owners put in. It's the most lavish thing about the house, besides the stunning view it gives of the woods and the lake beyond with a private dock.

When I saw this tub, I didn't care about the rest of the house or the fact that it needed a shitload of work done to it. I wanted this tub, this bathroom. It felt like a little oasis for me and my broken heart. The sad part is that the tub I thought I'd live in, I never use.

I glance at the frosted shower stall then at the tub. I should have a shower and take advantage of another child-free afternoon to get stuff done around the house before work, but the bath looks so inviting. What the heck, I can take a little time this morning to have a soak, especially since I cleaned yesterday.

I find the Epsom salts and bubble bath I bought last year along with some tea candles. Running the water, I dump the salts and bubble bath in the tub before setting the candles around the edge and lighting them.

Satisfied with the vibes I've created, I grab a towel and my phone once the tub is filled. I ease in. The water is near-scalding, but that's exactly how I like it. I sink all the way down, turn on the jets, and let out a moan into the white-tiled bathroom as the water pounds against my aching muscles.

The thrum of the jets lulls my eyes closed in no time, and I fully relax into the moment. I'm nearly asleep when the notification of a new email resounds loudly through the bathroom, startling me. I blink and wipe my bubble-covered hand on the washcloth before picking up my phone. My still-sensitive stomach drops as I read the notification.

DomInTheWoods

Re: Questions (This is WhyAmIHere33)

Hi, Lindsey, I'm glad you chose to email me...

I sit up in the tub, water dripping from the tips of my hair as what happened last night when I got home rushes back to me.

I drank some wine I found—a totally dumb idea—stripped, lay in bed, and started scrolling through DomInTheWoods's Loopr profile. One video after another played, starting with his very first ones. The more I scrolled and watched, the more interested and turned on I became.

I don't click on the notification. Instead, I go to the app I was looking at last night and tap the notifications section before reading through them. I started asking him questions on his old videos, and he responded.

I read over our last interaction.

@DomInTheWoods: Take your time to decide, but I wonder: Don't you want to find out why you're here, replying to me in the early hours of the morning when you should be getting rest?

@WhyAmIHere33: Yes, I do.

I check in with the drunk version of myself that thought it was a great idea to online-stalk a

Pro Dom. The version of myself who chose the very sad username of "WhyAmIHere" plus my age, and the one who apparently sent him an email. An email I don't remember the contents of completely.

Good god.

I squeeze my eyes shut. I've never been impulsive like this. Okay, I take that back. I impulsively moved here after my divorce, but I had good reason to. Kas liked Starlight Haven as much as I did after our mini vacation to the lake. They magically had an opening at the hospital, and I wanted to get as far away as possible from Jeremy and the woman he cheated on me with. But emailing an online Dom? That's a new level of impulsivity.

I debate if I should read the email I sent and his response or if I should delete it and forget it. I remember Morgan not telling us if he lived here, but it was clear to me he probably does. But so what? Even if he is a local, it's not like he knows who I am. If I delete it, I can pretend it never happened, move on with my life, and that will be that.

I open my email app, my finger hovering over his reply in my inbox with the preview *Hi,*

Lindsey, I'm glad you chose to email me… highlighted.

Chose to email me. An interesting choice of words.

Curiosity pulls at the corners of my mind, and his videos I watched on repeat replay in my mental eye. I should delete the email. I should.

But I don't. Instead, I open it.

To: lindsey_c@expressmail.com
From: info@dominthewoods.com
Date: July 16, 10:45AM
Subject: Re: Questions (This is WhyAmI-Here33)

Hi, Lindsey, I'm glad you chose to email me.

But first, I have to mention that I believe, after reviewing our interactions and reading your email, that you were drinking or under the influence when you wrote to me. If you wake up and decide you've made a mistake by contacting me, you can ignore this email. I hope you're feeling alright this morning.

With that said, please know that while you're a friend of Morgan's, and I'd be more than happy to enter into an agreement with you if we're a good fit, do not feel pressured in any way if working with a Dom is not right for you.

I'm going to answer your questions and give you a brief overview of what it would be like under my guidance.

I pause after reading over the first few paragraphs and sit back in the tub. It's so… formal. But maybe that's what I should expect from a Pro Dom? I'm also embarrassed he could tell I was drunk. Not that it was hard.

Before I read on, I scan the email I sent him first to see how bad I actually was and nearly pass out while I take it in.

I start off with how I never thought submission would interest me but that his videos make me think it does because of how I feel, quote, "tingly" after watching them. I then tell him my friend Morgan told me to say she sent me, which explains how he knew that information. Then I go on listing out my questions.

Despite my embarrassment over the whole thing, I scroll back to continue reading his response.

To start, Lindsey, I ask you to reflect on why you think the idea of submitting to someone interests you. Sometimes, the idea of submission is only a fantasy that gets people off. If this is the case, when you say you feel "tingly" at the idea, is it because fantasizing about it turns you on?

I wonder, if I were to ask you to do whatever the fantasy is in reality, would you not like it? Asking yourself this will help you determine if your interest goes beyond fantasy, if you truly have the desire to submit to someone.

One of the videos I watched of him last night comes to mind, and I vaguely remember touching myself to it. He was holding what looked like a riding crop and acting out a scene.

I think of his rumbling voice soothing me, the way he commanded attention with it. He was talking to the camera, but it felt like he was talking to me. When he said to bend over and take my punishment for not being good, it did something to me.

He's right; that *is* a fantasy.

Now, I'll go through your list and answer each question by number. These answers reflect my perspective and experience as a Dominant, but they're not the only way to view things—there's no one-size-fits-all in this lifestyle.

Again, so formal. Is it weird that it turns me on? I don't think I've ever met a man who speaks and writes this way. His perfect grammar is also a rarity. I tried online dating a couple of months ago, and the "Wuts up?" and "Want 2 come over?" messages made me delete the app straightaway.

Is grammar and full sentences a Dom thing, too? Or just a DomInTheWoods thing? I bank that question, saving it for later as I keep reading.

1. How do you give up control but still have control as a submissive?

   As a submissive, you intentionally choose when, how, and to whom you give control—and that choice is where your power lies. With your Dom, you create structure and boundaries, establish limits, agree on safe words, and communicate your needs clearly. That foundation allows trust to grow, and with that trust, you're able to surrender in a way that feels safe, fulfilling, and fully your own. Keep in mind that everyone's version of submission looks a little different. The key is finding the structure and connection that works for your dynamic.

The word *structure* sticks out to me. It's something my life has been seriously lacking. The idea of someone holding me accountable while still respecting my limits and never using them to tear me down... it hits something in me I didn't know was raw.

My ex-husband was good at tearing me down. He micromanaged everything I did, made me feel like I was never enough. Pushed me to work more hours, to spend more time with Kas, to do more, *be* more, all while making it clear I was failing.

But what DomInTheWoods is describing? It doesn't sound like that at all.

2. What makes someone qualified to be a Pro Dom?

   Years of experience, training, and self-reflection. Personally, dominance and the desire for control and leadership are traits of mine I've had my entire life, but I've been a Dom since my early twenties, and I'm in my late thirties now. I've put in the work and hours to earn my clients' trust and submission. I'd be more than happy to provide you with references and my mentor's email if that will help you feel safe with me. I also have testimonials available on my website, which is linked here.

I pop some bubbles and lean back on a jet so it hits a knot in my mid-back, a laugh slipping from my lips. I can't imagine asking a stranger he worked with for a reference. And I already have one, anyway: Morgan. She wouldn't like someone or recommend them to me if they weren't good people.

3. How do you know if you're in need of a Pro Dom? Or that you're a submissive, for that matter?

   I can't answer for you personally, but my clients hire me because they need to be dominated. They want to experience power exchange, structure, and emotional release in a controlled setting where they feel safe. Some come to me to gain freedom from the choices they make in everyday life or to gain discipline and accountability to help them achieve their goals. For instance, building a daily routine, going to bed and waking up on time, or saving money. Some simply want to explore their submission in a safe container with me anonymously by conceding control to me. I do have to mention that I do not offer sessions online or in person that include nudity, sexual talk, or virtual sex.

I pause to look out of the picture window in front of me. The view is of the pine trees, and I can see the sparkling lake through some branches. Do I feel disappointed that he doesn't offer sex services? I'll admit, I'm a little confused, since the videos he puts online are very sexual. But at the same time, I don't know if that is what I really need. If I do this, I'll do this for more than just a fantasy.

Wait, am I really considering this at all? I don't listen to myself, and I don't listen to Nathan. Could I listen to a stranger?

I look away from the window back to my phone.

The second part of your question is another thing I invite you to reflect on before you make your decision to email me again. I obviously don't know you, but from your email and interest, I'm going to guess you may have submissive tendencies. However, that doesn't mean you want to submit to me or another Dominant.

I've attached a list of questions for you to journal on. If you read over them and react to them in a negative way, entering into an agreement with me is not for you. If you find yourself desiring to explore them and answer them truthfully, I think you will answer your own question. All that said, if you look at the questions and need further guidance or help, I'm happy to talk more as you explore.

When my natural instinct is to open the attachment straightaway without thinking more on it, I know that I really am considering doing this. It's nice that he's not forcing anything on me, that he's urging me to figure this out for myself. It feels safe. But for now, I hold myself back from immediately opening his questions and decide to keep reading his response to my email.

4. How much does it cost?

I want to smack myself on the head as I read the question I asked. Did I really ask that? Apparently, I did because it's there, and he answered it. I'm sure it's not cheap, considering he's a sought-after Dom, and there's no way I can afford to spend money on something for me right now, even if I end up wanting to go through with it. But I read his answer anyway to torture myself.

4. How much does it cost?

    Having this question listed means it's a concern of yours. Let me take that off your shoulders now. Not only are you a friend of Morgan's, but she's also helped me in many ways over the years. Consider the first month of our dynamic covered. If our relationship continues long-term, we can revisit this. But for now, I don't want you worrying about money or feeling like you owe me something if we move forward.

I'm not exactly sure how I feel about this offer, since I'm not great at accepting help, especially "free" help.

But I do remember Morgan saying that he

owed her a favor, and I suppose I could always pay the money back when I get a better hold on my finances.

I look back down at my phone and continue reading.

> Now, I will leave you to your thoughts. Please journal on the questions if you're open to it. This will help you truly consider if this is right for you or not. If you find yourself looking for more information, you can visit the website sublife.com to find answers. It's run by a friend who lives the D/s lifestyle twenty-four seven and is an experienced submissive.
>
> Have a good day, Lindsey. If I don't hear from you again, I wish you nothing but the best. If I do hear from you, and this is something you want to explore, I'll send you the next step in moving forward.
>
> - DomInTheWoods

I read the email repeatedly. Each time I read it, I find my body responding more. Reacting in a way that leaves me wanting, a desire building low in my stomach for what he could offer me and how he could help me.

I check the time. It's nearing one, so I have time before I need to be at the ER for my three-to-eleven evening shift. I ignore that nagging voice in my head telling me that I have things to do instead of playing games with a man I don't know, but I'm intrigued by what he said and asked me to do. I want to know why his videos and his email stirred that "tingly" feeling I embarrassingly mentioned to him.

I push back the nagging voice and open the PDF, starting with question one.

1. Do I feel relaxed or supported when I don't have to make all the decisions?

7

Dane

"WILL YOU SIGN MY cast?" Levi grins and bats his blue eyes with long blond lashes at me.

I could explain to him that signing a cast is what grade school kids do, but I'm not going to put him down for something that clearly has him excited, even if I think it's silly.

"I don't have a marker."

Levi whips one out from the top of his cast like a magician pulling a rabbit out of his hat.

"Hottie nurse gave this to me," he chirps as I take it from him and pull the cap off.

He points to the side of his cast where there's an LC and a heart drawn in black marker. "Wish she would have put her number, but I didn't want to get the cops called on me for unwanted advances."

I bend down to sign right under where the nurse did. Unlike the nurse, I don't doodle any cute hearts.

I hand the marker back to him and put my hands in my jean pockets, drifting my gaze toward the clock on the wall above the bed. It's a quarter to five, and last I checked, WhyAmIHere33, aka Lindsey, has not emailed me yet. I didn't expect her to reply as quickly as she emailed me early this morning, but I've been curious all day if she will.

"How much longer till they release you?" I ask.

"Eager to get back to the woods?"

"You forget that I like the woods."

"I do, too, but the non-woods are nice as well."

"Back to this again?" I ask. The last thing I want is to rehash our conversation from the tent yesterday. We will only get the same end result.

"Just looking out for you. You know, you could see if you could get that nurse's number. She said she works in the ER—you could go find her. Hell, I'd go find her, but"—he looks down at his broken leg, then back to me—"I won't be having that kind of fun for a while. Which means you can have fun for me."

His tone is hopeful and, dammit to hell, endearing. I don't know how he does it. Regardless, he's still on his way to annoying me again.

"Levi, enough," I warn in my gruff tone.

"Fine, fine. Don't go find the hot nurse. But I do have a favor to ask you."

"If it involves giving you sponge baths, the answer is no."

"But what if I—"

"The answer is still no."

He chuckles to himself and leans against his pillows. "Okay, fine. But in case you were worried about me, my friend Sven was back in town for the games, so he's going to stay and help me out. He's not going to give me sponge baths, but none of that has to do with the favor I was going to ask..." Levi runs a hand over his jaw, blue eyes staring at me.

"What is it?"

"I think I mentioned yesterday that I'm running a summer program for kids?"

My brow furrows, the words he said while lying on the mat yesterday coming back to me. "And?"

"It's this once-a-week afternoon obstacle course program that has some lumberjack-type games in it. I need a replacement."

"Okay, and?"

"Don't act dumb, because I know you're not. I'm asking you to take over for me."

A bark of laughter bursts from my lips, and before long, I'm laughing with my entire chest and stomach until the rough sound echoes throughout the small white room. But Levi isn't laughing.

I pull myself together and cross my arms over my chest. "You can't be serious."

"Serious as a preacher on Sunday."

"What about Hunter or Jimmy?" I ask, mentioning the other loggers here for the summer.

"They can't."

"Levi, I don't do well with kids."

"Bullshit. You may be broody and like to spend time in the woods, but the people who do know you know you're a nice guy. You're trustworthy, too. I already asked the city council director that runs it, and he thought you'd be a great fit."

"You *what*?"

"Look, man. Do it for the children," Levi pouts.

I run a hand through my hair and groan. "There's got to be someone else."

"Not someone who has experience with the course and the games. The whole draw was having a real 'lumberjack' work with the kids. They'll be disappointed if David-from-the-bank shows up to teach them."

"David-from-the-bank is a nice guy."

"With horrible aim. He could end up getting one of those kids' eyeballs axed out. Come on, man. If you won't do it for me, do it for the kids who will cry and be sad if it has to be canceled."

"There is really nobody else?"

"Can you think of anyone you'd trust with kids?"

"Fox?" I say.

"Already asked. Said he's planning his wedding and helping out with his niece or something? I didn't ask questions."

While I know Fox and Morgan have a new partner in their lives I haven't met, I had no idea Fox had a niece. Maybe she's related to their new man.

The muscles in my jaw tick. "It's only on Fridays?" *I can't believe I'm really considering this.*

"Yep. From one to three PM. Two hours of your life, once a week. It's only for a month. Four classes total."

"How many kids?"

"Nine—no, wait, ten! I got a text that there was a late sign-up."

"You'll tell me what you had planned?"

Levi grins sheepishly. "I was sort of going to wing it."

"Of course you were."

His grin turns devilish. "Does this mean you'll do it?"

My jaw ticks again before I exhale and relax the muscles.

"Is that look on your face an agreement?"

"I'll do it."

Levi smiles wide, holding out his hand, and I force myself to shake it.

"I have your discharge papers here to sign. We've got a wheelchair coming to take you to your car." An older nurse walks to the side of Levi's bed and hands the stack of papers to him. He signs as she gives him some instructions to take care of his leg.

When the wheelchair arrives, I help Levi down, and before long, we're ready to go. While

I won't be taking care of him, I offered to bring him back to the cabin he's renting since it's not far from mine.

The nurse begins to push his chair, and when I try to take over, she bats me away, claiming hospital protocol.

We exit the room, and I follow close behind. The Starlight Haven Hospital is small, and we have to walk through the ER hallway to get to the parking lot. It's louder in here, and I can hear someone complaining about their stomach hurting while a female voice tries to calm them.

"I told you when you were in here last week that you can't eat nuts anymore, Mrs. Crane. Diverticulitis isn't to be messed with."

"I know, I just really like my nuts."

My cheek twitches as I hear the exasperated nurse or doctor reply, "I know, but you can't eat them because you'll keep ending up here in the ER. I'm going to get you something for the pain; I'll be right back."

As we pass the room, the woman who I can now see is a nurse pops out from behind the curtain in evergreen scrubs that hug her curvy body. She pulls her phone out from her pocket and starts to walk toward us while typing something on it.

I know she's going to touch me before it happens. Her arm brushes mine, and she apologizes without looking up. My steps don't falter as I look back.

I've seen that brown hair with blond highlights before. She's the woman I ran into yesterday at the games.

"Hey, was that Lindsey?" Levi asks the nurse pushing his wheelchair.

Lindsey. LC with a heart. Lindsey_c@expressmail.com.

"Yeah, that was her. Poor thing has her hands full with the ER today. Must be a full moon," the older nurse says with a chuckle to herself.

I look back over my shoulder again, but she's no longer in my sight. Well, damn. What a coincidence that Lindsey, my possible client Lindsey, is the woman who ran into me yesterday. That she's also a nurse and I'm here on a day that she's working seems serendipitous, too.

The back of my neck prickles as I remember the way her body felt against mine at the games, how her nipples responded to our closeness. Now her comments about my nose make sense. That's what she recognized.

I wonder if she put it together after the alcohol

cleared from her system and if she'll say anything. If Levi figured me out, she could easily if she looked at more than my nose yesterday. The peony and sparrow tattoos on my neck along with my silver-and-dark-brown beard aren't exactly easy to forget, especially if you're watching my videos like she was. But she didn't exactly take time to study my attributes yesterday.

Though I sure as hell noticed hers.

The doors of the hospital slide open, and we step into the warm early evening air. I tell Levi I'll go grab the car, leaving him with the nurse while I walk away. I pull out my phone and see I have a new email notification.

Lindsey C
Re: Re: Questions (This is WhyAm-IHere33)
Okay, I want to work with you. What is the next step?

A grin spreads on my face.

It occurs to me that taking on a client who lives and works in my town puts my anonymity at risk. But besides this kids' program I agreed to do, my weekly grocery run, rare bank stops, and the dinner I pick up at the diner on Sunday evenings, I don't come into town.

Then there is the little fact that I find myself attracted to her. If I were to describe my type, Lindsey is it, and one thing I do not do is fall for my clients. I've had some people say they wanted to hire me to help them with their daily lives only to reveal later they had hopes of starting a sexual or long-term relationship with me. I ended those dynamics immediately. Because as I told Lindsey, I do not offer sex as a service, virtual or otherwise.

This boundary keeps professional lines in place. Sex can muddy the waters, especially when a relationship is virtual. It's harder to read people's physical cues and emotions. It can make people mistake arousal for trust as well, and when your entire dynamic is built through a screen, the last things you need are blurred lines and broken boundaries.

Besides all that, my online persona is sexual, which can further confuse things. My Loopr account is an outlet for me, a way for me to explore that sexual part of myself and another source of income beyond my Domming services. It's why I'm very clear with my potential clients about what I offer and what I don't. Beyond that, I create content that explains my two sides to my audience so I'm not misleading anyone.

The weight of my phone in my hand is noticeable as I look up at the hospital's façade, imagining the voluptuous brunette inside.

I don't know much about Lindsey, but sometimes I get a sense about people just from the questions they ask. And after putting together our run-in yesterday and seeing her minutes ago, I truly do think she needs what I have to offer. No matter what happens from here, I'm going to make sure she gets the support she needs.

And the attraction? I can manage it. It's not like we'll see each other again. This will be just like all my other virtual D/s dynamics.

8
Lindsey

The sound of my phone pinging jolts me from sleep. You'd think my body thought a murderer was in the house with the way I sat up on the couch, heart beating rapidly in my chest. But no, no murderer. I've been on edge since I emailed DomInTheWoods, waiting for him to email me back.

I check the time—I've only been asleep for fifteen minutes, which explains why I feel so groggy. I got home from work and plopped down on the couch, too tired to do anything else.

My shift felt longer than usual with my lingering hangover. Not only that, we were busy tonight, and every free moment that I did have, my mind wasn't on work.

Prior to my shift, I journaled vigorously on the questions he'd sent me. With each stroke of pen to paper, I discovered things about myself that I'd never even thought about. Like the fact that I personally enjoy when I earn approval, awards, or praise.

Another thing I learned is that the reason I find DomInTheWoods's formality appealing is because it earns my respect. It makes me feel safe, like I could and want to submit to him. I even imagined him praising me for doing something right, and I got wetter than I ever had in my life. Which is saying something considering nobody was touching me.

I got so into answering and fantasizing about working with him that I was almost late for work. When it was time for my first fifteen-minute break, I nearly ran to the break room to finish journaling.

While I was helping Mrs. Crane with her diverticulitis, my mind raced with the only question I had left to answer, one that was not on the list but one I needed to answer for myself: If I'm truly a submissive, do I want to submit to DomInTheWoods?

Ultimately, the answer I kept coming back to was yes.

The questions he had me journal on spoke

to me in a way that I didn't think they would. Nearly every question was a *yes* or a *maybe* depending on the situation.

That had to mean something, right?

My phone notification goes off again, and my heart thumps, figuring this is a new email from him before I even look down. I spoke to Kas on my dinner break, and she's long asleep by now, so it wouldn't be her. And Nathan would call me if something was wrong.

Nervous excitement builds in my lower belly, and I inhale a breath and look.

It's him.

DomInTheWoods.

I click the notification and open his new message. It doesn't escape me that I'm acting like a teenager with a school crush on a man that I've never met nor seen his full face, even if his nose—and, for some reason, his voice—is familiar.

I pull the fuzzy blanket off the back of my couch and pull it over me, settling in to read his long-awaited email.

To: lindsey_c@expressmail.com
From: info@dominthewoods.com
Date: July 16, 11:50PM

Subject: Re: Re: Re: Questions (This is WhyAmIHere33)

Hi Lindsey,
I'm so pleased you chose to email me back.

My skin buzzes as I imagine his voice saying that to me. And I'm not going to lie; I like that he said he was pleased with me. It only makes me crave him saying it more.

I see that you also attached pictures of the answers to the questions I sent you. I did not ask you for those, but I appreciate them nonetheless, and it makes me happy that you sent them. It will give me insight into who you are and how you view yourself. I'll review them.

I press my thighs together, heat creeping up my neck. Is it normal to get turned on by this? I've been asking myself this a lot over the last twelve hours. He hasn't technically done anything for me. All I've done is read his emails and answer his questions. Yet my body responds to him.

> Before we move forward and get contracts signed, I ask that you review the below to see what I do and do not do with my clients. I let you know a few of them in my last email, but it's very important that I lay out everything I offer from the beginning so there's no confusion. I pride myself on being open and transparent, always.

I pull the blanket up to my chin, too eager to keep reading and sick of questioning my every thought and action. It's getting old.

"Let's see what things you can help me with, DomInTheWoods. I hope it's everything, because I need it," I say as I begin reading. It's a very thorough list of things he can provide—including discipline, physical training, behavioral correction, and control—and what he cannot—including professional therapy, twenty-four seven power exchange (where Dominant and submissive roles are permanent), and, perhaps most importantly, sexual services.

I balk a little as I read the comment next to that no-go:

> While I don't provide sexual services, sexual release or arousal can be natural responses. If

those physical or emotional responses happen, there is no shame in that. However, I do ask you don't share any sexual reactions with me.

As if I'd share *that* with him.

I know this is a lot of information, and if you have questions, please do not hesitate to reach out and ask. If you would still like to move forward, email me a written confirmation of consent. After I receive it, I'll send you a questionnaire that will help me set up our agreement. This will be about limits, safe words, etc. Once that's completed, we'll have our first call.

I look forward to hearing back from you, Lindsey.

- DomInTheWoods

The blanket I pulled over my body at the beginning of the email is on the floor. My chest rises and falls, my breathing heavier than usual. I guess I'm not breaking rules already by getting turned on by this, which is good.

Because I don't think I could stop the reactions I'm having. My body feels as if it's been lit on fire, and for the first time since I read his email this morning, I'm questioning if maybe I'm considering this only because I'm lonely and horny.

Like I did in the bath earlier, I read his email again and again to make sure that's not why, fully absorbing what he says he offers. Discipline and accountability, structure and routine, stress relief and mental unloading, chore enforcement. Those are all things I've been struggling with and need help with. When I imagine him supporting me with these goals and receiving praise from him for it, it makes me feel... calm. For the first time in a long time. Maybe ever, if I'm truly being honest with myself.

There are some things I don't really understand, but I'm sure he'll explain them to me. Like etiquette and obedience and protocol training. I also know I'll spend the rest of my night looking up those things on the website he linked.

If there's one thing I'm good at, it's research. I was at the top of my nursing class. I like information, and I like to be good at whatever it is I'm doing.

I'm not just considering this because it turns me on; I'm considering this because I do think it will better my life—and, by proxy, Kas's—in so many ways.

I lift my gaze from my phone and look around my A-frame cabin that's sparsely decorated and filled with secondhand furniture I got thrifting. It's two floors and a loft, the layout simple like most A-frame cabins in the area. When I moved in, I had so many dreams of how to fix it up. I wanted to paint the walls from the beige color they are now to a white. I wanted to redecorate the loft above my room into a reading nook for me and a gaming nook for Kas. I wanted to get a pontoon boat or something to have at the dock. Make it our own little oasis.

While we haven't lived here long, only two years now, I could have at least painted the walls. But one thing after another got in the way.

My attention drops back to my phone, to DomInTheWoods's email. Yes, I do think I need this. What's more, I want it. I want structure, accountability, and routine. I want to feel like I did a good job when I go to sleep each night. I don't want to feel...well, how I feel now. Tired, overworked, and stressed. I want to feel how I felt while journaling. How I felt reading DomInTheWoods's formal emails. I want to be calm and unburdened.

I hit reply and send an email back to him with

the written consent he requested. It isn't until my head hits the pillow a while later that he emails me back.

To: lindsey_c@expressmail.com
From: info@dominthewoods.com
Date: July 17, 12:30AM
Subject: Re: Re: Re: Re: Questions (This is WhyAmIHere33)

Lindsey,
I'm so happy you want to continue and that you sent an email back so quickly. It shows me how willing and eager you are to work with me. I think we will fit together quite well. Please see the attached questionnaire and answer the questions after a night of rest. Do not do these now if you are still awake, which I have a feeling you are. I want you to have a clear heart and mind, as these questions are important to our success together and require honest thought.

I'd like to note that there is a section of the questionnaire that includes questions of a sexual nature. You are not required to answer them if you don't feel comfortable. The reason

I include these is that, as mentioned in the services I offer, some clients seek support in working through blocks or anxieties related to intimacy, desire, or submission—particularly within their personal relationships or dynamics outside the professional one they share with me.

While I do not offer sex or submission/punishments involving sex, understanding how someone relates to those aspects can be valuable in supporting their personal growth and goals. These questions are entirely optional, and you're encouraged to skip anything that doesn't feel aligned with your goals.

Sleep well.

- DomInTheWoods

I read over the email, my heart pounding like I find it does every time I get a message from him, and reply back.

To: info@dominthewoods.com
From: lindsey_c@expressmail.com
Date: July 17, 12:32AM

Subject: Re: Re: Re: Re: Re: Questions (This is WhyAmIHere33)

DomInTheWoods,
Do I have a time limit on filling out the questionnaire?

To: lindsey_c@expressmail.com
From: info@dominthewoods.com
Date: July 17, 12:33AM
Subject: Re: Re: Re: Re: Re: Re: Questions (This is WhyAmIHere33)

Hi Lindsey,
I can't tell you how happy your question made me. I like when my submissives ask for clarification, especially when it relates to doing things for me on time.

Please return the questions back to my inbox by tomorrow at midnight. If you need more time, please email me and let me know. I'm always happy to accommodate when asked.

Now, if you can, get some rest for me.

- DomInTheWoods

That now-familiar tingly feeling sparks between my thighs, and the urge to watch one of his videos on Loopr overtakes me. But instead, I obey his command to get some rest. I plug my phone in on my nightstand and flip onto my belly, forcing my eyes to close.

It occurs to me as I fall asleep that I'm already trying to please him.

9
Dane

THE MUSCLES IN MY back tense and release as my axe cuts into the massive log. I swing again in the spot I hit before, and the wood logs clunk and clatter to the ground.

I cut a few more logs, then set down my axe, moving to the tripod that's holding up my phone. It's Monday, which is always the day I batch film outdoor content unless the weather is bad. But today is a perfect day. The sun is shining, and it's seventy-eight degrees, a little hotter than I normally like but not hot enough to make working unbearable.

I look through the videos I took to make sure my face isn't showing in any of them. Satisfied, I decide to go down to the river. It's about a ten-minute walk from here, and a bit of exercise and a cool off in the water sound great.

My modest two-bedroom cabin is deep in the forest, which I prefer. I don't have a lakefront property, and it takes me about twenty minutes to get to the General Store by truck, but I don't mind the drive.

I can also trek a thirty-minute trail that will bring me to Fox and Morgan's doorstep. I don't use it often, but when I worked for them, I liked that I didn't have to drive, which was nice when the snow was bad or a mudslide hit from too much rain.

I pick up my T-shirt from where I'd thrown it on the ground and wipe my forehead of sweat. My muscles twitch from the exertion of chopping, but I invite the bite of pain. It makes me feel alive, and I like the feeling of being strong and in control of my body.

I slip my phone in my pocket and stretch my quads, deciding to run the short distance to the river. I take a deep breath and pump my arms as I begin to run, my lungs burning the farther I get down the path. The sensation only fuels me to want to run a greater distance than I planned.

My feet pound on the dirt, echoing in my head. I've never been a huge fan of music while I run, something I've been told by Levi makes me a psychopath. But music has its purpose, like everything else in my life. I listen to classical music when I want to focus and enjoy punk rock or metal when I'm filming content.

My lips turn up as a bead of sweat drips down my forehead. I grab my shirt, which I'd tucked into the side of my shorts, and wipe it away. I've tried to listen to music while I run, but I'd rather hear each intake of breath, the pounding of my heart in my ears, and the beat of each foot hitting the ground. It's meditative, which is something I need with the workload I've committed to. Especially when my workload involves caring for other people.

The sun above shines on me, heating my skin. The muscles in my legs and biceps tingle, the sensation causing the image of a certain curvy nurse in green scrubs to enter my mind without my permission. In her first email to me, Lindsey mentioned she felt "tingly" thinking about submission. That isn't an uncommon reaction for someone who either is a submissive or has submissive fantasies when talking or thinking about the act of it. But as I told her, being one and having fantasies are two different things.

I spent time reading over her journal answers,

and while she's never submitted before, at least mindfully and with a Dom, there is no denying that what she craves is more than a fantasy. The true test will be when we officially start working together. But I do get feelings about people, and the feelings I have about Lindsey have only gotten stronger now that I know her mind a bit better.

She answered the journal questions I sent her in great detail, more so than anyone I've sent them to before. She doesn't know it yet, but I'll have her keep a journal while we're working together. I'll ask to see it each week, so the fact that she has already shared her private and inner thoughts pleases me more than she knows.

I ease myself into a slow jog, my mind no longer in a meditative space. Instead, it's completely on Lindsey. I'm already curious to know more about her. The questionnaire I sent her will give me more info, but that's more to help me understand her limits and her desires. Not her personality. Not what makes Lindsey, Lindsey.

I bring myself to a walk as I approach the riverbank. We had a good amount of snow the last two winters, which means the water is running beautifully. The sound of it flowing through the riverbed and over rocks soothes my overworked mind.

I stop at the edge of the bank and remove my clothes and shoes. I pull my phone from my pocket and stop when my phone screen lights up. When I see the notification is from Lindsey, I smile.

"So eager," I say, though no one's around to listen.

I take my phone and tap the screen, fully aware I'm standing in the woods naked. While this river runs through my property, it wouldn't be uncommon for someone to follow the river's edge and end up getting an eyeful of my dick. But nudity is something I'm not ashamed of, and this is my property, so I can do what I like. If someone comes along, they'll just have to deal with it, though the likelihood is low.

I walk into the waist-deep water. It's cold, but my sticky skin and sore muscles welcome it. Once I'm acclimated, I lean against a tree root at the opposite side of the bank and open Lindsey's email. "Let's see what you have to say, beautiful."

To: info@dominthewoods.com

From: lindsey_c@expressmail.com

Date: July 17, 1:01PM
Subject: Completed Questionnaire

Hi Dom,
Can I call you Dom? Or is there a certain way I'm supposed to address you? I know you mentioned Sir, but I read on that website sub-life.com all the different titles you can call your Dom. However, I'm not sure what you like.

Anyway, I've completed the questions, and I've attached them. I answered all of them, and I think I've learned a lot about myself.

I hope the answers are satisfactory.

Best,
Lindsey

I splash some cold water on my chest and chuckle. Lindsey's opening question amuses me, delighting me in a way that hasn't happened in a long time. It's a fair question, but it's rare that I work with brand-new submissives. I get a lot of inquiries because of my Loopr videos, but a lot of them fall into the "I have submissive fantasies, but I am not actually submissive" categories, so we don't end up working together.

In fact, all but one of my current clients have been in the lifestyle previously, and a lot of my subs are referrals from past clients. They emailed me with specific goals and reasons they needed my help. But I admit it's nice to start fresh with someone, and it excites me.

I wonder how she'll be when we truly start to work together. Will she give me pushback? Maybe have a little brat in her? Could her eagerness to please me at this moment come from perfectionism rather than the true desire to please? These are things we will figure out as we go.

I set my phone down on the bank near the tree I'm leaning on and sink into the water. I dunk my head under, scrubbing at my hair and beard before breaking the surface. After wiping off my face and blinking water from my eyes, I consider floating for a bit but find myself staring at my phone. I guess Lindsey isn't the only eager one.

I run my hand over my face again. The feeling is a bit unsettling since I pride myself on being able to withhold pleasure, specifically instant gratification. One of my earlier self-practices as a new Dom was ordering something I really wanted, like new oil paint or an expensive cognac, then delaying partaking in it until the eager itch went away. I stare at the phone again and grit my teeth.

"Fuck it," I say to the trees.

What's the harm in answering a client's email right away? I did the same late last night after she sent her consent. In this email, she asked questions, ones I can answer without it meaning anything more than what it is.

I grab my phone and lean back against the tree, the sun warming my chest as I answer.

To: lindsey_c@expressmail.com
From: info@dominthewoods.com
Date: July 17, 1:11PM
Subject: Re: Completed Questionnaire

Hi Lindsey,

I'm very happy to see your email before midnight. Thank you for sending me the completed questionnaire; I'm glad it helped you learn more about yourself and your desires. I'll review the answers and send you a link to schedule our first call.

To answer your other question, if you're comfortable with it, please address me as

Sir from now on, both in writing and verbally. In power exchange dynamics, titles like Sir are called honorifics. They're not just labels but intentional acknowledgments of authority, trust, and mutual respect.

Please find that I've attached the same questionnaire I sent you but with my answers. I ask that you review it before our call.

Thank you, Lindsey.
Till then,
Sir

I go to send the email, but, at the last second, add a P.S.

P.S. It pleases me greatly that you did your own research.

I attach my questionnaire I have in a folder on my phone and hit send. Once it goes through, I put my phone back on the bank and resist the urge to look at her questionnaire.

I lie back in the river, floating in the water so I feel weightless. My eyes train on the blue sky through the forest of trees, and I push all thoughts of work—of Lindsey—from my mind. Even if I find it hard to do.

This is simply another client, another person I'm going to build a relationship with and help through my dominance. It isn't and won't be more than that.

10
Lindsey

THE PINGING OF MY phone makes my heart rate spike. I put the spatula I'm holding on the counter and pluck my cell out of the back pocket of my jeans, finding a response from DomInThe-Woods. *That was fast.*

A smile lifts my lips as I open it up and read over the email. *Sir.* He wants me to call him Sir. I think I can do that.

My eyes scan the rest of the email, and my body heat rises.

He sent me his questionnaire? The urge to open it is strong—I want to see how we match up. But I can't open it now.

"Who's the text from?"

My eyes find Nathan, who's on the couch with a book, some paranormal wolf shifter series

Morgan got him into. It's now face down on his lap as he stares at me with curiosity.

My brother is exactly why I can't open it now, and I'm thankful that Kas is in her room playing video games. Every once in a while, Nathan and I will hear her yelling about something or another.

I'm in the kitchen making grilled cheese for the three of us before I go to work. My neighbor cancelled, so Nathan came over to watch Kas. He deserves a Brother of the Year Award at this point for how often he saves my butt. He's also continued to bug me about setting up the calendar with times he can help with Kas, which I still haven't done.

"Oh." I shove my phone back in my pocket and pick the spatula back up. "Just a spam email."

I study the grilled cheeses, but I know Nathan hasn't stopped staring at me. I can feel his eyes burning into me.

"Why are you lying?"

I swallow the lump in my throat and look up at him. "I'm not."

"Linds." He chuckles. "You look like you're about to jump out of your skin."

I place a hand on my hip and stare at him. "It was nothing."

Nathan puts the book on the coffee table and walks to the kitchen. I flip the grilled cheeses again as he stands near me, hip against the red granite counter. "Who was it?"

"Nobody." I scoop one of the sandwiches onto a paper plate and hold it out to Nathan. "Will you take that to Kas?"

Nathan takes the plate, but instead of walking toward Kas's room, he moves to the dining table and puts it down. "She can eat at the table with us."

My skin flushes. "She's not going to like that. You heard how into her game she is."

"Too bad; she can pause it. We always eat at the table together."

I want to say *not recently*. Especially since Mom moved away. But I bet Kas eats with Fox, Morgan, and Nathan at the table when she's with them. So why shouldn't she do it here? I've just been too tired to fight her on it, so I let her eat in her room.

Nathan walks back to me, and I hand him another plate. Once all the plates are on the table and I've added some store-bought tomato soup to some bowls, I make a move toward Kas's room to convince her to join us, praying she won't fight me.

Nathan steps in front of me before I get too far. "Before you get Kas, I have to say…" He places his hands on my shoulders. "You don't have to tell me who messaged you, but I don't think I've seen you excited like that in a long time. Whoever it is, I hope it goes well for you."

I smile softly at Nathan and almost tell him what the email was, but this is too personal to share. It's not exactly something you tell your brother. It's also something I want to keep private. It's for me and nobody else. Not to mention, I never saw myself doing this. It's a new side of me that I'm only now just learning about, and I don't want to share it. I don't think I need to share it, either, even if Nathan is dying for me to.

"Nathan—"

He leans in and hugs me, which takes me off guard. When my brain catches up to what's happening, I put my arms around his waist and inhale his woodsy scent.

Nathan pulls back a moment later. "Just promise me that if it's a man, you'll let me know if I need to kick his ass."

I shove him playfully. "I told you, it was a spam email."

He chuckles and steps away. "Must have been a good spam email, then."

"Sure was," I say, even though I don't know the entire contents of the email. Gosh, I'm going to be thinking about his damn questionnaire for my entire shift. I could read it on my breaks, but I don't know if that's a good idea. Dom—*Sir*—wasn't lying when he said that some of the optional questions were sexual in nature. My body once again started getting turned on just answering them, so I can only guess what reading his answers will do to me. It's going to be a long night.

Nathan opens his mouth to say more but then closes it. "I'll go get Kas. Food is getting cold."

I shake my head. "No, you sit and start. I'll grab her."

Nathan nods. "I'll wait for you two."

I consider arguing and telling him I don't know how long this will take before I nod back.

Kas's room is on the bottom floor next to what's now the guest room—or Nathan's when he stays over. The door to her room is ajar, and when I enter, you'd never guess I cleaned it on Saturday.

It's only Monday afternoon, and it looks like a bomb went off. Her books and toys are everywhere, articles of clothes thrown on the floor. I know they're clean because some of them are still folded. I told her to put them away for me, but clearly that didn't happen.

I step up next to Kas, her Critter Cove game on the screen, one where she's a critter of her choosing tasked with building a village. On the screen, Kas's critter, a badger with a backward cap, is trading with another villager, a fox. She's got her big pink headphones on, and she's sitting in the pink-and-white gaming chair Nathan gave her for her eighth birthday this past January.

Candy wrappers are on the ground next to her with a juice box. While I let Kas have whatever kind of food she wants and never shame her for anything she eats, I try to limit sugar intake since she's growing. I don't even remember her grabbing those from the kitchen, which means she did it while I was upstairs.

I walk closer to her massive computer screen, a gift from her dad. Same thing with the new game console.

"Kas," I say loudly. "Time to eat."

She doesn't look up from her game; instead,

her eyes remain on the screen. I know she sees me; I'm standing right next to her. But this isn't the first time I've asked Kas to leave a game and eat with me. It's why I told Nathan she wouldn't like it.

We've duked it out a few times in the last couple of months, and instead of taking away privileges, I let her do what she wanted. I didn't want to fight, didn't want to make things between us tense. I wanted things to be smooth and easy. Especially since I know she took not seeing her dad more than once a month hard.

Sometimes I wonder if she blames me for that. She's too young to understand why she needs to stay here as often as possible despite my hardships with childcare. It's not like I'm going to tell her that her dad's a cheating dick who makes me feel like gum on his shoe, that he's late for his child support payments because he's always fighting the courts on how much to give me. It's not like he doesn't have the cash—he's a partner at the sports agency where he works. He's just a cheap asshole who loves to stick it to me for divorcing him even though he cheated.

"Kas!" I pull away one of her earphones, and she glares at me. "I said, time to eat."

She looks back at her game. "I'll eat here."

"No, Uncle Nathan is here. Come eat with us before I leave for work."

I swear Kas's shoulders fall, but it's so minuscule I wonder if I imagined it. Is she mad I'm working so much? I thought she didn't care. She's always happy to play her games and spend time with Nathan or JoJo. At least I thought so.

"I want to eat here."

She goes to put her earphone back in place, but I stop her, stepping in front of her game at the same time.

"Mom!" she whines. "Not cool."

"Your critter is fine."

"I'm in the middle of an important negotiation."

The way she says it is so serious, I want to either laugh or scream. Maybe both. "You can negotiate after lunch."

"Mom." She groans. "I'm not hungry."

"I'm not asking now, Kas. You need more than sugar for food. Come eat with me and your uncle. I miss seeing you."

She groans. "You're seeing me right now. Now move, Mom! I'm gonna lose out on this sale."

Her reaction makes the bridge of my nose

sting. Is this rock bottom? My kid choosing a critter video game over spending time with me? Yes, I've asked her to come eat with me before and she's declined, but I've never told her I missed her and been rejected outright.

"Kasandra Rose Wilson, you can play games in ten minutes."

"Mom!" she yells, standing from the chair. "The fox left!"

I cross my arms over my chest and glance at the screen. Sure enough, the fox that was there before is now gone, leaving only Kas's badger.

"He'll come back later."

She throws her controller and headphones on her chair and stomps out of the room. I blink away the tears in my eyes and collect myself. I know I shouldn't feel bad, but I do anyway. She's gonna be pissed at me for at least a day, which is what I was trying to avoid by coming in here. God, how did things get this bad?

You know how, Lindsey.

I rub my stinging eyes and pull air into my lungs. Yep, I think this is rock bottom.

I walk back to the dining room to find Kas shoveling soup into her mouth like it hurt her personally.

"Slow down, kid, or you'll turn into a tomato."

Kas slurps her soup and smirks up at Nathan. "Yeah, right, Uncle Nate. That's impossible."

"I don't know, is it?"

Kas successfully holds her laugh in, but now she's grinning toothily at him. "You tell me; you're the adult."

Nathan laughs. "You're too smart for your own good."

"You can say that again," I add.

Nathan turns in his chair to smile at me, but Kas keeps her eyes on her plate, her smile now a frown.

"Come, eat," Nathan says. "Your cheese isn't gonna cheese-pull anymore."

"That's the best part of the grilled cheese," I respond. Thankfully, my voice sounds calmer than I expected it to.

I sit across from Kas and pick up my sandwich. My daughter won't look at me, but Nathan does. When we make eye contact, he mouths, *I'll talk to her*.

I guess he heard what happened in Kas's room. That's not surprising, since her room isn't far from the dining table. I nearly flush with embarrassment but manage to keep it at bay, shaking my head and mouthing *leave it.* Nathan doesn't need to play dad. I know he doesn't mind it, but it's not his responsibility. He should be the fun uncle. Kas deserves that in her life.

I take a bite of my grilled cheese, which has indeed gone cold. I shrug at Nathan, and he smiles sadly from the lack of cheese-pull.

"Next time," I say.

He nods. "Next time."

11

Dane

I SAID *TO HELL with it* and lit a fire tonight. It got down into the fifties, and while I tend to run hot, the flames sounded like a good idea while I finished up some current client work.

The song over the new speakers I installed in my cabin switches, and I close my eyes to listen to the instrumental music playing. Tonight, I'd gone for my favorite film composer, Dustin O'Halloran, over Bach or something similar. I found I needed a more modern soundtrack to focus me.

I open the attachment on Lindsey's email. I scan it to double-check that she answered everything like she said and then open my standard agreement template.

The questionnaire has two parts. The first part is about what she wants from our relationship, the things she needs help with. The second is about hard and soft limits and contains the optional questions that she answered.

I read the first part, making notes in the draft agreement for what she's seeking help with. It's standard. Help with schedule and routine, like waking up without snoozing her alarm multiple times and moving her body more. She also says that she feels out of control in her life, like she never has time for what's important because she's always working or taking care of others. I make a note to ask her more about that on our call, because that could mean a lot of things.

She also wants financial advice, getting her finances in order so she doesn't have to work as often.

There's a sentence about not liking her body, which makes me angry. Her body is perfect, and I'll make it a mission of mine to help her love it, to help her love and accept all parts of her.

I continue to read and make note after note, coming up with a simple plan for her to follow in the beginning that we'll adjust as we go. I do that for the next hour until I reach the second part of the questionnaire. This part will help me understand her further and adjust anything I need to in my plan.

Unlike the first part of the questions, in this section, my clients rate their experience level for each item listed from zero, which means no experience, to five, a lot of experience. Then there's another column where they rate their limits and interest. A zero means a hard limit, a line not to be crossed. A five means it's at the top of their list.

It starts off with an easy question about praise. In this case, I ask if she likes praise—i.e. being called a good girl when she's done something that pleases me. In the box, she rates a zero on experience level and a three with limits and interest, which means she's willing to try. Good.

I mark that note for our call she scheduled on Wednesday, eager to see how she responds to it. In my eyes, this doesn't have to be sexual, and it isn't for many of my clients. It's about my tone and how I use it.

I read further through the list. Her answers are pretty standard for someone new to submission. Following orders and rules both get fives, while more restrictive behavioral rules are marked with a three.

She's given a clear no to things like humiliation and certain types of teasing, which aligns with my own limits. I don't believe in tearing a submissive down. I'll never call them worthless or anything like it.

My eye catches a note she left beside the teasing question, which she marked as something she's open to: "But not in a mean way, like calling me stupid or something like that."

My skin prickles, and I wonder who hurt her in the past. Lindsey's not worked with a Dom before, so it can't be that. Ex-boyfriend, maybe? Or a friend? Could even be a family member.

The burning desire to protect her flares in my gut as my gaze drifts to the fire that's nearly out now. I mull over everything I've learned about Lindsey from her questionnaire, unable to deny that some of her answers aroused me. We're compatible in many ways, having many of the same likes and dislikes.

My thoughts drift to the memory of her soft body pressed to mine that afternoon at the Lumberjack Games. I shift in my chair, painfully aware of how tight my jeans have become... and how long they've been that way.

That nagging voice in my mind from earlier returns, poking at me, asking me why I'm having such a strong reaction to a new client—not only physically, but emotionally. I don't know her past, and I don't know her.

I inhale and exhale multiple breaths. Within a few minutes, I've convinced myself that I'm simply horny. While what I do with my clients isn't sex, I know that many of them derive sexual pleasure from our sessions, and it's nothing to be ashamed of. But it's why I reiterate both before and in our agreement that they can do what they want once our call ends as long as they respect my boundaries and do not tell me about it.

It's important to me to keep things professional and that my clients feel safe with me and I with them. Lindsey won't be any different.

With that thought looping in my mind, I assure myself that, like my clients have natural reactions at times, I'm having one, too. There's nothing to be ashamed of. The fact that it's been too long since I've let myself have a release plays into it as well. It's the best explanation for how I feel right now. It has nothing to do with Lindsey being beautiful and that I haven't been able to stop thinking about her since our run-in at the games.

I close my laptop and set it on the side table. I can finish our agreement in the morning with a clear head. For now, I need a cold shower and a reality check. Lindsey is a client. If I wanted to have "fun," as Levi calls it, or pursue a relationship—which is not in the cards for me right now given how busy I am—I should have declined her emails and made a move at the hospital. But I made my bed, a bed without a warm, full-figured body next to me, and now I must lie in it.

time I go to work and come home, something has changed about her. The one positive when I was with Jeremy was that while I still worked, I did work less. I was able to watch her grow up, but now I'm missing it. Soon, she'll be eighteen and going to college far away from here.

"Why don't you stay home with me? We can make our cinnamon popcorn and watch a movie."

"You'll fall asleep halfway through."

"I won't." While she'd usually be right about that, I have my meeting with Sir at ten PM. There's no way I'll fall asleep, no matter how tired I am.

Kas rolls her eyes, and I sigh. "You really want to go to Moira's instead of spending time with me?" I know that sounded pathetic and manipulative, but I miss my kid.

"Please, Mom." She pouts. "I already said I could come."

I should argue, put my foot down like I did the other day with lunch, fight for her to stay and watch a movie with me. But I don't want my kid to hate me. "Okay."

Kas jumps up and down, excitement lighting her features as if I said I was taking her to Disneyland. I wish she got that excited about watching consensual. RACK, as it's called in the kink world: Risk-Aware Consensual Kink.

Am I part of the kink world now?

I've always considered myself kind of vanilla. Since I grew up going to church, and it took me awhile to get over the "sex before marriage is bad" line I was fed, Jeremy was only the second man I had sex with. Nearly everything I've tried in bed has been with him. We mostly had missionary sex, sometimes doggy.

Then after I had Kas, our sex life fizzled out to near nothing. Later, I found out he was cheating, but I try not to think about that because I'll end up spiraling, and I don't need to do that right now.

"Mom!"

I lift my head from my pillow as Kas appears in my doorway.

"Yeah, honey?"

"Can I go over to Moira's and spend the night?"

"It's seven thirty, and I just got home."

Kas shrugs. "We're gonna play a new game she got."

I sit up and make eye contact with my eight-year-old. She's maturing more every day. I swear, each time I go to work and come home, something has changed about her. The one positive when I was with Jeremy was that while I still worked, I did work less. I was able to watch her grow up, but now I'm missing it. Soon, she'll be eighteen and going to college far away from here.

"Why don't you stay home with me? We can make our cinnamon popcorn and watch a movie."

"You'll fall asleep halfway through."

"I won't." While she'd usually be right about that, I have my meeting with Sir at ten PM. There's no way I'll fall asleep, no matter how tired I am.

Kas rolls her eyes, and I sigh. "You really want to go to Moira's instead of spending time with me?" I know that sounded pathetic and manipulative, but I miss my kid.

"Please, Mom." She pouts. "I already said I could come."

I should argue, put my foot down like I did the other day with lunch, fight for her to stay and watch a movie with me. But I don't want my kid to hate me. "Okay."

Kas jumps up and down, excitement lighting her features as if I said I was taking her to Disneyland. I wish she got that excited about watching a movie and eating cinnamon popcorn with me, something five-year-old her would have been all for.

"I'll ride my bike there."

"No, the sun's going down. I'll drive you."

Kas jumps again. "Thanks, Mom, I'll go pack a bag!"

I flop back down on my bed and stare at the high ceiling with exposed beams. Another point in the bank of "bad parenting." I'm racking them up real fast.

With an audible sigh, I grab my phone and check the time. Not long now until I meet DomInTheWoods. I really hope he's ready to whip me into shape.

Too bad his rules won't let him use real whippings. I probably need one for being such a pushover of a mom.

I'm sitting at my desk in my living room, legs bouncing. It's two minutes before ten PM, and I've already logged on for the video chat via the link Sir sent me—I didn't want to be late and give a bad first impression. I've got my camera off, figuring if he isn't showing his face, I'm not going to show mine, either. Plus, if he does live in Starlight Haven, it's better to stay unknown.

The clock on my laptop switches to 9:59, and my stomach rolls over. Sitting here, staring at the screen that says "Waiting for the host to join" makes everything more real. I mean, it was real when I filled out the two-part questionnaire and even more real when he sent me his, but this is *real* real. We're about to talk to each other with our words, and if all goes well, I'm signing an agreement with him. To be his submissive. I never thought I'd be excited about something like this, but here we are.

At exactly ten PM, the wheel on my screen spins, and the black square turns to an image. Not a static image like I expected; it's moving. Oh god, it's him. I mean, of course it's him, but I thought it would be a black screen.

While I can't see his face, the camera shows from his chest down. He's wearing a black T-shirt that's tight across his chest. His biceps are huge, and his forearms look like they could have their own porn site. Bet they'd make a lot of money, too. They're veiny but in a hot way.

"Hi, Lindsey."

I shiver from the echo of his deep voice, and I'm grateful my camera is off because it's a visible shiver. "H-hi." I clear my throat. "Hi, Sir." This is the first time I've addressed him as such out loud, and I said it directly to him. It feels a little weird, but it's not bad.

Then I realize I'm not sure if I was supposed to say that yet. Should I have only said hi?

Before I can ask, the low sound of a hum echoes through the speakers, the timbre of it zipping straight to my clit. "Very good, Lindsey."

A blush rises to my cheeks, and I take a sip of my water next to me. If I'm going to last this entire hour with him, I need to keep it under control. This is a professional relationship, nothing more.

"Um, thank you." I flush harder, glad he can't see me turn the color of a lobster.

His arms flex, and I notice an interesting compass tattoo on his left forearm. "You're welcome. Thank you for being on time. Punctuality is a trait I appreciate in people, especially my submissives."

"I'll always be sure to be on time, then."

He chuckles, the same warmth of his hum moving through my body. There's also a familiarity to it I can't place.

"Good." He shifts in his desk chair. The background behind him is a simple black backdrop. Smart of him—nobody can guess his location.

He continues. "Before we get started, I'd like your verbal consent. You'll sign the agreement after we review it here together, and I'll countersign once you've sent it to me. But before that, I want to make sure you're here of your own free will and that I have permission to speak to you as a Dominant."

I squeeze my thighs together under my desk and nod. Then I remember he can't see me. "Yes." I suck in a short breath when the *yes* comes out high-pitched, then clear my throat. "I am here of my own free will. And I give you permission to speak to me as a Dominant."

"Good. Please know that while you've given me your consent, you can tell me to stop at any time. We'll discuss a safe word you may use in the future, but for now, the word *stop* will suffice. How does that sound?"

"Yes, that's fine."

"First lesson." His voice somehow gets deeper. "If you're comfortable with it, I ask that you answer with 'Yes, Sir' or 'No, Sir.' How does that sound to you?"

I wet my lips. "I think that sounds good."

"Hmm, I never like when the answer has the word *think* in it. It means you're unsure or you haven't thought about the answer before you spoke it. Can you tell me which one it is?"

His gruff and commanding tone means business, and I sit up taller in my chair. It feels weird to have someone question me this way, and a swell of embarrassment builds in my stomach. At the same time, I can't deny that my throat itches to answer him. To please him. And he's right, I hadn't thought about my answer before speaking.

"I answered without thinking," I say. There's silence on his end, and the itch in my throat tells me I missed something. Once I figure out what it is, I swallow and speak again. "I answered without thinking, Sir."

He lets out a pleased hum, and my body tingles with what I can only describe as the feeling of happiness.

"Does it feel uncomfortable to call me Sir as my honorific? We could try something different."

"Like King or Commander?" I muse with a tone of sarcasm, the words out of me before I can stop them. I want slap my hand over my mouth, but I've already said them.

To my surprise, he chuckles. "There's the woman who commented on my videos and emailed me while inebriated."

Inebriated. He could just say drunk, but maybe that's too informal for him. "What do you mean by that... *Sir*?" I see the muscles of his forearms flex, and my mouth automatically waters.

"You've been so agreeable since our first interaction. Your emails are perfect, your answers are perfect. But that first time we talked, and in your very first email to me, your guard was down. Your smart-aleck question just now reminded me of what I believe to be underneath the personality you've carefully shown me. Some answers in the questionnaire revealed it to me as well."

"And what did they reveal to you, Sir?" I ask, suddenly feeling bold.

"What do you think?"

I start to answer with something along the lines of *you already know, so tell me* but then remember his words from before, so I pause and think. I consider all the research I've completed on sublife.com, all the journaling I've done, and the questionnaires I've filled out. I even took a BDSM test I found that said I was one hundred percent submissive and eighty-four percent brat. Awareness tingles up my neck, and I know now what he's looking for.

"A brat."

His forearms flex again. "You thought about it that time, very good."

My skin warms, and I tuck a strand of hair behind my ear. "Thank you, Sir."

He leans forward on his desk, his strong pecs closer to the camera. "Thank you for being honest. Now, correct me if I'm wrong, but addressing me as Sir is getting easier the more you say it, yes?"

"Yes, Sir."

"Hmm." He leans back in his chair. "If Sir does not work, you can call me Dom. King and Commander are not titles I identify with, though I would never shame or judge Dominants who do."

"If you like Sir, I can address you as Sir. It was only uncomfortable because it's new."

"I appreciate your honesty. Is there a way you'd prefer me to address you?"

My heart beats faster in my chest. "I—what would you call me besides my name?"

"Pet, sub—or if there's something else you think of, we can discuss it."

I sit with each name and remember how, on his videos, he would call his pretend sub "baby." But if he called me that, I think I'd end up falling in love with him.

"You can call me Lindsey."

"That pleases me just fine."

Warmth stirs in my belly, and my head dips naturally, my gaze falling to the keyboard. I really need to get a grasp on my bodily reactions, or I'll fall in love with him regardless of what he calls me.

"Do you have your email open, Lindsey?"

I look back up at the screen. His arms are now folded in front of him. I click over to my email and reply, "Yes, Sir."

"Good. Open the agreement attached, and we'll go through it section by section. Let me know if you need any further explanation or if you don't like something. We'll discuss it and edit it together. Does that sound good?"

"Yes, Sir."

"Tell me when you're ready, and I'll begin."

I click open the attachment, and everything becomes more real when I see the letterhead.

DomInTheWoods, INC.
Professional Dominance and Submission Agreement

This agreement is entered into on Wednesday, July 19th between:

- *Dominant (hereafter referred to as "Dom"): D. Woods*
- *Submissive (hereafter referred to as "Sub"): Lindsey C.*

Purpose: *This agreement establishes a structured and consensual dynamic between Dom and Sub ensuring that all interactions remain consensual, professional, and nonsexual while encouraging discipline, accountability, and self-improvement.*

There's a part of my brain that says *Are you really doing this?* But a larger part is screaming *You're really doing this, yay!*

I smile softly and I fill my lungs with air quietly. I focus my gaze back on the screen where the agreement stares at me. D. Woods. Is his last name really Woods? What if his first name is really Dom? Dom Woods. I almost snort. That can't be it.

"Lindsey?"

"Sorry."

"Do you want to continue?"

"Yes, Sir," I say without hesitation.

"Then let's begin."

13
Dane

Lindsey's "Yes, Sir" echoes through my speakers, and the hair on my arms rises. A small part of me wondered if, when this got real, she'd bolt. If she'd discover she wasn't ready for this level of commitment. But she's proving to me that was a silly thought.

Lindsey's already shown she's eager. And I bet that if I could see her, I'd see that willingness in her eyes. Even if I believe I'm right and she has bratty tendencies that I look forward to uncovering and reforming.

"I'd like to preface that while this is an agreement, it would not hold up in a court of law," I say. "This is a personal agreement between us, and legal systems do not recognize power exchange agreements as legally binding. I invite you to see this as a consent document. It's fluid, and if at any time you'd like to change something or revoke that consent, it will end. Same goes for me. I can end our arrangement at any time if I see fit. Any questions about that?"

"No, Sir. I understand."

"I'd like to add that we both hold power in this relationship, and it's important we understand that everything we do is with mutual agreement. Consent is not one-sided."

"That makes sense. I wouldn't want to do anything that upsets you or makes you uncomfortable."

My chest rumbles in appreciation. If I could see her, I imagine her head would be tilted down in gentle submission. I bet she's smiling, too.

"I've divided the agreement into sections: Consent & Communication, Boundaries & Limitations, Responsibilities of the Dom, Responsibilities of the Sub, Rules & Discipline, Duration & Termination, Confidentiality & Privacy, and lastly, our signatures. We'll start at the top and go to the bottom.

"As I mentioned, and as it states under Consent & Communication, this dynamic is fully voluntary and can be terminated by either party at any time. You'll see that I require open and honest communication at all times as well. I cannot read your mind, and you cannot read mine. We also have the added hurdle of anonymity."

I stare at her dark screen, wishing she'd chosen to show her face, but I can also respect why she didn't.

I continue. "I cannot see your reactions to me, nor can you see mine. It's very important that we use our words. Do you think that will be an issue for you?"

I hear a soft exhalation through my speakers before her warm voice follows. "I will do the best I can, Sir. I admit that sometimes I have a hard time with that."

I lean back in my chair. "In what way?"

There's a long pause, and it pleases me that she's now thinking before she answers. "I, well, sometimes I lie about how I'm feeling. Or that I need help with something."

"I see. Do you want to change that?"

"I thin—" She pauses and changes her words. "Yes, I'd like to be more honest."

Good girl. I think the praise to myself. We haven't discussed if that is an affirmation she'd like me to use, so I won't yet.

"It's not uncommon to feel shy about being

honest. But if you can promise me that you'll do your best and admit to me when you've lied or have the urge to lie, we can work together to improve on it. I do ask, however, that you're always honest if something I do makes you uncomfortable or if you do not like something I ask you to do. *That*, I do not want you to lie about. Is that something you can agree to?"

"Aren't Dominants supposed to make you uncomfortable, make you do things you don't like?"

I lean forward in my chair, staring at the dark screen. "Yes, but let me clarify. I may push you into things that feel uncomfortable, especially if they challenge you or help you grow. That's part of the dynamic. But I'll always encourage you to tell me how you're feeling before, during, and after. A healthy D/s relationship is built on mutual consent, trust, and respect, not fear or coercion. As your Dom, I'll push your limits but won't violate your boundaries. You'll never be forced into anything you haven't already given me permission to take."

"I feel silly now," she says.

"You don't need to. It's a thoughtful question, and I'm glad you asked. I'd also like to point out that you were honest with your feelings just now. You've made me happy."

I imagine Lindsey is blushing from the praise, even if I don't truly know if she is. But I've been doing this long enough to know what a blush sounds like, and her hitched breathing on the other end of the connection clues me in to her reaction before she responds with, "I'm glad, Sir."

Fuck. I should not be thinking about how much I like the way she says Sir. It's warm, her voice reminding me of the classical music I love so much. I notice she puts a different inflection on it each time, depending on what she's responding to.

Sir is the honorific all my submissives use for me, and Lindsey using it should not be any different. But it is.

I clear my throat and refocus. "Moving on to safe words."

Lindsey decided to keep the traffic light system. Red to stop, yellow to slow down, green to keep going. It's good to have them if something I say or do becomes too much for her or she wants me to stop immediately. I also like to use them to check in, confirm she's liking something I'm doing.

"Do you feel good about our chosen safe words?" I ask once more.

"Yes, Sir. Do you?"

Her question is sweet and a little sassy. "Yes, I do."

"Good," she says.

I smile as I move on to the next subject. "On to communication. I recommend a weekly video check-in to start, but our daily work can be done online using an end-to-end encrypted messaging app to ensure privacy. I request that you journal on your thoughts and feelings daily. This will not only help you stay on track with your goals, but it's also something that will help with your honesty. If you can't tell me your thoughts and feelings directly, you can write them in your journal. You will send me your pages every Sunday night for me to review. Does that work for you?"

The pause on Lindsey's end is longer than usual. I wait another thirty seconds before I ask, "What's going on over there, Lindsey?"

"I—" Another long pause. "My life is a little complicated, and I'm worried that I'll fail before I even start."

"First, that's very normal when you're starting out. This process can be overwhelming. And second, I think you're better at being honest than you give yourself credit for."

She laughs, but it's not a light laugh. It's a sad one.

"Tell me what you're worried about, and we'll adjust accordingly," I say.

"I, um... I—um..."

"Take a deep breath for me, Lindsey." I wait to hear the inhale, and then praise her for listening. "That's it. And another." She does as she's told, and I feel satisfied at the ease with which she submits to me. Even if I don't think she realizes she's doing it quite yet. That's an awareness she'll build over time.

"Good," I say when her breath sounds calmer and easier. "Do you think you can tell me what made you so upset just then?"

"I work at a hospital."

I did know that already. Not only because I saw her there the other day but also because I asked her for basic information, if she was willing to give it, in the questionnaire. Single, thirty-three years old, and occupation: ER nurse.

"Yes, you said that on your questionnaire."

"Oh, right."

"Are you worried you won't be able to find time to do what I require because of your work, or is it something else?"

She pauses once more before she continues. "I...well, as I mentioned in the questionnaire, I've been dealing with some financial issues. I've been working more, taking on extra shifts. Like I said, I just don't want to fail."

There's a pull in my gut, one that says there's something she's not telling me. But I've asked her to be honest, so I'm going to have to trust her.

"Can I let you in on a secret?"

"Okay," she answers.

"You're going to fail, Lindsey."

"What?"

She sounds so offended that my cheek twitches. "You are. And since we're being honest, you have been failing already, have you not? It's why you wanted to work with me."

She does the smart thing and thinks before she responds. "I'm not going to lie; that made me uncomfortable."

"Uncomfortable good or uncomfortable bad?"

"There's a difference?"

"Let me ask, do you want to use your safe word?"

"No, of course not."

"As I said, I'm here to push you out of your comfort zone, and that can make you uncomfortable, which is a good thing. But if what I said made you uncomfortable in a way that violated your boundaries, then you use your safe word, and we evaluate how we move forward."

"I see what you mean, Sir. I just do not like to fail, and you're right; I have been failing in my life. It's not been easy."

"I understand and hear you, but I think it's important to know that you will continue to fail because it's part of learning. I'll fail, too. Neither of us is going to be perfect, which is why honesty and communication are important. The question is: Are you willing to learn how to be comfortable in the uncomfortable, even derive satisfaction from it?"

"Yes, I do want to learn."

"I think you forgot something."

She corrects herself quickly. "Yes, Sir. I do want to learn."

"Lindsey?" I hum.

"Yes, Sir?"

"Look at you, failing and learning already."

I hear a soft laugh, and it warms my chest. "I suppose you're right."

"I am right," I banter back. "Are you ready to continue?"

"Yes, Sir."

"Let me know how this sounds to you. Our daily check-ins on the messaging app will be nonnegotiable due to the virtual dynamic we're establishing, but they do not have to be very long. You can start your daily journaling at an easy five minutes a day and will send your pages to me on Sunday before midnight. We'll have the video calls once a week, but if you need to cancel because of a shift or because you're in need of sleep, we can connect that day on the messaging app instead. How does that sound?"

"I th—" She stops herself again. "It sounds good, Sir."

"A quick learner," I commend. "Then that is what we'll do."

Again, I can't see it, but I'd bet money Lindsey is blushing from my praise. The idea shouldn't delight me as much as it does—at least, not beyond a Dominant receiving his sub's submission—but it does.

I take a drink of my water to wet my dry mouth. "Now, on to Boundaries & Limitations."

14
Lindsey

"DID YOU MEET SOMEONE?"

I look up from my phone at the hospitalist, Dr. March—or Billie, when we go by first names. One of her hands is on her round hip, and she's smirking at me. I slip my phone in my pocket and pick up a clipboard from the nurse's station desk.

"No, why would you think that?"

She snorts. "You've been glued to your phone every time I see you, and when we passed each other in the hall earlier, I said hi, but you didn't hear me because you were engrossed in something on it."

I bite the inside of my cheek. Nathan asked me a similar question the other day, and now Billie. I really suck at being discreet; I'm going to have to get better.

"Not a guy," I say, which is technically true. Sir is not simply a guy—he's a Dom. Officially my Dom after we finished our meeting and signed the agreement just after midnight last night. It's still surreal to think about, but it happened. Which is why I've been glued to my phone.

"You sure?" she asks.

I look up from the clipboard. It's an intake form for a patient in the waiting room. They have a stomachache and a runny nose, probably the stomach bug that's been going around. That will be an easy one to take care of—fluids, electrolytes, maybe an anti-nausea medication.

"Yeah, I'm sure," I say.

"Then what's got you so interested?"

"I'm reading a new thriller," I respond almost too easily. "Can't put it down."

Billie's eyes narrow. "I love thrillers—what's it called?"

I rack my brain for the name of Elijah Astor's book, a semi-local here in town. I know it, but it's the last thing I've been thinking about, and by the look on Billie's face, she knows it, too.

"Dr. March, you're needed in room three," another nurse calls from down the hall.

Billie walks past me and grins. "Text me the

title of that book. By the look on your face, it seems titillating."

If she'd stuck around to see my reaction, she'd have seen my blush. The book, aka my messages with Sir, are *very* titillating, but not in the way she's thinking.

I set down the clipboard, grateful today so far hasn't been as busy as it was yesterday. But I'm only a couple of hours into my shift, and some people are just waking up for their day since it's just after nine AM. It could get busier, but it's hard to know when you live in a small town. Some days we have nobody, and other days? It's as if the entire town gets hurt and sick.

Before I go and get my next patient, I take out my phone and check the messaging app I downloaded last night upon Sir's request. There's a new message from him, and my stomach flips upon seeing it. I wonder if I'll ever get used to seeing notifications from him or if I'll always be excited and nervous when they pop up. In this case, I'm more nervous.

Why? Because I sent my morning check-in right before the extra shift I took started at seven, even though I was supposed to message him at 5:15 AM. I'd agreed to text him as soon as I woke up, confirming I was up and starting my new routine on time. It sounded easy enough when we were negotiating it last night, but apparently, not so much.

I was to wake up at least one-and-a-half hours before work or wherever I needed to be for the day. Stretch for ten minutes, meditate for ten minutes, have my coffee, shower, get ready, pack my meals for the day, then go to work or do whatever else was on my schedule for the day. Then at night, I'd reserve an hour before I went to sleep for winding down. That could include a bath, my nightly check-in with Sir, and my five minutes of journaling. I still had a chance to get the evening routine right, but I'd screwed up the morning one royally.

I attempt to shove down my embarrassment along with my nerves as I open Sir's message.

Sir

Good morning, Lindsey. I see your message to me came in late. What happened?

He knows I'm at work and will not always be able to answer right away, just like he clarified he won't always be able to see and respond to my messages immediately. We both have lives outside of our agreement, and I know he has other clients and his online persona, too. But since I'm on the app, he can see that I've read it. Might as well answer now before I take in my next patient.

Me

I had a hard time falling asleep, Sir. When my alarm went off, I didn't think twice before I hit snooze.

Sir

I see. And why did you have a hard time falling asleep?

Would saying "Because I was thinking about you" be inappropriate? Probably. Especially in the context I was thinking about him. I may have stayed up a bit too late after our meeting scrolling my platonic Dom's channel and looking at his new wood-chopping videos. He said we had to be honest, but I don't really want to be honest about that.

Me

I was keyed up after our meeting and went down a Loopr wormhole.

Okay, that was honest. I don't have to give him the content of said Loopr wormhole, but what I said was true. The little bubbles that indicate he's typing pop up for a few seconds before his new message appears.

Sir

I'm going to assume that the rest of your planned morning routine fell apart due to your later wake-up, which means you probably forgot to pack food as well?

Dang, he's good. But I guess that's why people hire him, why he has a waiting list. It's a reminder that he's taken me on due to my friendship with Morgan, that he owes her a favor—another reason I don't want to fuck up. I want to get this right.

Too bad I already screwed up on the first

morning. I know he said failure is going to happen, but that doesn't mean I want it to happen. I quickly type out my response, keeping it plain and simple.

Me
It does, Sir.

Sir
That's not what we planned for, is it?

Me
No, Sir. I'm sorry.

Sir
I'm not here to reprimand you or make you feel bad, but I do expect you to take responsibility for your choices. We set up your morning and evening routines for a reason, yes?

Me
Yes, Sir.

Sir

I know you want to please me, Lindsey, and truly, that pleases me in itself. But these routines are for you; they're in place to set you up for success. When you break the routine, I'm not the one who feels the effects. Tell me, how do you feel this morning?

I feel like an annoyed kid for a moment, honestly. It's how I imagine Kas feels when I attempt to hold her accountable, even though I've sucked at it recently.

I brush that thought away and attempt to answer his question truthfully. I don't feel like he's scolding me, but I do feel bad that not only did I not do something right, I disappointed him. I'm also disappointed in myself and feel out of sorts from rushing to get here. Even two hours later, I still haven't shaken it.

Me

Disappointed in myself and stressed.

Sir

Do you like feeling those things?

Me

No.

Sir

If I said the routines we outlined are there to prevent those feelings and not to punish or control you, would you believe me?

Me

Yes, Sir.

Sir

Good girl.

I think I break out into a sweat. I'd told him during our chat last night that I'd be fine with him using praise in that way, but him saying it for the first time is...well, maybe having him call me "baby" would have been easier.

I nearly type out the blushing emoji then remember this is my professional Dom, not a guy I'm flirting with. Bubbles pop up again, and another message from Sir comes through while I'm lost in thought.

Sir
Was that okay for you, Lindsey?

Me
Yes, Sir. I liked it.

Sir
Good, let me know if that changes.

Me
I will, Sir.

Sir
Back to the topic of you breaking your morning routine. Tonight, I'd like you to set two different alarms. One to wake up and one as a backup. Is that possible for you?

Me

Yes, I have an alarm I can use besides my phone.

Sir

That's perfect. Along with that, you're going to start packing your meals for work ahead of time. I know this will change depending on your shifts, but we can adjust on those days as needed. How does that sound?

It sounds annoying. But I know he's right; it will make my life easier. It will also be good to get in the habit of doing it since Kas goes back to school in mid-August and she's not a huge fan of Starlight Haven Elementary School's lunches.

It's a reminder that I haven't told Sir about Kas yet. It was on the tip of my tongue last night, but I held back, not wanting to reveal that part about myself yet. I'm not ashamed of Kas in any way, but I am ashamed of how bad of a mom I've been. I've also been grappling with revealing it because of the nature of this relationship and not truly knowing if this man lives here or not.

Sir

Did you get called away to work or does that feel uncomfortable?

I smirk to myself before answering, almost typing *Impatient much?* but holding myself back. Pretty sure that would get me in trouble, even if the idea does excite me for reasons I'm not going to touch right now considering I should be working, not messaging my Dom by the nurse's station.

Me

Sorry, making lunch ahead of time does sound annoying, but I know it will be good for me.

I don't know why, but I feel like I can hear him chuckling through the phone, and I realize I was still a bit snarky by saying it was annoying. The little bubbles appear on-screen as he types, my stomach fluttering as I wait for his answer.

Sir

You can feel annoyed, but remember, you're not doing this because it's fun, you're doing it because it sets you up for success. And I expect you to follow through because you agreed this was important.

My skin prickles as I read the message, hearing him say it in that deep and commanding tone of his in my mind. I stand up straighter as I answer.

Me

You're right, Sir. I did.

Sir

I'd like you to message me when your meals are packed for tomorrow. Send me a picture to show me you did what I asked of you, understood?

A little bit of that annoyance flares in my gut, but this is what I signed up for. I need someone to hold me accountable. And I'll admit, there's a pull in my gut—despite my annoyance—that needs to do what he asked, that wants so desperately to do it. That's even excited to send him the picture and get his praise.

Me
Yes, Sir. I understand.

Sir
We need to address the commitment you broke and how to rectify it so you think twice before doing it again.

So much for not imagining naughty things at work. Like lightning, an image of him putting me over his knees, his sexy forearms flexing as his hand comes down on my bottom flashes behind my eyelids. I know that's not the kind of punishment I'm going to get for breaking my commitment, but…I can't help but think it would be nice.

I suck in a breath, the sterile antiseptic smell of the ER reminding me I'm at work and that this agreement with him is not going to get me spanked, laid, or both. I type out my answer, a simple…

Me
Okay, I'm ready.

...even though I'm not sure I'm ready. His response comes a minute later, and I read it thoroughly.

Sir

No scrolling Loopr or any social media tonight. I'm going to send you a locking app to download. Once you have it set up, give me your password so I also have access. This will allow me to lock you out of your social media apps and tell me if you access them with the password against my command. If you break it, there will be consequences. I would also like you to write a reflection while journaling tonight. It can be a few sentences on how today felt and how you'll do better tomorrow.

It sounds like a lot, but in reality, I know it's not. He's here to help me. He has my best interest at heart. Even if this feels hard, I know it wasn't meant to be easy.

This was something we talked about at length on our call last night. He warned me there'd be a lot that came up while working together, feelings I may have never felt before or have revolted against in the past. Like when I was a kid and got grounded or had privileges taken away. But thinking about that part of our conversation only reminds me why I signed our agreement. By doing this, I not only help myself but Kas, too. It doesn't hurt that it's also something I truly want, something that excites me even in these uncomfortable moments.

Me

Yes, Sir.

Sir

Remember, Lindsey. This isn't about punishment, it's about making sure this lesson sticks. Now, go do your job, and we'll check in tonight. I expect you to hold yourself to the standard we both know you're capable of.

I expect you to hold yourself to the standard we

both know you're capable of. Well, dang. When he says it like that...

My shoulders shift back, and I smile a little.

Me

Thank you for having faith in me, Sir.

Sir

I'm here to support you when you don't and to help you build that faith in yourself. Now, go to work, and we'll talk later.

Me

Yes, Sir.

"That thriller book again?"

I fly five feet in the air as I turn to see Billie, who's smirking as she walks past me. I know my cheeks are pink, not only from her comment but also at the fact that I'm still standing in the same place I was when she was called away. I'm lucky our charge nurse wasn't the one to find me; I don't need to be looked at as a slacker or questioned about why I'm not doing my job.

"Yeah," I lie.

"Definitely send me that title."

I clear my throat and pick up the clipboard I had earlier. "Will do."

She chuckles, and I walk toward the waiting room to collect my next patient, who has already been assessed by a triage nurse. I decide right then and there I can't converse with my Dom outside of breaks, even if the desire is strong. Very strong, clearly. I need this job, and I can't risk it.

15
Dane

It's another nice day out, the late-morning heat not unbearable and a gentle breeze flowing through the trees. I'm on my porch, sitting in an Adirondack chair that I got from a local artisan a couple of years back, my phone in hand.

I scroll through the comments on my newest videos, my usual responses flowing from my fingers. But my attention isn't completely on what I'm doing. Instead, I'm wondering if the Loopr videos Lindsey was scrolling last night happened to be mine. I looked through the past twelve hours of notifications to see if she'd accidentally liked one or maybe even commented, but sober Lindsey is careful. If she was, in fact, looking at them.

I finish an answer to a commenter that isn't her then upload my newest video with all the appropriate hashtags. Once it's done, I check my emails and messaging app. I reply to the clients who have sent me their check-ins for the day.

When I'm done, my fingers itch to flip to Lindsey's chat. There are no new messages, so I shouldn't want to look or reread them. I shouldn't have reread them twice already. My pointer finger hovers over the chat, but at the last second, I don't look, placing my phone in the chair's cup holder.

I rest my head back, stomach growling. I need to go in and eat lunch. I ran again this morning and lifted weights before that. But the hunger pains don't force me out of my chair; they only make me think of Lindsey.

It occurred to me the moment she messaged me with her misstep that she did not bring lunch, snacks, or any other food to work. I know enough about her now to know that money is tight for whatever reason. We haven't dug into her finances yet; that will come later after she gets acclimated to me as her Dom. It's easier for someone to share more personal and sensitive information once we've connected on a deeper level, built trust and respect for each other.

Morning and evening routines are always a

great place to start. It helps me learn more about my clients and what they struggle with.

The growl of my stomach brings me back to my earlier thought. Would Lindsey buy food for herself at the hospital? Or would she go the entire day without, ignoring her hunger to save money? The thought of her not eating while working long hours on her feet and doing hard work pisses me off.

If our D/s relationship was not restricted to online, I would have already dropped food off for her at the hospital. I would have ordered her to eat it, even stayed to watch her consume every bit of what I brought her. Even better, I'd have fed her some of it from my hand. Then I would have given her a punishment disguised as a reward. Maybe a toy she'd wear all day at work that only I'd have control of.

My dick strains against my jeans, and I blink open my eyes, which had closed of their own volition while I imagined the scenario. That was inappropriate for me to think about.

I take an inhale of fresh air. I need to think logically about this.

This is not the first time I've thought about Lindsey in ways that I should not. But I also have never before met—if you could call our run-in that—my online clients before we started working together. I've never felt their bodies against mine or been attracted to them in the way I was immediately attracted to her.

There's also the fact that I have not had sex for over a year or indulged in masturbation in quite some time. I haven't needed that release. I've had other things to channel my energy into, like running and working out.

I palm my cock through my jeans, hissing at the touch. I could open my fly right here, imagine it's not my hands touching my heated shaft. It wouldn't take long for me to find release, and I know I'd feel better in the short term.

But I'd be disgusted with myself afterward. Lindsey deserves more than that. She deserves more than being a client I jack off to when I'm horny, something I've never done or even thought of doing before. If I've gotten turned on in the past, I've just let it be what it was with no judgment and gone on with my life.

Fuck. I remove my hand and stand up. I'm not going to give in to myself in the way my body craves, but I can be the Dom Lindsey deserves. The Dom she expects me to be.

I call Levi, and he answers on the first ring. "Dane, my man. You called early."

Fuck. I'd forgotten briefly that I was going to call him after one o'clock to talk about the obstacle course gig I said I'd take over for him starting tomorrow.

"I have a favor I need to ask you," I say.

"Alright. It'd better not be asking me to get someone else to volunteer—I told you, you're it."

"No, I need you to call the General Store. Ask Carlee or Hollyn to deliver as many premade sandwiches and chips as they can to the ER nurses at the hospital."

"Um, that's an odd request."

My jaw flexes. "Tell her it's a thank-you from the loggers for all the work they did during the games. You know the nurses were not taking care of only you during the weekend."

"Dane, I can't pay for that."

I want to reach through the phone and throttle him. "I'll pay for it."

"Why can't you do it?"

"As a favor to me, just do it, and keep my name out of it."

"Damn, you're rich, aren't you?"

I'm not a millionaire, but I'm not hurting for

cash. Between the services I offer and the money my videos on Loopr pay out, buying lunch for nurses isn't going to put a dent in my bank account. Not in the slightest.

"Levi, as a favor to me, will you do it or not?"

"On one condition."

I rub my hand over my face, pacing across my deck. It's already after eleven, and I want this done as soon as possible so Lindsey eats.

"What is it?"

"You don't complain about the obstacle course. Not one more peep or groan or grouse."

"Fine," I answer without delay. I wasn't going to, anyway. I put my phone on speaker and open a pay app, finding Levi by his name. I send him five hundred dollars and hear his gasp on the other end.

"I don't think it will cost that much."

"Keep the change or donate it, I don't care."

"So grumpy."

"I'll call you later. Text me when it's done."

"Okay, boss, you got it."

"And remember, don't say it was from me."

"Okay, weirdo."

I hang up before I say something asshole-ish, grateful he's at least doing what I requested. I put my phone in my pocket, not allowing myself to question if what I'm having Levi do is the wrong move. All I care about is that itch to take care of my submissive is scratched. Lindsey will eat, and the rest of the nurses will, too.

That's what I'm choosing to focus on.

Lindsey

Thank you, Sir. It feels good to know you're happy with me. And while I was annoyed at first with your request to pack my future lunches, it did feel good to get it out of the way before tomorrow.

Lindsey's reply to my most recent message came later than I expected—around eleven, nearly two hours after she first sent it. I answered the photo of the cute purple lunch box she sent with my praise within minutes, but then there was nothing. As the time dragged on and I went through my usual nightly routine—settling into my chair, messaging my other submissives, answering emails—I started to wonder if she'd been called back into work.

I already know from the schedule she sent me that she's running herself ragged taking extra shifts and working overtime. I'm not surprised she hit snooze on her alarm this morning. Even without her scrolling social media late into the night, she probably would have done it anyway. She's exhausted. I'd be exhausted if I was her.

I type out an answer after reading over her response again.

Me

It pleases me to hear that. Have you done your nightly routine yet? It's getting close to midnight.

I'm surprised when the bubbles pop up right away given her last response took so long to come in, but I'm happy to see them. Happier than I probably should be. But I brush it off as me being glad she's okay after not hearing from her for so long.

Lindsey

I did. I'm in bed right now.

Me

Good girl. How did the routine feel for you?

The bubbles telling me she's typing pop up and then stop. Then pop up again. And then stop. This happens a few more times before one word comes through.

Lindsey

Hard.

I recline in my chair. All my other submissives are taken care of for tonight, and my work is done, which I'm glad for. I can give my focus to Lindsey, who seems to very much need it.

Me

Would you like to tell me why it was hard?

Again, the bubbles reappear then disappear multiple times, showing me she's struggling to find the answer. Several minutes later, it finally comes through.

Lindsey

It's hard for me to take time for myself, even if it's something as small as doing my new nightly routine.

Me

Why do you think that is?

When no answer arrives after a minute, I become irritated. She needs guidance, and a messaging app isn't the place for it.

Me

I'm going to call you, is that alright?

Her answer comes through quickly this time.

Lindsey

Like on the phone?

I chuckle to myself as I answer.

Me

Is there a different way?

Lindsey

Walkie-talkie.

My fingers itch, and I won't deny the image of spanking her comes to mind. She really does have a smart mouth when she wants to.

Me

Answer my question, please, Lindsey. Can I call you?

Lindsey

Yes, Sir.

Warmth blooms in my chest from her agreement, and I tap the call button on the message app. It won't show video on either end, but we don't need visuals for this conversation. Even if it would be nice to see her face.

"Hi, Sir." Her warm voice echoes through the phone's speaker.

"Hello, Lindsey. Thank you for taking my call."

"Aren't I supposed to do what you ask?"

I press my lips together, and my chest smarts. "You only submit to me if you want to. You can always say no. Always."

I hear the creak of her mattress as she shifts on her bed. "I know, I'm sorry. That was a bad attempt at me being playful."

My chest aches for a new reason now, and my frown turns into a smirk. "I see. I'm sorry I took it the wrong way. In that case, you're being smart with me."

She laughs softly. "Maybe I am."

I lick my lips. There's so much I could say, but being playful back would lead down a rabbit hole that I don't need to fall into. I also know when a submissive is attempting to cover an uncomfortable emotion. Lindsey is doing that now.

"There's a time and place for cheek," I say with a deeper, more commanding tone to my voice. "But may I be very honest with you?"

"Obviously. That's why we're here, right?" she says with a saucy lilt to her voice.

The sass again. "Lindsey," I say in warning. "A time and place, remember?"

She exhales, and I visualize her sitting up straighter against her headboard. "Yes, Sir. You can be honest."

"Are you telling me the truth?"

"Yes, I'm telling the truth."

"Good, I'm happy to hear it. It's important to

know that while I'll always be honest, I'm going to continually ask for your consent. Not only for enforcing your routines but also during our conversations. It's important to know that while I may push you, I do not cross your boundaries."

"I understand, Sir. I appreciate that."

"Being playful, teasing, sassing—it all has a time and a place. But you're using it now to cover up what you're feeling. Does that resonate with you?"

There's a pause on the other end before she says, "It does."

"Why is it hard for you to take time for yourself?"

"You cut right to the chase." She chuckles.

"Lindsey," I reprimand.

She sighs. "Sorry, Sir. I—" I hear her mattress creak again.

"It's alright. Take your time."

Her soft breathing comes through the phone for several seconds before she answers. "Things in my life these last few years have not been easy. I have someone who depends on me."

"Besides your patients?" I ask curiously. Her questionnaire said she's single, so if not a partner, then who?

"Yes." She exhales. "Every time I do something for me, I feel like I'm taking away from them."

"I see. And do they feel that way?"

"No. At least, I don't think so. But I work a lot, and when I'm not working, I'm catching up on things around the house. So I don't see them as often as I'd like."

I won't deny an emotion that feels a lot like jealousy sparks. I want to know who this person is, why they take so much of her time, and why she cares so much for them, even if it's none of my business. My submissives aren't required to tell me about every little thing in their lives. The more I know, the easier it is for me to help them, but with the kind of D/s relationship we form, it's not required.

I run my tongue over my teeth and check myself. These aren't things I should be feeling right now.

"Have they expressed anger at you for taking time for yourself?" I ask.

"Not directly, no."

"Yet you assume they'd be mad if you took only an hour for yourself?"

"I guess it sounds silly when you say it like that."

"It's not silly if that's how you feel. It is

obviously something that bothers you, that is true for you."

"It's in my nature to care for others. It feels wrong when I do things for myself."

My impulse to take care of her as her Dom wells in my chest. She's not ready for a firmer hand, so I intentionally keep my tone soft and gentle. "What if I told you that when you do something for yourself, you're not taking away from others? You're making sure you have something to give in the first place."

She laughs softly, and the sound relaxes the muscles in my shoulders. "I would say that sounds logical."

"If you give and you give and you give, eventually, you will have nothing left."

"Do you take time for yourself, Sir?"

Her question stuns me for a second. I've gotten so used to my submissives never asking about me. Some tried when we first started working together, but I always reiterated I was there for them. They only knew what they needed to know to build a foundation for our relationship, and that was that.

"Are you asking to avoid what you're feeling or because you want to know?" I ask.

Her soft laugh floats through the phone again, but this time, it sounds a little nervous. "Both, I think. You seem like a busy man. How do you take care of yourself when you're caring for your submissives and"—I hear her lick her lips—"filming all your online content?"

I decide to answer her, justifying it by telling myself the information will help her see it's okay to take care of herself. "I make myself a priority. I have a schedule, and I follow it."

"But what do you do?" I clear my throat, and she corrects herself. "But what do you do, Sir?"

"Do I get a please with that?" I retort.

Her intake of breath tells me that playfulness was out of line. I don't know what it is about this woman, but she has thrown me off my game—a game I've become an expert at playing. Until now.

"Will you please tell me what you do to take care of yourself, Sir? I'd love to know."

I shift in my chair, her obedience not helping to keep me on track. I pull myself together as much as I can and answer, "I give myself time to work out every day. It's not always at the same time, but I run. I chop wood. Sometimes, I paint."

"You paint, Sir?"

Fuck. Why did I tell her that? I've never told

anyone that before, not even Fox and Morgan. I rub my hand over my jaw and know I need to get this conversation back on track.

"I do. I may be busy, Lindsey, and I may have people depending on me, but I'll reiterate: When you do something for yourself, you're not taking away from others. You're making sure you have something to give. If giving is important to you, you must make time to give to yourself. Taking a bit of time in the morning and evening is not something to feel guilty for."

"Easier said than done, Sir."

"But you did it tonight, did you not? Even though it was hard?"

She exhales. "I did."

"If you take away the guilt, how did it feel?"

"I suppose it felt good."

"You suppose?"

"It felt good, Sir. Especially when you said it made you happy."

"It did make me happy. You know what else would make me happy?"

"I don't know, Sir."

"If you learn to put yourself first."

"I don't know if that's possible. It feels wrong to do that, at least in my life."

"It doesn't feel wrong because it *is* wrong. It feels wrong because you've been taught to put yourself last. But let me be clear: In this dynamic, I won't allow that."

"Sir—"

"I was not done speaking yet. May I finish?"

"I'm sorry. Please finish, Sir."

I hum a warm sound and hear her smile over the phone. "When you're with me, you put yourself first. Is that understood?"

"I can try, Sir."

"No, Lindsey. You will."

"And if I can't?"

"You will because you want to. You will because I ask you to do it and you want to please not only yourself but also me, don't you?"

There's a sharp intake of breath on the other end of the line, and I have no doubt she's crying. If she were here, I'd pull her into my lap and play with her hair until her tears dried, but that will never be possible.

"I'm sorry." Her voice reaches my ears, thick with emotion.

"Why are you sorry?"

"I didn't want to cry."

"You can cry, Lindsey. Feeling your emotions

is important. I don't think you've let yourself feel them in a long time."

"No, I haven't," she admits through a gasp.

"Cry, then. I'm here for you. Let me take care of you."

I hear sniffles and what sounds like a muffled sob. "That's it, such a good girl. Lean on me."

Lindsey lets her emotions flow, and I visualize sitting on the bed next to her, wiping away her tears. I don't know how long we sit on the phone, but by the time her sobs end, I know she's exhausted herself to near sleep.

"You did good today. You took care of yourself, put yourself first. Now get some rest."

"Is that an order, Sir?"

The huskiness of her voice makes my cheek twitch. "Rest," I say in a harder tone. "That is an order."

"Thank you, Sir."

"No, thank *you* for trusting me. I'll be looking for your check-in tomorrow morning."

"It will be there."

"Good. Now rest."

"You, too, Sir."

She hangs up before I can say anything back, and I stare at my phone for a long while after the call ends. There's something different about Lindsey, and if I'm not careful, I'm going to fuck things up between us.

She obviously needs me. But as of this moment, right now, I can't find it in myself to question anything I'm feeling further. Helping her feels right, and my fingers itch to do something I haven't done in a while.

I get up from my chair and head to where I keep my paint supplies, pulling out a blank canvas.

16
Lindsey

Who knew that having a good cry over the phone to your online Dom could be as much of a release as a good orgasm? Not me. Though an orgasm would've been a lot more fun and kinder on my eyeballs. They have felt sore all day from my late-night sob fest, but I do feel lighter in a way I haven't in a long time.

When I woke up late this morning, I thought I would feel embarrassed. But to my surprise, I didn't. While I cried and raged when I found out Jeremy had cheated on me, and I've cried since then, I haven't cried the way I did last night. I haven't simply let myself feel and get it out. There's something about DomInTheWoods that makes me feel safe, even if we've just started working together. His voice is like a warm hug, and when he said he was here for me, that he'd take care of me, I believed him.

I think it was easier, too, because we don't know each other, because I don't have to worry about facing him. I could let myself go without someone staring at me or giving me a pitying look. I didn't feel the need to hide from him like I do with my family. I didn't have to be strong for him, I could just... *surrender*. And isn't that why I decided to work with him in the first place?

One thing the cry did prevent me from doing was telling him about Kas. While packing my lunch and doing my routine, I'd thought about it and had planned to come clean. But with a clear head this morning, I realized that I don't need to. I told Sir I have someone who depends on me, who needs my attention. That was enough for him to help me see I need to take care of myself, too, even if I know that will take time to learn.

I did better this morning, which I was proud of. I got up with my alarm, no snoozing. I let Kas sleep in as I did my morning routine, sent Sir my check-in, and then got Kas ready for the first day of her obstacle course. We even went for brunch and then to the General Store together. I was able to thank Carlee and Hollyn for their delicious sandwiches that also saved me from making dinner last night since there were enough to take some extras home. Carlee joked about how the rest of their customers were upset since the anonymous donor cleared them out at lunchtime. But she was happy that we were all fed and enjoyed the food.

Now, Kas and I are heading out the door for her obstacle course class. They're holding it at the public park in town. Thankfully, it's free and will run for four weeks until school starts back up. She'll miss one week when she visits her dad, but she still wanted to do it.

Kas is buzzing in the car, and I still find it hard to believe she's this excited over an obstacle course. Especially when she's been spending so much time with her video games.

"Did you drink my coffee?" I ask her as we drive away from our cabin.

We make eye contact in the rearview mirror, and she scrunches her nose. "No, that stuff tastes like dirt smells."

I chuckle as I turn onto the road that will take us into town. "When were you drinking enough coffee to decide that?"

"I wasn't. I tasted it once, and that was enough."

"I think it tastes good."

"Good to know you like dirt, Mom."

I shake my head at my kid. "If you didn't drink coffee, were you eating sugar?"

"Just the pancakes earlier. Why?"

"Because you're practically vibrating back there. Are you excited or nervous about the course?" I ask while maintaining my focus on the road. It's a short drive to the park, which is nice. It also means I can come back home and take a nap before my shift—if I can get my brain to calm down enough to let me rest, that is. *Put yourself first, Lindsey*, I remind myself, though it's in Sir's voice when I hear it.

"Excited, I think."

"You think, or you are?" As the words leave my mouth and repeat in my head, I see Sir has already rubbed off on me. I smile a little as I look in the rearview mirror back at Kas.

"I am. I just hope it's not a lot of running. I hate running."

Kas is definitely my kid. When Sir said he ran for workouts, I wanted to cringe. Not my cup of tea. It's why I chose stretching as a way to move my body every day.

Kas looks out the window, and I observe her through the mirror when I can. Now she looks pensive, and I do think she's nervous. I want to ask her more, but we pull up to the park before I can.

I see a bunch of obstacles laid out across the lawn of the park, which is surrounded by forest. There are some tires, a bunch of logs, and what look to be rubber axes. Not sure how those are going to cut wood, but I wouldn't be okay with my eight-year-old swinging a real axe, anyway. There's a bunch of other stuff, too, and I know one day they're going to go to the public pool and do a log roll.

Kas has her seat belt unbuckled and is already opening the door before I can even fully stop the car. "Kas! At least wait until I—" But she takes off running before I can finish, the car door slamming in her wake. I sigh as I turn off the engine and look out the front windshield to see Kas nearly sprinting toward a group of kids that has already gathered, including her friend Moira.

I would never guess she hates running by how fast she sprints to them. I unbuckle my seat belt as she waves to Moira, but instead of stopping, she goes to the boy I saw at the games. What was his name again? Tim? Ted? No, Tyler.

Suddenly, everything makes sense. Is this boy

the reason she wanted to do this? Why she even wanted to go to the course at the games?

Goodness, isn't eight too young to have a crush on someone already?

I release a groan and push open my door. I'm not ready for my kid to have crushes. She was supposed to wait until she was a teenager. I was supposed to have several more blissful years until I had to deal with teenage stuff.

I glance at the reflection of myself in my car window and tuck a strand of hair behind my ear. The other moms are probably wearing makeup, but I didn't see the need to just to drop my kid off. Now, I'm kind of regretting it. While I did get some sleep last night, I can see dark circles under my eyes from lack of rest, and the whites of my eyes are still a bit red from all my crying. I need to pick up some eye drops in case this becomes a regular thing.

I tug my jeans up around my waist and exhale a breath, turning to see Moira's mom, Mandy, with a few other parents standing near the entrance of the park. Sure enough, Mandy looks flawless. She's thin, blond, and very bubbly. She's a nice woman who is always kind to Kas when she comes over.

"Hey, Lindsey!" she calls as I approach, waving at the other parents.

"Hey, Mandy, how are you?"

"Good, good. Just another summer day. Can't wait till school starts."

"No kidding." I laugh.

"Can you believe our girls wanted to do this?"

I chuckle. "I was thinking the same thing." I look at Kas, who's still standing next to Tyler. Tyler is talking to another girl, and Kas is staring at the side of his face like she can see through it. Damn, my kid's got it bad. That's how I used to look at Jeremy when we first started dating. Totally and completely obsessed. I guess I passed starry-eyed looks down to her, too.

"Have you met the teacher yet?" Mandy asks.

I shake my head. "Just got here."

"Oh, right, duh. Mom brain." She leans over so only I can hear. "Wait till you see him. He's *whew*!" She snorts.

It's loud in my ear, and I cringe. "Who is he?"

"Honestly, I forgot what he said his name was. I was looking into his eyes, and I think I forgot how to speak. Tyler's mom said he's the guy who won the speed pole event this weekend, and apparently, he lives here but rarely comes into town. I know I definitely would have remembered him if I'd met him."

"Are you blushing, Mandy?"

She snorts again and whispers, "Don't tell my husband."

I shake my head and look around the park in an attempt to spot this man. I'm not one for jokes or anything alluding to cheating, but I know Mandy loves her husband. She's just being—well, Mandy. She moved here around the same time I did when her husband got a job as the new sheriff when the other retired.

"I'm surprised you don't know him," I say. "You know everyone."

"That's what I said, but I guess he's good at avoiding people. I tried to talk to him, but he doesn't speak much. For every question I asked, he gave me short and concise answers. That young guy, Levi, was supposed to teach the course, but he broke his leg at the games. This guy is filling in."

"Levi," I repeat. "Oh, yes, he had me sign his cast." I laugh. I'd met him once before in town at the diner; he was a sweet guy. Super flirty but too young for me.

I rack my brain to think who else could teach this course. I know it's not Fox or Nathan, so—

"Oh, there he is!" She points to a part of the course made of ropes. My eyes track her finger, and I'm met with the jean-clad ass of a man who's bent over. I can't tell what he's doing, but I'm guessing he's tying his shoe. None of that matters, though, because his ass is what I and the other moms are focusing on.

"Okay, I should go before I have a hot flash," Mandy says from beside me. "Go say hi to him. I didn't see a ring, so I bet he's single. Maybe he'd come out of the woods for you."

Mandy's words and soft laugh fall on deaf ears, because I *know* that butt. It sounds ridiculous to think, but I do. Because I've stared at it on Loopr for far too long.

My mouth goes dry as DomInTheWoods, my Sir, stands to his full height.

He's even more massive in person, and the afternoon sun highlights his broad shoulders covered by a fitted white T-shirt. When he turns, all the air leaves my lungs, and I'm speechless.

Salt-and-pepper beard, cut jaw, perfect nose, and determined eyes. A nose I've seen before. Eyes I *know* I've seen before. I would bet millions of dollars that if I got closer, I'd see their hazel color, the pretty mix of blue and green with flecks of golden brown and a dark-brown ring around the iris I found so fascinating while he was staring back at me.

Everything clicks into place all at once. The reason I thought I recognized DomInTheWoods's nose, why his voice sounded familiar and safe. My gaze trails down his neck, the tattoos I studied online greeting me. Peonies on the right and a sparrow on the left. On his left forearm is the unique compass tattoo I couldn't stop looking at during our video call.

I feel lightheaded as it all makes sense. How could I not have realized it before? He's the man I ran into at the games this past weekend. Not only that, Mr. Perfect Nose is my Dom and now my kid's obstacle course instructor. I don't swear a lot, but *what the fuck?*

I flick my gaze back to him, and his eyes lock on mine. The way he's watching me says he recognizes me, too. He visibly tracks his gaze over my curves then back to my face. Is he remembering how my nipples got hard against his chest, how his hands held me firm to keep me from falling over?

My heart pounds wildly, and my blood pressure has got to be spiking. I stare, unblinking, taking in the full experience of him. He's intense. Beautiful. And there's no question in my mind why he's a Dom. His mere presence commands attention, and his focus remains zeroed in on me. The corner of his lips tips up a bit, and my skin prickles.

That near smile tells me he knows who I am to him, that he knows I'm Lindsey, his submissive. Did he know as soon as he found out my name when I emailed him? Has he seen me before? Did Morgan tell him? Did he already know I'm a mom?

I have so many questions, and it's becoming hard to breathe. My brain tells my feet to move, to grab him and find out the answers I need to know.

"He's staring at you," Mandy says giddily.

"More like eating you with his eyes," another mom adds, and the group laughs.

I inhale a sharp breath as my cheeks heat. Mandy bumps my shoulder, and I pry my focus from Sir to look at her.

"Do you know him?" she asks.

"Sort of." I would've preferred to say no, but it would be obvious to everyone that that's a lie.

"He's coming over here," the same mom from before whispers.

Goose bumps break out over my arms, and I turn my head to my approaching Dom. The group of parents next to me all stand up straighter, and the air around us seems to vanish.

"Ladies." He addresses everyone before stopping my heart with his next word. "Lindsey."

His deep voice zips through my body, and my mouth goes dry. He does know it's me. I don't know what to say back, though. I don't know his name, and there's no freaking way I'm going to call him Sir or DomInTheWoods. Mr. Perfect Nose might be even worse.

He turns his gaze from mine back to the parents. "For those of you who haven't met me, I'm Dane. I'll start in a minute; you're welcome to stay and watch or pick your kids up at three."

The parents mumble their thanks, but their attention is on me and the dominating man before us who I now know as Dane. *D. Woods.* I guess that is his real last name. I want to roll the full thing around in my mouth, let it fall from my lips and hear it out loud. But I don't need to say it to know it suits him. Dane Woods.

"Can I talk to you for a moment?" he asks me directly.

"The kids..." I say.

"We've got them," Mandy chirps, pushing me toward Dane. It catches me off guard, and I almost fall forward. He comes to my rescue, grabbing onto my bicep much like the first time we ran into each other. His touch is searing, and my damn nipples harden like they've been conditioned to pop out when he touches me. Thank god I'm wearing a real bra with pads today so they're not visible through my shirt.

"You okay?" he asks as he rights me.

I nod, pulling back so we're standing side by side and I can avoid his eyes. His hand drops from my bicep to my lower back, not touching me but hovering over my skin. The phantom feel is hot against my body, and even though I don't know what to think right now, I wish he'd just touch me.

Dane dips his head until his lips are by my ear and says, "Let's go next to the bathrooms."

I wordlessly agree. We walk away from the other parents, and I glance at Kas. She's not paying attention to me, her eyes still on Tyler. They're talking about something, and she's smiling so wide I smile, too.

"Which one is yours?" Dane asks, his hand still hovering above my lower back, its force field guiding me to the bathrooms. God, he's tall.

I lick my lips, and I don't miss how he observes the action. "Auburn hair, pink shirt, jean shorts. Her name is Kasandra."

He nods but doesn't say anything else. A moment later, we're next to the bathrooms, the cement structure blocking us from the prying eyes of the other parents. Maybe I should have said no to talking alone or lied about knowing him, but they're going to have questions regardless and will probably start rumors.

Not that they wouldn't have anyway. The visible reaction I had to Sir—I mean, Dane—and the way we stared at each other, they're going to talk no matter what. The downside of a small town.

I find it's better to accept your fate and let people think what they want. That's what Morgan, Fox, and Nathan do when people talk about their poly relationship, and it's worked out for them. That's what I did when I first moved here and people wondered where Kas's dad was. Eventually, the gossip blew over, and people got to know me. Now, it's old news.

Dane stands with his back to the cement wall of the bathrooms, and I face him. I don't know if he placed us this way on purpose, but I appreciate that I'm not boxed in and that if I want to, I can flee. Not that I will, but it still feels safer.

A warm breeze blows through the strands of my hair, and the corner of Dane's lips lifts.

"Hi, Lindsey," he says. The warm rumble of his voice, a voice I cried to last night, seeps through my skin.

"You know who I am." It's not a question, it's a statement of truth.

He sticks his hands in his pockets, veins in his forearms straining. "And now you know who I am."

I want to say *How could I not?* but instead counter, "How long have you known it was me?"

"Not long. We ran into each other at the games. Then I saw you again at the hospital, and that's how I put it together. You signed my friend Levi's cast."

That day, I'd been so in my head about making my decision to work with Sir, the very man standing in front of me. I remember when Levi asked me to sign his cast, but I would remember if Mr. Perfect Nose had been in the room, and he wasn't.

"I don't remember meeting you. And trust me, I would have remembered."

His mouth forms a full smile. It's disarming.

"You passed us in the hall on our way out. You were looking at your phone, and Levi asked the nurse with us if that was you. He said your name, and I put it all together."

More pieces click into place, and heat rises in my cheeks. Was I emailing him at the very same time I passed him in the hall? My mind feels as if it's about to explode.

"You knew this whole time?"

"What did I know the whole time, Lindsey?"

His question, the way he asks it, the way he says my name with so much authority, don't help my nipple situation, but they also anger me.

"That I was *the* Lindsey emailing you," I say.

He shakes his head. "I couldn't have. Not until I saw you at the hospital."

"You should have said something."

"I didn't want to make you uncomfortable. You know my business is based on anonymity. There wasn't a reason for me to tell you."

I could argue a million points in the other direction, but I can also understand his. I nibble on the inside of my cheek before I ask, "Did you know I have a daughter?"

He shakes his head. "Of course not."

"You didn't google me or something?"

Dane's lips twitch in another near smile and his eyes sparkle with amusement. "No, I didn't. What I know about you has come from you. That's it."

"And you live in Starlight Haven?"

He nods. "I do."

"And you've never seen me?"

"I would have remembered if I'd seen you before last weekend."

The back of my neck prickles, and my body tingles. Is he . . . attracted to me? This is bad. He's my Dom and now my kid's instructor.

"Lindsey."

I look into his eyes, which should be drawn by every artist on the planet and captured in photos. They're insanely beautiful and intense, the kind of intense that scares me but also sends all the moisture from my mouth to my vagina.

"Yes, Sir?" My response slips from me so easily that I slap my hand over my mouth. Dane shifts on his feet, his chin dipping slightly.

"Oh my god, I'm so sorry," I mutter. "I don't know why I said that."

"It's okay," he says calmly. "This is an unusual situation."

I inhale a calming breath, refusing to look him in the eye again. "I should go." I turn to leave, but his hand snags mine before I can fully turn around. I look down at our hands together. His skin is tanned from hours in the sun, and mine is pale from a lack of vitamin D. When he squeezes my hand gently, I look up at him.

Our eyes meet, and he drops his hand. I want to grab it back, but I keep the urge locked down. I was about to leave; I shouldn't want to hold hands with a man I hardly know. Or want any of the things I've thought about with him beyond what our agreement stated.

"The kids are waiting, but I'd like to talk to you more about this," he says.

"About what, exactly? That the man I agreed to do—*you know what with*—is now my kid's instructor?"

Dane's face is emotionless, but his eyes sparkle again as if he finds this entertaining.

I roll my shoulders and force myself to stare directly into his eyes. "I'll make this easy," I say. "Everything between us stops now."

The sparkle in his eyes dim and his reply comes out even and quick. "That's not necessary, Lindsey."

"It is."

He steps toward me, his voice quiet as he says, "Are you saying your safe word then?"

The air around us grows tense, and we're standing close enough that if I were to lean in, our lips would touch. My heart flutters, the word *red* on the tip of my tongue. I should say it, withdraw consent and end it here and now. But I can't make myself because I know that's not what I want. I'm just reacting to the shock of everything.

Dane exhales, and my shoulders ease a bit. "Would you take time to think about it for me?" he asks.

We stare at each other for another long moment. Time slows, and the blues, greens, and golds of his eyes hypnotize me. Eventually, I release the breath I was holding, and I dip my chin.

"Yes, Sir," I reply. It's quiet, and I don't know if I should have said it again here in public, but it already feels so natural. That realization rips a shiver up my spine.

He releases a low hum, and he shifts his body so his mouth is near my ear. "Good girl."

Another shiver undulates through me, and

he steps back, his features a mask of confidence. "After you." He gestures back the way we came.

I wet my lips and force my Jell-O legs to walk. Dane looks at me one more time before we reach the point where we part ways—him to the children and me back to the other parents, who I plan to avoid like the plague.

"Message me later with your decision, yes?" he asks before we part.

"I will," I answer, making sure to leave the *Sir* out this time.

He nods and walks away to where the kids are while I face the group of parents watching me as if I'm their new favorite movie.

"You were back there for quite a while," Mandy comments as I approach.

"It's nothing," I respond, probably too quickly. "He's a friend, and he had a question about Levi's leg." The lie is an easy one, but I know the women don't buy it.

"Really?" Mandy smirks. "What did—"

I cut her off. "I need to get home, but I'll see you all later."

I pull my car keys from my pocket and ignore their chatter, looking out to find Kas before I leave. She's still standing next to Tyler, but now she's looking up at Dane, who's speaking to them. The ten kids are all paying attention, a rare sight to see, completely into whatever Dane is talking about.

I study my daughter's profile and see her mouth is slightly parted in awe, enough that she could catch bugs in it. I don't think I've seen her look at anyone like that except for maybe the first time she met Fox. And that was because of his sheer height, long hair, and tattoo-covered body.

It doesn't take a genius to see my kid is already completely taken with her lumberjack instructor. *Me, too, Kas.*

My attention shifts to Dane one more time, and our eyes meet briefly as his lips curl into a smile. My stomach flips, and that tingly sensation in my body flares to life. Who am I kidding? It hasn't left in days.

God, I am so screwed.

17

Dane

Levi didn't mention when he asked me to take over that not only would I be teaching ten kids once a week for the next month, but I'd also become a spectacle for parents.

I said they could stay out of courtesy, but I didn't think they would. I'd given them two free hours of childcare, and the only ones who left were Lindsey—the only person I would have wanted to stay—and a woman named Mandy, who said she's the sheriff's wife. The rest stayed, parking themselves at picnic tables and benches.

It puts me on edge, an emotion I haven't felt in a long time. It's one thing when you're being watched anonymously online; it's another thing entirely when it's happening in person in real time, especially after spending so much time alone. There goes my anonymity, though I do recognize a few parents I've seen from time to time at the store. I just don't know their names.

"Are you a real lumberjack?" a girl named Moira asks.

"Duh, he won that speed pole climbing competition last weekend. Like for the millionth time, my dad said. He's a real lumberjack, no cap," a boy who looks older than the other kids says. I think his name is Max.

"Just because you climb a pole doesn't mean you're a logger." My attention turns to the girl who I've learned is Lindsey's daughter, Kasandra, or Kas, as she told me she likes to go by. My lips twitch at her response to the boy. She has one hand on her hip and rolls her eyes.

I haven't known Lindsey for long, but even if I hadn't been told which one was her kid, I would have known right away. Not only do they look like each other with their brown eyes and round faces, but she's also smart. This isn't the first time in the last hour that she's responded to other kids with quick wit and a sass in her tone that reminds me of her mother.

The group of kids giggle at her retort, and my twitching lips turn into a small smile.

"That would be so sus if he wasn't," Max adds. "He's teaching us lumberjack stuff."

"Logger stuff."

"Whatever. Don't be extra, Kas."

This time, Lindsey's kid does roll her eyes. "I'm not being extra. My Aunt Morgan says that's what they're called now instead of lumberjacks. It's gender neutral."

"Then why don't they call them the Logger Games instead of Lumberjack Games?" Max retorts.

My mind is trying to keep up with their chatter and slang, but one thing I do know is Kas doesn't have an answer to Max's question. The spark in her eyes dims, and she frowns.

It doesn't slip past me that she called Morgan her aunt. Is Lindsey related to Morgan, then? I don't know much about Morgan's personal life beyond that she and Fox have added a new man to their dynamic. Maybe Kas is his niece? Which would make him Lindsey's brother.

I clear the thoughts from my mind that are none of my business and put my fingers between my lips and whistle before a fight breaks out between the kids. The group of them all stand up straight and stop talking, their eyes widening as they give me their attention.

"Kas is correct; we're called loggers," I say in a stern tone. "I am a real logger, and the Lumberjack Games are called that because of the history of the games in the town. Though maybe they need an update. Now, do you kids want a history lesson or to continue learning the course?"

The group grumbles out some version of "ew, history" while Kas smirks and sticks her tongue out at Max. Max responds back with the same expression, and I curse Levi again for breaking his goddamn leg and putting me in this situation, a situation I had no idea would potentially fuck up my dynamic with Lindsey. I have hope, however, that she'll give us a chance to talk it through. I understand her hesitation, even her anger at me for not disclosing that I knew who she was, but she also didn't tell me she had a kid.

The moment I found out, everything made sense. The long hours she keeps at work, the hardships she faces both personally and financially. How she told me someone in her life depended on her. It wasn't a boyfriend, husband, friend, or parent—it's a child. *Her* child. Who she's apparently raising alone and with a full-time job. I wish she'd felt comfortable enough to tell me, and it's bothering me that she didn't. Even if, logically, I can understand why.

"Logger Dane?"

My eyes shift to Kas, and the kids all giggle at her new name for me. I suppose I walked into that one. "Yes, Kas?"

"Are you going to teach us speed pole climbing?"

I point to the ropes course that was set up. Part of it is vertical ropes that are only eight feet high. That way, no harness is required, but they can start building their upper body strength by climbing them.

"That's where we'll start."

"Those aren't poles," Moira responds.

"It's a good place to start, trust me." The last thing we need is a bunch of eight-to-ten-year-olds climbing poles in gear and getting injured. This is a very beginner course intended for the kids to have fun and learn some basics, not to get them jobs as loggers in the future. It's honest work, and there's nothing wrong with it, but it's not exactly the easiest path in life.

"Can we try climbing now? It looks *soooo* easy," Max says.

I raise an eyebrow at him. "Have you done it before?" I challenge. This kid is a know-it-all. He kind of reminds me of Levi. Maybe he has a kid I don't know about, too.

"No, but I go on the monkey bars all the time," he throws right back.

"Yeah, and you fell on your stomach last week." Tyler snickers.

Kas giggles the loudest of all the girls at Tyler's comment. I noticed earlier that she kept looking at him. It's clear now that she's crushing on the boy. I wonder if Lindsey knows…I push that thought out. Not going there.

"Alight, alright. Follow me. We'll do the ropes, and then we'll move on to the log balance section."

The kids all nod, and I buckle up for what I know is going to be an interesting rest of class. At least this will distract me from thoughts of Lindsey and what we need to talk about later. And the fact that she called me Sir in public. And that I called her a good girl right back.

All the kids have been picked up but one: Kas. I nearly messaged Lindsey, but it's only seven minutes past three. The rest of the parents besides Mandy stayed for the entire two hours, but Mandy picked up her kid on time.

Thankfully, the rest of the class went smoothly, and nobody got hurt on any of the obstacles we went over today. The parents seemed happy with what I did, too, so I'm going to call it a success.

"She'll be here," Kas says from her place beside me. "She probably was napping because she's gotta work tonight and is on her way now."

I nod, putting my hands in my pockets as we stare out at the parking lot. The warm afternoon breeze ruffles Kas's hair, and I wonder what to say. It was easier when I had something to talk about—the course—but now, we're just standing here. I don't have siblings, and my experience with children is zero.

"Do you live here, Logger Dane?"

I almost laugh at her name for me, one that's now stuck with all the kids—minus Max, of course, who insists on calling me Lumberjack Dane.

"At the park?" I ask.

Kas puts her hands on her hips and stares up at me, the sun shining in her eyes. I notice her nose is a little pink from the sun. I wonder what the SPF was on the sunscreen Lindsey put on her and if she needs a higher one.

She rolls her eyes. "No. Do you live in Starlight Haven?"

"I do."

"How come I've never seen you before?" she asks.

I was asked this question multiple times today by the parents and now by her, but I answer the kid. "I don't come to town often."

"Why?"

"Because I like my privacy."

"Why? Don't you like people?"

I press my lips together. Do all kids ask this many questions? "Depends on who the people are," I say.

Her brow squishes together before she nods. "I can respect that. People are annoying sometimes, like Max."

It's difficult, but I manage to keep in my laugh. I like this kid. I debate what to say next, but I'm saved by a truck pulling into the parking lot. It's not the same car I saw Lindsey leave in, but I know whose truck it is. Fox's. My hackles rise, and I hope nothing happened to Lindsey to prevent her from picking up Kas. Worry builds in my stomach, but when I look down at Kas, she doesn't look worried at all.

"That's my uncle, or at least one of them." She squints, clearly trying to see who's in the driver's seat. When they pull up, I know right away it's not Fox. It's a brown-haired man that I've never seen before. He leaves the truck running and gets out, walking briskly toward us. My first instinct is to step in front of Kas and protect her, but before I can, she's running toward the guy.

"Uncle Nate!" She launches herself into his arms, and he grabs her with a chuckle. He hugs her before he places her on her feet and ruffles her hair. She bats his hand away, but a grin remains on her face.

"Sorry I'm a little late; I went to the other side of the park."

"Where's Mom?" Kas asks.

"She asked me to come get you since you were coming over later anyway."

I study the interaction between the two and know they're related without having to ask. They have the same brown eyes and facial features. Nathan is smiling, but while Kas was smiling a second ago, she isn't now. "I don't have a bag. I thought I was going home first."

"I stopped and grabbed it before I picked you up. Your mom's got you covered, even put a suit in there for playing in the stream later if you want."

"Did you get my gaming headphones?"

"Like I would forget."

Kas's smile returns, but it's not as bright as before. It's clear to me—and by the way Nathan's smile falters, it's clear to him, too—that Kas wanted to go home. Guilt gnaws at my stomach, knowing I'm most likely the reason her mom obviously switched plans on her and sent her uncle to pick her up.

"Are you going to introduce me?" Nathan asks Kas.

"Oh, yeah! Uncle Nate, this is Logger Dane. He's cool."

Nathan walks the rest of the distance toward me, his eyes assessing in a way that reminds me of a wolf. He's got a well-trimmed beard and tattoos marking his left forearm that look like a forest scene. I notice a tattooed band around his left finger with what looks to be the letters O U R S spelled out on his knuckles.

It doesn't take a genius to put it all together. This is Fox and Morgan's fiancé, the man she's been wanting me to meet. He's much shorter than me but built. His eyes are friendly yet calculating, much like mine.

"I'm Nathan, Lindsey's brother. Nice to meet you."

I take his extended hand, and we shake. His squeeze is firm, and the moment his eyes take in my appearance, studying the tattoos on my neck, I see a spark of recognition in his eyes. "I'm Dane," I say.

He shakes my hand for another second before pulling back and shoving his hands in his jean pockets. He looks me up and down again, and I know what he's going to say before he says it. "I think you know my partners, Fox and Morgan?"

I hold his eye contact and nod, not wavering or letting him know that he's figured me out. By the way he keeps glancing at my tattoos and jaw-line, he knows who I am online.

It's neither here nor there, but this again reminds me why, beyond my desire to be alone, I don't interact much with people in town. My tattoos make it easy to figure out who I am if they've seen my Loopr account.

"I do. For a long time now."

Nathan squints as if he's attempting to read my mind.

"Uncle Nate, can we go? I'm hungry."

Nathan shifts his gaze from me to his niece. "Yeah, Fox made some cinnamon rolls, and Morgan made a salad."

"Gross." Kas gags.

"It's called balance," he responds with a chuckle before turning his attention back to me. "I'm sure I'll see you around again, Logger Dane. Thanks for waiting with her."

The nickname is annoying coming from him, but I nod. "No problem. See you next week, Logger Kas."

Kas's cheeks tinge pink, and then she's tugging Nathan toward the running truck. Once they've pulled away, I take out my phone and walk around the park to grab some loose items—like the rubber axes—that I'll keep in my truck so they aren't misplaced. The rest of the course will stay up for the month while we're using it.

I stop in front of the pile of axes and look at the notifications on my phone. I have several from my clients with their check-ins but none from Lindsey.

My jaw clicks from the force of my grinding, and I exhale. My patience is thin, and I don't like it. I told her to message me when she had an answer for me, and while my fingers demand to ask her for one right now, I've already given her an order. It was my fault I didn't specify *when* I wanted her answer.

Time to exercise my patience.

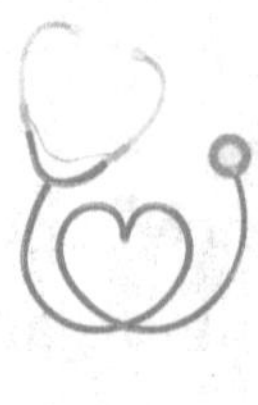

18
Lindsey

Sir

Hi, Lindsey. When I said to message me later, I should have been more specific. Do you have an answer for me?

(message delivered at 7:05am PT)

The message from Sir, who I now know as Dane—a very nice name, I may add, one that suits him and his salt-and-pepper hair, square jaw, strong arms, and toned ass—stares at me as if it's going to jump out of my phone and spank me.

Now that's a weird image. Weird and inappropriate thoughts are floating all around, actually. Ones I'm going to blame on a lack of sleep and being overworked.

I yawn and pour myself a glass of red wine, the cheap stuff that tastes *meh* but does the job. It's after seven in the evening, and Kas and I finished a dinner of frozen pizza a bit ago.

I take a sip of the wine and look down at my phone again. The screen is black now, but it's as if I can still see Dane's earlier message I've yet to respond to. Which means it's been over twelve hours since I read it the first time and over twenty-four hours since I saw him at the park.

When his question came through five minutes after my shift ended this morning, I was too focused on wrapping up paperwork and getting home to sleep before Fox dropped Kas off to give it much thought. But I don't have an excuse for ignoring it the rest of the day.

The truth is, I'm still unsure and guilty. The uncertainty comes from all the reasons I know I should end our dynamic and all the reasons I know I don't want to. I need his help, and I was already starting to see the benefits of working with him.

That's where the guilt comes in. I didn't follow through with any of the routines or check-ins I promised. I let stress take over, and now I'm even more overwhelmed—and guilty—not just for breaking the commitments I made to myself but for ignoring Dane's texts, too.

My phone buzzes on the counter, and my gut tells me who it is before I look at the screen. I think it's time to face the music. I can't ignore Dane—*Sir*—any longer. I don't think I want to, either. The guilt is becoming too much to handle. And I'd be lying if I said I didn't miss talking with him.

I take another sip of my wine and go to the living room, snuggling up on the couch under a blanket. Kas is playing her game in her room on the condition that tomorrow, we'll spend time together since today was a day for me to rest and play catch-up around the house.

I set my wine down on the coffee table and tap my phone screen to unlock it. Nerves swell in my stomach, and I open the message app and prepare for whatever his message says.

Sir

You've missed your planned check-ins, and I have not heard from you. Should I take this as your decision to not move forward, or would you like to talk?

Well, damn. I've made him mad. Or at least, I think I have. That's the tone I read it in.

Before I can decide how to answer, another message pops up.

Sir

Or do you want to get in trouble, Lindsey?

I read the message again and again, and my heart races faster each and every time I read it. Do I want to get in trouble? That's not what I want, right? I mean, I don't want him to be mad at me, so I wouldn't want to get in trouble, either. I like it too much when he calls me *good girl.* Especially when he said it in person.

I've thought about that moment a lot in the last twenty-four hours. How the husky timbre of his voice made me feel. How the praise made my body react.

Sir

I see that you're in the chat and have read my messages. Did you forget I have that ability? Let me know if you would prefer we talk on the phone.

I shift on the couch, not quite understanding why this is turning me on. It shouldn't. I'm not even saying anything back to him. But maybe it's because he's being so attentive and because his messages make me feel wanted, even if I do feel like I'm in trouble.

His messages read as if I could be more than just a client to him, like the way he's disappointed that he hasn't heard from me is somehow more than just because he's my Dom.

But that's a silly thought, right? We hardly know each other, and we only started working together recently.

My fingers hover over the screen, and a new message comes through before I can decide what to say.

Sir

I'll give you ten minutes to decide.

I know right away that I don't need ten minutes. I do feel guilty for not responding sooner, but that seems silly now. Because if I imagine never getting a message from him again, never speaking to him again, or simply awkwardly staring at him from afar when I see him every Friday then maybe sporadically in town, it feels… wrong. Like I'd be giving up something good, something important.

I type out my message and hit send before I can fully think it through.

Me

You're impatient, Sir.

I nibble on the inside of my cheek, analyzing why I chose to say that instead of apologizing. The bubbles pop up, and his answer comes through without pause.

Sir

Is that what you wanted to say to me, or would you like to try again?

I sit up on the couch as if he's here beside me or watching me through the window. In a way, I thought I was being cheeky, but now, I want to please him, and he hardly said anything at all.

Me

I'd like to try again.

Sir

Please do, Lindsey.

Me

Can I call you in five minutes, Sir? I'd like to talk to you.

Sir

If you promise to be on your best behavior for me.

I itch to say I can try, but I know that will only make things worse for me. Maybe he's right; maybe I do want to get in trouble. But again, I ask myself why. I've never liked being in trouble before.

I shake that thought away.

Me

I promise, Sir.

Sir

Very well. My clock is set for five minutes.

I sit up from the couch, grab my wine, and run up the steps to my room, fluffing my pillows and sitting on the bed, placing my glass on my side table and grabbing my earbuds so our conversation will be private. I left the door open a crack, but it's mostly closed to muffle any sounds of my voice. Not that Kas will hear with her headphones on.

With less than a minute left, I hit the call button, finding out too late I hit the video chat. When my Sir's, *Dane's*, face fills the screen, I'm shocked for a moment before I realize there's no reason to hide now. We've met. We know what the other looks like. The walls are gone, and it's just us now.

It should be impossible for a man like him to get more beautiful, especially when looking at him via a screen, but somehow, he manages it. Unlike last time, where he had a plain black background, he hasn't hidden his surroundings.

He's outside, from the looks of the back of an Adirondack chair in a deep green. The July sun won't go down completely for another hour, but the golden light of the impending sunset only makes him look like some lumberjack god, lighting the planes of his sharp features and black-and-silver hair that's trimmed tight at the sides and styled on top.

"Lindsey." His voice rumbles. "Thank you for being on time."

"Hi, Dane. Thank you for giving me another chance."

He cocks an eyebrow, the corner of his lip curling up. "I was feeling lenient."

Heat pools in my belly, and despite myself, I pretend as if he only smiles like that for me and not for every person he's ever said that to. I suppose I'm the only one who's seen it, however, and I can't help but feel a bit smug about that.

I dip my chin so our eyes lose connection, and Dane clears his throat.

"Look at me, Lindsey."

My head snaps up, and my brown eyes meet his beautiful hazel ones.

"Now that we can see each other, keep your eyes on me unless I tell you otherwise," he says sternly.

"Yes, Sir." I say the Sir part quietly, nervous with Kas being in the house.

Dane's eyes flick behind me as if he's looking for someone. "If you're worried about Kas hearing us, you can call me Dane unless we're alone or messaging."

Relief washes over me. Not only because I won't have to be worried about Kas hearing me call someone Sir but also that I get to use his real name. It suits him, and I like the way it feels to say it. I've gotten used to Sir already, but it will be easy to get used to Dane now that we've officially met and I know every part of his face.

"Thank you."

"You're welcome."

The gentle sound of crickets comes through my earbuds, and it soothes my nerves. Dane stares at me, and while I was hoping he'd start the conversation, I know he's waiting for me to begin.

"I'm sorry for not getting back to you and for breaking my commitments again." I pause for a second and look down, but when he clears his throat, my eyes snap to his. He doesn't look angry, but his gaze holds mine as if he's letting me know he's here to support me, urging me to continue. I swallow to wet my dry mouth. "I'm sorry for not responding to your messages, and I'm sorry for sassing off."

"That is a lot of sorries," he purrs, the natural hum of his voice making my toes curl in my socks.

I continue to hold his gaze, my cheeks heating. "Should I not be sorry?"

"Yes, if you truly are. But I'd prefer if the apologies came with a way to hold yourself accountable so you don't continue this behavior."

I bristle. "I think my behavior was warranted though, wasn't it?"

Dane doesn't flinch, and his gaze remains even. "I don't know, Lindsey. You tell me. Was avoiding me the way you truly wanted to respond? Or did you respond that way because of how you were feeling?"

"Are you going to respond to everything I say with a question?"

"Are you going to continue to deflect or be honest with me?"

I huff, frustration building in my core. "You weren't honest with me, Dane."

"If you want to go tit for tat, we can do that." He pauses, the planes of his face softening slightly. "But maybe take a breath and ask yourself why you're so eager to argue with me. Why do you need to steer the ship when you know you prefer letting me take the lead? That's why you came to me, yes or no?"

"Yes," I say without hesitation. I don't want to

steer this ship; I'm tired of steering it. Obviously, it has not been working for me.

He doesn't respond right away. He shifts in his chair and holds his phone so his face is closer to the screen. "Checking in, do I still have your consent?" he asks.

While I'm feeling a lot right now, I don't want to stop. "Yes."

"Green or yellow right now?"

I pause to check in with myself and then answer. "Green."

He hums. "Good, then let's go back. I know you're new at this Lindsey, but I expect you to take ownership of your choices. Just as I will take ownership of mine."

"I thought by apologizing I was," I answer honestly.

"Apologies are nice, but they lack the awareness and understanding that you went against your word, your agreement with me."

"I don't know how to respond otherwise."

"Then you can ask me for help instead of pushing back and being a brat. I want to help you, Lindsey."

I ignore how him calling me a brat ignites something low in my belly. "I told you before, it's hard for me to ask for help."

"I know, and that's why you have me. When we speak, you can let go."

"I wish it were that easy."

"You're thinking too hard about this. Let your natural instincts as a submissive guide you. We would not have gotten this far in our dynamic if that wasn't there. Now, take another breath, and let go of your fight. Remember, you are still strong in choosing to surrender, and you are still in control by choosing to surrender. Trust me to catch you." There's a heavy pause as emotion builds in my throat and the bridge of my nose starts to tingle. "Can you do that for me?"

His voice breaks through the emotion, and I nod.

"Use your words, baby."

Baby. I suck in a small breath, my eyes seeking his. Does he not realize what he called me? Is that something he calls everyone he works with at some point? I could ask, I could question it, but I liked it too much to want to. Because I want him to do it again.

"I can do that," I finally say.

"Good girl. Now, would you like me to give you an example of what I expect?"

"Yes, Sir." The *Sir* slips out so naturally, but

my eyes dart to the door to make sure Kas isn't there, even though I know she won't be.

Dane's warm chuckle sends sparks from the soles of my feet to the top of my head. My eyes focus back on his hazel ones through the screen, and I match his small smile.

"I'll use myself as an example," he says. "I want to acknowledge that I wasn't honest about knowing your identity. In keeping that from you, I broke a key part of what we've been building—your trust. And I recognize that trust is the foundation of this dynamic.

"I also acknowledge that I didn't give you a clear timeframe to respond to my request at the park, which left things uncertain. That lack of structure was on me, and I understand it made things harder for you. As your Dom, it's my responsibility to lead with clarity and integrity, and I take full ownership of where I fell short. Moving forward, I will be open with you and set clear expectations so there's no confusion between us. That starts now. Does that feel right to you, Lindsey?"

"Yes, Dane. Thank you for saying that."

His eyes are warm. "I want to be clear that there is a time and place to question me, to push back. If ever you feel you can't trust me, if I let you down in some way as your Dom, it is your responsibility to be brave and tell me. Can you do that for me?"

"Yes, I think—" He clears his throat, and I laugh a bit. "Yes, Dane. I can."

"Very good. Now, would you like to try again?"

"Yes, I would." I adjust on my bed, my arm getting sore from holding my phone. I make a mental note that next time, I need to use my laptop to call him.

My eyes hold his as I do my best to articulate my thoughts in the way he's requested. Then I take a breath.

"I took advantage of the lack of boundaries you set. I allowed my anger and fear to dictate how I did and did not respond to you. I ignored your messages when I should've answered, and instead of being honest and explaining myself, I pushed back with an attitude. I know that's not how we should communicate. I broke trust, and I need to do better."

"And do you want to do better?"

"Yes, Dane. I want to."

That warm hum of his resonates between us.

"Does that mean your answer to continuing our relationship is a yes?"

I thought I wasn't sure before, but deep down, I never wanted to stop. Our conversation only shows me how much I need this. Need *him*.

"Yes," I say with certainty. "If you do."

"I never wanted to end it."

His words ring through the line and warm me from the inside out. "You're not mad I didn't tell you that I'm a mom?"

"Not mad, disappointed."

"That's worse," I groan. "Everyone knows that."

"Then what do you think you could do to ease my disappointment?"

If I thought my mouth was dry before, it is now. *Ease his disappointment*... What I'm thinking is *not* what he's picturing. Because there is no way he's picturing me on my knees in front of him, reaching for the button of his jeans.

God, I need to get laid or something. This is getting out of control.

I reach toward my nightstand and pick up my wine glass. My lips press to the cool glass, but before I can take a sip, Dane's voice rings through my phone in a cool command. "Do not take a sip of that wine."

The bark in his tone brooks no argument. I put down the glass and look at him, feeling that tingly feeling low in my body. "Did I do something wrong?" I ask.

"Have you had a lot to drink tonight?"

"No, a couple of sips."

"Good, you are to drink water for the rest of the night."

"What? Why?"

He raises an eyebrow, and my chin dips, but I force my eyes to remain on his like I know he wants.

"Are you talking back again?" he asks.

I press my lips together and shake my head. "I'll only drink water the rest of the night, Sir."

His lip twitches at my slipup, and I realize how bad I am at calling him Dane when he's in Sir mode.

"Have you forgotten I want you to remain sober when we speak?"

There is a clause about that in our contract, but it's not like this session was planned. I know it's not a time for me to argue that, though, so I nod. "I remember."

"Good. Can you tell me why you reached for your wine when I asked you how you could please me?"

Please me. Eff my life. "I—" What do I tell him?

The truth. He did want honesty. But this is not supposed to be sexual, and what I'm thinking is definitely sexual.

"Lindsey, I'm asking you a question."

My heart races in my chest, and before I can think again, I say, "It was something sexual, Sir."

My cheeks burn pink, and the buzzing sound of crickets and cicadas seems to intensify through the quiet of the line, my confession along with my Sir slipup hanging between us.

"I see."

"You know what?" I chuckle nervously. "Maybe I should hang up for tonight. I'm tired, and this has been good. I'll journal and send you—"

"Lindsey, stop."

His demand ceases my words, and I stare into his sharp eyes.

"You will not hang up."

"Okay," I respond.

"If you're comfortable, will you share with me what it was?"

That was . . . not what I was expecting him to say. I thought it was against his rules. My heart thuds in my ears, and I wish I had a glass of cold water to drink. Very cold water.

"I, um... I wanted to kneel in front of you and—" I can't finish the rest, and he knows it. Dane shifts in his chair slightly, so slightly I would have missed it had I blinked. My toes curl in my socks again, and I attempt to wet my lips with my dry tongue.

"Your desire to submit is clear." He inhales. "It was brave of you to share, and your honesty pleases me."

"I want to please you, Dane." The words feel as if they've come from an entirely different part of me, yet they feel right. I rub my thighs together, and there's no missing the way Dane's masculine jaw ticks before he nods.

"You should get some rest."

His command brings me back to my body, and I blink several times as his words settle in me. He's ending the conversation, which is probably a good thing considering all that's going through my mind now.

I nod in understanding. "Okay."

"Take the night to recover from all the work you've been doing. Drink water only, and send me your check-in for the evening once you've completed your routine."

"Yes, Dane."

"I know you have tomorrow off. If I give you an assignment, will you have time to complete it?"

"Like a test?"

His shoulders ease, and a warm, soft laugh drifts through the phone. The sound of it eases me, too. "Not a test. I'd like to focus on rebuilding trust between us. I will send you questions to reflect and journal on that pertain to this conversation, and from there, we'll figure out a proper punishment for your avoidance. If you have ideas, you'll write them down for me to review. How does that sound?"

"I can handle that."

Dane nods and leans forward in his chair so his face is closer and I can see his eyes clearly. "I'm glad we spoke."

"Me, too, Dane."

Our gaze remains locked until he finally breaks it. "Be good for me and hang up now. I'll look for your check-in."

I smile softly and dip my chin. "Good night."

"Good night."

I do as he says and hang up, dropping my phone beside me and leaning back against the pillows. I expect my mind to race, to analyze every second of our conversation, but instead,

I feel content, the urge to do my check-in and receive his praise present in my mind.

I climb out of bed and pick up my wine glass, heading to the bathroom. I shut my eyes for a moment and check in with myself. Where before I felt unsure and afraid, now I feel hopeful.

Dane's smile and hazel irises swim behind my eyelids, and I grin to myself. It surprises me, but I'm excited for the future, a feeling I don't think I've felt in a long time. I pick up my wine, the urge to drink it gone now. I dump it down the drain and snap a picture to send to Sir. His answer comes through right away, and my heart flutters.

Sir

Good girl, now go do what I asked.

I respond without hesitation.

Me

Yes, Sir.

19
Dane

I STARE OUT THE window of my office, the midmorning sun streaming through the glass panes. The sunny day doesn't match my thoughts because I'm unsure of myself and brooding like a grumpy asshole.

Fuck, it's been a long time since I've felt this way, since I've felt like I've failed a submissive the way I failed Lindsey. I let my attraction to her cloud my judgment, and I've slipped up, not only in not giving her clear instructions and boundaries but also in our interactions. I should never have asked her to tell me what she imagined. I should have done what I always do on the occasion a submissive has a sexual desire or fantasy and gently diverted away from it. Instead, I had her lean into it.

Her response eased my disappointment alright,

but it also made me feel like a horny shithead, like I was a captive to my baser instincts and couldn't fucking control myself around her. It's not a feeling I like, and it never has been. Feeling out of control reminds me of how I felt as a child, and it upsets me.

I also called her baby, a nickname I reserve for my online persona to call the internet at large, never a submissive I'm working with. The moment I said it, it felt right, and it's why I didn't react in the moment. It should have been my hint to stop the conversation, but I didn't.

I feel drawn to Lindsey, and I crave her now, more than I crave a good run or the taste of rich cognac. Cognac the color of her eyes, which always suck me in.

My phone buzzes in my pocket, and as if she sensed I was thinking about her, there's a message from her waiting for me. I tap it open, going against the itch inside my gut that tells me to deny myself, to put some distance between us.

Lindsey

Good morning, Sir. I hope you slept well. I woke up this

morning and did not hit snooze on my alarm. I did my stretching and journaling on the questions you sent me. I'll email them to you in a minute.

Me

I'm happy to hear that. How do you feel?

Lindsey

Still a little tired but good. I needed to sleep.

Me

You work very hard, and your body deserves rest. Do you need time for a nap later today?

Lindsey

Are you enforcing a nap time, Sir?

I chuckle to myself because I know she said that with no less than a little sass.

Me
I wasn't, but now I am.

Lindsey
Are you serious?

Me
I don't say things I don't mean.

Lindsey
I can try to fit one in.

Me
You will if I say you will.

I expect a sassy answer again or for her to say something along the lines of "I'm not a child" even if she is acting like one. But that's not what I get.

Lindsey
Okay, if you are asking me to, I will.

Pleasure from her submission washes through my body, and I ease back in my chair.

Me

Find a time in your plans today to sleep, Lindsey. Your body, your mind, your health; they're as important as those you take care of if not more.

Lindsey

It's difficult with what I do and taking care of Kas.

I think of the little girl I met at the obstacle course the other day. Smart as a whip, sassy like Lindsey. I have no doubt she has her hands full with her. I think of her brother and wonder about her family and Kas's dad. Does she have anybody to help her?

Me

Do you have help with childcare?

Lindsey takes a moment to respond, the bubbles dancing for some time before her answer comes through.

Lindsey

It's . . . a long story. I can share another time, but long story short, I do have help, though I feel guilty asking for more.

Me

Tell me why you feel guilty.

Lindsey

I have a neighbor, a teenage girl, who watches Kas, but I mentioned money is a little tight for various reasons. Then there's my brother, Nathan, who's engaged to Fox and Morgan. The three of them help with Kas a lot, but they have their own lives, you know?

Me

Have they expressed that they don't like helping you?

Lindsey

No, the opposite. Nathan said he wants to help more during the summer, but he's already done so much. I feel like shit taking more from him.

Me

But he's offered his help?

Lindsey

He has. He told me to send him a calendar so we can make a plan.

Me

Did you send the calendar?

I ask the question although I know what her answer will be. Lindsey wants help, but she doesn't want to ask for it or take it when it's offered. Her pride is admirable but has no place here.

Lindsey

It's not that easy.

Me

That isn't what I asked. Did you send the calendar, yes or no?

Lindsey

No.

Me

Send Nathan your calendar, and I'd like a screenshot when it's completed. Have you had your coffee yet this morning?

Lindsey

No, why?

Me

You will not have your morning coffee until your calendar is sent to your brother. Is that understood?

There's silence, and I know I've chosen the right consequence for her. Eventually, an answer comes through.

Lindsey

I'll do it now.

Me

I'm here to make your life easier. To take care of you when you can't take care of yourself. This is me doing that.

Lindsey

Thank you, Sir.

A few minutes later, a screenshot of the email to Nathan with a time stamp is sent through, and not long after, she sends me a picture of her drinking a cup of coffee. There's a demure smile on her face and a light in her eyes that wasn't there yesterday. She does look tired, but she looks happy.

Satisfaction pools in my chest at her obedience, and if she were here in front of me, I would have rewarded her with a kiss that made her knees weak.

Me

That's my good girl.

I typed and sent the message as if it were a knee-jerk reaction. My heart stops beating, and I know I've fucked up again. "Good girl" is one thing—"that's my good girl" is another.

Lindsey responds a moment later with a smiley face emoji, the one that's blushing. I turn my head to the ceiling and let out a groan of frustration. My dick is threatening to tent my fucking pants, and the urge to run it out overtakes me as quickly as my urge to say inappropriate things to Lindsey.

I stand, making my way through my cabin and entering my room. I remove my pajama pants and throw on a pair of running shorts, a T-shirt, and socks. A couple of minutes later, I've sucked down electrolytes and put my running shoes on. I swing open my door and inhale the mountain air, my body feeling better as I fill my lungs with the scent of summer.

My feet pound on the ground, and I get lost in the rhythm of it.

My heart beats loud, and my breath comes hard. My lungs burn, and I keep running. I pass tree after tree as my eyes track the ground for rocks and fallen branches. The ground is rich, and there's green grass, various plants, and earthy soil on the forest floor. Before I can stop it, the beautiful brown color of Lindsey's eyes invades my mind, and I almost trip.

I come to the fork in the path ahead of me, and instead of taking the one I know will lead me home, I take the one that will lead me to the only person I know I can talk to: Fox.

20
Dane

"You're lucky I didn't have a shotgun on me. I thought you were a rabid animal given the way you came huffing out of the woods."

Fox walks through the door of his cabin, handing me a mug with ice water in it. The cup reads "World's Biggest Grump" on the side. I ignore his friendly barb and take the drink, staring at the silly inscription.

"You drink out of this?" I ask.

"It was a present from Nathan on my last birthday, so yes."

"You've gone soft," I tease him.

Fox raises a thick blond eyebrow at me as we both take a seat next to each other on the top step leading to his front door. "You think I didn't punish him for it first?"

I chuckle and sip the ice water, the gentle breeze

and the water easing my overheated body. I ran harder and longer than I thought I did. My muscles are going to kill me later. "I imagine you did and that he couldn't sit for a week."

Fox is a Dominant I've always admired, someone who's been a good friend since we met. While one could be put off by his height, strength, and tattoos, I recognized a kindred spirit in him, same with Morgan.

Fox is similar to me but tends to be more aggressive in his style of punishment. I witnessed a scene with him and Morgan once and saw the way he handles his wife. It works for him, for them. I can go hard, and I enjoy being rough, but I tend to lean more on the forgiving side than Fox does.

"Nathan said he met you the other day." Fox folds his tattooed hands over his knees in front of him. "He came back and let us know he met the online lumbersnack Dom."

I chuckle. "Guess that confirms you told him about me."

He nods. "Not your identity—just the videos. He put that together when you met."

I nod back at him. I still work for Fox and Morgan from time to time during busy seasons.

Less now since my Loopr has become popular and my client list is long. But in the last two years, my friendship with the married couple has become more peer-to-peer than anything else, especially since I don't leave my cabin much anymore. I know Fox is someone I can turn to when I need someone to talk with. Morgan as well. But since she's the one who sent Lindsey to me, Fox is a better option to keep her identity sealed to the best of my ability.

"So are you going to tell me why you came over unannounced after I haven't seen you in months, or do I have to guess?"

I exhale and set the mug down next to me, dropping my hands between my legs, much like how Fox is positioned. "I came for advice."

Fox makes a low humming sound. "And you came to me instead of my wife?"

"It may not be smart, but I'll take my chances."

Fox's lips twitch, and I notice he looks more relaxed than I've ever seen him. Morgan felt much the same in our few interactions since Nathan came along, and I'm glad to see it. They're a couple who deserve to be happy.

"Alright. As I mentioned, Morgan and Nathan

are in town for a bit, so you can talk freely. It's just us."

"I'll save us both the small talk and cut straight to it." Fox nods as a gesture to keep speaking. It's true that I haven't seen him in a while, but we don't need to talk about the weather. We're simply not that type of people.

"I have a new submissive," I say. "Things have become complicated."

Fox's brow furrows. "Is this relationship in person?"

"It's—" I want to say the word *complicated*, but that won't help Fox give me advice. "They contacted me online, and we went through all the proper protocols, talks, agreements, and boundaries. We've only been working together for a brief time, but things have become hazy because we discovered each other's identities."

"By accident?" Fox asks.

I nod. "The details are unimportant. I do not want to say too much since I don't want to give hints as to who they are."

Fox places his hands on his knees and rubs his palms on his jeans. He may be wondering if he knows them, but knowing Fox, he's attempting not to. He's not a nosy person and never has been. I've always liked that about him.

"Do you feel at risk of them sharing your identity with others?" he asks.

I shake my head. "No, nothing like that. If I'd be worried about anyone spilling the beans, it would be Levi."

"He has a big mouth."

"That he does."

We both exhale a laugh before Fox asks, "Then what is it that brought you here?"

"I'm attracted to them, and I believe they are to me. The boundaries I set up in our dynamic are becoming blurred. I don't know what it is about them, but they make me want things I haven't wanted in a long time, maybe ever."

"Should I cut to the part where you tell me you're considering asking them to do scenes in person?"

My spine straightens as I stare at my friend. "That was not what I was going to ask."

Fox almost smiles as he smacks me on the back. "It wasn't?"

The sting of his pat shakes whatever veil has been held over my eyes, and the reality of his question sets in. "Asking them hadn't crossed my mind."

"Consciously," Fox adds. "But it's where we would have ended up. I've seen that look in your eye, because I've had it before. With Morgan and with Nathan."

"I'm not looking for a full-time, live-in submissive," I refute, which is true. While I love what I do, living the lifestyle twenty-four seven with someone has never been what I imagined for myself, not even if I decided to settle down someday. A twenty-four seven dynamic is a massive commitment. It demands constant time, attention, and energy from both partners. It's not just about control; it's about caretaking, management, emotional stewardship. You're essentially becoming responsible for someone else's routine, mental state, and growth every hour of the day, not just during scenes. I don't think it's something Lindsey would want, either, especially with the added responsibility of Kas.

"I never said anything about a twenty-four seven live-in submissive." Fox smirks. "I said *in-person* scenes. I know you know there's a difference."

My brain rewinds the conversation, and he's right. When I don't speak, Fox places his hand on my shoulder and squeezes.

"When was the last time you did an in-person scene with someone?"

"Over a year," I answer honestly.

Fox dips his chin, and I don't see any judgment in his eyes. "Because you don't want to?"

"Life, work; it's been busy. Starlight Haven is small, and I don't want to risk people talking. Usually, I'll drive to Los Angeles when I have the desire, which was the last time I did an in-person. The scene was fine, but it wasn't fulfilling. Since then, I've found my work to be enough."

"You don't have to explain yourself. Everything you're saying makes sense. I only asked because I think you forget you have needs."

"I don't want to use this person simply for my sexual needs."

Fox grunts. "I didn't mean to imply that. But Dane, you give and you care for so many people, but who is taking care of you?"

His line of questioning reminds me of my questions to Lindsey.

"I take care of myself," I say simply.

"You do, and I'm not saying you don't do it well. You're one of the most put-together and well-adjusted people I've ever met. But you know I've always taken issue with Domming being your main source of work. You need real-life connection to keep yourself sane and fulfilled in all areas of your life, not just sexually."

Now I'm the one grunting. "I hear what you're saying, but I haven't had this issue before. I haven't thought of my clients in this way or needed an in-person connection to keep me grounded. I have my routines for that."

"Exercise and work are good, but they don't replace what I'm talking about, and you're smart enough to know that."

I run my hand over my beard, jaw tense from clenching it. I know that's true, but I'm fighting it. "Even if you're right, it doesn't change the fact that I'm thinking of a client in a way I shouldn't. In a way I *can't* think about them."

"And what way is that?"

I run my tongue over my teeth. "You're going to make me say it?"

"Do I have to ask you to use your words?"

"You're a bastard sometimes, you know that?"

"You're the one who came to me for advice. Morgan is nicer."

My eyes shift to Fox. He's watching me like a predator watching his prey. I exhale and say what I shouldn't but know I need to get out.

"Like they could be more."

He nods slightly in approval of my words. "And you think they wouldn't want that?"

"They came to me for help, to structure their life and build discipline."

"You said that you believe them to be attracted to you as well. That tells me your feelings are not one-sided, yet now you're having me believe they are. Which is it?"

I think of all my interactions with Lindsey. The comments she left on my videos that started our interactions, the "tingly" feeling she mentioned in her email, the way she looked at me and called me Sir so easily at the park the other day, her admission of wanting to kneel in front of me and ease my disappointment with her smart mouth.

I blow out a breath. "No, I don't think they're one-sided."

"Then you're getting in your own way. Wanting this person, being attracted to them, it's not a crime or a sin. If you were some creep who collected subs online for your own perverted pleasure, that would be one thing, but you're not that. You're a good man, and a good Dom. Stop beating yourself up over what you're telling me is a mutual attraction. It sounds like what you need to do is speak with them and rewrite your agreement, if that's what you both want. That way, the lines will no longer be blurred."

I ruminate over his words and know he's right. I've spent so much time building my business, making sure my submissives are safe and cared for with me. I never want anyone to feel as if I've crossed a line or that I'm what Fox said: an anonymous man on the internet who gets off on telling people what to do. I've never been that and never wanted to be that.

I've also never wanted to be just a man who gets off on power and control like my father was. What I do has always been about a mutually beneficial relationship, exploring kink in a safe container.

Fox's hand squeezes my shoulder, and our eyes meet again. "You alright?"

I nod. "You're bringing up good points. It's making me think."

"Don't hurt yourself."

My chest shakes with laughter, and Fox drops his hand.

"You can be funny sometimes, Malone," I say, intentionally using his last name.

"Don't get used to it."

I look at the "World's Biggest Grump" mug sitting next to me. "Gotta keep up the persona."

His lip twitches. "Not a persona."

I smirk, knowing that Fox is a big softie on the inside. He may come off as a grump and be ex–Special Forces, but if you get the privilege of knowing the true him, you know he's one of the best men around. Which is why I take his advice to heart when he gives it.

We stare out at the woods for another few minutes, my brain processing everything he's said. When I hear the sound of tires on dirt and gravel, I stand, knowing Morgan and Nathan are on their way up the drive.

"I'm going to head out. Thanks for the chat."

Fox stands and claps me on the back in a brief hug. "Hope it helped."

I nod and start to walk away.

"Dane?" Fox calls.

I stop and turn. Fox is still standing at the bottom of the steps with his hands in his jean pockets, tattooed arms bulging under his T-shirt. "I don't know much about your past, but whatever is blocking you from being happy, kick it in the fucking ass. Don't let it control you."

My pulse quickens as I stare at my friend. There are many things Fox could say, but that was more than insightful.

"You a life coach now?"

He chuckles. "Thinking about being an online Pro Dom, actually."

"I know someone who could help you with that."

Fox flips me off as his truck comes up the drive. I flip him off right back and leave before his partners can see me, taking off into the woods at a jog.

21
Lindsey

That's my good girl.

I can't stop replaying Dane's message to me last week. Nor can I stop imagining him saying it to me in his deep and rumbling voice. It's all I've been able to think about every time I send him my check-ins and every time he praises me for following through.

Sometimes—okay, a lot of times—I go back and read the message to make sure I didn't read the wording wrong, but I hadn't. Then I sent him back a blushing emoji. I regretted it as soon as I did, but he started it, right? Or is that something else he says to his other submissives?

The thought makes me a bit jealous, even if it's irrational. I knew what I was getting into when I started working with him. This is his job, which means I'm a job. Maybe flirting is part of it? It's not like that counts as sex. If anything, what I said I'd do to ease his disappointment was crossing a line, but he wanted to know what I thought, and I was being honest. I haven't made a comment like that since then, and I wasn't able to drop off or pick up Kas at the obstacle course this past Friday due to work, so I haven't seen him in person, but our messages have been flirtier than they were.

Unless I'm imagining it?

"Mom?"

My gaze moves from my chicken Caesar salad to Kas, who's sitting across from me in the booth. I had a day off today, so she asked if we could come to the diner for dinner. It was an easy yes, and prior to this, we spent our time watching a movie. Eventually, she asked to play her game. I said she could but only if she taught me how to play. I thought she'd say no, but we ended up playing a bit of Critter Cove together before coming here. It's been a nice day, a day I wish we could do more often.

"Yeah, honey?"

"I go visit Dad soon, right?"

At the mention of Jeremy, I attempt to keep a calm and cool face. I'd nearly forgotten he existed with everything that's been happening recently. Dane has replaced my thoughts of him, which, until a second ago, I thought was a good thing. But maybe it's not so good considering he's supposed to be my platonic Dom.

"Yep. Next weekend."

She plays with her food. "Do you think he'd come here instead?"

The idea of Jeremy coming here, invading my mountain town, which has truly become my safe haven away from bad memories, makes my skin crawl.

"No, it's better if you go visit him in Santa Solana."

"Can I skip it then?"

My eyebrows lift, her question surprising me. "Why? I thought you liked visiting your dad. Did something happen last time?"

She shakes her head, and relief floods me.

"Then what is it, honey?"

"I don't want to miss the obstacle course."

I stab a forkful of salad, thinking this is my perfect way to ask about Tyler. "Oh?" She nods. "Does this have to do with a certain guy in attendance?"

Kas's brow furrows before she asks, "You mean Logger Dane?"

"Logger Dane?" I grin.

"Yeah, that's what we all call him now. He's nice for an old guy. Kind of reminds me of Uncle Fox but less treelike."

I laugh. Not only did she call Dane old, but she called Fox a tree. He does have legs and arms like tree trunks, come to think of it.

"Have you told Fox you compare him to a tree?"

"Yep."

I shake my head at my kid and eat a bite of my food before answering her previous question. "I can ask your dad if we can reschedule, but you start school at the end of August, so it gets a bit tricky."

"That's why dad should come here. Can't he stay at the motel or something? Or with us?"

I think of Jeremy and his prissy girlfriend in a cheap motel and almost cackle. Then I think about him in my home, and I want to throw up.

"He'd rent a house," I say. "But I don't think he'll have time with such short notice. And you know he works a lot, too."

"But so do you."

Kas doesn't say it with any malice, but I see the way her eyes lose a bit of their sparkle. Guilt over my work schedule and lack of time with her that I'd managed to shove down by hanging out with her today comes back in full force.

"I know. I'm sorry." I wish I could say something different, like if her asshole dad paid child support on time instead of being a dick, then I wouldn't have to work so much.

That reminds me, I need to call my lawyer and see if there's any update on that front. I just haven't had the time.

Kas picks up a french fry and plops it back down on her plate. I'm about to change the subject from me being a crap mom and her asshole dad to asking her about Tyler when the door to the diner jingles.

I'm sitting with my back to the door, but Kas looks up at whoever walked in, and the spark in her eye flickers back to life. I'm about to turn to see if it's Nathan or one of her friends when she says, "Logger Dane!"

The back of my neck prickles, and I know without turning that Dane is staring at the back of my head. I hear his booted footsteps, and a second later, he's standing at the head of our table. He's freshly showered, silver and dark-brown hair damp so it looks darker in color than usual.

The scent of his cologne, or whatever it is on his person, wafts to my nose, and my mouth waters at the masculine scent.

"Hey, kid."

"We were just talking about you," Kas says.

Dane softly smiles, his gaze settling on me in the intense way it does. Now I feel like I'm naked and under a microscope. I didn't dress up to come here. I'm not wearing any makeup, and I'm in a plain T-shirt and a pair of shorts made from stretchy material. Had I known I'd run into him, I would've at least put on some mascara.

"Were you?" he asks.

"Yeah, I told my mom you're less treelike than my Uncle Fox."

I press my lips together to hold in an embarrassed laugh, but Dane looks amused, the skin around his hazel eyes crinkling. "Am I now?"

"Yep." Kas grins before popping a fry in her mouth as if what she said is completely normal.

Dane's focus shifts to me, and he puts his hands in his pockets. I try to keep my attention off his forearms, but by doing that, I'm now focused on his face. His bearded jaw, that perfect freaking nose, and pretty eyes I can and do get lost in.

That's my good girl.

Inexplicable heat rises in my body, and I feel ashamed. Now is not the right time to think of that. Not in public. Not with Kas here. Actually, I should never think of it again. Ever.

"Dane!"

Both Dane and I look toward the source of the voice. It's one of the waitresses, Cheryl, and she's smiling as she walks toward us. She's a nice woman. Thin, blond, beautiful, younger than me, and a local. I've never had a problem with her, and I like her. But the way she's looking at Dane makes my skin itch. Do they know each other well?

My eyes study Dane's profile as she walks over with a bag in her hand. His eyes don't light up, and he doesn't smile. His face is neutral, and while it should satisfy me, it just makes me annoyed. Not at him but at me for even caring what or who he does in his free time.

"I was going to bring your order out to you like usual, but it's nice to see you come inside instead of handing you your dinner through your truck window." She giggles.

Dane nods and takes the bag from her. "I wanted to pay off my tab."

"Oh! Yeah, sure. Let me do that for you."

I guess that explains why I've never seen him here before. He doesn't usually come inside, which probably means my jealousy is for nothing. Again, not that I have any right to be jealous. I do wonder, though, as I look at the way Cheryl stares at him, if she follows him on Loopr and knows what he does for a living.

"Thanks, Cheryl." He reaches in his pocket and hands her cash from a dark leather wallet.

She looks surprised but takes it, looking at me then back to him before she says, "Thanks. Do you need change?"

"I'm good."

"Okay, then." She stares at him with a flirty smile, as if she's waiting for him to say something, but he doesn't. It's stupid, but I'm happy he doesn't flirt back. "See you next time."

Dane nods and turns back so he's facing me and Kas. Cheryl stares at his profile for a beat longer, and I swear she pouts at his easy dismissal. Before I can think about her reaction, she walks to another table, leaving the three of us.

"Are you going to eat alone, Logger Dane?" Kas asks.

I attempt not to laugh again at hearing Kas call Dane that to his face.

A hint of a smile plays at his mouth, and he nods. "Yes."

"Eat with us."

My eyebrows shoot up. Kas is friendly, always has been, but she's never invited a near stranger to eat dinner with us. But as I observe her, it's clear she's as taken with Dane as I am—and in such a short amount of time.

"It's okay, kid. You enjoy time with your mom."

"Mom's okay with it, aren't you, Mom?"

I attempt to stop my cheeks from flushing at being put on the spot. Kas looks so hopeful, and I don't want to deny her. It may be an awkward meal, but I'm not going to say no.

"Yeah, of course, *Logger Dane*. Join us."

He swallows, Adam's apple bobbing in his strong throat. He adjusts subtly on his feet. Dane is studying me, gaze boring through to my soul. I read what he's saying in his eyes: *It's up to you*.

I soften my expression and dip my chin. What can it hurt? Kas obviously wants him here, and who am I to deny her?

"Alright, then," he says. "I'll join you."

"Scoot over, Mom."

I shake my head and do as she requests,

scooting over so Dane can join me on my side. He stares at the spot then to a chair at a table next to us.

"It's fine," I offer. "There's plenty of space."

He eyes me to be sure before finally sliding in so we're next to each other across from Kas. I'd misjudged how much space we'd have. He's not a small man, and I'm not a small woman.

The heat of his body sets my skin ablaze, and our arms are touching. This isn't the first time we've touched, but we've never been in a situation like this.

"Is this okay?" Dane asks.

I turn my torso so I can look at him easily. His smell invades my senses completely, overriding the fried smell of diner food. I softly inhale, his woodsy smell calming me for whatever reason. It's probably not okay, but it doesn't feel not okay. In fact, having him here next to me feels the very opposite of not okay.

I clear my throat. "Yes."

Dane nods and turns to the bag in front of him, taking out his meal and the plastic utensils that came with it. There's extra silverware in a basket near me, so I grab him a fork and knife.

"Here," I say. "Might as well use the real ones."

He reaches for them with a thanks, and I swear he purposely brushes my fingers when he takes them from me. It sends a zip down my arm like lightning, and if Kas wasn't here, I think I'd throw myself at him like a rabid dog.

I pull my hand back and take a sip of my icy root beer, debating if I need therapy instead of a Dom. I swear that none of my reactions to him are normal.

"What is that?" Kas asks with a sour expression.

Her question makes me look at Dane's food.

"It's an egg-white omelet with chicken, spinach, and broccoli."

"Ew, Logger Dane. Gross."

Dane smiles softly at Kas, and my heart melts a little. "It's good."

"You're lying."

"Kas," I say. "Don't comment on other people's food like that or accuse them of lying."

"It's okay, I know it doesn't look appetizing," he says. "But I like it."

"I'm calling cap," Kas adds, eating a fry.

"No cap," he answers back easily.

She barks out a laugh, covering her mouth as she finishes chewing. "No, no, no, Logger Dane. It's so Ohio when you try to use our slang."

"I thought it was lit," he adds, taking a bite of his food. Food that, to Kas's credit, does look pretty gross.

She giggles again, and the sound is music to my ears. "Nooo, please stop!"

"Wait, what does Ohio mean?" I ask.

"Cringe," Dane and Kas say at the same time. They look at each other in amusement before Kas breaks out into giggles once more.

"How do you know that, Logger Dane?" she asks.

"Yeah, Logger Dane, how do you know that?" I add.

He swallows another bite of his food. "The internet."

Kas snort-laughs. "Logger Dane, that is Ohio."

Dane smiles like I've never seen him smile before he shrugs. "I have to keep up with you kids. I don't know what you're saying half the time."

"Please don't talk like that on Friday. You'll embarrass yourself."

"Kas!" I say.

"What? I'm saving him."

Dane eats another large bite of his weird omelet, then says, "I appreciate the advice. I'll take it under advisement."

Kas giggles yet again, and I think she says "It's your funeral" under her breath.

"Sorry," I say to Dane.

His gaze turns to mine, and the sparkle in his eyes mesmerizes me. "It's fine."

My eyes fall to his lips as his tongue darts out to lick away remnants of his food. I watch the action as if it's a documentary on National Geographic. I wonder what that tongue would feel like on my skin, or his lips sucking on my neck. My nipples tighten at the dirty thought, and I shiver.

"Cold?" he asks.

His rich voice resonates through me, and embarrassment floods my cheeks. I manage to meet his eyes, and I can tell right away that he knows I'm not cold. I'm the opposite. So very much the opposite.

"It's hot in here, Mom; how are you cold?"

Kasandra's question throws me back to reality, and I shift my body away from Dane as far as I can—which isn't far considering there's a wall preventing me from moving. Why did I say he could stay again? This was a stupid idea.

"I'm fine, honey. Just got a random shiver."

She eats a bite of her burger. "You want a fry, Logger Dane?"

My heart speeds up at her question. She really does like him, and I wonder if he's had any experience with kids or if this is new to him. While this is unexpected, I'll admit it's nice having him here. His presence is soothing, and I like when Kas laughs and jokes. I don't get to see much of it lately.

"Sure," he says. I know Dane is from here, and I'd bet money he's tried the diner's fries before. I know he's humoring my daughter, and I think I fall in love with him a little for it.

Kas smiles at his answer, looking like a cat who caught the canary as she pushes her plate closer to him. He takes one and pops it in his mouth.

"They're good," he says after chewing.

"Better than your egg whites?"

"Want to try for yourself?"

Kas screws up her nose. "No way."

Dane laughs. "You're missing out."

"Don't think so," she responds quickly.

Dane and I make eye contact, my cheeks blushing for a whole other reason now. This feels nice. Maybe too nice.

"You want a fry, Mom?"

I shake my head. "You eat them."

She nods, and I feel Dane watching me. I turn my head as I chew my bite of salad.

"You want to try my omelet?" he asks.

Kas laughs. "I dare you, Mom, it looks so nasty."

"Kas!"

Dane only laughs and cuts a bite of his omelet, making sure to get a piece of everything. I think he's going to put it in his mouth, but instead, he holds it out to me.

Kas covers her mouth to try and stop her laughter. I don't think I've seen her this excited since before Jeremy and I broke up, unless I count her excitement over the obstacle course, but this is different. This is more of an everyday type of excitement. And all over me potentially eating a bite of Dane's food.

"You really want me to try it?" I ask her.

She giggles. "Mom, it's so yucky looking. You have to!"

I shake my head and smile with her, turning my focus back to Dane. I expect him to hold the fork out to me so I can take it; instead, he's holding it up to feed me.

Kas giggles. "Zoom, zoom goes the airplane, Mom! Open wide."

Dane chuckles now, and his irises swim with amusement and something else I can't place. When I woke up this morning, my Dom feeding me in public was definitely not on my list of to-dos. But now?

Before I can overthink it, I part my lips. Dane lifts the fork to my mouth, slow and careful, and I close my lips around the warm egg and the cool press of metal. He draws the fork back with a measured hand, his eyes darkening as he watches me chew. His eyelids lower, heavy with something that looks almost reverent, like feeding me is the best thing he's ever done. Even if that's an odd thought.

"Oh my god, Mom. You ate it!" Kas snorts. "Is it nasty?!"

Dane's gaze lightens, and he lifts an eyebrow in question. I chew the food and inhale a breath through my nose. It's...not bad. But the egg/chicken combo is not my favorite. The more I chew, the more I think my daughter is right.

I swallow and reach for my root beer. "It's..."

Kas snorts again, and Dane shakes with his own laughter.

"It's not that bad," he says.

I pat Dane's hand that's resting on the table now. "If you like it, that's what matters."

He smirks at me. God, is everything this man does sexy?

Dane picks up his hand along with his fork, and he cuts into the omelet. He brings the bite of food, on the same fork that was just in my mouth, to his. His eyes stay on mine as his bowed lips close over the food and he eats it.

I shift in my chair, and when he swallows, he looks to Kas. "So yummy."

More laughter fills the air, and soon we fall into an easy silence as we eat our meals. Kas eventually starts to ask Dane what it's like to be a logger.

We both listen to him with rapt attention, learning that his dad was a logger and he followed in his footsteps. He talks about cutting down trees and reforesting to keep the planet healthy. He also mentions that he doesn't do much logging now but doesn't tell Kas what he does. Thank god.

My daughter hangs on his every word, and I have no doubt Kas will ask him to eat with us again sometime when we're done. Not that I would mind. I should mind, because he's my Dom. I shouldn't be having meals with him. A meal that has felt an awful lot like a date.

My mind starts to carry me away with ideas of the future. One that involves Dane and me together. One that involves meals at my kitchen table. Meals with Nathan, Fox, and Morgan. The image of Dane sitting next to me on the couch while Kas plays a game or he tells her a story and tucks her in at night is when I know my brain has gone too far for the night. Way, way too far.

"You good?"

I focus my attention back on Dane. There's concern in his eyes, and I blink away the haze of my stupid imagination. "Yeah, fine. Why?"

"Kas asked you a question."

I look at Kas. "Yeah, honey?"

"I was asking if we could go get ice cream now."

"I promised you we would."

Kas bounces in her seat and does a little cheer. "You want to come, Logger Dane?"

"I think I need to get back home, Curious Kas."

She snorts. "That is not a good nickname."

"Is it... Ohio?" he asks.

Kas groans, and Dane smiles easily. Their interaction makes my chest warm for what feels like the millionth time in the last half hour. There's a part of me that would love for him to get ice cream with us, but I don't need to feed my fantasy of him being more than what he is to me now. Our impromptu dinner already did not help my situation.

"Just say *weird* or *cringe*, Logger Dane."

He chuckles and steps out of the booth. Cheryl walks back over at that exact moment, and I swear she's attempting not to glare daggers at me.

"You're still here!" she says to Dane.

"Leaving now." He doesn't look her in the eye as he pulls out his wallet again. His eyes meet mine as he says loud enough for Cheryl to hear, "I've got this."

"Dane—" I start.

"Let me take care of it." His words are more than just words. They're a command. If the gentle edge to his tone didn't say it, his eyes do. He's asking me to submit to him, here and now. To let him not just take care of the bill, but to take care of me, something he said he'd do if I'd let him. I just never imagined it would be in this capacity.

I dip my chin, and emotion builds in my chest. When was the last time a man not in my family paid for my meal? It's been a long time, and while I think I should fight him on it, it feels good to let him do it.

"Thank you, Dane," I say while holding his penetrating gaze.

"You're welcome, Lindsey." The warmth of his deep voice curls my toes like it often does, and I imagine, if we were in private, he'd call me his good girl again.

He clears his throat as if he's imagining it, too, before turning to hand the cash to Cheryl. "Keep the change."

She takes the money and walks off again with that same pout on her face.

"See you later, Kas the Sass," Dane says.

Kas screws up her face. "Still cringe, Logger Dane."

He chuckles and smiles at me, his tone dropping deeper as he says, "Bye, Lindsey."

I don't think I can speak, so I wave, knowing I'll be messaging him later. For now, I'm wondering what the heck just happened between us.

22

Dane

A FAMILY WAS NEVER something I pictured for myself. Growing up an only child with a mom who loved me but treated me more like a friend and a dad who had not only anger issues but also a misguided idea of what dominance and control was, the idea of having children was not a dream. What I wanted was something quieter, a life without shouting matches or constant turmoil. Especially after a childhood spent listening to my parents fight nearly every day. Truly, all I ever dreamed of was a quiet life that made me happy. A life that fulfilled me and gave me a purpose. The one I thought I had now.

I take after my old man in many ways, but I've kept the good parts of him and rewritten the bad. Before I started doing what I do now, I logged full-time, just like he did, but on my own terms. I didn't log because I had to; I did it because I loved the solitude, the physical work, and the constant change of scenery. And when it came to my dominant nature, I found a healthier way to channel it. I didn't need control to feel powerful or to lord over anyone. I needed connection. Purpose.

I found the kink community in my early twenties while working at a logging company in Portland. I spent time at a local club, learned under one of their best Doms, and understood—for the first time—that dominance could be about trust and responsibility, not fear and control. I spent a few years bouncing around, including a stretch in New York, before I eventually ended up in Starlight Haven. I hadn't planned to stay, but there was something about this place that felt healing. Settling down here finally gave me the quiet I'd been chasing for years. Then my Loopr account exploded, and I started Domming full-time.

Over the last five years, I've grown into myself in ways I never imagined I could. I healed parts of me that felt broken—not only through the work I do but also with a therapist—and settled into the nice life I created.

I've been fine with limited human interaction,

satisfying any need for touch when it came by driving down to a club in LA, which, as I told Fox, I've stopped doing. Not only did the interactions feel empty, but they were not as fulfilling as my work online is. It didn't matter, though—at least, I thought it didn't, because I have my dynamics, my cabin, painting, and running. I also have my Loopr account where I act out scenes and have fun. I thought I had everything I could want, and I was content.

Cue the curveball I didn't expect: Lindsey.

If I did picture a potential partner coming into my life, I certainly did not expect them to be completely new to submission. I didn't expect them to be such a stunning yet sassy brat. I didn't expect them to live in this little mountain town I call home. And I most certainly didn't expect them to have a kid, a sweet and witty one I find endearing and funny.

Tonight, I went to the diner to pick up my breakfast for dinner, something I do every Sunday. It's rare I go inside; Cheryl sees my truck pulling up and brings it out. I know it's because she's hoping I'll ask her out or talk to her about my life.

She's tried to pry information out of me since

she started working at the diner a couple of years back, but I've given her minimal information. Sometimes, I think she watches my videos online, but I honestly don't know, and I'm not going to ask her.

When I drove up to the diner, I spotted Kas and Lindsey sitting at a booth through the window. Before I knew what I was doing, I'd parked my truck and made my way in. I don't know what I thought would happen when they noticed me, but I sure as hell didn't expect Kas to invite me to eat with them. I didn't expect myself to say yes, either.

But now I'm learning that I should expect the unexpected when it comes to Lindsey and Kas. On top of that, I do and say things that are completely out of character for me, things that lead me to believe Fox is right. I need to speak with Lindsey about moving our relationship forward in a different direction. I've been thinking about it all week, during every message, every bit of praise I send, but I've been allowing us to settle into our dynamic, wanting to ask her at the right time.

I open my laptop and go to my email to catch up on some work. My email is stacked full with new requests to work with me. Usually, that means a video has gone viral or at least gotten enough views for people to want to know more about what I do and see if they can get on my waitlist.

I pick up my phone and open Loopr, finding that a video has over eight hundred thousand views. There are thousands of comments, too. It's a minute-long one I uploaded earlier this morning that I filmed the night after I called Lindsey *my good girl*.

I kept my shirt on, the lighting dark so I could edit it in black and white. My button-up is black, and I have it rolled up on my forearms. It's one of my more erotic videos, where I'm pretending to talk to a submissive that needs punishment, which explains why it's done as well as it has. I'm sure my email is full of inquiries asking if I do in-person scenes. The internet is thirsty, and when I give them water, they drink. This video will pay out well, so it's done its job.

I go to exit out of the app when a new comment comes through on my notifications, and I stop in my tracks at the username. I look at the time on my phone and see it's seven. Lindsey's socials won't lock for a bit yet, so I guess someone is scrolling and looking at my page. I probably shouldn't be as happy as I am about it, but the fact she commented tells me someone wants to play.

I take a sip of my decaf coffee, almost choking on it when I read the comment she left on my video.

@WhyAmIHere33: How would you punish me?

I swallow down the hot liquid and read the notification again while I cough. Then I read it again.

It's no different from some of the other comments on the video, but my reaction is based solely on it coming from her. Did she drink that wine I told her not to drink the other night?

I sit up in my chair, deciding I can answer my other submissives in a minute. Lindsey is mine, after all. There's also the question that's been running through my mind since I left Fox's last week. If I were to do what he said, allow my subconscious thoughts that are now conscious to manifest into a relationship with her, an in-person one, would she say yes?

Part of me thinks she wouldn't. She didn't come

to me for more than what we're doing now. But then I read a comment like that, and I remember what she said about how she'd ease my disappointment and the blushing emoji she sent, not to mention the flirty undertones of our messages this week, and I think she would. Maybe she's even imagined it or wants it already like I do, even if I've been berating myself and attempting to deny it.

Fuck it.

I open up my messaging app and find Lindsey's name, typing a message before I can talk myself out of it.

Me
Are you drinking?

It takes less than thirty seconds for her next message to pop up.

Lindsey
No, Sir. Why do you ask?

Me
The comment you left on my video was brave.

Lindsey

Do you think I need alcohol to be brave?

Me

No, I think you're brave already. Maybe the better word is uninhibited.

Lindsey

I'm sorry, Sir. Did my comment make you uncomfortable?

Me

No, but you're playing with fire.

The bubbles pop up, and then go down again. Then they pop up and go down again. She does this for a while before a message finally comes through.

Lindsey

Will you tell me then, Sir?

Me

Tell you what?

Lindsey

What it would be like if I were your submissive.

A possessive clawing itches at my chest, and my desire to find out where she lives so I can remind her exactly who she belongs to takes over. The urge is unexpected, like everything with Lindsey, but instead of stuffing it down, I embrace it.

Me

You are my submissive, Lindsey. Or have you forgotten?

Her response comes quickly, and the clawing at my chest is satisfied for a moment.

Lindsey

I haven't forgotten. I know I'm your submissive, Sir.

Me

Then what is it you meant?

Lindsey

What would it be like if I was your submissive and you came home to find me starting without you. How would you punish me?

Fuuuck. Blood rushes from my brain to my dick, and I know this has already gone too far. We've already crossed lines that we can't come back from. In any other scenario, I would have ended it with a submissive who asked me this. I would have ended our relationship well before this because of my reactions to her, like when I called her baby.

Everything about this, about our talks, goes against my rules. Goes against what I've tried to maintain and build with my clients. But with Lindsey...

I want to break the rules for her.

Me

If you want the answer, we need to discuss it, and I need your consent. Not only that, I need to see your face and hear your voice when you say it. Are you able to do that?

I'm expecting a message. But instead, my screen flashes with an incoming video call. It rings once, twice, my heart thudding hard in my chest. Then I click accept.

23
Lindsey

WHAT AM I DOING? has been the question running through my mind since I typed out my unhinged comment on his video, a video that did things to me and made me want the world to know that he's mine. Even if he's not technically mine.

You are my submissive, Lindsey. Or have you forgotten?

"Hi, Lindsey."

The voice that was in my head now rings through the speakers of my laptop, and my pulse pounds in my throat. I nibble on the inside of my cheek as I stare at Dane—my Dom—on the screen.

"Hi, Dane."

He smiles softly, and I notice there's firelight dancing in his eyes. I wish I was there with him.

"Are you alone?" he asks, his eyes shifting

behind me. I'm not in my bedroom—I'm on the couch in the living room, a different background than what he's seen before.

"Yes," I say with a nod. "Kas is at Moira's—last-minute sleepover."

"Please address me as Sir, then."

And there go my nipples. They could seriously cut glass every time he's around me, especially when he talks like a stern general. "Yes, Sir."

"Good girl."

I exhale a breath at his praise and smile at him. There's a pause of silence and the sound of a log popping in the background. The pop breaks the haze I fall into every time he looks at me—let's be honest, every time he looks at or *talks* to me—and I realize that whatever is about to happen, it's real.

"Lindsey." He says my name as if it's something precious. "Before you give your consent and I answer your question, I need you to know this will permanently change our dynamic."

I frown. "I don't think I understand."

Dane shifts in the recliner he's in, his face coming closer to the screen. "Is what you asked me to tell you sexual in nature, or is it not?"

My skin heats, and I lick my lips. "It is, Sir."

"Did I or did I not say I will not cross into that territory with my submissives?"

"You said you would not, Sir."

"Do you understand now?"

My brow furrows. "Are you saying that if you answer, our agreement ends?"

"No, that is not what I want. But our dynamic will change, and so will our agreement." He pauses, his eyes penetrating into mine. "I'd say that it already has, but I want to make it clear that this conversation we're having will change it permanently. This will no longer be what it was when we started."

"What will it be, then?"

"We will need to figure that out. But things have already changed between us. You know who I am, I know who you are. We're attracted to each other, unless this is only on my side?"

Arousal zips through my body, and I shake my head. "No. It's not one-sided."

He smiles warmly. "I want to be clear, however, that if you do not want our agreement to change and you do not want to do anything involving sex with me, we can stick to our original agreement, and that is perfectly fine. We can also stop altogether, if that's what you want, or—"

"No," I interrupt him. The idea of walking away now, especially after the meal we shared tonight, feels wrong. "No, Sir. That's not what I want."

"Don't interrupt me, baby."

There it is again. *Baby.* I stare into his eyes, and within them, I see the question before he voices it. "Is it alright if I call you that?"

I swallow hard and nod. "Yes, Sir. I—" I swallow again, and he smiles knowingly. He already knows what calling me baby does to my body. "I like it."

He breathes out his satisfied hum. "Can I continue?"

"Yes, Sir."

"As I was saying." He clears his throat, though there's an amused tone to it. ". . . or we can create a new agreement. Have a dynamic that explores the sexual side of our relationship, which I think we both want."

"I know, Sir."

He cocks his head to the side. "You know what?"

I wet my lips. "You said you think. I'm clarifying that I know I want to explore it." The words that come out of my mouth shock me because *where did this Lindsey come from?*

Dane laughs, and I wonder if he's thinking the same thing. I could say it comes from the fact that I've been horny this whole time, that I've been attracted to him and been thinking of doing sexual things with him since I watched his videos. But he's influenced me so much already, even in the short time we've been working together.

I discovered tonight after we got home from dinner that I feel more like the old version of myself than I have in a long time, the one before Jeremy beat me down. And now, I see it even more. Because while it may be a small thing to say I know what I want, it's big for me.

"You're a fast learner," Dane says. "I like that about you, Lindsey. But we have to work on that smart mouth of yours." His tone is different than it's been before, darker and more sensual. It's the way he sounded in that video I commented on, a video that almost felt like he was talking directly to me. "Would you like to work on that, baby?"

Blood pounds in my ears as I nod. "Yes, Sir. I want to be good for you."

"Hmm, I think you do."

"Sir?" I ask.

"Yes?"

"Do you think or do you know?"

He laughs again, the sound making goose bumps fan over my skin. "In this case, I'll let that smart mouth slide because I should have been clearer with my words." He gets a bit closer to the camera so I can see his lips clearly as he says, "I know, Lindsey."

His words settle in my bones, and I want to ask him what about me made him want to do this with me. Maybe it's because he's drawn to me like I'm drawn to him, or because I'm here and it's easy. I wonder if he's done this with other people before?

I almost open my mouth to ask him but decide against it. That's his business, and it's not like we're going to date. We're just going to have a different D/s dynamic like he said, a more intimate one. No dating here. I almost laugh because that sounds like a romance novel, *Dating My Dom*.

"Everything okay?" Dane asks.

I nod, deciding I can and will do this. I want to do this. "Yes, Sir. Everything's fine."

He studies me for a moment before nodding. "The same safe words are intact as we explore this new side of our dynamic together. Because you answered both sections of the questionnaire I sent, I understand your limits and boundaries when it comes to sexual exploration, and you've seen mine. However, we'll discuss them again when we write up our new agreement. For tonight, I want to reiterate that I'm here to take care of you. If something feels bad, if you don't like something I say or ask you to do, now more than ever, it's important that you communicate with me. If you say your safe word, we stop, do you understand?"

Excited nerves well in my stomach, but I like the feeling. I like that I'm on the precipice of something big and new and completely unknown. I didn't know that by being bold and commenting on his video tonight, this is where it would lead. But I'm glad it did.

"I understand, Sir."

"Good girl." He sits taller in his chair. "I would like to confirm: Do I have your consent to take control tonight and lead you through a scene?"

"Yes, Sir. You have my consent. Do I have yours?"

He pauses, and his smile is warmer somehow. "Yes, baby. You do."

I smile back at him, watching as he transforms before my eyes. His eyes darken, and his shoulders square. "Now, ask your earlier question again. Refresh my memory."

There's a hard edge to his tone, one I don't think I've heard before. A shiver works up my spine, and I shift on the couch. I'm more aroused now. Painfully so.

I wish he was sitting next to me so he could touch me, but this is good for now, safer, easier. The screen is a barrier that allows me to feel more open and honest, which was why it was easy to agree to our arrangement in the first place.

I tuck a strand of hair behind my ear. "In your video on Loopr, you pretended you came home to find your submissive starting without you. You said you were going to punish them."

He hums, almost a low rumbling purr. "I did, didn't I?"

I swallow, feeling my panties grow wet. Holy crap, this is actually happening right now. We're really crossing into new territory, and surprisingly, I'm not afraid to cross into it. "Yes, Sir."

Dane's hazel eyes burn into mine through the screen, the fire still flicking in their reflection. "And what was the question you asked me?"

I swallow again, my tongue sticking to the roof of my mouth. "If that were me, Sir, how would you punish me?"

A sly smile lights his features, and he leans back in the chair. "Correct me if I'm wrong, Lindsey. But on your questionnaire, you said you'd be into exploring role-play. Is that correct?"

My nipples tighten almost painfully, and my breasts feel heavy with the need for touch. "I did, Sir."

"Your breathing picked up. Does that mean my question excited you?"

"Yes, Sir."

"Do you want to play together a little, or is that too much for you?"

"You want to role-play right now, Sir?"

He chuckles. "Do you have a better time? I can check my schedule."

"Now is fine," I say eagerly.

Dane steeples his fingers, a sly smirk on his lips. "Check in with yourself, and then let me know how you feel about it. Green, yellow, or red?"

I inhale a breath and close my eyes. I've never role-played before, but it's always something that's interested me. I tried to get Jeremy into it once by coming home with a naughty nurse costume, but he made me feel like it was stupid.

I know Dane won't make me feel stupid. I may not know him well, but he's only ever made me feel safe from the moment we started talking. I do believe him when he says he'll take care of me. He's already been doing that, even when I pushed back out of fear.

I open my eyes back up, breathing more evenly now. "Green, Sir."

"Remember, you can use your safe words at any time. They're there for a reason."

"Thank you, Sir. I trust you."

"I'm happy to hear that, baby. But even so, remember your safe words."

God, every time he calls me baby, I think my panties melt again as a rush of arousal courses through me. He sees me shift on the couch, my thighs squeezing together, and he licks his lips.

"Are you wet for me already?" he asks.

I don't know what I expected to come out of his mouth, but it wasn't that, and his words hit me right on the clit. My cheeks heat, and I nod.

"What was that?" he asks in a demanding tone.

"I am, Sir."

Dane rubs his fingers over his beard, and I want to be the one threading my fingers through the coarse strands. "You've been a very bad girl, haven't you?"

The simmer in his eyes along with the cock of one brow tells me the gears have switched. This is the role-play. The nerves I felt ball in my stomach like a rock.

I must look like a scared deer because he leans forward toward the screen a bit, features warmer. "Don't think, just play," he says. "There's nothing to be embarrassed about, alright?"

I nod. "Okay."

"Good, Lindsey. Now tell me, have you been a bad girl, getting wet without me?"

"I–I have, Sir."

"Hmm." He leans back in his chair, putting his laptop on his thighs. I can see more of him now at this angle. His torso, the strength of his forearms, and the fire flicking over his skin and bulging veins. God, he's hot. I can't believe he wants to do this with me of all people, but I push that thought away and try to be in the moment.

"I explicitly told you to wait for me until I got home from work. But here you are, touching yourself without my permission."

I suck in a breath, my heart pounding harder in my chest. "I'm sorry, Sir," I answer, playing along like he said. "I was impatient. You were gone for a long time."

"What did I tell you about being sorry?"

"That you'd prefer if apologies came with a way to hold myself accountable so I don't continue my bad behavior."

"But you were a bad girl the last time I asked you to wait, too. Were you not?"

"Was I, Sir?"

"You don't remember?"

I shake my head, falling into the role-play, my breaths still short but not because I'm nervous anymore. It's because I'm more turned on than I ever have been in my life. "Can you please refresh my memory, Sir?"

"Since you asked so nicely." He pauses. "I came home and found you touching that sweet pussy of yours without my permission. I put you over my knee and spanked your ass red. You were dripping and begging for my cock by the time it was over."

My breath hitches as I imagine it in my mind's eye. "I remember now, Sir."

"You couldn't sit for a whole day could you,

baby?" I bite my lip and shake my head in answer. "Apparently, that wasn't a good enough lesson, and I need to do better," he says.

"I'm sorry, Sir. I'll accept whatever punishment you have in mind."

His dark chuckle returns. "So eager to be punished. Maybe you did this on purpose, hoped that I would find you touching what belongs to me."

I swallow hard and rub my thighs together in need, jostling my laptop in my desire to ease the pulsing between my legs.

Dane tsks, the sound is menacing coming through the speakers. "Did you just rub your thighs together?"

I flush at being caught, even if it wasn't a completely conscious move. "I did, Sir."

"Poor thing, so desperate to be touched."

My chest heaves, and my skin feels hot. I think my clit has developed its own heartbeat, and I swear I might come from the role-play alone. That would be embarrassing.

"Had you waited for me, I'd already have my mouth on your sweet cunt."

My eyes widen at his dirty words. I'm not used to talking like this. Jeremy would have never called my pussy a cunt—I don't think he even called it pussy. Honestly, I don't think I would have liked it if he did. But when Dane says it? I like it. I like it a lot.

He continues. "But that won't be happening tonight. Why do you think that is?"

"Because I disobeyed you," I answer, near breathless.

"Yes, yes, you did," he tsks again. "And Lindsey"—I stare into his mischievous eyes—"bad girls don't get my mouth. Do you know what they get?"

"What, Sir?"

Dane strokes his long fingers down his well-trimmed beard. My eyes follow the movement with rapt attention. "They get edged by their own hand."

24
Dane

LINDSEY'S EYES WIDEN, AND my dick kicks against the zipper of my jeans. It's been awhile since I've done this type of role-play with a live person, not just talking to myself on a video. Even longer since I've done anything sexual over video chat with a partner. Thankfully, it's not something you forget how to do, and with Lindsey, it doesn't feel awkward. She's a natural, even if I can tell she doesn't think so. She's a bit nervous, but I would be, too, in her position.

"Edged, Sir?"

Her innocence, the way she asks questions, how she calls me Sir in that sweet fucking voice... goddamn. I'm a fucking goner for her already. It's why I'm doing this scene with her before we've revised our agreement, even though I know better.

But like everything with Lindsey, I do things I don't plan or expect.

"Hmm, someone always gets what she wants, doesn't she?" Lindsey's eyes widen, and I continue. "You're going to bring yourself to the edge of orgasm, then stop."

"Stop, Sir?"

My cheek twitches in a half grin. "Bad girls don't get to come, remember?"

"I promise I'll be good, Sir."

Despite her questions and newness to this dynamic, when she says things like that, I'm reminded she's not only a quick learner, but a natural. Lindsey has submission in her bones. She just needed the right partner to nurture it, to give her a safe space to lean into it. I'm happy as fuck that right partner is me.

"Promises are empty, baby. I need you to show me you'll be good."

"Tell me how to show you, Sir."

Her eagerness makes my dick harder, and it takes everything in me not to touch myself. If I was a less-practiced Dom, I would have. But this isn't about me. This is about Lindsey and building our new dynamic.

"Say please," I command.

"Please, Sir."

I make a satisfied rumbling noise in my chest as a response and study Lindsey's features through the screen. What I wouldn't give to be with her now, to feel her warm breath on my cheek and her soft body against mine as I held her open for me. Made her touch herself again and again while I pinned her thighs open so she couldn't close her legs.

I wet my lips, hoping she'll want to do in-person sessions. I could make that dream a reality if she's open to it, but this will do for tonight.

"Pausing to check in, Lindsey. Green, yellow, or red?"

"Green," she says easily.

"I'm not going to ask you to undress, but please let me know if anything goes too far, yes?"

I can see a lovely flush rise from the collar of her T-shirt even through the screen. I wonder if her entire body flushes that rosy-pink color when she's turned on. I bet it does.

"I will, Sir."

"Good, do you have a coffee table in front of you or somewhere you can put your laptop so I can see you but your hands will be free?"

"Yes, Sir."

"Do that then position yourself in front of the screen with your legs spread open so I can see you."

Lindsey blinks at me as if I asked her to strip and bend over, ass to me.

"Too much?" I ask. She shakes her head, and I snap my fingers twice. "Then get to it, baby. I won't ask again."

The sound along with the command throws her into action. She places her laptop down on the table, and a second later, she must put a book or something under it because the angle changes.

She sits back on the couch and positions herself like I asked. She's wearing tiny pajama shorts that leave little to the imagination, and when she spreads her legs, I see a peek of underwear.

"Turn on the side lamp; I want to see you better."

Lindsey hesitates, and a flash of anger zips through my veins. Not at her but at whatever thought made her pause. I don't technically need her to turn on the lamp—there's a soft, dimmed overhead light that gives me enough to see—but the lamp would allow me to view all of her, including the color of her underwear and the dips and valleys of her curves. All things I want to appreciate.

"Lindsey," I say, bringing her attention back to me. When our eyes meet, I make sure my facial features are soft. "If you don't want to turn on the lamp, you don't have to. But I'd love to see your beautiful body better. It would make me very happy."

Lindsey's shoulders ease. Trepidation I wish wasn't there is still on her face, but I see the instant she makes her choice. She shifts on the couch to turn on the lamp, and the light floods over her, highlighting her curves the way I hoped.

"That's my good girl," I praise. "Now back into your position, legs spread for me."

She does as I ask, body still tense. When her thighs part and her shorts creep up, they expose the sides of her underwear. They're a pretty pink that reminds me of the flush of her cheeks.

My erect dick aches, but I ignore it. Ideas of things I want with Lindsey in the future start to rack up in my mind, though.

"Take a breath for me, baby," I demand.

Lindsey does, but her shoulders still don't completely ease the way I'd like. I study her further, noticing her pupils are shifting as if she's attempting not to look at the part of the screen where her image resides. That makes me angry, too.

I pack that away for another time, knowing what I have to do for now. Normally, I'd have my submissive look at me during this, keep eye contact to make it more intense for them. But that is not what Lindsey needs. She needs to drop into her body and allow herself to feel without worrying about seeing her own reflection.

"Rest your head back on the couch, and close your eyes," I say.

Lindsey's shoulders finally relax once she's in position, and the tightness in my chest lessens a bit.

"Good girl. Now exhale and spread your legs wider. Let me see what you're freely giving me, what belongs to me."

She smiles as she does what I ask. I noticed that before, that she likes when I claim her. Fuck if I don't like it, too. It satisfies my Dom, but it also makes me want to do very dirty things to her.

The image of her at my feet wearing my collar comes to mind, but that's not something she's ready for yet. She may never want that. I mean, fuck, do *I* want that?

My dick twitches as if it's answering for me, and I refocus on the beautiful woman submitting through the screen, waiting for my next command.

"Keep your eyes closed, and tell me how you feel," I say.

She swallows, her arms at her sides. "Exposed, Sir."

"Green, yellow, or red?"

"Green, Sir."

"It's time for your punishment, baby. Are you ready to atone for your bad behavior?"

"Yes, Sir," she responds, chest moving up and down in clipped breaths of excitement.

I can see the disks of her hard nipples protruding through her thin white T-shirt. I remember how they felt against my chest that first day we ran into each other—I've never been able to forget.

Now, in the light, with her at my mercy, I can study her chest. Her tits are small, maybe not even a handful, but they're fucking perfect. Suckable, bitable. Exactly right for nipple clamps or suction cups.

"Bring your hands to your chest and play with your nipples through your shirt. Get yourself wetter for me."

A whimper leaves her lips and goes straight to my groin. I shift on my chair but remain focused on the woman giving herself to me so willingly.

I'm about to ask her if that's too much, but her hands lift up, and she tentatively rubs her fingers over the hard nubs. A soft moan echoes through the speakers, and it's nearly my undoing. I'm too fucking old to come in my pants, but it might happen.

"That's it, baby. Are you imagining my hands playing with you?"

She nods, and I chuckle. "Was that a yes?"

"Yes, Sir."

"If you had listened to my command, those would have been my hands, wouldn't they?"

"Yes, Sir."

I tsk. "Such a naughty girl. Now pinch them for me, tell me how it feels."

She does as I ask, her butt gently shifting on the couch. "It feels good, Sir."

"Do you like the pain?"

She pinches her nipple again, and I know the answer before she moans out, "Yes, Sir."

"If you had been good, I'd have my mouth on your tits right now. I'd bite your cute nipples until you screamed. Would you like that?"

She nods before remembering her words. "Y-yes."

Her butt shifts again, her legs inching closer

together. I snap my fingers, and she stops. "Don't you close those legs, Lindsey."

"I'm sorry, Sir."

"Pinch your nipples again, harder this time."

She does what I ask, a soft gasp leaving her mouth.

"Good girl. Now use one hand to keep playing with *my* nipples, and use your other hand to touch *my* cunt."

I put emphasis on *my* because I want her to know that her body now belongs to me while we're playing. That the only reason she gets to touch herself is because I'm allowing it.

I observe her carefully, and once again, I know I've turned her on. Lindsey's chest and collarbones are completely flushed, all the way up her neck, and her breathing has remained heavy. I bet she's soaking through her underwear and messing up her couch. Good thing it looks like leather. Next time, I'll have her get a towel.

She keeps her left hand on her chest while she begins to trail her right down, over the soft rolls of her stomach. I wait with bated breath to see what she'll do next. I didn't give her clear instruction to touch herself over her underwear or under, but that was intentional. I want to see where her thoughts go, how comfortable she is right now without using words.

Her hand gets to the elastic band of her shorts, and she doesn't pause, slipping her hand beneath it. I suppress a groan as her fingers make contact with her pussy. She sighs in pleasure.

"Tell me how wet my cunt is."

"So wet, Sir."

"Hmm, do you need to come, baby?"

She nods vigorously. "Yes, Sir."

"Too bad you were naughty, then." She growls in frustration, and my sadistic side preens. "Circle my clit for me. Tell me when you're about to come."

"It won't take very long, Sir."

"Such a needy girl," I reiterate. "Now do what I asked you to do."

Lindsey's hand moves beneath her underwear, legs spread wide for me. It takes less than thirty seconds before her thighs begin to tremble, and I know what's happening.

"Sir, I'm about to—"

She doesn't finish her sentence, and I bark, "Remove your hand."

The command is loud, and she startles, yanking her hand from her shorts.

"Look at me." She does, and I rumble out praise. "Good girl. Now show me your fingers."

She shifts and holds them out, cheeks flushed and pupils dilated. The light in the room makes her hand glisten, and I'd give a kidney to suck the digits into my mouth.

"Taste yourself," I command.

I expect her to hesitate, to balk at the idea—some people would. But her lips part, and she slides her pointer finger into her mouth. Confidence exudes from her as she sucks on it, making a show of it. I know what she's doing; she's teasing me. Only proving that she is very much a naughty girl.

"What do you taste like, baby?" My voice is husky, dark and edged with desire.

"I taste like yours, Sir."

Sparks ignite under my skin, her words satisfying me more than I can say. "That's right. Because your cunt is mine. Now touch that pretty little clit again."

Lindsey doesn't hesitate to bring her hand back to her shorts. Her shoulders stay relaxed, and her eyes remain on mine as she inserts her hand beneath the elastic.

"That's it," I say, leaning back in my chair to enjoy the show. Her eyes hood, and another whimper escapes her when she touches her swollen nerves. "Green, yellow, or red, Lindsey?"

"Green!" she cries.

"Stop!" I bark. Her hand stops moving, and her eyes pop open. "You were about to come, weren't you?"

"I was, Sir."

"Pinch those nipples again for me. Harder this time." Her hand reaches up, and I add, "With both hands."

She huffs. If she's already this wound up, she's in for the ride of her life because I'm far from done yet. She pulls her hand from her shorts, bringing it along with her other to her breasts. Once in place, she follows my order, fingers pinching the hard buds. Her moans of pleasure reach my ears, and I wait until they turn to whimpers. Then I tell her to stop yet again.

"Sensitive?"

"Yes, Sir," she whines.

"Hmm, I bet. But you're being such a good girl for me."

"Thank you, Sir. I want to be good."

"I know you do, and you're making me very happy. Now touch yourself again, but this time, put your fingers into that tight pussy."

A sound akin to a whine filters through the speakers, and I have no doubt I'm going to come in my pants by the time this is over. But I'm beyond the point of caring.

Lindsey reaches her hand down again, pressing her head back into the couch. My gaze zeros in on the space between her legs, and I watch as the fabric of her shorts moves, getting a peek at the dark hair covering her soft mound. I know the exact moment her fingers enter her cunt because she moans, and I can hear how fucking wet she is.

God-fucking-dammit. I rest my head back against my chair, cock throbbing. "Does that feel good?"

"Yes! God, yes!"

"Pinch your nipple while you fuck yourself."

Lindsey pinches and moans, her hips bucking off the couch.

"That's it, baby."

"Sir, I—oh god, I—"

I yell out a command to stop again, and she groans, body deflating back against the cushion. I let her come down from her near orgasm, have her sit with the feeling of frustration before I bring her attention back to me. "You're doing so well. I'm so proud of you."

Her cheeks flush a deeper red, and I note that she liked that praise for the future.

"I think my good girl deserves a reward for following directions. Would you like that?"

"Yes, Sir."

"Of course you would," I remark.

Her chin dips, and if I were in the room with her, I'd grab it to make her look at me. "Lindsey," I say sternly. Her eyes snap to mine. "Have you learned your lesson?"

"Yes, Sir. I'll be good, Sir."

"If you touch yourself again when I tell you not to, I won't be as forgiving. Do you understand?"

"Yes, Sir. I understand."

"You have sixty seconds to make yourself come."

She blinks at me, and I cock an eyebrow back.

"Now it's fifty-five."

Lindsey's eyes widen, but she lays back again, her hand working her clit faster this time. Her eyes flutter closed, and I let her do it. I want her to enjoy her first orgasm with me in whatever way is most comfortable for her.

I hadn't planned on letting her come this soon. I wanted to edge her longer to punish her for her fake transgression, but seeing her now, teetering on the edge, I don't want to deny her. I know she needs this release just as much as I need to see her have it at my command.

"So beautiful," I say, loud enough so she can hear.

"Sir—" She whimpers.

"Clock's ticking," I tease.

"Sir—I, I don't think—"

"Bring your free hand to your throat." She does as I ask, and her hips start to rise off the couch as she places it there. "Now pretend it's my hand. You can feel the calluses on my fingers, the heat from my grip, can't you, baby?"

"Oh, fuck, I—" she cries.

"Grip that pretty throat for me."

Her fingers tighten, and her other hand circles her clit faster.

"Come, Lindsey," I growl.

"Dane!" she cries. My name sounds like a melody as it spills from her lips. She shouldn't have called me Dane during a scene, but I'd be a fucking liar if I said I didn't fucking like it.

Lindsey whimpers, still holding back, and I focus on her final seconds before release.

"I've got you. Let go and come." The command

in my tone is final, and her back arches off the couch. I press the heel of my palm over my jeans without thinking. I grunt quietly as her thighs shake and her body twitches and trembles as she comes. She cries my name again, loud enough that it echoes through my speakers like the last note of a song.

My own orgasm rips through my body, and warm cum coats my lower stomach and soaks my boxers, my cock twitching as my submissive's stunning body begins to float down from her high.

Lindsey's staccato breaths fill my ears as she sags back into the couch, her eyes still closed. I ignore the fact that I came in my pants and keep my attention on her.

I let her float in her post-orgasm high for a few more minutes before I break the silence. "You did so well, baby. Can you open your eyes and look at me?"

Her eyelids flutter open; her pupils are still dilated. If I was there, I'd clean her up and hold her against my chest until she fell asleep, but that's not possible for us now. Aftercare will look a little different virtually.

"Green, yellow, or red?" I ask.

"Green," she breathes, her voice husky and sated. "Very green."

"That's good. You made me very pleased."

"I'm glad, Sir."

Her voice is sleepy, and I know that dreams will soon take her if I don't get her moving. "Do you have water beside you?" She nods. "Drink that now."

Lindsey shifts and grabs a cup from next to the lamp. I make sure she drinks it all before I give my next order. "Do you have enough strength to wash up?"

"Yes, Sir," she says, a little more awake now.

"Good, go do that, and I'll wait for you."

She shifts on the couch but stops before she gets up. "What about you, Sir?"

"What about me?" I ask.

"Shouldn't I take care of you, too?"

My pulse quickens. "You're such a good girl for asking, but you already took care of me." I don't elaborate by sharing I came in my pants. All she needs to know is I'm satisfied. "Now go, wash up."

She opens her mouth to say more, but I send her a look that tells her she won't get any more from me. She smiles softly, then stands.

A few minutes later, she's back, a sleepy look on her face. A face that looks relaxed and at ease, which makes me happy. "How are you feeling?"

"Good. Really good. Thank you, Sir."

"Was everything we did okay for you?"

She nods. "Yes, more than okay, Sir."

"I want you to drink more water before you sleep. If anything comes up that you need to talk about, call me."

She flushes a bit. "I will, Sir."

I hum before relaxing back in my chair. "You can call me Dane now that the scene is over."

She sighs happily and ducks her chin. "Dane."

My spent cock twitches, reminding me of the drying cum in my pants. "Speaking of rest, I want you to go straight to bed after we get off the chat."

"My routine—"

"It's okay, you can skip it for tonight. But I expect you to check in with me as soon as you wake up. We'll discuss more about our new dynamic when we've both gotten some sleep. Does that sound good to you?"

"Yes, that sounds good."

"Good. Now go rest; you earned it."

"You, too, Sir—uh, Dane."

My chest shakes with silent laughter. "Good night, Lindsey. Sleep well."

I end the video call and get up. After cleaning myself up and settling back into my chair, I find myself thinking. Not only about the last hour with Lindsey but also dinner at the diner and every moment we've shared so far.

My earlier thoughts of what I expected my life to be come rushing back to the forefront of my mind. I didn't expect her—or Kas—to come into my life. And I sure as shit did not expect to feel my control slipping the way it has with Lindsey.

Before now, it felt frightening and forbidden. But after we agreed to change our dynamic and she shared her body with me in such an intimate way, it feels less like a leap and more like fate. Because Lindsey is…much more than I ever thought I'd have in my life. More than I've allowed myself to have.

I take a drink of the water I brought with me after I cleaned up, the cool liquid easing the heat in my body. Fox's words from our conversation repeat in my mind: *Whatever is blocking you from being happy, kick it in the fucking ass. Don't let it control you.*

Fox is right; I have been blocking myself from happiness all while thinking I was content and happy. And in so many ways, I have been. I've found a purpose in my work and enjoy the silence of my routine, but in doing so, I've kept people at arm's length so nothing could develop into more. It was another way for me to stay in control.

But with Lindsey, I've let that control slip. Not just in our dynamic and the scene we just did but tonight at dinner, too. I told her and Kas a bit about my life, how I came to be a logger and live in Starlight Haven. My past is not something I share freely, yet I did with them. And I didn't think twice about it.

I think about letting Lindsey in more. Not only telling her more about my past, but also doing in-person scenes with her and having her in my cabin. Having Kas in my home teaching me about the video game she mentioned while we chatted and ate.

It strikes me that while the thought of having someone like Levi or anyone else in my space makes my pulse pound, and not in a good way, the idea of having Lindsey and Kas here does the opposite.

It tells me all I need to know.

I pull out my phone and see a message from her with just one word. A word that has me smiling to myself.

Lindsey

Green

Green. Keep going. I have the green light with her.

I heart her message and lean back in my chair, feeling more grounded and connected to myself than I have in years, maybe even since I started my journey as a Dom.

I type out a quick message to Fox, thanking him for the push before I open my agreement with Lindsey in my email. I'm going to review it and make notes and adjustments. Once we've both discussed our new dynamic and signed the revised agreement, I'd love to try a few ideas I have with her. One in particular I know she'll like.

25

Lindsey

I'm floating. My feet are on the ground, but I feel as if my body is in the clouds. My problems are a million miles away, and for the past four days, I've woken up every morning to my alarm feeling like my life is finally heading down the right track. It's wonderful.

My phone buzzes, and like an addict, I grab it off the table in the break room, opening my message app to read my new message from Dane.

Sir

I've read over your journal entries, and I'm pleased you're feeling good about our new dynamic and that you feel satisfied with the routines we're establishing. You're doing so well, baby.

My stomach flutters at his praise along with the endearment. Since we discussed new boundaries and signed our amended agreement on Monday, one that removed the clauses about no sex or sexual activities happening between us, things have been great.

We went over every question on the second part of the questionnaire when we revised the contract, and I still can't believe how many things I marked as "willing to try." Medical play, schoolroom scenes, voyeurism—even shaving and erotic objectification. Dane was professional the whole time, like he always has been. Asking thoughtful questions, adjusting things, and, from what I could tell, filing ideas away for later.

I've been journaling not only about the role-play experience but any feelings that have come up with our new dynamic. Dane and I haven't had another scene like the one on Sunday, but beyond talking about the sexual questions and our agreement, we've continued flirting over messages, building more trust with each other through our daily interactions and my check-ins. I swear I've had to change my underwear at least once a day with the sexual tension between us, but I haven't come since Sunday. I'm hoping that will change soon, however, because playing with him again is all I've been able to think about.

I type out a message and sit back in my chair, nibbling on a carrot stick I packed. That's another thing I've been good about—packing lunches. I even made Kas premade ones for when she's with JoJo so they don't eat frozen stuff. She complained to me yesterday that she'd rather have chicken nuggets, but I'm trying to be better about putting my foot down even if it's uncomfortable. Something Dane is helping me with.

I smile as I swallow another bite. When I started working with Dane, I had a feeling it would help me, but I never expected to feel so good. With every text and action, I'm more hopeful instead of down on myself all the time.

I've also been speaking to myself better and feeling more confident in my parenting as each day ends. Amazing what routines can do—what having Dane in my life has done.

Me

Thank you, Sir. I wanted to let you know I've got Nathan's days set for watching Kas until school starts at the end of the month, and I said no to covering a shift tomorrow so I can take her to the obstacle course before she heads to see her dad.

I managed to convince Jeremy to let Kas come a day later for his weekend with her. She'll stay till Monday instead of Sunday; that way, she doesn't have to miss the obstacle course tomorrow. He gave me hell, but I used Kas's pouty face to my advantage. It messed up my work schedule a bit, but Nathan, Fox, and Morgan came to the rescue, going above and beyond for me. They're going to drive her down to Santa Solana and stay for the weekend; that way, I don't have to worry about picking her up on Monday. Nathan was happy to do it. He wants to try to teach Fox how to surf, and they claimed they needed a little vacation.

I finish typing out the text with a wider smile. Dropping off Kas wasn't my only reason for saying no to the extra shift. I need rest from work so I don't completely burn out, but I also want to see Dane in person when I drop her off. A little pathetic? Probably. But the idea of seeing him, even if we can't touch or talk, has me more excited than I'd like to admit.

His message pops up a second later, and I read it eagerly.

Sir

Good girl, I know that must have been hard for you to do. But shouldn't you be working now?

I giggle at his message, knowing he would have said that in his growly voice if he were here with me.

Me

On my break.

Sir

How long do you have left?

Immediately, I wonder why he's asking, and I can't help but imagine what he could possibly have me do in twenty minutes while I'm at work. Does he want me to send him a titty pic or something?

I don't see Dane asking me to do that, even

though I wouldn't mind. In fact, I'd find that a little hot. The idea of *forbidden* is fun. I also did say on my questionnaire I would be interested in public play, even if I don't know what that looks like.

I realize time is running out the more I think, so I send him an answer.

Me

About twenty minutes.

Sir

We haven't taken a look at your finances yet. Do you have time to send me over what you need help with?

The floating feeling I felt before dies. Like a balloon losing helium, I slowly come down to the ground until I'm a sad, wrinkly blob.

Me

I'll admit, Sir, that was not what I thought you were going to ask.

Sir

Oh? And what did you think I was going to ask?

I debate exposing my thoughts or keeping them to myself. But our relationship is about honesty.

Me

Something fun.

Sir

Being financially responsible is fun.

I snort as I type out:

Me

Says who?

Sir

Your Dom, smarty-pants. Did your lesson the other night teach you nothing about what your smart mouth gets you?

I shift in my chair, feeling a little bit of that float return to my body.

Me

Maybe I need a reminder.

My phone rings, and I know it's him without looking at the screen. My heart flutters as I answer. "Hi," I say.

"If you were being serious, tell me you consent to a scene right now."

My heart thuds against my chest. "You know my answer is yes."

We may not have been playing together long, and the sexual part of our relationship is new, but I think I'll always say yes to Dane. He's proven more than once that I can trust him. He's always checking in and making sure I'm good.

There's a reason I said yes to that scene with him over the computer, even before a new agreement was in place between us.

When we revised the contract together, he brought that fact up and apologized for moving forward without an official agreement, even though he got my consent beforehand. I told him

I didn't regret it and felt good about it, which says a lot about how I feel about him, given my past.

"Is there anyone in the break room with you?"

Heat rises in my body, and I shake my head. "No, I'm alone."

"I put something special in your locker for you."

"What?" I ask, blinking. "When?"

"Do you want to ask me that, or do you want to find out what it is? Time is ticking."

Instead of answering, I stand up and go to my locker, double-checking I'm still alone. There are no locks on our lockers. This town is so small, and we all trust each other. I'm never worried about anyone stealing something, so it's never bothered me.

When I open mine, I don't see anything at first. But then I notice a bag behind an extra pair of scrubs I have inside.

"Do you see it?"

"Yes, what did you get me?"

"Take the bag, and go to the bathroom. Don't open it until you're inside."

My fluttering heart beats faster as I do what he says, grateful there's a one-stall bathroom in the break room that also houses a shower. I have no idea what could be in this bag; I'm completely drawing a blank.

I click the lock then go to the sink where I can place the present on the edge of the porcelain.

"Okay, I'm opening it." Dane doesn't say anything, but I know he's still there. I can hear birds chirping from wherever he is.

I open the simple white gift bag with white tissue inside. Then I pull out the box, blushing the moment I read what's inside.

"Sir," I say quietly. "You can't be serious."

"I was going to save this for later, for after you got out of work, but I think you're in need of a lesson."

"Sir," I whisper even though I know nobody can see or hear me. "A panty vibrator?"

"I've cleaned it for you and set it up. It's connected to an app on my phone, so I can control it from anywhere, even another state."

I swallow. "You want me to wear this at work?"

His low hum comes through the phone, and I know without feeling it that I'm wet. Very wet. "What if I'm with a patient?"

"Then I guess you'd better practice your poker face, baby."

"You're serious?"

"Would I tell you to do something if I wasn't serious?"

"No, you wouldn't."

"Remember, Lindsey. You can tell me no. I will not be upset."

I believe him, too. "I'm not saying no."

"Then put that little toy inside your panties and tell me when it's done."

His low command sends a shiver up my spine, and I place my phone on the sink. I take the little ridged silicone toy that will fit snugly against my clit in one hand and pull down my scrubs and underwear with the other.

I was right: I'm wet, nearly as wet as I was the last time we played. I wipe away the wet spot with a paper towel then put the toy where it's meant to go, pulling up my underwear to help keep it in place. Once my scrubs are secure, I wash my hands and pick my phone back up.

"It's done, Sir."

"How does it feel?"

It's a strange sensation, having an odd-shaped piece of silicone between the lips of your vulva. The textured part presses against my clit, and while it's not comfortable, it's not horrible, either. But I haven't walked yet.

"Interesting, Sir."

"Bad interesting or good interesting?"

"I don't know yet."

He chuckles at the same time the toy comes to life against my clit. I stifle a cry and almost drop my phone. The buzzing is intense against my sex, and my eyes water.

"Dane," I choke.

"Still interesting?" he asks in an amused tone. The bastard.

"Intense," I manage to get out. The buzzing stops, and I inhale a long breath.

"Are you alive over there?" he asks.

"Barely."

His laughter comes through the phone again before the buzzing starts in a bold pattern that hits hard then retracts before buzzing for a few long seconds. I grip the phone in one hand and the sink in the other, clamping my thighs together while trying not to cry out.

"I'm giving you five minutes to come," Dane announces. "Then you need to eat something and get back to work, understand?"

"Yes," I say breathlessly. I didn't think he was going to let me come so soon, but I'm grateful for it and am not going to question it.

"Remember to be quiet; you don't want someone to hear you." The moment he finishes speaking, the pattern stops, and he must put it on the highest setting because I can hear it buzzing.

I grip the phone harder and move to press my head against the tile wall, clamping my hand over my mouth.

"I'm imagining you right now, baby, in your cute little scrubs, your cheeks flushed. I bet you're making a mess in your panties, aren't you?"

"Yes," I squeak out.

He chuckles again, deeper and more mischievous this time, and it's almost my undoing. The high-speed buzzing lowers, and I inhale a shaky breath. My clit is tingling, and my hard nipples rub against the cups of my bra.

"Lindsey, Lindsey, Lindsey," he chants. "Such a good girl when you want to be."

"Sir," I whimper. "I'm going to—"

"Do it, baby."

He switches the setting of the toy to high, and I bite my hand as a strong orgasm rips through me and I whine in pleasure.

"I wish I could see you right now. I bet your body is craving my touch. I bet you'd do anything to feel my hands on you, isn't that right?"

My "Yes, Sir" is strained, and my eyes are stinging from all the sensations. Dane hasn't stopped the vibrations yet, and my orgasm won't quit. I almost drop the phone as another, more desperate whimper leaves my lips.

"You want me to stop?"

"Y-yes, oh fuck," I say as the vibrations become almost painful against my clit.

"Give me another one."

"Sir—"

"I said, give me another one, Lindsey," he growls through the phone.

The vibrations pulse in high and strong patterns, and despite thinking I can't, my body listens to him. "Shit," I moan as a second one hits. "Fuck."

"Shhhh, baby," Dane coos. "Don't want anyone to come running."

I'm about to ask him to stop when the vibrations cease and my body sags. My forehead is still pressed against the cool tile as I drag air into my lungs and try to calm down.

"You did so well, coming twice for me at work."

I almost sob from his praise, my body floating high like it did the other night. I never thought full-body orgasms like this were possible, and he's not even giving them to me directly. I decide that for his birthday, whenever that is, I'm getting him a plaque that says "Orgasm God" because that's what he is.

"Still alive?" he asks.

"Barely, Sir."

"Was that too much?"

The concern in his tone makes my chest feel warm. "It was a lot, but..."

"Use your words, baby," he says when I don't continue.

God, I love when he says that. "It was a lot, but I liked it. I liked it a lot, Sir."

"Good." He hums. "Because I liked it, too."

I smile at his admission and want to ask if he came, too. But I don't think he did, just like I don't think he did the other night. There's a pressure in my chest, one that makes me want to ask him why he's not touching himself while I'm getting off. Is that a Dom thing or does he not want to?

"You should go eat, and make sure you drink your water. You have seven minutes left on your break."

"I will," I say softly, my heart pounding at his care. I should've known he was actually timing the rest of my break. I inhale another calming breath and step away from the wall, my legs mostly solidified now. My underwear is ruined, though. Thank god I keep extra sets here, because they're no longer wearable for the rest of my shift.

"Good girl." I'm about to hang up when his voice comes through the line. "And Lindsey?"

"Yes?"

"Remember that poker face." I groan through the phone, and he chuckles. "Did you think I got you this gift for your pleasure?"

"You didn't?"

"No, baby, it's for mine."

I bite my lip, my sensitive clit throbbing.

"Now go. We'll speak later."

26
Dane

Fox

Checking in with you.

Me

About what?

Fox

Don't play coy with me.

Me

Since I'm in a good mood, I'll answer you. I'm good.

Fox

I take it everything with your sub is good, then?

Me

We've amended our relationship and contract to include deeper intimacy.

Fox

Did you use AI to answer that?

Me

You're a bastard sometimes, you know that?

Fox

So I've been told.

Me

We're working it out.

Fox

You didn't ask them to do an in-person scene yet, did you?

Me

I'm working up to it.

Fox
Do you need me to top you?

Me
I don't think your partners would be into that.

Fox
I'll ask them.

Me
Fuck off.

Fox
Be a good boy, and use your words.

Me
I did.

Fox
Next time I ask you, I hope your answer is different.

Me

Fox sends me back a gif of a man slapping a paddle against his hand, and I smirk.

Me

You wish.

I exit out of my messages and walk into my kitchen. It's nearly seven, which means Lindsey will be ending her shift soon.

Since our little scene in the bathroom earlier, I haven't stopped thinking about her. I've been itching to play with the toy inside her panties, but I'm waiting. I wouldn't tease her while she was with patients, putting her job or the people in her care at risk, but the idea of making her wear the toy was for her to wonder when and if I would click the button. Not only would she think of me all day, but it was also the ultimate surrender of her control.

It was a little lesson for her, of course, but it was also for me to see how far she'd go to please me and how deep her trust is. But her luck will run out soon, because at a minute past seven, I'll send her a little pulse to remind her that she's mine to play with. That had I wanted to, I could have clicked the toy on while she worked, even if I never would.

I grin and open my fridge, pulling out some chicken breast, sweet potato, and green beans I meal-prepped on Sunday. It makes me think of Kas and our interaction at the diner over my protein omelet. She'd probably think this meal is just as disgusting. It's not bad, but it's not great, either. It's fuel and does the job. It's also easy to prep for myself and keeps well for reheating. It's practical, just like most things in my life.

What's not practical, however, is the way I'm thinking of feeding Lindsey a bite of my food. I open my utensil drawer and remember how her lips closed around my fork when I fed her a piece of my food at the diner. She chewed slowly, almost sensually, which made me think about all sorts of things, most importantly, how nice it was to feed her. How she took the bite I offered so easily.

Feeding her wasn't just about the food. It was about care, control, and trust, all wrapped up in one small moment.

That thought leads to Fox's texts, and I know he's right to call me out about the in-person scenes. While the amended contract we signed includes a sexual dynamic between us now, I have not asked her to come over.

I thought it best we work up to it and let it happen naturally, even if the desire to ask her on a date has been on the tip of my tongue. Not that we've had the time between our busy schedules. Lindsey's, in particular, is chaotic, something I hope we can fix once I look at her finances. She may have sent me what I requested on one of her breaks, but I have yet to check my email.

I pop my food in my toaster oven and lean against my counter as my phone alarm goes off, telling me it's time to play. I open the app to the toy and wait for it to connect. I've never played with a toy like this before, not in this way, at least.

I've used toys in scenes in the past, but I saw this online and had to get it, knowing it would be the perfect toy for this virtual relationship Lindsey and I have been building. I even drove down the mountain to a larger town to pick it up at my PO box—along with some other toys for the future—so I'd get it faster.

I open the different controls and click the one that will send one sharp pulse then pause and move into a low and steady vibration. I imagine her filling out her end-of-day reports or maybe talking to a coworker. I wonder if she made a noise and blew it off as a cramp or something. Or maybe she's alone and is pressing her head against the cool metal of the locker, attempting not to come.

There's no way she's not turned on. Even though I didn't touch the toy all day, she'll be wet for me. I can guarantee it.

Fifteen minutes later, as I'm finishing up my food, a message on my encrypted app comes through.

Lindsey

I'm sending you a bill for new underwear.

I smile around my food and type a message back.

Me

I'd be happy to buy you some. As long as I get to pick them out.

With the new dynamic we're building, I don't feel like a creep imagining dirty things with her anymore. Like what her shapely body would look like in lacy underwear I'd buy her or how I'd make her jack me off with a pair she'd soaked. And hopefully, one day, me stuffing a pair in her smart mouth while I spanked her ass red in punishment—or purely for my pleasure alone.

Lindsey

What will you pick out for me, Sir?

Me

It will be a surprise. But you'll wear whatever I get for you, won't you?

Lindsey

Yes, Sir. I'll do anything you ask.

Her message comes through fast, and laughter rumbles through my chest.

Me

Are you saying that because of the toy driving you mad or because you mean it?

Lindsey
Because I mean it, Sir.

Me
Good girl.

Satisfied, I take a drink of water. When my phone buzzes again, I smile as I read her question. I knew she'd be wet and ready. I'm happy that I was right.

Lindsey
Can I come, Sir?

Me
No.

Lindsey
Please, Sir. I don't know if I can hold it back.

The image of her squirming and pleading to come doesn't help the hard-on I have, one that's been constant today thinking of her wearing my toy. If she were here with me, there are so many things I could do to make sure she didn't come.

But she's not, and I know I'm being mean by not letting her come. But I like the idea of pushing her boundaries further, of testing the depths of her submission to me, especially while she's learning to submit and I'm learning her.

I think for another few seconds, knowing she's teetering on the edge, waiting for my answer.

Me

What will you give me if I let you?

The bubbles appear on the screen, and my brows lift when her answer appears.

Lindsey

Anything, Sir.

I love her innocence in all this. She truly doesn't mean *anything*, because I can think of many things she'd probably hate.

Me

That's a dangerous thing to say to your Dom. I'll give you one chance to take it back.

Lindsey
I'm not taking it back.

Me
You're brave tonight, baby.

Lindsey
You make me want to be brave.

Her words stop my fingers from replying right away, hitting something deep in my chest that makes it warm and tight. It's a reminder that Lindsey is unlike most submissives I work with and what we're developing is new territory, even for me. But it's a connection I want to explore, one I've dived headfirst into. Her words show me that she has, too.

Me
I'm glad to hear that.

Lindsey
Sir, I, I can hardly type. I'm using voice to text.

Deciding to have mercy on her, and because I need to hear her voice while she begs on the edge of release, I call her. She picks up before the first ring ends, breathless.

"Sir, please. I don't think I can wait. The vibrations are too much!"

I stand up straight, leaning against my counter. "You said you'd give me anything. I'm curious as to what you'll give me if I let you take what's mine."

She groans through the phone, "I don't—I don't know, Sir." She sobs, and I appreciate her will to hold off. I truthfully thought she'd already have given in by now.

"Lindsey, if you don't know, then I'm afraid I won't let you come."

"Please, please, please," she chants. "I don't know if I can wait."

I put my phone on speaker and open the app to the toy, clicking the dull vibration to a higher setting. I know what will happen, but if she can't use her words after such an offer, this is what happens.

"Fuck!" Her curse filters through the line, and I know she's coming. I don't let up the vibration as she cries out. I imagine her gripping her phone and pressing her thighs together, clit sensitive. I like it, though, because it's another reminder of me she'll carry with her.

"Such a bad girl," I say loud enough for her to hear me. She whines, and I finally ease the vibration, but I don't turn it off completely.

"I'm sorry, Sir. Oh god." She groans again as I send another pulse at her apology.

"What do I do with you now, Lindsey? You disobeyed me." Her breath comes hard and fast, and I continue. "I could make you come again and again until your clit is sore and puffy. Until your pleasure is no longer pleasure. Do you think that would teach you a lesson?"

"Yes," she says quietly, though from her tone, I know that is not what she wants. It's far from what she wants.

"You're lucky I'm in a forgiving mood tonight, and I know you've had a long day, so I'll settle for this. You said you'd give me anything to let you come, and now I'm owed. So what will you give me?"

"What is it you want, Sir?" she asks through a deep breath.

I send a pulse of vibration to her clit, and she gasps. "Tell me what you'll give me. And don't make me ask again, or I'll make you wear this toy for days, maybe even an entire week, with the vibration so low that you'll be on the brink of release until I see fit to let you come. And if there's one thing you should know about me, Lindsey, it's that I can be a patient man when I need to be."

She releases a low, whimpering sound that makes me think she both loves and hates the idea, which is exactly the response I was hoping for.

There's a pause on the other end of the line, and finally, after a few labored breaths, she speaks. "My mouth, Sir."

It's so quiet, I hardly hear it. "What was that?" I ask to make sure I heard right.

"My mouth, Sir."

My dick does a full-on jerk in my pants at the image, an image she's put there before. She's already said she wanted to kneel at my feet, to ease my displeasure with her smart mouth. Fuck if I don't want that, but—I thought easing into in-person would be best. It's one of the reasons I got the toy.

I wet my lips and inhale. I know that once Lindsey's in my presence and I can touch her how I want, do with her what I want, that will be it for me. It wouldn't just be the image of her in my life; she'd physically be there, in my space. Is she truly ready for that? Am I?

"Sir?" Lindsey's voice is unsure and hurt.

Fuck.

I swallow hard and release my clenched jaw. "That's a generous offer." I may not be able to see her, but the energy that seemed to crackle between us even through the phone ceases, and it's as if she stopped breathing.

She took my silence as a rejection.

"I should go, Sir. I need to get home."

"Lindsey," I say sternly, "we aren't done talking."

"It was a stupid offer; one you don't want. I didn't realize how late it was. Kas is waiting."

"Lindsey," I bark, but she's already hung up.

I put my phone down on the counter, my almost-finished meal staring at me. I took too long to answer. She was offering herself to me, and instead of speaking to her about what it would mean to do an in-person scene together, I froze.

My appetite shot, I dump the leftovers in the trash and wash my dishes while fuming.

I don't like that she hung up, and she knows that from my boundaries we've discussed previously, but I also screwed up. I may not know Lindsey well, but I know enough to gather that she has confidence issues. A big indicator of that beyond her questionnaire was the way she didn't want to look at herself on the screen during our virtual role-play.

I wipe my hands off on a dish towel and pick up my phone, opening the messaging app and clicking on her name to text her.

Me

In the future, please do not hang up on me. Remember my boundaries? This is not how we handle our emotions or feelings. We talk through things, even if they're uncomfortable. That being said, I didn't mean to upset you and would like to talk about this more. Please let me know when we can discuss what happened.

I hit send and close out of the app for now. She's driving, and I don't expect an answer. I also need time to cool off. I'm not used to my submissives hanging up on me, but I also do not have this type of dynamic with them.

I blow out a harsh breath and click to send classical music flowing through my speakers, hoping my nightly routine and work will reground me. I doubt it will, though, because my recent routine involves talking to a certain smart-mouthed brunette with eyes the color of rich cognac and lips that are wholly kissable.

Lips I just fumbled like an idiot.

27
Lindsey

Dane's message from last night replays in my head in the comical voice Kas uses when she's sassing back. *In the future, please do not hang up on me. Remember my boundaries? This is not how we handle our emotions or feelings.* While the boundaries part sucker punches me every time—because I was a jerk for crossing those and do feel bad about it—the rest of his words remind me that being an adult blows. I don't want to be one. Especially since I feel rejected.

"Mom, can I get these for the car ride later?"

I look down at Kas, who has a packet of something in her hands. We're at the General Store, grabbing a few things that she can take on her mini road trip with Nathan, Fox, and Morgan to see her dad after the obstacle course.

"What is it?" I ask. She holds up the packet,

and I see it's wasabi dried edamame. "That's spicy; I don't know if you'll like it."

"I'll like it," she insists.

"Have you had it before?"

"Tyler eats it."

I click my tongue against my teeth. "Does he now?" Kas stares at me, and I wiggle my eyebrows. Her response is to roll her eyes, but I don't miss how her cheeks flush—oh yeah, the girl's got a crush. I knew it already, but this is confirmation.

"Don't be cringe, Mom."

I laugh. "Is there a reason you want to buy something Tyler likes without knowing if you like it or not?"

"I just want to try it," she huffs, throwing it in the basket without waiting for an answer from me. "He eats it all the time."

"Is that the only reason?"

She crosses her arms over her chest. "What other reason is there?"

I lower my voice even though there isn't anyone around. I think we're the only ones in the store besides Hollyn, who's working the front. Her wife might be in the back.

"I don't know, maybe because you like him?" I ask.

Kas turns red, her eyes darting around the store. "Mom!"

"I'm just asking."

"You're being so cringe."

"I'm not trying to be. I'm just asking a question."

"It's just a snack, okay?!" she snaps.

"Kas, don't raise your voice at me."

"Then stop, Mom!"

My eyes dart up and down the aisle. There's still no one around, which I'm grateful for. Nothing like being scolded by your eight-year-old in the grocery store. I didn't think my question would upset her so much, but I was wrong.

"Okay, I'm sorry. I was only trying to talk to you."

Kas rolls her eyes again, and the sadness and frustration I've been carrying since my conversation with Dane last night—even if he didn't outright reject me—only deepens. Kas used to tell me everything, but since Mom moved, I started working more, and things got harder with Jeremy, it's been difficult to get her to tell me about her life. I didn't think my question would upset her this badly, let alone make me feel more rejected.

"Can we go now?" Kas says.

I swallow back tears, not wanting to cry in front of her or in public. "Do you want anything else for the trip?"

Kas shakes her head, so we make our way to the front. Hollyn spots us and waves. "Well, look who it is! My favorite eight-year-old!"

Kas smiles and returns the greeting, her frown disappearing. I immediately feel jealous that Hollyn can get my kid to smile that easily but apparently, I just embarrass her. Mom of the Year right here. Tears prick my eyes as I set my basket on the counter.

"Hey, Hollyn," I manage to choke out.

"Hello, hello. Good to see you, Lindsey."

I avoid her eyes and look down at Kas. "Can you check us out, honey?" I ask, handing her my credit card. "I need to use the restroom before we go." Kas's eyes brighten, taking the card from me. "That okay?" I look up at the older woman.

She studies me, and I wonder if she can tell I'm on the verge of a breakdown. She dips her chin. "Of course, I'll make sure Kas doesn't buy the store while you're gone."

I mouth a thank-you before I turn and head toward the bathroom at the back. The bridge of my nose stings, and I keep my head down in case someone else actually is in here. I don't want to make eye contact with someone I know and have them ask me if I'm okay.

When I'm almost to the door by the premade food and drinks section, my eyes fill with tears at the knowledge that I'm close to safety.

"Lindsey."

My skin prickles at the sound of his deep voice, and I stop in my tracks. Had any other person said my name, I would have been able to pretend I didn't hear it. But not him. I lift my head from the ground as Dane comes to stand in front of me, blocking my path to the bathroom.

I stare into his hazel gaze, and despite him being the source of part of my frustration and sadness, my body relaxes, and the first tear slips from my eyes.

"What are you doing here?" I ask, wiping my cheek. It's a dumb question. He's here to buy groceries; why else would he be at a grocery store?

Dane frowns and holds up a pack of twenty individual trail mix packs. "Thought the kids might want a snack when we take a break."

I look at the treats and back to Dane. Him getting a snack for the kids shouldn't be the thing that completely does me in, but it is. Not only is he hot and kind, but he cares enough to come buy the kids a snack, too?

"Excuse me," I say in an attempt to get around him, but he doesn't move. "Dane." My voice is weak and thick with tears.

Instead of moving out of my way, he puts the package of trail mix down next to one of the displays of premade food and takes my hand. I'm so blinded by the warmth and safety of it that I don't realize until the door is closed and locked that he's pulled me into the bathroom and I'm now against the door, the heat of his body pressing into mine.

"What happened, baby?" His face is angry, and if I didn't know him, I'd be frightened by it. But all I can focus on is the sweet way he called me baby and how his eyes are filled with concern.

When I don't answer, he squeezes my hand still in his. I look down and see our fingers are laced together. I don't remember doing that, but I become mesmerized by the way it looks—his large hand, tan from being outside, slotted together with mine. The contrast between our skin tones stupidly reminds me I should get some sun. I don't know why, but that makes me sad, too, because it's hard to find time for myself, and the person I give all my free time to doesn't even want to talk to me.

"Lindsey." Dane's free hand gently grasps my chin and pulls my gaze up to meet his. "Tell me what I can do to fix it."

I blink, and more tears fall. My heart flutters in my chest as he moves his hand from my chin to wipe away a tear. There are a million things I could say right now—that he can't fix me, that he can't undo my mistakes or soothe the guilt I feel or take back what I said to Kas that embarrassed her.

My lips part, and I take in a small breath. The action draws his eyes to my mouth, and it reminds me of what triggered this feeling in the first place: his response to my offer.

"You rejected me."

I expect him to step back, to pull his hands off my body, but he doesn't. Instead, the hand wiping away my tears cups my cheek, and his features harden.

"When did I reject you?"

"You know when."

"I don't remember saying those words."

Frustration stacks in my throat. I've played

our conversation from last night a million times over in my mind. While he didn't reject me, it was the way he responded, the words he said and the silence.

"You didn't say it directly, but it was clear to me you didn't want what I offered," I say.

"How so?"

I want to roll my eyes at him. Men really are blind sometimes. "Your silence told me."

Dane leans closer and tilts my head up so the space between our lips is minimal. "Unlike my bratty sub, I will use my words if I don't want something."

My breath catches in my throat, and damn my body, but I feel it heat at not only his closeness but also the implication of his words. His grip on my cheek tightens, and the smell of him invades my senses. Our closeness reminds me of that day we first met, when my chest was pressed against his.

My tears have stopped, and as I stare into his dilated pupils, I take air into my lungs, pulling some of the bravery I've felt around him as of late into my chest. "Then use them," I demand.

One of Dane's dark eyebrows lifts. "Are you giving me an order, baby?"

Damn him calling me baby again. It makes me want to melt and get on my knees for him right here. Which is not what is going to happen right now.

"Yes," I say. "Or do you have another bratty sub you want to use your words on?"

The moment the words leave my mouth, I regret them. I know he has other clients, and his relationships with others is not my business.

"I shouldn't have said that; I'm sor—"

"Lindsey," Dane cuts me off. His hand on my cheek slips to my throat, and his palm grips it gently while his thumb presses into my fluttering pulse point. His eyes penetrate mine. They're full of heat, a little sadness, and what I can only call lust. A lust I feel, too.

"You're the only bratty little sub I use my words on," he says.

For a second, I think he's going to kiss me, but his lips remain over mine, the heat of his breath ghosting over my mouth. If possible, my heart beats faster as what he says sinks in. *The only one.* I want to clarify what that means—I think I know—but my words are lost as we stare into each other's eyes.

"I want to be clear, Lindsey. You've been a

very"—he traces the tip of his perfect nose over the side of mine—"very"—he continues, his lips now at my ear—"bratty girl."

My breath escapes me, and his hand gently squeezes my throat. "You hung up on me last night, you didn't respond to my message, and you didn't send me your check-ins, did you?"

I shake my head, and his thumb presses into my pulse a bit harder.

"You want me to use my words, so use yours," he orders.

"I didn't send you my check-ins, Sir. I was upset."

"Then you talk to me. We figure it out. But what I won't accept is you acting out every time you don't get what you want."

I swallow against his hand and nod, knowing he's right. "I felt rejected, and I acted out," I explain.

"I wasn't rejecting you, I was thinking." His thumb strokes my throat, and my hips automatically press into his. I feel it then, his erection against the zipper of his jeans. My mouth goes dry, and Dane's grip on me tightens.

"What were you thinking about?" I ask quietly.

"That this is new territory for me."

Surprise lights in my chest, and the desire to ask him more questions about his life and work sparks in my mind, but now isn't the time for that. "It is for me, too," I reply instead.

His smile is soft, but there's a mischievous look in his eye as he asks, "Do you want to know what else I was thinking?"

"Yes," I whisper as his lips get closer to mine again.

"That there's nothing I want more than to put that smart mouth of yours to good use."

Arousal lights in my lower belly, and all I can feel and think about is the heat of Dane's body, the spark of his words in my veins, and images I know we're both seeing in our minds' eyes.

Knock! Knock! Knock!

The surprise of the knock makes me jump, and Dane and I nearly bonk heads.

"Mom! Are you pooping or something? We're going to be late to the course!"

Heat flushes my cheeks, and Dane bites his lips to keep from laughing. I guess Kas and I are even on embarrassing each other now, even if she doesn't know that she's embarrassed me.

"Mom? Are you in there?" she calls again.

"Yeah, honey. I'll be right out."

Dane's still smirking, and I gesture for him to get behind the door. He does as I ask, and it hits me that if Kas were to see him here, she'd have a lot of questions, questions I can't answer.

I put my lips to his to tell him to be quiet, and before I can open the door, he pulls me to him until his body is against mine, the heat of him pressing into my back. "Answer my messages."

I turn my head, look him in the eye, and nod, mouthing *Yes, Sir* with a small smile. He releases me and hides behind the door. I turn off the light for good measure before opening it just enough so I can get out.

Kas is standing there with our reusable grocery bag on her arm, looking annoyed. "If Logger Dane gets mad that we're late, I'm blaming you and your IBS."

"Kas!" Knowing Dane is in the bathroom just made that comment so much worse. "I don't have IBS, and how do you even know what that is?"

"Moira said her dad has it, and sometimes he—"

"Okay," I stop her. "We're not going to talk about the sheriff's bathroom habits or make light of his health. That's rude. Now let's go." I point to the exit and pretend I can't feel Dane's presence still behind me and that my kid didn't just reveal that our sheriff has IBS.

What a weird day.

28
Dane

For someone who's never taught a class, much less a class to children, I think I'm doing well. Today, we did some more balance work, and they also learned how to hold the rubber axe and throw it at the special target that grips the axe's edge so it will stay in place if they hit it.

Once we were done with that, I gave them a ten-minute break, and I think they were more excited about a bag of trail mix than they are about the course as a whole. I wasn't sure how to feel about that, but I guess kids like snacks.

"Okay, for the last twenty minutes, you can go practice whatever obstacle you want." They all cheer, but before they take off running, I stop them. "Only use the ones we've gone over so far." There are a few groans, but they all run off in groups toward different stations.

It isn't until I look to my side that I see Kas is still here, staring at a group that went to the axe throw. The group includes her friend Moira, another girl, Sara, and one of the boys named Tyler. Her usual happy expression is gone, and in its place is a sad one, one that looks so similar to how Lindsey's was when I found her in the grocery store earlier. My brow furrows, and my first thought is to see if Lindsey is here yet, but she's not. Most of the parents chose to leave today, leaving only a couple of them watching from the benches.

I step toward Kas, who's sort of wandering aimlessly now, kicking at imaginary rocks in the grass. She was fine when she got here, sassy and funny like she's been the last couple of times we've interacted. Obviously, something's changed, and it looks like it has something to do with Tyler by the way she keeps looking over at him.

"You okay, Kasnado?"

She scrunches her nose. "Logger Dane, no."

I chuckle, but the dumb nickname did the trick. She's smiling a little now. "I'll keep trying till you like one."

She nods and looks away from me, her feet going back to kicking at the grass.

"You don't want to go play on the course?"

She shrugs. "Been there, done that."

God, this kid. The more I get to know both her and her mom, the more I see how much they are alike. "You haven't done all of it."

"You said we had to stick to the things we've done already."

She's got me there, so I gesture to her group of friends. "You were good at the axe throwing, but your stance needs a little work. Why don't you go practice with your friends?"

She shrugs. "Nah."

Alright, she's not going to make this easy on me. "Then you'll have to stay here and talk to me."

She shrugs again. "You're not so bad, Logger Dane."

"Are you saying I'm Gucci?"

Kas giggles like she did at the diner, and I smile at the sound. "So embarrassing! Just say cool. That's what old people say."

"I'm not that old," I retort.

"Your hair is silver."

"I grayed early."

Kas turns to me, her eyes squinting in the sunlight. I brought sunscreen for all the kids today, too, and made them all put on an extra layer even if their parents did. It makes me happy that her nose isn't red today like it was last week.

"How old are you?" she asks.

"Thirty-eight."

"You're older than my dad, and he's old, which means you're super old."

My laugh is tempered at the mention of her dad. I know Kas has one, obviously, and that Lindsey is no longer with him, but that's most of what I know.

"When you're my age," I say, "you'll realize it's not that old."

"That's like a gazillion years from now, Logger Dane."

I shake my head at her and cross my arms over my chest. A second later, Kas has gone back to looking at her friends. It takes a split second for the smile I put on her face to turn back into a frown.

My eyes follow hers, and I see she's looking at Tyler once more. He's holding hands with Sara as Moira throws one of the axes. Kas doesn't look away from their hands, and a moment later, her eyes turn glassy with tears.

It doesn't take a genius to see she's feeling

rejected, just like I made Lindsey feel. But in this case, Tyler has eyes for another girl, and I have no fucking clue how to make Kas feel better. How do you make kids feel better about their crush liking another person?

When I was a kid, my dad would've told me to get over it and stop being a pussy. He was an asshole and didn't care about my feelings. My mom would've told me not to worry, that I was cute, and that there are plenty of other fish in the sea. That wouldn't have made me feel better, so I don't think that's the right thing to say to Kas.

"Logger Dane?"

Her voice is small, not like that of the brazen kid I've come to know. "Yeah?"

"Do you have a girlfriend or boyfriend?"

Her question surprises me, and what surprises me more is that I almost say yes. I think about what Lindsey and I are, what I told her in the bathroom earlier. We have a lot to talk about, but after thinking nonstop and seeing her today, I know, despite my earlier reservations, what I want with her. And it's more than just a virtual relationship that includes sexual scenes over a computer.

"It's complicated," I say to Kas.

"Adults always say things are complicated."

My lips twitch. "Life can be complicated sometimes, Kasadilla."

"That's your worst nickname yet," she groans playfully.

"Made you smile, though, didn't it?"

She rolls her eyes then says, "Do you like them?"

"Like who?"

"The person it's complicated with."

"I do," I answer easily, wondering how this turned into a conversation about me.

"If you like them, you should tell them." Kas looks out at Tyler, and my heart breaks a little for her.

"That's sound advice," I say.

"My uncles and aunt tell each other all the time how much they like each other. It's annoying, but I think that's why they stay together."

My brow furrows at her comment and the turn in conversation. "Relationships take work. Liking each other is only part of it."

She shrugs. "I think if my mom and dad said they liked each other more, my dad wouldn't have started seeing someone else."

Well, this went into territory I was not prepared for. It also explains a lot about Lindsey's past. I don't know if Kas knows she just told me that her dad cheated on her mom, but that's the clear implication.

"That steps into very complicated territory, kid. I bet it wasn't that simple."

She shrugs. "That's what Mom says about it, too."

"She's a smart woman; you should listen to her."

"That's also what my Uncle Nate tells me," she huffs.

"Sounds like you have a lot of smart people around you."

"I guess so."

I gently bump her on the shoulder with the back of my hand. She looks at me, and I see the sadness and confusion in her eyes. "Take it from me, Chaos Kas." Her smile comes back at the nickname, and I continue. "You're young. You're going to like lots of people, and some might like you back, and some might not. But that doesn't determine how likable you are. Remember that."

Her eight-year-old brain works around what I said, and I don't know if she gets it completely or not, but I meant what I said.

"Is this one of those self-esteem speeches teachers love to give us?"

I huff a laugh. "I don't know, is it?"

She shrugs. "My teacher likes to make us these mantras about being enough and brave and stuff."

"Sounds like a smart teacher."

She rolls her eyes. "You like calling people smart."

"I call it like I see it. Now, why don't you throw an axe or two? You've still got ten minutes. Someone who likes you a lot is waving you over."

Kas looks to where I'm pointing and sees Moira smiling and waving her friend over. I expect her to say *that's not the same* or make an excuse not to, but she smiles and nods at me, telling Moira *one minute* by holding up a finger.

Kas faces me, and before I know what's happening, little arms are around my waist, and I'm being hugged. My body stiffens in surprise, but then I relax.

Kas pulls back and looks up at me. "Thanks, Logger Dane."

I don't have time to react before she's off again, making her way to Moira. She ignores Tyler and Sara and picks up an axe. She says something to Moira that makes them both giggle, then a determined look appears on her face.

She squares up with the target and stands in the form I showed them. A second later, she lets the axe fly, and it hits the center of the target with ease. She and Moira jump up and down in celebration, and I clench my jaw to keep from laughing.

When she glances back at Tyler, I know with one hundred percent certainty she pretended that was his face. I don't know if that's healthy or not, but I can't deny the kid has talent. I'd also much rather her pretend the target is his face than throw the rubber axe at his real one.

Twenty minutes later, all the kids have been picked up, including Kas, who was picked up by Nathan so she could go to her dad's for the weekend. Now alone, I take my phone from my pocket and see I have several messages; a few are from clients, but those aren't the ones I'm after. I see Lindsey's thread has notifications, and I click it open. She messaged me an apology for her disobedience and said she's going to journal on why she did what she did and didn't check in with me. All of that pleases me, and I acknowledge what she sent and praise her before I type out what I've been itching to say. What I know is the next step in our relationship.

Me

If it wasn't obvious, I'm going to say it now: I like you, Lindsey. I like you a lot. I'd like to show you how much, if you'd let me. Are you free tonight?

I reread the message, finding it's so unlike me in many ways. It's sappy, but my conversation with Kas is fresh in my mind. Lindsey needs to know that I like her and I'm not rejecting her.

The bubbles that indicate she's typing pop up, and a few seconds later, her response comes through.

Lindsey

You have my schedule; you know I am.

I laugh at her smart mouth, and I have to think she's being sassy on purpose.

Me

I'll send you my address. We'll eat at seven, but arrive by six thirty.

Lindsey
Yes, Sir. Any other requests?

Me
Wear the toy I sent you.

Lindsey
Yes, Sir.

Me
And Lindsey?

Lindsey
Yes?

Me
Don't be late.

29
Lindsey

I'VE SHAVED AND EXFOLIATED every single part of my body that I could possibly think to shave and exfoliate. If I still lived in a big city, I would have gotten a full Brazilian wax, but that's not something the Starlight Haven's local salon offers. Even if it did, I wouldn't go.

The woman who owns it, Sandra, would go on to tell the entire town I was getting lucky. I swear that woman has a phone tree set up just for gossip. Not that it would matter much. I've already had a few of my coworkers, including Billie, ask me if I was dating the mysterious lumberjack in the woods.

I couldn't even be surprised at the questions considering the public run-in at the obstacle course and then our impromptu dinner at the diner. It seems people have seen him more in the last couple of weeks than they have the entire time he's lived here. It makes me wonder if that's solely because of me or because he replaced Levi at the course.

I don't have time to think about it more because my GPS tells me to turn onto a winding road, and his cabin is only a couple of minutes away.

The nerves I've felt since he asked me to come over are a ball in my stomach, bouncing with each rock of gravel my tires go over. It's been a long time since I've been on a date—if that's what this is—and even longer since I've had sex.

If that's what is going to happen. I have no idea, but between the dormant toy resting against my clit, his comment about my mouth in the bathroom, and everything that's gone on with us in the last week, I'm going to guess yes? At least oral?

I also can't forget the fact that he said he likes me.

My pussy gets wet, and despite my clit still being sensitive from his toying yesterday, I wish the vibrator would turn on so I could get some relief before I knock on his door.

I glance at the clock on my dash and see that it's six twenty-five. We don't live too far from each other, but he lives farther into the woods than I do, closer to Fox, Nathan, and Morgan.

It took me about fifteen minutes to get here. As his cabin comes into view, more nerves rack my stomach.

"Freaking calm down," I tell myself. "You like Dane; you feel safe with him. He said he likes you." I smile at that. It was such an odd thing for him to message, but it was needed, nonetheless. Especially after the rejection and near meltdown I had before he intercepted me at the General Store.

I haven't been able to stop thinking about that interaction since we parted. The way his breath felt on my lips, how my body reacts every time I'm around him or hear his voice. And tonight, there's no computer between us. There's no kid to interrupt us or even Nathan. I told my job I'm unavailable unless it's an emergency where the entire staff is needed—which has never happened in our little mountain town, thank god.

When I pull up and see his black truck, I park in the empty space next to it. His cabin looks fairly new, built in a similar way to the one Nathan lives in. I obviously can't see the inside, but there's a porch with two green Adirondack chairs in the front with a small table for drinks between them. It's one-story, and I'm guessing it only has two bedrooms like most of the cabins in this area. That was the case when I was looking for housing, at least.

I glance at the clock on my dash and see I have two minutes to get to the door. I check my makeup and my hair one more time. I wanted to be comfortable, so I kept it light. A bit of foundation, mascara, eyeliner, brow pencil, blush, and a pink lip. He didn't say what to wear beyond the toy in my underwear, so I chose a yellow halter-style sundress that has a deep, low vee. I added a gold necklace with a wave charm that Nathan gave me last Christmas, which sits near the valley of my breasts, which are currently being held up and pushed together by the halter strap. Hopefully this is sexy enough for tonight; it was the best I could do on short notice since I had to shave everything and then dry and curl my hair.

The clock goes down to a minute, and my adrenaline spikes. I have to get out of the car and to the door, or who knows what he'll do. The idea of being punished doesn't sound all that bad, but since we're in person, maybe I should rethink that.

I get out of my car, locking it and rushing toward his door. I walk up the four steps and knock at exactly six thirty. My chest heaves a bit from rushing and nervous excitement, and my skin prickles when I hear movement coming toward the door.

It swings open, and the little breath I had exits my lungs. Dane is a very attractive man, but in his element, here in his home, he's breathtaking. His hair is styled, and he's wearing a black button-down shirt with the top few buttons undone. I can see a bit of his skin and a smattering of dark chest hair through the opening. His throat works as he swallows, and my eyes drift from the tattoos on his neck to his forearms, which I can see because he has his shirt sleeves rolled to the elbows. Below the waist, he's wearing a pair of dark-wash jeans that may even be black.

He clears his throat, and my gaze snaps to his. "See something you like?" His eyes sparkle.

"You look nice." It feels like a dumb answer, because the man is like sex personified.

He rubs his hand over his jaw and steps back just enough so he can look me up and down. His eyes drag slowly from the simple nude pumps on my feet, to my bare legs, and then to the hem of my dress. I swear his eyes pause at the space between my legs as if he can see the toy waiting to be used through the fabric.

His simmering gaze trails to my chest, and when he finally meets my eyes, there's a depth of lust in his hazel pools that almost has me lying down on the porch and asking him to take me.

"You look good enough to eat," he purrs.

A short laugh escapes my lips as he invites me in with a playful grin.

"I feel like I'm entering the Big Bad Wolf's cabin."

He closes the door and locks it, then gets close enough to me so that I can smell the masculine scent of his cologne mixed with the spices of whatever he's cooking for dinner. The heat of his body is intoxicating. "Who says you aren't?"

My clit throbs, and my gaze flicks to his lips, lips I've been dreaming about kissing for far too long now. "Am I?"

"I guess you'll find out." He takes my hand, a mischievous grin still gracing his features. "Do you want a tour, or would you like to sit and chat before dinner instead?"

His question pulls me from my horny haze,

even if my clit is still begging for attention. That part of me wants to skip dinner and get to the good stuff.

I look around his cabin. There's a living area, dining area, and kitchen. It's not a lot of space, but it's well decorated. It has a masculine feel to it, strong yet sleek. It's cozy while not being too cozy, the colors dark green and navy. He's lit a fire in his brick-lined fireplace despite it being warm outside, and above the mantel lined with white candles is a painting.

"Is that one of yours?" I ask, walking toward it, his question forgotten.

"It is," he answers softly.

My feet seem to carry me of their own accord, and as I get closer, I see it's not a normal painting one would find above a fireplace, like a landscape. It takes me a minute to see it, but my mouth goes dry at the sight when I do.

It's an erotic painting done in black, white, and gray. My eyes trace from the dark hair of the woman down her back, her curvy body made of rolls and dimples like mine. Eventually, I put together that it's a painting of a woman kneeling. Her back is to the viewer, but she's naked, the only thing on her body a black leather collar around her neck and matching cuffs circling her wrists. Her legs are spread open, and her hands are placed palms facing upward on her knees. Her chin is also dipped with her eyes trained on the floor.

"Do you like it?"

I jump, turning my head to look at the man beside me. "It's beautiful." I mean it, too; he's very talented. I can't deny, however, that part of me wants to be jealous of the fact that he has a painting of another woman above his fireplace, one he clearly took time and care to create. Maybe she's a past lover? Whoever she is, she obviously meant something to him since he not only painted her but also hung her image where he sees it night after night.

"I'm glad you like it." My eyes meet his, and he studies my face, gaze penetrating. "Everything okay?"

"Yes, of course."

He observes me for another second before he nods. "Do you want a tour then, or to talk first?" He restates his question with a grin.

"We can talk first," I say. I'd like to see the rest of his place, but my curiosity over what he wants to talk about wins out. I would rather not see if his bedroom has another painting like this one.

Dane gestures with one of his hands toward the dining table, and I step forward. When I'm next to him, his warm palm lands on my lower back, the heat of it searing. It focuses my thoughts and grounds me, reminding me why I'm here: that he's invited me to his cabin because he wants me here.

He guides me to one of the wooden chairs and pulls it out. It's nice, and I appreciate the gesture more than I probably should. Especially since it's the bare minimum a date should do.

If this is even a date.

Dane's fingers brush the tips of my lightly curled hair as he moves to sit near me at the head of the table. The action sends a shiver up my spine, and as he takes his seat, a grin is still playing at his lips. The light above us casts a warm glow over the table, one that isn't set for dinner yet.

Dane folds his hands on the table, leaning toward me. "I'm glad you decided to come tonight, Lindsey."

I smile softly at him, his heated stare reminding me of the nervous excitement fluttering in my stomach. "I'm glad, too."

"I thought it would be good to talk now so that we're both on the same page about how far you'd like to go tonight, what you're comfortable with."

Heat blooms up my neck. "We already have our new agreement, and we've gone over our questionnaires about what we like and don't like."

"We do, but since being in-person is new territory, I want to make sure you're comfortable. There's no screen between us now."

I lick my lips. "I'm comfortable."

Dane's gaze drops from my eyes down my body, his focus zeroing in on the redness of my skin. "Are you?"

I shift in my chair. "I'm just nervous."

His gaze softens. "I have an idea, and it might be uncomfortable at first because it's new, but I think you'll enjoy it. Do you trust me?"

I stare into his eyes. He knows I do. I wouldn't be here if I didn't. "I do."

His features transform to that of the Dom who ordered me to touch myself through a computer screen. His eyes are harder, his lips devoid of a smile. But I still sense a comfort and safety in his demeanor, one that screams that he'll take care of me, that I can let go and let him be my support. It's the entire reason I started this relationship with him in the first place.

"Remind me of your safe word," his deep voice rumbles.

"Red."

"Do I have your consent to use and take care of your body tonight in whatever way it pleases me?"

My pulse flutters wildly, and I swear my heart is beating out of my chest. This is really happening. "Yes, Sir."

"I'll be checking in with you throughout the evening. If anything is too much, tell me immediately."

"I will."

He hums in pleasure. "You'll stay the night," he says definitively, no question in his tone. Not that I want to leave before the sun rises, anyway, especially if we have sex.

Dane shifts on his chair, pulling out a paper from the back of his pocket. Unfolding it, he places it in front of me. My eyes scan the document: test results.

"I want you to be comfortable with everything we do tonight. If we get to the point of penetration, I'll use a condom, but I wanted you to see this."

The formal use of the word *penetration* is

amusing to me, but it also fits Dane's way of being. I look at the paper again and then to him. "Thank you, Sir. I'm sorry, but I don't have anything to show you."

"It's okay. I didn't ask you to. But if it's alright, will you tell me if you're on birth control?"

"I am, Sir. I don't have the results available, but I haven't been intimate with anyone in a long time, and I was tested this past year. Nothing to report."

I swear his pupils darken at my words. "Thank you for sharing that with me."

My chest warms, because I know I've pleased him. Immediately, I crave more of that feeling. "Thank you for sharing yours with me, Sir."

There's a pause, and Dane inhales. His chest expands as his lungs fill, and with his breath, the air around us changes. I automatically sit up straighter in my chair, and my eyes fall to the table, focusing on the grain of the dark wood.

"Eyes here, baby."

My chest squeezes at the pet name, and I focus back on his sharp features.

"Stand and come here," he commands, crooking his finger at me. When I'm in front of him, he surveys my body slowly. "Did you dress up just for me?"

"I did, Sir."

"Hmm." His hand reaches out, and my knees try to buckle when his fingers ghost over my pointed nipple. This halter-style dress has a built-in bra, but it's lacking pads to cover how hard my nipples are for him. "I like that you thought of me when putting this on."

His touch moves to my other nipple, and I suck in a small gasp of air.

"You like having these pretty nipples played with, baby?"

"Yes, Sir."

Dane tweaks one, and I gasp, arousal flooding my already wet panties, reminding me the toy is still against my clit. He does it once more before his hand drops, and I nearly ask him to bring it back, but he's the one in charge right now. "On your knees."

My hooded eyes widen at his command, and his head cocks in question.

"Are you going to make me ask you again?"

I shake my head, my eyes dropping to the ground. It's then I see a rectangular pillow near his feet. Dane gently nudges it forward, and I awkwardly shift to the ground. When my knees are on the pillow, I'm grateful for it. The hardwood floor would have been uncomfortable for more than a few minutes.

Dane's finger lifts my chin up, and his thumb strokes my jaw until my muscles relax. "You look like you were meant to be at my feet."

My lips part, and emotion wells in my chest. It's an odd reaction to an odd situation I never thought I'd be in. His words not only arouse me but also make me feel powerful. I don't know that I fully understand it, but it's a feeling I could get addicted to.

"Thank you, Sir."

"I'm going to teach you a submissive pose. When we play and I ask you to kneel, this will be how you present yourself to me. Understood?"

"Yes, Sir." The response comes out of my mouth, but my brain is still stuck on the idea that we will have more than just tonight.

"Good girl." He strokes my jaw again, the feel of his rough hands mixed with his praise curling heat in my lower belly. "Now, rest back on your haunches with your knees spread." I adjust on the floor, my dress parting and riding up my thighs. The cooler air of the cabin drifts between my legs, and the contrast on my heated skin makes me shiver.

"Perfect. Now place your hands palms up on your knees and relax into the pose."

I do as he asks and take a calming breath. My eyes are still on his, and the pleasure I see radiating from them only eases my body further.

He hums a low sound when his eyes take me in. "Stunning," he says, fingers tucking a strand of hair behind my ear. "If I ask you to take this pose and wait for me, your head will be down, eyes trained to the floor. But when I'm with you, I'll ask you to look at me unless I instruct you otherwise, understand?"

"Yes, Sir."

"Good." He continues to stroke my jaw, the rhythm methodical and calming. He does this for a while longer, the quiet of the cabin and the way he looks at me—as if I'm something to be treasured—sinking me further into what I could only liken to a meditative space.

"How do you feel now, Lindsey?"

I check in with my body, and the nerves are gone. In their place is a soothing calm. "I feel good, Sir."

"Still nervous?"

"No, Sir, just excited now."

"That's good." He strokes my cheek once

more before pulling his hand back. "The point of this pose is not only to show your submission to me but also to calm you. If you're feeling nervous or need to be grounded, I may have you kneel or submit in a different pose. But this is a good place to start, and it's one we'll use often."

"Thank you, Sir."

He shifts back in his chair. My eyes remain on his as he stands. He had the power prior to this, but with him over me now, I feel the power exchange even more so. He's tall, broad, and strong. His thighs are thick, and at this level, I can see the clear erection in his jeans.

My fingers itch to open his belt, to make good on my offer to use my mouth to please him, but he's the one who dictates when I get to touch.

Dane's finger slips under my chin, and when our eyes meet, he's amused. "I know you're hungry for my cock, baby. But first, we need to eat real food. I have plans that require you to keep up your strength."

Heat blooms beneath my skin, but it would be silly to argue; I know it won't get me what I want. Dane holds out his hand, and I stare at it in confusion.

His warm chuckle washes over me, and my

eyes move to his again. “Would you like to feed yourself dinner while seated? Or if you’d like to stay there, I’d be happy to feed you, but it will be by my hand only.”

My cheeks burn at the idea of him feeding me at his feet. I think I remember reading that Dominants like to feed their submissives as a way to show their care for them. I’ll admit I’d like to try it sometime, but not tonight.

I put my hand in his. Dane helps me up, and when I’m standing, his lips press against my ear. “In time, you’ll eat only at my feet and by my hand unless I allow otherwise. But for now, let’s get to know each other first, hmm?”

My pussy flutters. I fight back a moan, surprised that his words turned me on as much as they did. I guess I do really want to try that sometime.

I wet my lips. “Sounds good, Sir.”

Dane presses a lingering kiss on my forehead. “You’re too perfect, Lindsey.”

30
Dane

If I had less self-control, dinner would have been Lindsey's cunt. A sweet cunt I could smell as soon as she opened her legs for me while kneeling.

I'd imagined her at my feet, kneeling so perfectly for me, since the moment we started talking. I've even painted what I imagined she would look like, and I loved the end result so much that painting now resides above my fireplace. The one Lindsey stared at and, if I assumed correctly, was jealous of. Eventually, I'll reveal that it's her, but I don't need to show those cards now. Not when we're just getting to know each other.

"I'm glad you like your food," I say as I chew a bite of my grilled lemon chicken.

She smiles around a bite. After she swallows,

she says, "I'll admit, I was a little worried you'd be serving me a chicken and veggie omelet."

I sip my glass of dry white wine, the one five-ounce glass I'm allowing each of us tonight so we are both clearheaded. "I thought about it."

She chuckles. "Thank you for sparing me."

"Come on," I tease. "It wasn't that bad."

"Tell that to my taste buds," she jokes, eating another piece of chicken.

I watch with rapt attention as the fork slides from her mouth like that day at the diner, and my cock jumps. To avoid cutting this dinner short and fucking her over the table, I ask her a question. "How long have you lived in Starlight Haven?"

She sips her wine, her brown eyes finding mine. "About two years. You?"

"Five."

Her eyes widen. "I can't believe we haven't met before now. You'd think we would have."

"I keep to myself, as I think you know by now."

"This town is so gossipy that I'm surprised, honestly. Especially since you know Fox and Morgan."

"Like Fox and Morgan, they know I like to

keep my life private. It's easier with my work, and I also like the quiet."

"I do, too. It took me some getting used to after growing up in a city, but it's why I ultimately decided to move here. For Kas as well. We needed a change of pace, and this was about as different as we could get without moving states while also staying close enough that she can see her dad." Lindsey grits her teeth at the mention of Kas's dad, and it puts me a bit on edge. I don't like seeing her upset.

"Does she see him often?"

"Just one weekend a month. If I had my way, it would be never."

"Is he not a good parent?" I think of what Kas told me today. Her commentary led me to think he's not a great guy, but I want to hear it from Lindsey.

She sighs. "He's fine. He treats Kas well, but he's an ass to me, and we don't get along. What annoys me most, though, is his parenting: He tends to treat Kas more like a friend. That means when she comes back from his place, she's always a little more defiant of me and the rules. Which is already something I've had a hard time enforcing, as you've started to find out."

I nod. Lindsey's already gotten a bit more confident in keeping routines since we started working together, but it's good to have more information so I can help her better in the future.

"My mom was like that with me," I say. "I felt more like her friend than her child."

"Really?"

"She was a sweet woman. I loved her, but she was a shit parent." I cringe as soon as I say it. That's probably not something Lindsey wants to hear.

"Did she pass on?"

I nod. "Both my parents."

"I'm sorry."

"It's okay," I say. "It's been awhile now." I don't need to get into the fact that my relationship with my parents, especially my dad, was strained long before they died. It's not something I need pity for, and I've had time to grieve and heal.

"My dad passed away a few years back of a stroke," Lindsey says.

"I'm sorry for your loss," I say softly.

"Thank you." She takes another drink of her wine. "My mom is still with us—she actually moved with us to Starlight Haven for about a year, but she missed Santa Solana and moved back. Nathan lives here now, though, as you know. Do you know his story?"

"I don't know how he met Fox and Morgan, but I know they're all engaged now."

Lindsey smiles. "He was coming up to see me two Christmases ago when his car crashed into a snowbank, and they rescued him. He was snowed in with them for a couple of nights, and, well, I don't need to imagine what happened from there to get them to the point of moving in with each other as fast as they did."

I smile. I *can* imagine it. And knowing Fox and Morgan, it must have been a wild experience for Nathan, especially if he was new to kink like Lindsey is.

"They love each other," I say. "That's what's important."

Lindsey dips her chin. "To be honest, I'm a little jealous."

I swallow another bite of chicken. "Of what?"

She wipes her mouth. "Of how much they love each other. I don't know if I've ever been loved like that. The way they look at each other, it's like...I don't know. Like their souls were meant to be together."

My chest smarts for the beautiful woman in

front of me, and I want to comfort her, to tell her that she'll find that love. Because there's no way the world could be so cruel as to let her suffer as much as I'm guessing she already has with her ex. But something in me won't say it, because I don't like the idea of her with anyone but me. And it's too soon to tell her that.

"Fox and Morgan are special people, and I'm sure Nathan is, too. I'm glad they found each other."

"Me, too." She sighs. "Anyway, I shouldn't complain. I have Kas. She loves me—most of the time, at least." She chuckles to herself. "And, of course, Nathan and my mom."

"I didn't think you were complaining. You have a right to want to be loved like you deserve."

Lindsey's eyes meet mine. We hold each other's gaze for a long beat before she asks, "And you?"

"And me, what?"

"Have you had a love like that?"

I have loved, at least like a Dom loves his partners. I've also had silly first loves as a teenager. But I've never loved so deeply that I wanted to have that person in my life day in and day out.

"I haven't."

"Really?" she asks, her eyes wide.

"I've lived mostly by myself since I was eighteen. I traveled a lot, spent time in different places logging. Most of my work is done online now, and before you, none of my online dynamics have been intimate."

"You're serious?"

"I don't lie, Lindsey."

"I—sorry, I just thought . . . I don't know what I thought."

"That I have submissives here every night?"

"You were pretty friendly with Cheryl. I swear she was ready to throw her bra at you when we were at the diner. Thought you might know her better than you know most people in this town."

I cock my head at her jealous tone. "Careful, baby. You're on my clock now, and everything that comes out of that mouth of yours has consequences."

Her cheeks blush a darker pink at my warning, and I slide my hand across the table so that my fingers brush over the knuckles of her hand around the stem of her wine glass.

"There's nothing going on between me and Cheryl, and there never has been. Moreover, the boundaries I have in place with my clients have remained intact, always. You're the only person I've changed them for. Ever. You're the only one who's been in my cabin." I take her hand into mine and gently hold it, her eyes once again widening in shock.

"You're serious?"

"Not even Fox and Morgan have been here." I lay her palm open on the table and begin to trace the lines of it. "And I told you, I don't cross lines with my clients."

"Except for me."

I want to say it's clear she's more than a client, but I don't. Truthfully, I don't think she's ever been one. We've always been more.

"Except for you," I reiterate. "But if you're worried about my experience level, don't be. I have had partners in the past, but none of them have been my clients. And none of them have been to my cabin, either, nor will they be invited in the future."

She bites the inside of her cheek, and I didn't think it was possible, but her skin looks even pinker now. "That's good to know, Sir. And I wasn't worried."

Satisfied with her answer, I eye her nearly finished plate. Mine looks about the same. It was a light meal, something I did on purpose because of what we're about to do. Nobody wants to do a scene on a full stomach. I'll provide snacks for her later if she wants them.

"Are you finished?" I ask, pulling my hand from hers and sitting back in my chair. I put a hand in my pocket where I placed the controller to what lies in her underwear. I picked this toy not only for what it does and how discreet it is but also because it has both an app on my phone and a remote I can use in person.

Without looking at her plate, she nods. "I am, Sir."

I click the remote on, the toy in her panties buzzing at the lowest setting. Watching her face transform from shock to pleasure, her hands gripping the edge of the table, is a picture I think I'd like to try to paint. Maybe I'll start an entire Lindsey collection.

"Look at me," I command.

Her eyes open, pupils dilated so her irises are near black in color. Her hands still hold the table, and I up the vibration. A gasp, followed by a moan, spills from her lips, and I decide this experience is way better in person.

"You've been very naughty as of late, Lindsey."

She bites her lip, eyes starting to hood as she squirms in her chair. "Not only have you talked back to me, but you've disobeyed me, too, haven't you?"

She nods.

"Words," I remind her.

"Yes, Sir."

"It's one thing to be playful; it's another thing to purposely ignore me. To shirk your responsibilities. To go against your word. You've done it more than once, and I think it's time you learned a little discipline, don't you?"

She whines as I increase the vibration again. "Yes, Sir."

Her breathy tone goes straight to my dick, and I'm done waiting for this evening to truly begin. "Repeat your safe word."

"Red."

"If you want to keep going, what do you say when I ask?"

"Green, Sir."

"And if you want me to slow down?"

"Yellow, Sir."

"Good girl. Now get on your knees." I sit forward in my chair and spread my thighs. "And crawl to me."

31

Lindsey

"C-CRAWL, SIR?" I FUMBLE over my words.

He lifts a dark eyebrow. "Is that a problem?"

The vibrations against my clit pulse, and I shake my head. It's not a problem per se, but it *is* embarrassing. I know that's kind of the point, and while I said it interested me on my questionnaire, I don't need to remember that to know it excites me. The wetness that floods my underwear is proof of that. I've just never done it before or ever thought I'd hear a man say those words to me.

"No, Sir," I say.

"Then don't make me ask again."

The force of his words clicks something into place in my brain, and I push my chair back from the table. My knees touch the hardwood floor, and I stifle a groan. This position lightens the vibrations against my clit but somehow makes them ten times more intense.

I inhale and place my hands on the ground. My dress is short, so it no longer covers my ass, and the air of the cabin brushes against the backs of my thighs and my heated sex. It's a reminder that I'm about to crawl to a man.

Deeper heat pools in my belly, and my nipples are painfully hard like they always are around Dane. I don't lift my gaze, knowing if I look at him, the rational side of my brain may tell me to stop. But I don't want to stop. I want this; I want to please him.

I put one hand forward and begin to crawl the short distance to him. It only takes me a few seconds, but in those seconds, I take another inhale and exhale, allowing myself to sink into the feeling of surrender.

When I'm in front of his spread legs, I stop, and he reaches out and lifts my chin with his pointer finger. Our eyes connect, and all my feelings of embarrassment and humiliation go away when I see the approval in his gaze.

"Such a pretty thing when you submit. Do you want to continue?"

"Yes, Sir."

He strokes my chin before he pulls his hand back to his knee. "Kneel in the position I showed you, eyes on me."

I sit back on my haunches, spreading my knees and placing my palms open on top of them. The vibrations from the toy ebb and flow against me, but he's turned it to the lowest setting so I'm able to keep my focus on him.

Dane's hand reaches out again, and I think he's going to touch my chin, but instead, he takes hold of the wave necklace I'm wearing. He tugs on it, not hard enough to break it but enough that the delicate chain bites into my skin. His eyes simmer, and whatever he's thinking is something he clearly likes, because his breathing turns heavier. I want to know what it is, but it's not my turn to speak. Like he said, I'm on his clock now.

He drops the chain a moment later. "Undo your halter."

My heart pounds in my chest. I knew when I came here that there was a strong potential for getting naked. It's why I scrubbed and shaved everything down. But now... now, it's real. He's here, I'm on my knees in front of him, and he's going to see my body for the first time.

Dane must see my hesitation, because his

gaze softens. "Those tight little nipples have been taunting me since the first day we met." His eyes trail down to my chest. "Put me out of my misery, and let me see the beautiful tits that belong to me."

I bite the inside of my cheek and lift up my hands. If I hesitate any longer, I may chicken out, and I don't want to. I want to be good for him. I reach behind my neck and quickly untie the knot of the halter.

The top of my dress falls, pooling at midwaist. The cooler air brushes across my already tight nipples, turning them into hard buds that hurt.

"Good girl," Dane praises. "Now take a breath for me." I do as he asks, and my shoulders ease. "That's it, you're doing so well."

My muscles relax further, and after another breath, I almost forget I'm nearly naked and kneeling in front of the hottest man I've ever seen in my life. A man who's chosen me. A man who's also chosen me to be the first one to be in his space. The man who, by his words and actions, has told me we're exclusive—at least intimately.

The thought gives me a bit of confidence, and my chest pushes out as if I'm offering my breasts to him. In a way, I am. Not just this part of me, but everything. Mind and body.

"Can I touch you?" he asks.

"Please, Sir."

Dane chuckles, and my cheeks warm at how pathetic that sounded. He leans forward in his chair, the wood creaking under his weight. His fingers brush my hair back then ghost down my neck. Goose bumps break out over my flesh, and he traces them down until he's brushing the crest of one mound. Air gets trapped in my lungs as his fingers smooth over my nipple, this time with no fabric between us.

He takes the hard bud between his fingers and pinches, and the sensation of it, mixed with the low vibrations against my clit, have me crying out.

"So responsive," he says. He pinches again then brings his other hand to join, both hands cupping and teasing my breasts now. "Does this feel good, baby?"

He pinches both nipples at the same time, and the bite of pain floods my pussy with arousal. "Yes, Sir!"

"Hmm, I love how you fit in my hands, how warm you are, how sensitive. I have no doubt I could make you come from playing with your tits alone." He pinches again. "I bet your cunt is wet for me, huh?"

"Yours," I whisper.

Dane stops his teasing, hands stilling on my chest. "Yours, what?" he asks.

"Your cunt is wet, Sir."

A deep growl rumbles from his chest, and his eyes turn so dark, I wonder if he's possessed. His touch moves from my chest, but before I can miss the warmth, he shifts to the edge of his chair, and his hands dive into my hair. Then his lips hover over mine, and the way he's breathing makes me think he's not in control of himself.

He presses his forehead against mine, and our noses bump, our breath mingling together. "I was going to save the reward of my mouth for later, but you deserve a kiss for knowing what's mine."

Dane's fingers dig into my skull, and I'm overtaken by his scent of cedar and spicy vanilla mixed with the spices of dinner clinging to our bodies. His lips ghost over mine as if he's asking me for permission, but he already has it.

"Green," I whisper.

His fingers tug me the rest of the way in, and

my hands grip his shins so I don't fall over from the force of his kiss. I don't have time to think if that's going against the rules because, in the next moment, his lips crush to mine.

I've had a few first kisses, and all of them were tentative, sweet. Two people attempting to figure out each other for the first time. But there is nothing tentative or sweet about Sir's kiss.

He consumes me, his beard tickling my skin. I gasp, and he uses the opportunity to slip his tongue inside. His groan vacillates through my body, the sensations of it mixing with the vibrations against my clit. His fingers in my hair attempt to tug me closer, but there's nowhere to go. Our mouths are fused together.

He tastes like wine and lemon, and the heat of his tongue and the strong grip of his hands nearly send me over the edge. My body tenses, but Dane keeps going, the fabric of his shirt brushing against my nipples as he massages his tongue against mine and kisses me until there's no air left in my lungs. My clit throbs as he pulls back and sucks on my lower lip; I take in a short breath of air and cry out. My body starts to crest, but a sharp tug on my hair stops my orgasm from happening, and I gasp.

Sir's low chuckle is akin to sinister as he pulls away from me, hands still gripping my hair so my head tips back from the tension. His lips are red and puffy from our kiss and the stain of my pink lipstick. He looks good, like I've claimed him. But I can't focus on that, because he's smirking like the devil, and my body is trembling with the denial of my release.

"Bad girl. My reward didn't include permission to come." He releases my hair and sits back. I miss the heat of his body, but I can still taste him on my tongue. He continues to grin as he adjusts the roll of his sleeves, the veins of his forearms somehow more prominent.

The vibrations on my clit haven't ceased, but I do my best to ignore them. He keeps his eyes on me and reaches his left hand into his pocket, pulling out a chain. He holds it up for me to see, and it looks like two clamps on the ends of one long chain.

"These are nipple clamps. Have you ever tried them before?"

"No, Sir."

He sits forward again, his rough fingers ghosting over my pointed nipples. "It's going to hurt, but I think you'll like the pain. Are you willing to try?"

"Yes," I say without hesitation. "I trust you."

His eyes soften. "Good. Now arch your chest forward, and put your hands back on your knees, palms up."

My fingers are still gripping his shins, and my skin prickles with embarrassment. He smiles at me knowingly, and I do as he asked. When I'm in position, he pinches one nipple, placing the clamp on before doing the other. The chain connecting them hangs down, the light weight adding to the subtle pinch. It's not comfortable, but I also don't hate it.

"Green, yellow, red?" he asks.

My nipples throb, but so does my clit. "Green, Sir."

Dane tugs on the chain, and I gasp from the sharp sting. He grins and does it again before sitting back, his hungry gaze taking in my half-clothed, kneeling form. I'm sure my hair is a mess, and my lipstick is gone or smeared, but with the way he's eating me up, I don't care. His gaze is satisfied, and there's no missing the massive bulge that presses against the zipper of his jeans.

Another moment under his stare passes before he stands. He looms over me, his presence dominating. I fight the natural urge to look at the ground, because he didn't tell me to look down. I also fight the flash of disappointment, because I'd be lying if I said I wasn't hoping he'd make good on his threat to use my smart mouth. But I'm putting my trust in him and letting him lead.

Dane takes a moment and clears his food and glass from the head of the table so they're out of the way before holding out his hand to me. "Stand up."

His command is strong and gives no room to argue. Not that I would.

I put my hand in his, grateful for the help. Once I'm up, the toy in my underwear presses more firmly against my sensitive core, and I grit my teeth so I don't come. His smile is knowing, and I can see he revels in my struggle.

"Bend over the table, Lindsey."

My lips part to argue, but his stern glare stops me. I fight another wave of embarrassment and do as he asks.

"That's it," he says. "Chest flat, arms out, and press your palms against the surface by your head."

The cool wood makes me shiver, and the chain

on the clamps bangs against the table. When my nipples press to the surface, it's not comfortable, and the clamps bite into my skin. I turn my head so my cheek is also against the table and I can see Dane.

He runs his hand down my back in a way that feels like praise, then he walks around me and starts to shift my body into the exact position he wants, moving my hands wider. Once he's done, he stands behind me. His feet gently kick at mine, forcing me to spread my legs slightly apart. I would have thought something like this would feel clinical, but all I am is excited. The humiliation of it is turning me on in ways I can't explain.

A second later, he rucks the bottom of my dress up around my midsection, completely exposing my butt and the pair of yellow, high-waisted lace underwear I'm wearing to him. They've ridden up, and the cheeks of my ass are exposed. When I shift under his gaze, the movement reminds me that my nipples are clamped and pressed into the table.

Dane remains behind me, and while I can see his hair and parts of his body, I can't see his hands. I know where they are a moment later, though, because he ghosts his fingers over my now-trembling thighs. I bite my lip to keep from moaning, but his touch feels so incredibly good, and I know I'm beginning to crave it like an addict. I want him all over; I want to feel his chest against my back as he slides his dick inside me for the first time.

My hips shift against the edge of the table as if they're chasing friction, and a gentle slap against my ass stops my movement.

Oh my god, he spanked me.

"Such a needy little brat," Sir tsks. "Did I say you could move?"

"No, Sir."

Sir isn't touching my body. In fact, he's not moving at all. If I was blindfolded, I would have thought he'd left the room. But just when I'm about to beg for a touch, any kind, his fingers ghost over the band of my underwear.

He gives me space to tell him to stop, but I don't. His fingers curl under the elastic and he pulls them down. The toy drops away with them, but he must catch it, because I don't hear it hit the ground.

He works the wet lace down, stretching them over my parted legs, but when he gets to my knees, he leaves them there, trapping me with the tightly drawn fabric. He moves again and steps into view, placing the toy that was just on my pussy near my face. It's no longer buzzing, but it's glistening, and I understand this is a way to show me he's in control, that what's happening to my body is because of him.

"Are you ready for your punishment?"

My focus moves from the toy to my Sir's heated gaze. "Will it hurt, Sir?"

He comes closer to me, his fingers tracing down my cheek. "It will." My body shivers, and his thumb shifts to press against my lower lip until it slips against my tongue, the salty taste of his skin warming my taste buds. "But you want it to hurt, don't you, baby?"

My fantasies of him spanking me have filled my mind since before the idea of us ever being intimate became a possibility. He removes his thumb so I can speak. "Yes, Sir. I want it to hurt."

"We'll start easy. Ten spanks, and I want you to count each one. Don't be afraid to use your traffic colors—I need you to be honest with me if it's too much. Can you do that?"

"Yes, Sir."

"That's my girl." He strokes my cheek then holds out his palm. "Now kiss my hand, and tell me you want it. Tell me you want me to teach my smart-mouthed girl a lesson."

I kiss his palm without hesitation and respond, "I want your hand, Sir. Please, teach me a lesson."

His rumbling hum of pleasure fills the space before he steps back to begin.

32
Dane

Lindsey Clark is fucking perfect. I nearly lost my goddamn mind when she called her sweet cunt mine. I kissed her, claiming her, and I fear I won't ever come back from tonight. Because that kiss... it solidified what I've been trying to deny. That the reason she ran into me that day is because she *is* mine.

I run my palm down her back, over the dress bunched at her waist, then to her round ass. Her skin is flushed from everything she's feeling, and I'm practically salivating from the mental image of her ass soon to be covered in my marks.

I step back to let Lindsey feel just how at my mercy she is, that I could truly do whatever I wanted to her in this position with her legs trapped by the soaked panties around her knees. Panties I plan to keep when our time here tonight is done.

My hungry gaze takes in her cunt, *my* cunt. She's wet, arousal coating her inner lips and thighs. If she takes her punishment well, I'll get on my knees and lick her dry until she's begging to come against my tongue.

A few more long moments pass as I dream of the many things I can do to her in this position. My cock is leaking pre-cum, begging for me to give in, but that's not what she needs right now. Right now, she needs to become comfortable in her submission, to learn her lesson and her place in our dynamic.

I step forward, my body at her side. Her face is turned toward me, and she blinks slowly and wets her lips. Everything in her body language tells me how much she wants this. Her skin is flushed, and her eyes are soft, yet her muscles are slightly taut in anticipation of my strikes. It propels me forward, and I gently place my left hand on her lower back while I drag my right over the skin of her ass. "Remember to count, baby."

Her lips part as if she's going to respond, but I don't wait. I bring my hand up, the air rushing against my palm before it lands on her skin in a loud smack.

"One!" she cries.

Pride at her obedience fills my chest as her shout along with the slap ring through the cabin loud and clear. I purposely chose not to play music tonight, wanting her to feel and hear everything we do, for us to be in the moment with each other. Hearing her cry at the strike of my first spank, I know it was the right choice.

I smack her again, this time on the other cheek. Her ass bounces and jiggles, the skin flaming from the hit. Fuck, I missed this. Being with someone in person, not simply through a screen.

"Two!" Lindsey exclaims.

"Good girl." I caress my fingers over where I just hit. I study her face but see no signs of her stopping me. I stroke her heated skin, teasing her into a false sense of safety before I bring my hand back and spank her again, this time with a bit more force and an upward motion.

Her fingers dig into the wood of the table as she counts out the third strike. I don't give her a break as I swat her sweet ass three more times in rapid succession. She almost doesn't keep up her count but manages.

I stop after the seventh, laying my palm on her hot skin and squeezing the flesh. Lindsey whines, and my lips tip up in a grin from the pain I know I'm inflicting. My gaze drops to her slit, and I notice it's wetter than before. Looking down at the floor beneath her, I see she's making a mess.

I meet her hooded gaze; her eyes are glassy with tears. I stroke her, my fingers creeping toward her pussy. She sucks in a short breath, but her safe words don't leave her lips, so my fingers brush against her back entrance. The tight ring of muscles tenses as I tease the sensitive flesh.

"Sir," she says, her voice quavering.

I trace the ring again. "You've done anal before, correct?"

She nods. "Once, Sir."

I gently press the tip of my thumb against the muscle, not going inside, and she pushes back as if she wants me to. "Fuck, baby. I like that you're so eager to let me use all of your holes. But your ass is for another time." I bring back my hand and spank her, the sudden slap jolting her body forward, her cry louder than before.

"Eight!" she yells, though her response was a bit delayed.

I release a low chuckle, moving my hand lower, past her puckered hole to her weeping pussy. I brush my knuckles over the plump skin, her arousal wetting me. She sighs as I use a finger to trace over her slit, dipping my pointer finger inside until I'm met with fluttering muscles.

"Oh god," she moans.

"You like that?" I tease.

"Yes!"

I insert my finger deeper, and my needy girl pushes back against my finger. God, she's perfect. I pull it out before she can get herself in trouble and spank her ass for the ninth time.

Her cry as she counts this one has more pain mixed in with the pleasure, and I know she's nearing her limit. I wouldn't put it past Lindsey, however, to ask for more as a way to prove something to me. It's a behavior I've experienced in newer submissives, and I won't let her put herself at risk in an attempt to please me or because she thinks she deserves it.

I drag my finger through her cunt again before grabbing her ass with both of my hands and squeezing. "Last one. You ready, baby?"

She nods and tells me yes, her curvy body shifting against the table as if she's trying to present her ass even better. Fuck me.

I grip her cheeks again before pulling back,

using both my hands to spank her at the same time. I revel in her red skin shaking, my new and final handprints blooming on the already abused skin. Lindsey cries out her final count, and I stroke my hands over where I've spanked, soothing the skin.

When I hear a soft gasp, I shift so I can see her face clearly. Her eyes are closed, but tears cling to her lashes. It's not uncommon for people to cry during a spanking session; it's normal. But I don't like it, and my chest aches much like it did when I saw her tears earlier today at the store.

I move so I'm on the side of the table and sweep my hand down the side of her face. She sucks in a breath as I wipe a tear from her pink cheek. "Open your eyes, baby." When she doesn't, I lace more command into my tone. "Open your eyes."

She finally does, and I hold her chin between my fingers, searching the brown depths for answers.

"Did I go too hard?" I ask.

She shakes her head. "No Sir, it's...I don't know why I'm crying. I'm embarrassed."

"You're releasing; it's normal. Breathe through it." She inhales as she nods. "You did so well." I wipe away a tear. "I'm proud of you."

"Really?"

I smile softly. "Really. You've made me very happy." She blinks back her tears, and I stroke her cheek. "Can I help you up?"

"You're done?"

Her quick change is only further proof of how perfect she is. The more time I spend with her, the more I realize she was born to be in this role, and I can't wait until she sees it for herself.

"Do you want to continue?"

She presses her lips together, and I see the wheels turning behind her eyes. "More spanking?"

"No," I assure her. "I think my good girl deserves a reward for taking my hand so well, don't you?"

"If you think so, Sir."

I huff a laugh, staring at her lips. "God, I can't wait to use this mouth."

Lindsey's eyes flash to my crotch, and her tongue darts out to wet said lips. I stifle a groan, and she notices, a coy smile consuming her features.

"Can that be my reward?" she asks.

Desire pools in my belly, and I press my thumb against her lower lip. "You want me to use your mouth instead of making you come with mine?"

I expect her to say something smart or to say she does but wants me to come, too. "I want to make you come, Sir," she says instead.

My dick swells and digs into the placket of my jeans. Her request is simply too sweet to pass up, and I'd be a fool to do so.

"Ask me nicely," I say.

"Please, may I use my smart mouth to make you come, Sir?"

"Hmm, when you put it that way..." I slip my thumb into her mouth, and, like the minx she is, she sucks on it. I pull back so I don't blow my load in my pants and leave her on the table as I move to her backside. She's left drips of arousal on the floor, and her thighs are shaking from the strain of this position.

I bend down and tap her ankle, having her move her legs together. Once able, I pull the underwear off one leg, making sure not to snag it on her pump, then do the other one. I put her panties in my pocket and remove her shoes. She won't need them for the rest of the night.

When I'm done, I help her off the table. Her flushed face is still wet from her tears, and I wipe them away with my thumbs, leaving her mascara slightly smudged under her eyes. She looks fucked and satisfied, and we haven't even gotten to that point yet. I like that she's received pleasure from pleasing me and from my strikes alone, even if she hasn't come yet.

I leave her dress rucked up around her waist, my fingers trailing from her neck to her collarbone until I reach the clamps still on her nipples. It's going to hurt when I take them off, so I decide to leave them for now. They may still come in handy while I use her mouth. To prove my point, I gently tug on the chain, and she yelps.

"You know," I say, dropping the chain, my hand now tracing the gold necklace she's wearing. "I think next time I'll give you a training collar and a leash." I don't miss the way Lindsey's eyes light at the suggestion. "Would you like that?"

"Yes to the training collar, Sir. Maybe to the leash."

I keep tracing the necklace, my heart kicking up at her answer. We'd briefly spoken about what a training collar is when our dynamic shifted last week and we renegotiated our agreement. While it can mean different things to different people, I told her if I were to give one out, it would be a symbol of commitment, learning, and the potential for a deeper, more permanent bond between me and my sub.

"But the idea excites you?" I ask.

"Yes, Sir."

"What about it excites you?"

"I—" She stops and thinks for a second. "I like the idea of being owned by you."

"I already own you, Lindsey." I pull her necklace gently and seal my lips over hers. She squeaks in surprise, and I dominate her mouth, tangling our tongues together. She submits to the kiss easily. My pulse bangs in my throat at the fact that I just told her I own her, that it truly feels like I do. She is my submissive, we do have an agreement, but owning her, truly owning her—that's much more. It goes beyond a training collar and doing a scene with a leash. We will have to talk about it later, but for now, the idea of it clearly excites us both.

I rest my forehead against hers, my fingers still gripping the chain. Her breath puffs against my lips, and eventually, I lean away from the intoxicating scent of her floral perfume and the sweat of her skin. Her eyes stare up, wide and no longer glassy.

I release the necklace and inhale a breath before barking my next command. "On your hands and knees, baby. Then follow me like the good girl I know you are."

33
Lindsey

For the second time tonight, I'm crawling. It's easier than the first time but different. This time, I'm following him like a pet follows its owner. And not only did I ask to use my mouth to make him come as my reward, but I admitted I'd accept a training collar and maybe a leash, too?

Who am I, and where did Lindsey Clark go?

The only thing I can think of right now is that I've changed. Or maybe this is who I've always wanted to be, and I needed to meet Dane to open my eyes.

For years now, I've simply gone through the motions, and in the last year, I've been trying to keep my head above water. I've been so focused on work, caring for Kas, and dealing with Jeremy's bullshit that I've lost *me*—or maybe I've never been able to find out who I was in the first place.

Jeremy and I got together when we were in our twenties, and during that time, I was focusing on my career and him. Then after we had Kas, my attention was on raising her and my career, plus always trying to please Jeremy, who was unpleasable. Not like Dane, my Sir. He makes me feel like the smallest things I do make him happy, and I haven't even known him for a month.

Sir stops walking, and I'm so focused on my thoughts, I almost run into the backs of his legs. He turns and takes a seat in his recliner, the one I recognize from our video calls. My stomach jumps in anticipation of what's to come. I've been wanting this, to please him in this way—so much so that I chose it over my own reward.

It's once again an interesting realization, because I would have never offered something like this to Jeremy. He might have liked it, but I would have pretended I had cramps or sickness to avoid giving him a blow job. Not with Dane.

"Get in your kneeling position," he commands as he takes a pillow from behind his back and places it in front of him on the floor. "But place your hands palms down on my knees."

I do as he asks, moving so my knees are on the pillow before I sit back on my haunches and spread my legs the way he showed me. When my ass smarts from the sore skin touching the backs of my legs, I must give myself away somehow, because Sir grins. I bite the inside of my cheek, not giving him the satisfaction of cringing. He must realize what I'm doing because his chest gently shakes, but I stay strong.

When I'm settled, his gaze drops down my body, over my clamped nipples to my stomach with my dress still rucked around it, then to my spread legs. There's no underwear to hide my pussy from him now—or should I say *his cunt*. It's a vulnerable position, but not any more vulnerable than the other positions he's had me in already.

He's also touched me intimately; his finger has been inside me. Trying to close my legs now would be silly. Not that I'd want to, because he's eyeing me as if he wants to devour me.

He's done it all night, and while it's intense, I like it. It makes me feel desired and wanted, a feeling that's foreign to me. In a lot of ways, it reminds me how Fox looks at Morgan and Nathan, as if they're his. As if they're treasured. And I know they both are.

Dane did say he owns you. He also mentioned

a training collar, which I said I'd accept. From my research and our brief talk, I know it can be a big deal for some, and when we're not in a scene, I want to ask him what that means for our future.

I swallow to wet my dry mouth and place my hands on his knees, knowing I have time to think about that later. I want to be in this scene with him now. Completely.

"Comfortable?" his deep voice asks with a lilt of playfulness.

"Yes, Sir." As comfortable as I can be on my knees with my dress around my waist, nipples pinched and weighted by the clamps, and my ass on fire. But I really am fine. I'm finding I like the pain, more than I imagined I would. I see why all the submissive forums I looked at online often talked fondly of being spanked or reprimanded. How they like the pain their Dom inflicts because it reminds them not only of their Dom but also to be good. To submit.

Sir places his forearms on the arms of his recliner, leaning back with ease. Somehow, his aura remains strong even though he's relaxed, as if he's the king and I am his servant at his feet—and a willing one, at that.

"Tell me, Lindsey: How many times have you imagined being in this position?"

"Many, Sir," I reply.

"And in that imagination of yours, what did you do?"

I clear my throat. I'm not used to talking this much before a blow job. Jeremy didn't like talking while we were having sex. During oral, he'd just sort of lay there, and oftentimes, he'd take so long to come, it felt like a chore. It left me feeling unattractive and useless, like I was bad at them.

The confidence I was feeling a moment ago evaporates. "Lindsey."

My name draws my gaze up, and I realize I was looking down during my gross memory. "Yes, Sir?"

"Where did you go just now? Your energy changed."

My fingers grip his knees. Damn him for being so attentive. "It's silly. I'm fine."

"Nothing you think or feel is silly. I want to know what upset you about my question."

"I'm not used to talking about sex like this. Then I got to thinking about how giving my ex blow jobs felt like a chore, how he made me feel like I was bad at them."

The muscles of Sir's throat tense, and his fingers grip the armrests of his chair. "Your ex was an asshole. Trust me when I tell you I'm nothing like him."

"I know you're not, Sir," I respond easily. Dane has never compared to Jeremy in any way, shape, or form. Not in looks, not in demeanor, not in anything.

"I'm going to start over. You'll do what I say, Lindsey. I've told you that you're mine, and that includes your smart mouth. But now you're going to prove it to me, understand?"

My pulse speeds up, but his command eases my mind. "I understand, Sir."

"Good. You need to be told what to do, don't you?"

I wet my lips. "I do, Sir."

My fingers tense and release against his knees in anticipation of his next command. I appreciate that he pivoted, that he saw my struggle and knows I need someone to take my thoughts away, not ask me to narrate what I plan to do to him. I don't want to plan or think about anything. I want him to be the one to do that.

"Take my dick out."

I don't hesitate. I slide my palms up his thighs, muscular ones that are strong and that flex under my touch. Sir remains attentive, and I know he's making sure I don't dissociate.

When my hands get closer to his erection, I feel the heat of his shaft through his jeans, the bulge large and unlike anything I've ever felt before under my palm. I have no doubt if and when we do have sex, this man is going to split me in half.

My lips tip up in a smile, and as if he read my mind, he grins back. "Don't linger, baby. I told you to take my dick out. I meant now, not tomorrow."

My skin burns from his cocky comment, and I so badly want to sass back, but the sting on my ass and the pinch of my nipples reminds me not to. My fingers find the button of his jeans, and I pop it open.

Sir's breathing is even, but mine is feathery with anticipation as I find the tab of his zipper and begin to pull down. The sound of the metal teeth opening shoots a spark straight to my clit, and I decide that this might be my new favorite sound. When I part the fabric, I want to say

I'm surprised he's not wearing underwear, but I'm not.

My fingers venture beneath the rough fabric of his jeans, the back of my hand scraping against the cool zipper. I'm not looking at him, but I feel his heated gaze on me as I wrap my palm around his hard cock and pull it out, exposing him to me for the first time.

I was correct in my assumption he could split me in half. He's large, larger than I've had before, and thick. The shaft is curved, the tip is broad, the skin is flushed red, and the slit is leaking precum I want to lean forward and taste. I don't think I've ever considered a dick beautiful before, but Dane's looks like something that would come up in a search for *perfect cock*. Just like his perfect nose and face... his perfect everything—goddamn him.

"You like what you see?"

By the way my mouth is watering, my first answer is almost *duh*. But that would get me in trouble, too, so I answer without the smart attitude. "Yes, Sir."

He expels a low hum of praise before he barks, "Stroke it."

My left hand rests on his right thigh while

my other starts to pump him. The silken skin shifts up and down, his dick pulsing in my hand because he's so hard.

Dane's eyes simmer as he watches me, veins in his neck tense. "That's it. Now swipe your finger over the crown, use my cum to get your hand wet."

I jack his cock, doing what he says. He groans when my thumb swipes over his slit, the whitish liquid coating my finger. It's not enough to lubricate my hand, but he likes it, so I do it again.

"You've never deep throated a dick, correct?"

I shake my head while I continue to pump him in a slow rhythm, enjoying how his dick feels in my hand and the way Sir's looking at me as if I'm the best thing to ever happen to him.

It's . . . powerful.

"Correct, Sir."

"I would like you to try. We'll take it slow, and if you need me to stop, tap my thigh three times. That will take the place of your safe word since your mouth will be occupied. Understood?"

"Yes, Sir." Nerves swell low in my stomach. He's right, as usual; the idea of deep throating does excite me. When I filled out the questionnaire, I didn't know what it was, so I looked it up and watched a few videos. At first, it seemed violent, but the more I read and the more I watched, the more I knew I wanted to try it with Dane. In a way, I guess I manifested it.

The idea makes me smile a little, and Dane catches it. "Something funny?"

My cheeks flush. "It's silly."

He leans forward, his dick still in my palm. His hand shoots out, and he tugs on the chain still connected to my nipples. I yelp, the sharp pain both hurting and creating a fresh wave of wetness between my thighs.

"I told you, nothing is silly. Tell me what it is."

I grip his dick harder at his command, and he hisses.

"I'll get you back for that when your mouth is stuffed with my cock, but first, tell me." He tugs on the chain again, and I groan.

"I was just thinking that I manifested this."

"Did you now?"

"I watched some videos and imagined it."

"Hmm, did you come thinking about it?"

I flush. "No, Sir. But I did get wet."

He pulls back slightly and runs his fingers over my lips. "I bet you did." Dane leans back in his chair and flicks his gaze to my cock in his hand. "Did I tell you to stop stroking?"

My hand slides up his shaft, then back down, my rhythm continuing. A second later, he leans over to his side table, and I see it has a drawer. He takes something out of it, a box he holds up to show me. The label reads "Mitt's Mouthwatering Mints." He opens the brand-new package and pulls out one round, pink tablet.

"I ordered these just for you," he says as he holds the mint between two fingers. "Do you like the taste of cherries?"

"I do, Sir."

"Open your mouth and stick out your tongue."

My mouth parts, and he praises me, placing the pink tablet on my tongue.

"Suck on it," he says.

I close my lips, the cherry flavor of the mint that isn't minty at all bursting over my taste buds as the tablet dissolves.

"This is low strength, but you're going to start salivating more than usual. Don't be embarrassed by it. I want you messy, baby."

My pussy likes what he says, because not only is my mouth getting wetter but so is down below as well.

"Open your mouth," he commands.

I hesitate for a moment because I know when I

do, there's no way I won't start to drool on myself given the amount of spit starting to collect inside my mouth. But Sir cocks his brow again, and that does the trick. My lips part, and he smiles slyly.

"Come on now, you can go wider than that. Show me the pretty hole I get to fuck."

His words only add to my arousal. From our discussions, Sir knows I have the desire to be objectified during sex, and like the amazing Dom he is, he's delivering. My clit throbs, and I part my lips wider for him, saliva dripping from my open mouth. It would be embarrassing if I didn't feel his cock pulse in my hand or see more pre-cum leak from the ruddy tip.

"Keep your mouth open, and get up on your knees."

The spit continues to drip out of me, and when I sit up taller so I'm more level with him, my saliva hits my chest, sliding down the valley of my breasts.

"Beautiful," he hums. "Nod if you remember what I said about three taps on my thigh if you need me to stop."

I nod.

"Good girl. Now put that smart mouth to good use, and suck my cock."

34
Dane

Lindsey's wet, warm mouth slides over the crown of my dick, and it takes all my strength to keep from coming the moment she sucks.

The action pulls a guttural groan from deep in my chest as my hands find the strands of her silken hair. When I cup her skull, she moans around my length. I grit my teeth; the mint I gave her made her mouth nice and wet. Her saliva drips on to my balls and entire pubic area, making a mess of my jeans.

"Yes, baby. That's it." I grip her hair tighter, pushing her head down a tiny bit so she gets used to the motion. "You're just a pretty hole for me to use, aren't you?"

She moans again in reply, eyes down as she focuses on her task.

"Look at me while you suck your Sir's cock."

Lindsey looks up as best she can, her hands digging into my inner thighs. It's a sight to see. My submissive between my knees, her mascara smudged under her eyes as they water. Her lips are puffy around my dick, which is soaked with her spit, spit that won't stop coming. "Have you ever had this much dick in your mouth, baby?"

Lindsey tries to shake her head.

"Breathe through your nose."

When she does, I guide her down further so she's nearly halfway. My dick is long and thick, and I know she's not going to take it all, not at this angle and not her first time trying. That will take practice and time to rid her of her gag reflex.

Lindsey's mouth suctions around me as I bring her head a bit farther down. I sense her panic before she has time to fully react.

I pull her off my cock, and she sucks in air. Her mouth is messy, her chin and chest slick with her spit. Holding her head in my hands, I make sure her eyes are on mine. "Keep your mouth open," I bark. "Good, now stick out your tongue."

Her pink tongue sticks out, and more spit dribbles from it.

"Now relax it, keep it flat." She does, so I

continue. "Breathe through your nose, give me complete control of your movements. Nod if you understand."

She nods, and I bring her mouth back to my erection, pressing on her head until she's halfway down once more.

"Fuck, yes," I praise. "That's it. Eyes here."

Her eyes flit back up, and I watch with careful attention as I push her head farther down. Her fingers dig into my thighs, but she's not tapping out.

"Good girl," I groan. "Relax your throat; don't use your teeth."

Her cheeks redden, but she does as I say. When her throat relaxes, I push her further down until my crown hits the back of her throat. She gags, her shoulders tensing. I attempt to let her up, but she resists me.

"Hmm, someone wants to choke on my cock, huh?" She keens, eyes watering enough that a tear leaks out. "Such a good girl, letting me use her pretty holes however I want."

She moans once more, but it's cut off when I push her head back down. She gags again, but this time, she doesn't tense as much. I pull her back up then do it over and over. On the fifth time, I thrust my hips up slightly until I hit the back of her throat.

The choking sound is stronger, her nails, which I've noticed are blunt from what looks like nail biting—something to address later—dig deeper into my thighs, and I pull her off my cock.

Lindsey audibly sucks in air as I move my hands to cup her red, wet cheeks. I swipe at the tears and spit, and she pulls in my grasp, trying to get back to my straining dick.

"Wow. You are a cock-hungry slut, aren't you?"

Lindsey's eyes saucer at the title, but I wouldn't have said it if I didn't know beforehand that she'd be into it and open to me calling her that.

Her already-blown pupils darken, and I smirk when I see her squeeze her soft thighs together and moan before nodding. She opens her watering mouth wider without a command and sticks her tongue out flat in submission.

I bring two of my fingers to her open hole and press down on her tongue so more spit drips from the corners of her lips. "I bet you'd beg me for my dick if I gave you permission to speak."

She whines as I slide my fingers farther into

her mouth. Her breathing picks up. I press down at the back, and her mouth waters more, but she holds back her gagging.

"How about my cum, baby? Would you beg for that, too?" She nods her response and rubs her needy thighs together once more. I remove my fingers and grip her chin, practically growling. "Use your mouth to show me how much you want it. Work for it. Then I'll give you a reward for being such a good cock slut."

Lindsey's chest heaves, and I release her chin, seeing what she'll do. Her glistening eyes, almost black with arousal, gleam with determination. Her hands on my thighs begin to move, but I stop her.

"Mouth only. No hands." I can see she's not pleased with that, so I add, "I just showed you what I like. Now get me off before I turn that ass red again."

She groans a little, and I lean my head back against the chair and place my hands on the armrests so I can enjoy the show. Lindsey is a quick learner, and she's eager to please. She just needed my help to boost her confidence and get her going.

She keeps her eyes on mine as she slides her

mouth back over my weeping cock. Her fingers dig into my thigh muscles as she slowly starts to work up and down my shaft, the veins of my dick disappearing between her swollen lips as she blows me.

"Fuck, yes," I grunt. "What a perfect cock slut you are."

Her moan around my cock spurs me on, so I lift my hips up slightly. "You're mine to use, aren't you, Lindsey?" She moans again. "I bet if I asked you to keep my dick warm with just that sinful mouth all day, you would, wouldn't you?"

Her responding sweet whimper is so deep, the vibrations almost have me coming down her throat.

"Take me deeper. I know you can do it."

Lindsey's fingers dig harder into my thighs, and I watch with satisfaction as she tries to take all of me on her own. She can't, but I like her determination. She gags, and I expect her to let up, but she doesn't. Her nostrils flare as she breathes and tries again, taking nearly three-quarters of me.

"Oh, fuck, baby. That's it."

Her mouth works up and down my dick, and I know I won't last much longer. I move my fingers to the back of her head, keeping the pressure light.

"Keep sucking."

Her cheeks hollow, and the sloppy sounds of my cock moving in and out of her slippery mouth along with her sucking is the best kind of music.

"This is your warning," I grunt. "If you don't want to swallow, tap my thigh three times now."

She answers by trying to take me all the way down. My fingers tangle in her silky tresses. I moan when her throat muscles contract around my crown and her fingers grip my jeans. Fuck me, I'm never going to come back from this. Lindsey is incredible.

"I'm coming, baby," I say through gritted teeth. Her eyes look up, watery yet mischievous. Her cheeks hollow, and my lower spine tingles, my balls tightening. If I could, I'd hold off and make good on my threat to have her keep my cock warm, but there's no way in hell I can stop. Her mouth is too good, too wet, and the way she's fucking looking at me—

I let out a string of curses as I hold her head in place. I come with a force I never have before. Lindsey's cheeks bulge a bit, and she gags as I shoot down her throat, so I let up on my grip.

She doesn't move off my cock, though. Some of my cum slips out from the side of her lips along with saliva, but her throat tenses and releases as she attempts to swallow all of me down.

My fingers flex against her skull, and my eyes remain open to watch every second of her being the cock-hungry slut I told her she is, that she's proven to be. I keep coming, and my muscles twitch as she sucks me dry like I'm her last fucking meal.

"Goddamn." I groan, spending the last of my lust into her mouth. Lindsey takes it down, and I exhale a satisfied breath as my body sags back against the chair. But Lindsey doesn't let up, her mouth still on me. Warmth and pleasure fill my body knowing she's waiting for me to give her an order.

I take my hands from her hair and cup her cheeks. While I guide her off my length, she sucks the entire way, popping off it like I'm a goddamn lollipop. I continue to hold her face with one hand as I collect the cum she missed on my finger.

"Open up," I say huskily. Lindsey doesn't hesitate, licking the leftovers from my finger, making my spent dick twitch. I trace her swollen lips when she's done. "You did so good, baby. My perfect cock slut."

A soft smile warms Lindsey's face, and I use my thumb to stroke her flushed cheek.

"Thank you, Sir." Her voice is scratchy from the abuse her throat took, but I'd be a fucking liar if I said I didn't like it.

"Are you ready for your reward now?"

She nods. "If you think I deserve it, Sir."

A surge of pride swells in my chest, and I nod. "I do. You've made me very happy." I tuck my cock back in my jeans, the front wet with Lindsey's saliva. She watches with a near pout, and I chuckle.

"Stand up." She blinks at the abrupt command, but despite her confusion, she obeys. Her face pinches in discomfort at the myriad of sensations I'm sure she's experiencing. "Remove your dress."

Lindsey stares at me as if I've asked her to get naked and jump up and down.

"Do you need another spanking?" I warn. "I'm happy to remind you that your sexy body belongs to me. Every part of it."

Lindsey wets her lips and steps away from my knees slightly. Her fingers find the bunch of fabric on her waist, and she starts to push it down. It falls, pooling at her feet. The light above us isn't at full strength, and the fire that needs tending to flickers behind her.

I take her in, wanting her to know how attractive I find her, needing her to know, so that anyone who's told her otherwise—her asshole ex included—fades into a far and distant memory, then hopefully disappears altogether.

Her hands move to cover her soft stomach, where I see a long scar on her lower abdomen, one that is, no doubt, from the birth of her daughter. It's beautiful, just like the rest of her.

I clear my throat before she can fully hide herself from me. "Cover what's mine, Lindsey, and I'll tie your hands behind your back and edge you all night." She gasps, which tells me all I need to know. "You'd like that, wouldn't you?"

"Maybe, Sir," she concedes quietly.

"Noted. Now come here, and sit on my lap."

"Sir?" she questions.

"Do it." She hesitates, and it doesn't take a genius to know what she's thinking. I sit up and reach out, grabbing her around the waist and tugging forward. She nearly falls on me, her sound of shock turning to a groan as her nipples brush against my shirt. "That's what you get for not doing what I ask when I ask."

Her muscles ease a bit as I pull her against me, helping her situate herself so her ass is seated in my lap and her legs are over the arm of the chair. I have her cuddle into my neck and then ask her to take a deep breath so she can relax.

I look into her eyes. "Your body is perfect. Whatever you think I'm thinking is wrong. If I ask you to do something, you do it. I'm going to want you in my lap a lot, and despite my allowance of your clothes earlier, I will expect you to be completely naked if I ask. Do you understand?"

"Yes, Sir."

"Now," I say, fingering the chain between her nipples. "Would you like me to take these off?"

"Please, Sir."

I tug, and she bites her lip, her ass shifting against my cock. "Hold on to me," I say. "It's going to hurt."

One of her hands is on the back of my neck, and she places the other on one of my forearms. Her nails dig into my arm like they did on my thighs as I bring my hand up to undo the first clamp. When it releases, her lips part, and she lets out a yelp followed by a low "Fuck."

"I know, baby," I coo. "You're doing so well. Take a breath for me now." The moment she exhales, I remove the second one. She cries out, burying her head into my neck. I drop the clamps to the side of the chair and brush my fingers over the marked, red skin. Her teeth bite into my shoulder, and damn if that doesn't send blood rushing to my dick. Fuck, I'm going to get hard again already.

"Is the pain too much?" I ask.

She shakes her head, face still buried in my neck. "No, Sir. It's a lot, but I like it."

I smile as I brush my thumb over each nipple again. She squirms at the sensation, and I shift my hand to tease the skin near her rib cage.

"I'm going to make you feel really good now, alright?"

"Okay." She moans softly as I stroke my thumb under her breast.

"If you don't like something—"

"Green, yellow, red," she interrupts.

I tweak her nipple, and she arches into me with a loud cry. "Still running your smart mouth, I see. Even after it's been thoroughly fucked."

I lean forward to capture her lips in a kiss, showing her who's in charge with my mouth.

She opens for me without pause, her moan filling me as her ass shifts on my lap. My hand around her lower back holding her outer thigh keeps her close to me as I slowly trail my free hand down her chest until I reach her stomach.

She tenses against my lips but doesn't stop kissing me. I tangle our tongues before sucking on hers, gently tracing down her soft rolls and to her lower abdomen. At this angle, her stomach covers the scar, but I act as if I'm tracing it.

The longer we kiss and I caress her, the more she becomes a puddle against me. Her warmth seeps into my skin, and I can't deny it feels good. I hadn't realized how much I missed being touched, how much I needed it.

I pull her tighter to me, my fingers digging into her thigh.

"Dane," she whimpers. "I need you to touch me. Please."

The sound of my name hits me square in the chest. I should correct her, but I don't want to. I also should make her ask me exactly what she wants, but I'm done teasing for the night. I want to watch her come on my hand.

I kiss her harder this time and tap my hand on her outer thigh. "Open up," I demand. She parts her legs with my help, and I shift her so she's still on my lap but her legs are parted, each one resting on either side of my knees.

I wrap one arm around her waist, and the other presses against her inner thigh. She rests her head near mine, and my lips brush her ear while she slides a hand behind my neck, her other arm at her side.

I brush my palm up her inner thigh until I find her slick pussy. She's soaked for me, the neatly trimmed curls wet with her arousal. She's so slippery, you'd think she'd come multiple times tonight already.

"You got this wet just from me fucking your mouth, baby?" I brush my thumb near her clit but don't touch it yet.

"And the way you spoke to me, Sir."

"You liked being called mine?" I start to circle the bundle of nerves between her legs, and she jackknifes off my lap. She would have toppled over if I wasn't holding her steady.

"Yes, Sir." I pinch her clit, and her chest arches forward. "And when you called me a—" She pauses.

"A what?" I slap her pussy.

"A slut!" she cries.

"Hmm, that's because you are. But you're

my slut, Lindsey. Remember that. I'm the only one who gets to utter that word to you, isn't that right?" I stroke her in a circle before dipping a finger inside her fluttering cunt.

"Yes, Sir."

I pull my finger out and slap her clit again. She moans and arches, and I turn my head to bite her earlobe. Lindsey whimpers, so I go back to circling her clit, faster this time.

"I'm going to come, Sir."

"Already?" I chuckle, even though I knew it would not take long. But she likes the teasing, as evidenced by the flush of her chest and the wiggle of her hips against me.

"I don't know if I can hold it." She squeezes her eyes shut.

I insert two fingers inside her and pump them up and down. "That's because you're a slut for me. Your body sings for me and only me."

Her hooded eyes open, and she bites her lower lip while she nods her agreement. I take the hand not on her pussy and move it up her waist and over her breasts until I'm at her throat. When we played over the computer, I asked her to gently grip herself and pretend it was me. Now we don't have to pretend.

I continue to thrust my fingers in and out, my hand wrapping around her throat. "Green?" I ask her.

"Green," she confirms, near breathless.

I gently grip the smooth column that's wet from spit and sweat, feeling her pulse thrum beneath my hand. I remove the fingers inside her and go back to her clit, circling harder this time. She swallows beneath my hand and groans in pleasure, so I pick up my speed.

"Such a good little slut," I praise her. "*My* slut." I squeeze her throat harder, and her hips thrust into my hand. "Greedy, too."

"Sir," she moans through the pressure on her throat. *"Please."*

"Do it," I demand. "Come, baby."

There's a pause in her breath, and I hold her throat just tight enough to constrict some of her air. Her lips part, and her hips buck as she falls into her release. As her body shakes against mine in pleasure, I slide my hand from her clit, placing two fingers inside her so I can feel her inner walls pulse around my fingers.

"So pretty when you come," I curl my fingers to brush her G-spot so she twitches in my hold. "I can't wait to feel this cunt I own choking my dick."

Her pussy clenches around my fingers, and I know she did it on purpose. I grip her throat one more time and release, sliding my fingers in and out of her before rubbing her clit. She jumps from the touch on her sensitive nerves, so I have mercy on her, holding her body to mine as she rides the waves of her orgasm.

A few minutes pass before her muscles have stopped spasming, and I run my hand up her thigh, my other arm wrapped around her breasts. My dick is half-hard beneath her, but I don't mind.

My eyes scan her spent body. It's flushed, and she's sweaty. I am, too. The fire has burned down to embers, and at the first sign of a shiver, I kiss her cheek. Lindsey's eyes are hooded, and there's a sleepy smile on her face as I shift to get up.

"I'm going to take you to my room and clean you up."

She starts to move, her heavy eyes opening all the way, but I can tell she's fighting off sleep. I had a feeling this was where her orgasm would lead, and I have no doubt she's in her floaty sub headspace. Tonight has been a lot for her, not only in body but in mind, too. On top of that, she works too damn much, and she's exhausted.

"I've got you," I say as I grip her.

"Sir—"

"Shh." I slip out from under her, and before she can argue, I lift her up in my arms easily. I know again what she's thinking as her eyes widen and she panics, throwing her arms around my neck to hold on to me with a death grip.

"I've got you, baby. Just relax."

"Dane!" she tries again, using my name, but I take a step forward and ignore her weak protest. If she didn't want it, she'd tell me her safe word. Of that, I'm sure. But Lindsey wants and needs to be cared for, and I'm carrying her to bed. End of story.

After another few steps, she finally relaxes against my chest and accepts my gesture. I carry her down the short hallway, and by the time I'm setting her on the bed, her eyes are drooping shut again.

I lean down and kiss her forehead. "I'll be right back."

I'm walking toward the bathroom when I hear her say, "Thank you, Sir."

35
Lindsey

I WAKE UP TO the mattress moving beneath me. My eyes peel open, and I blink away sleep to see Dane sitting up against the dark, wooden headboard, morning light flooding the room. He's shirtless and . . . wearing glasses.

Jesus, how does this man keep getting hotter?

I blink another few times, and when I try to move, I find that I'm tucked under covers. The last thing I remember is him carrying me—yes, carrying me—to bed, then him cleaning me up with a rag and warm water as I floated in a space of half-awake and half-dreaming while my body felt all tingly and wonderful. That apparently led to me actually dreaming, except I was dead asleep and don't remember a thing I dreamed about.

"Good morning," Dane's gruff voice greets.

I stare at him, blushing for some reason. I

don't know if it's because he's wearing square, thick-framed glasses that make him look extra delicious or if it's because I fell asleep on him last night after we did very dirty things together.

"Morning," I answer back. My voice is hoarse, and when I swallow, it feels like the back of my throat is a little bruised. The reminder of his cock hitting that spot before he came in my mouth makes me flush a deeper red.

The corner of his lips lifts up a little, and he reaches to the side table next to him where he has a cup with a metal straw. So not only is this man hot, caring, and sweet, but he also cares about the environment? I think I'm screwed.

Dane holds out the drink, and with my arms trapped by the covers, he puts the straw to my mouth. My body heats under all this attention, but I wrap my lips around the straw, sucking down the cool water. It feels good against my used throat and dry mouth, and I drink almost half of it before I tell him I'm done.

"Thank you," I say.

"You're welcome." He puts the glass down, and my eyes drift to his chest. I realize it's the first time I've seen him without a shirt on, which seems ridiculous after all we've done. He notices me looking and flexes. When I look up into his eyes, he's smiling at me, a gleam in his hazel orbs.

"How are you feeling?" he asks.

I shift under the blanket to pull my arms free, and the first thing I notice is how my nipples smart while rubbing against the sheet. My ass isn't much better. The movement is also a reminder that I'm completely naked under his lightweight, slate-gray comforter and sheet set.

"A little sore," I say honestly. It's not like I can lie—I clearly cringed.

"I'll get you some cream. I put some on you last night, but it's good to reapply."

"You don't have to."

"Maybe not," he says, "but I'm going to."

Dane shifts on the bed, and that's when I notice he has a laptop on his lap. How long has he been up for? I don't even know what time it is. Then I remember I have a short shift at work tonight, and I should call Kas and check on her before that, even if that means I have to talk to Jeremy. He hates when I call, but I do it anyway.

I grab Dane's forearm to stop him. "It's okay, really. I should probably get up and get moving."

"Why's that?" he asks as he closes his computer and puts it on the side table next to the water.

"I didn't mean to fall asleep last night."

He raises an eyebrow. "So because you didn't mean to fall asleep, now you need to leave as fast as you can and be in pain?"

He makes a good point, but I argue anyway. "I'm okay, really. It's just... you probably have things to do." I motion to where he set his laptop.

It hits me that he was probably talking to his other submissives. Not that it's any of my business—it *is* his job, even if the thought makes me question what exactly I am to Dane. A lot of things were said last night, but in the morning light and with my brain now coming back online from sleep, all my insecurities begin to bubble in my chest like lava.

I clear my throat. "I do, too. So, I'll get out of your way." I remove the hand that was still on his forearm and start to climb out of bed. I don't make it far, though, before I'm being tugged back and Dane is rolling on top of me, pinning my arms above my head.

"Did I say I wanted you to leave?" Dane's voice is deeper in the morning, if that's even possible.

"Dane," I mutter.

His hazel eyes are dark, and framed by his glasses, they somehow pop more than they usually do. "Lindsey." He parrots my name in the same tone. "Did I say I wanted you to leave?"

I run my tongue along my teeth and groan. "No, you didn't."

"Do you want to leave?"

I suck in air, allowing myself to feel the comforting weight of Dane's solid body and his strong hands holding my wrists above my head. I'd woken up and started thinking too quickly. I didn't even get to enjoy the fact that this is the first time I've slept next to someone who wasn't my kid in years.

Now that I really think about it, that was the best and deepest sleep I've had in . . . I don't remember. I feel good, despite the soreness of my nipples and my ass, but even that feels good in a different kind of way.

Dane's hands tense against my wrists, and my eyes refocus on his questioning gaze.

"I asked you a question." His breath, which smells like mint, fills my nostrils, and I curse him for waking up before me and getting the opportunity to get rid of his morning breath.

"I don't want to leave," I say honestly. "But . . . "

"But?" he asks when I take too long, and I'm surprised he didn't tell me to use my words.

"I had a plan of things I was going to do today before I work tonight. I was going to wake up early and do my routine then clean my house and maybe start on a project I've been wanting to do. Maybe nap."

He smiles at the last one. "It's only eight. You have plenty of time to do what you need to *and* take a nap. Even if you don't rush out on me."

"When did you get up?" I ask. "I thought it was way later than that."

"Around five."

I scrunch up my nose. "Is that a usual thing for you?"

"It is. My body naturally wakes me up around that time."

"Is that a Logger Dane thing or a Dom Dane thing?"

His grip on my wrists tightens, and his knees, which are bracketing my legs, pull in tighter against my thighs, his way of reminding me we're in a precarious position. One where he has all the power.

"It's a Dane thing." He smirks.

I swallow hard, and his gaze flicks down to watch my throat. The memory of his hand there, cutting off my air supply while he made me come, sends a lightning bolt to my core. Before I know what I'm doing, my hips shift up as if I'm trying to hump him, and Dane's warm laughter fills the air.

"None of that," he tuts. "You said you have things to do, and playing with me wasn't one of them."

Dane gets up as quickly as he pinned me and rolls off the mattress so he's standing near the side of the bed. That's when I see the damn man is only in a pair of gray boxers. My eyes drag down his muscular body, noticing everything is cut and massive. When my gaze reaches his thigh, I find a black-and-gray tattoo of a large stag, the tops of the antlers covered by the hem of his underwear.

He clears his throat, and I sheepishly meet his gaze. "I like your tattoo."

"Is that all you like?" he asks cheekily.

I almost roll my eyes but stop myself. I don't need another spanking right now, even if the idea does make my pussy wetter than he already made it by pinning me to the mattress and being stupidly hot in those damn glasses.

I turn my eyes down to the comforter. "It's not all I like."

Dane is quiet at my answer, and I don't look

up, shifting on the bed as I think of all the things I like beyond his tattoo. I should really get out of this bed before I embarrass myself. I didn't plan to spend the night, and now things are going to get awkward.

I still don't know what Dane and I are. He said a lot of things last night, and I said I'd wear his training collar, but what are we, really? Are we dating or just doing sexual scenes along with my daily check-ins? If I think too much about it, my head hurts. It's all way too confusing for this early in the morning.

"Put this on," he says.

I push my thoughts away as I look up at him. He's holding out a neatly folded mustard-colored robe. I take it from his hands, the silky material soft against my fingers. I know right away this is a woman's robe. My nagging insecurities attempt to bubble back up, but then I see it has tags on it.

"I got it for you," he says before I can wonder if that was the case or if he simply had a robe lying around for a woman to wear.

"There's also a new toothbrush for you in the bathroom. If you'd like, you can take a shower, or I can bathe you," he adds with a devilish twinkle in his eye. "Regardless of your choice, you'll put the cream I mentioned on to help with the pain."

I swallow and look down at the robe in my hands, rubbing my thumbs over the fabric. When I look at the tags, I see he's removed the price, but I recognize the brand as an expensive one. It's also my size. I don't know how he knew or if it was a lucky guess, but I've never had a man do something so kind for me.

Then it strikes me—we only planned this time together on a whim last night. How did he order everything for me in time? He had to have done it before. We don't get things shipped to Starlight Haven in one or two days like in a big city.

"Is something wrong?" Dane asks.

"When did you order this?"

I expect the question to make him uncomfortable, but he simply says, "When our dynamic started to shift, I ordered your favorite new remote-controlled toy and that, along with a few other things." He grins. "Like the mints."

My mouth waters as if I've been trained Pavlovian-style, and I have to swallow down the saliva collecting in my mouth.

"How did you get it so fast?"

"I drove down to the PO box I have at the base of the mountain. That's where I had everything delivered."

My heart squeezes, and I pull the robe against me, looking down at it. He did all that for me? I clutch the fabric and fight off a wave of tears stinging my eyes. I've cried with this man too much already, and I don't want him to think I'm weak.

I blink away the emotion before I look back up at him. He's observing me carefully, and I know he knows I'm fighting back tears.

"Thank you." I swallow again. "That was really thoughtful."

"You're welcome, baby. I told you I'm here to take care of you, and I meant that. Though..." His eyes flash down my body, the one still covered by the sheet. "I meant what I said last night, too. Eventually, I won't allow you to have clothes on when it's just you and me. I prefer to see what I own. So don't get used to the robe."

My sensitive nipples tighten into buds, and I bite the inside of my cheek. I know I'd be even more turned on by his words if my brain wasn't focused on what he said—not only the reiteration that he owns me but that he also wants to do this again.

It's on the tip of my tongue to ask him if this means that we're dating or if seeing each other like this is simply casual or normal for this type of D/s relationship. I also want to know if he tells other submissives he owns them, even though their relationships don't involve sex. But I don't, because I'm not sure I'm ready for the answers, especially if they aren't what I want to hear. Because, dammit, I think I'm falling for Dane. Not Logger Dane, not Dom Dane—just Dane.

"Well," he says, taking off his glasses, which I'm guessing are readers. "Are you going to stay in bed, or did you want to do your routine and have breakfast before we go to your place?"

My brow furrows at the same time my heart speeds up. "We?"

"If it's alright with you, I'd like to spend the day with you."

I think my heart fully stops in my chest. "I need to clean, and the projects—I don't know if they are something you'd want to help with."

"I wouldn't say 'we' if I didn't want to help you. I don't say things I don't mean," he says.

I study his face a moment longer and know he's really not joking. My shoulders ease, and I smile softly. "Are you doing this because you'll get to nap with me?"

He chuckles. "It's a bonus."

"Don't you have work?" I eye his computer, attempting to keep my face neutral.

"I did what I needed to do until tonight. But if you want, you can help me film a video or two later."

I imagine filming Dane as DomInTheWoods, and I'm not going to lie, that sounds like fun. Especially since when I watch the videos he posts, I'll secretly know I was the one who filmed them, who he was looking at while doing them. It calms this weird jealousy I've been feeling over a man I'm not sure is completely mine.

"Okay. But you can't judge me for how messy my house is."

"I won't, I promise."

"Then turn around, Sir. I need to put my robe on."

Dane huffs a laugh, and I can tell he wants to challenge me over the not-watching bit, but he salutes me instead. "I'll see you in the bathroom." He points to it with the glasses in his hand.

When he's out of sight, I flop back onto the pillows, pulling the soft fabric to rub on my cheek. I have no idea what I'm doing or why I agreed to let Dane into my home to help me clean and do projects of all things, but I can't say I'm mad about it. I'm probably more excited than I should be.

36

Dane

"Welcome to my humble abode," Lindsey says as she lets me into her A-frame cabin. I step through the peeling wooden door behind her, my gaze taking in her space as I inhale what smells like her floral perfume mixed with cinnamon or something else just as sweet and spicy.

While I'm only seeing the living area and kitchen from this vantage point, it's a beautiful home with a cozy feel. It's the type of place I would have lived in had it not just been me. But as a single man, I didn't need much space, so this isn't a home I would have picked when I moved here.

"Sorry again about the mess," Lindsey says sheepishly, tucking a piece of hair behind her ear.

I look around and note that it isn't messy, at least not to the eye. It looks lived in, but with the way she's been warning me for the last couple of hours, I wondered if maybe she was a hoarder or something. The only "messes" I see are some dishes in the sink and stuff that could be straightened along with laundry that needs to be folded on the couch.

"Your home is beautiful," I say, my eyes meeting hers. She shifts on her feet, hiking her purse over her shoulder and holding it in front of her. She's in her dress from last night, which is wrinkled and dirty. I would have washed it if there had been time for it to air-dry overnight. I also offered her clean clothes of mine, but she refused, for whatever reason, and I didn't want to push her more than I already have in the last few days.

While I would have loved to see her in my clothes, I do like seeing her in the clothes I punished her in. There's also the fact that I didn't give her her underwear back. Those, I told her I was keeping, and to my surprise, she just flushed and didn't ask again.

"Um, thanks." She smiles shyly. "Why don't you make yourself at home on the couch, and I'll go change."

I almost order her to stay in her dirty dress so I can watch her clean and bend over in it, but I want her to be comfortable, especially since this is my first time in her home, and I essentially invited myself over. I nod, and she runs off, her cute ass jiggling with the fabric of her dress as she runs up the stairs. I wait until she disappears from my sight before I walk around her space.

The home is casual and cozy, as I observed initially. It's fairly simple, not a lot of decor, but it's definitely lived in. There are shoes and coats by the door as well as a couple of umbrellas. Above a fireplace that looks as if it's never been used is a large family photo that's professionally done.

I walk over to it so I can get a closer look. Lindsey and Kas are in the middle, while Nathan and a woman I'm going to assume is their mom stand on either side of them. They're all smiling, and the picture must've been snapped last year, since Kas looks a bit younger than she does now.

I focus my attention on the central mother/daughter pair. I'd be lying if I said I hadn't thought more about what my life would be like with the two of them in it in the last twenty-four hours. It would be different, and it would no longer be only me and the quiet of the woods.

I'd have a family to take care of, and that would mean things in my life would need to change—not just in my day-to-day but with my clients. I don't think Lindsey is the type of person to ask me to give up being a Pro Dom, but I would do it not just for her but for all of us. Especially if she truly wants to wear my training collar.

The idea of that alone gives me a greater peace than I've ever known. The concept strikes me deeply. I never thought I'd want to give someone any kind of collar, much less share my space with someone and their daughter. But the image of Lindsey wearing one I gave her hasn't left my mind since she told me the idea excited her.

We haven't spoken of it yet, but she said she's mine, and I believe her. Not only did our scene together last night prove it to me, but her complete and utter submission to me did as well, even more so during her aftercare.

I don't think she remembers much of what happened after I brought her to my room, but in her half-asleep state, she gave her full trust to me. I cleaned her up, made her drink water, and put soothing arnica cream on the places where I knew she'd be sore in the morning. Afterward, I pulled her into my arms, and she fell asleep easily, her soft body pressed to mine as I whispered praise in her ear.

I stayed up as long as I could force myself to. I watched her breathing, studied the blond highlights in her hair and the faint laugh lines around her mouth. In rest, Lindsey was completely at peace. There was no anxiety or stress on her features; she was simply herself. And if I hadn't known it before, I knew, at that moment, our night together wasn't our last. I knew I'd do anything for her, because even without completely realizing it, Lindsey is changing my life for the better.

I guess Levi was right all along. His words were different, and his idea of fun isn't exactly mine, but the more time I spend with Lindsey and Kas, the more I see I needed to get out from behind my computer, step out of the woods, and start building real connections. More specifically, a connection with a curvy, smart-mouthed, brown-eyed nurse. One I plan to collar soon—a training collar, sure, but in my mind, it's still a promise of commitment.

"Oh god." Lindsey's groan cuts through my thoughts.

I adjust so I can see her come down the last few steps until she's standing next to me. She's changed into a blue-and-white striped tank top and pair of jean shorts, her hair is up in a ponytail, and she's put a tiny bit of makeup on. She doesn't need it, but whatever she's done highlights her brown eyes, round cheeks, and plush lips.

My gaze travels to her bare neck, and I wonder if she'd be open to wearing a day collar, too, one that only she and I would know the significance of.

"My mom made us take that picture last year since we didn't have any without my ex. Then for Christmas, she gave me the big version, and I would've felt bad not hanging it."

"It's a nice picture," I say.

"I had to put so much makeup on. I'd just worked overtime, and I was exhausted. Then Kas was being a pill that day about something. I'm surprised we're all smiling."

I look at the picture again, and after hearing Lindsey's story, I can see she *is* wearing more makeup than she is now and that Kas's smile *does* look a little forced. "Does that happen a lot?"

"Taking family portraits?"

I turn to fully face her, and she flushes. I don't know if that's simply her natural reaction to me or if it's because I'm raising my brow at her.

She knows that's not what I meant. She's simply being cheeky.

"I know you've been exhausted, but has that been combined with Kas being a pill lately?" I ask.

I see her cheek indent as if she's biting the inside of her mouth, and her gaze drops to her hands, which she now has laced in front of her. I've seen her do that before, and I don't like it.

"Lindsey."

I say her name sternly, which has the effect I want. She stops biting on her inner cheek and looks at me sheepishly. I step closer to her and take her chin gently in my grasp, my pointer finger stroking her jaw before I tip her face up so our eyes are level.

"Don't chew on your cheek. I don't like when you hurt what's mine." I grip her chin a little harder. "And please don't look away from me when I ask you a question, understood?"

She swallows before answering. "Yes, Sir."

I loosen my grip but keep holding her face, leaning down to kiss her cheek before placing a soft kiss on her lips. I pull back before I give in to my desire to kiss her for longer but keep holding her gaze with mine.

"Now be a good girl, and answer my question."

"Yes, it happens a lot. More so in the last year with my mom moving away and me having to take extra shifts and do overtime to pay bills. Because of that, I'm home much less and even more exhausted. That leads to me being less of a mom to Kas, which I think is why she's become so much of a pill. I let her do what she wants, and I know I've mentioned that she plays video games too much."

The guilt in Lindsey's eyes is evident along with pain and tiredness. I take her hand and rub my thumb over her knuckle. "Do you truly believe that?"

"Which part?"

"That you're less of a mom to Kas because you're doing your best to take care of her."

"Yes, I—" Lindsey stops when my words register in her brain. She exhales a loud breath. "I'd argue that I'm not doing my best. That this is less than my best. Which is why I'm a bad mom."

She parrots the words like they don't hurt when she says them, but I know Lindsey well enough now to know that by saying she's a bad mom, she's trying to hide how much that thought not only hurts her but also how much she believes it to be true.

"Do you have proof that you're a bad mom?" I ask.

Lindsey pulls her hand from mine and chuffs. "Do you see this house?"

I don't look around like she wants me to. Instead, I stay focused on her. "What about it?"

"It's a mess!" She throws up her hands.

"Are you not allowed to have a messy house sometimes?"

She blinks at me as if I've just said something in an alien language. "Says the man whose cabin is perfectly neat and tidy."

"I don't have a child, and I live alone."

"You could still be messy," she counters.

"I could, but I have many years of practice keeping my home the way I want it, maintaining my routines, and practicing discipline. But I'm not perfect, Lindsey. Nobody is. And to expect yourself to be is out of reality."

"How are you not perfect?"

My lips twitch in a near smile. "You think I'm perfect?"

She puts her arms over her chest and looks me up and down. "Perfect hair, perfect nose, perfect body, perfect dick, perfect Dom! I could go on."

I hold back a laugh, stepping closer to her so

she's overtaken by my presence. Lindsey doesn't shrink back, but her skin does pink up at my nearness.

"That's a lot of perfection to live up to."

"You don't need to live up to it; you just are," she responds, her voice a bit quieter now.

I brush a few baby hairs off her forehead tenderly. "I love that you think I'm perfect. As your Dom, it pleases me greatly. But..." I soothe my finger down her cheek, and she shivers. "I'm not perfect. Far from it. I've made mistakes with you; I've not been the best Dom I could be. Lately, I've been failing a lot, actually."

"How so?"

"Did I not cross lines for you, baby?"

She blinks. "I'm sorry—"

"No." I stop her. "I'm glad to have crossed them. But I'm seeing more and more that we've skipped a lot of important things, and in doing so, I've failed you."

"You haven't," she insists.

I trace her lips with my thumb. "Why did you email me?"

"So you could be my Dom," she answers.

"Yes, but what did you want from our time together?"

"You know what," she says.

"I want to hear you say it."

"I wanted to get my life together."

"Which meant what to you?"

"More discipline, setting up routines, getting my schedule and bills organized. And to be a better mom to Kas because of it."

"Do you feel like any of that has improved?"

"I do feel more confident in some things. I like my morning and night routines—now that I've been doing them," she mutters with a cringe. "I also have put my foot down with Kas a couple of times, like when she wanted to eat chicken nuggets instead of the lunch I packed her."

"That's good," I say. "But I'm not happy with how you feel otherwise or that you've not been consistent. I think it's time we change that, don't you?"

"Does that mean we're not going to be intimate anymore?"

I shake my head. "Far from it. We made an agreement, unless you'd like to change it again?"

"No, Sir. I don't want that."

A spike of anxiety I hadn't realized had flared calms at her words. "I don't, either," I assure her. "In fact, we made claims on each other last night and today. Do you remember what they were?"

She smiles softly. "You said I'm yours, Sir."

"You are." I reach out and touch her throat where her necklace was earlier. "And what else?"

"I said I'd accept a training collar."

"Hmm, you did. Now that you've had some distance from last night, is that still what you want?"

"Yes, Sir."

I nod. "Good to know." I brush her chin again. "And you understand what that means to me?"

"It will show my commitment to you: that I want to learn and grow with you."

"And I you." She smiles, and I softly smile back. "Before we take that next step, I'd like to focus harder on your goals with you, dig into ones we haven't touched yet. It will help build our trust and deepen our connection further, but it will also help you gain confidence within yourself and with parenting Kas."

Her face falls a little, and I can understand why. There's a huge part of me that wants to skip straight to collaring her, too. But she's showing me how much she needs to build on the things she's learned so far, to slow things down a bit.

"This isn't a step back, baby. It's a step forward. Do you trust me?"

"You know I do."

"Good. Now, fair warning. With our growing dynamic, you're going to rethink how perfect I am."

She smiles and laughs softly. "I doubt it."

"Famous last words. Now, kneel."

"What?"

"Don't make me repeat myself. I know you heard me."

Lindsey stares at me for another moment before she sees I'm serious. A second later, she's dropping to her knees and into the submissive pose I taught her last night. My chest rumbles in satisfaction, and I touch her head, brushing my fingers over her hair.

"Inhale for me, and relax." When she's completed her breaths, I tip her chin up. "That's my good girl. I want you to repeat after me, understand?"

"Yes, Sir."

Already, her eyes are softer and her shoulders are relaxed, showing me yet again that Lindsey was born for submission, and that she's meant to be mine.

"I may not be perfect, but I'm doing the best I can," I say.

She swallows then repeats, "'I may not be perfect, but I'm doing the best I can.'"

"I'm a good mom, and I'm loved."

Lindsey pauses, and I notice her eyes have gone glassy, but she repeats, "'I'm a good mom, and I'm loved.'"

"It's okay to feel overwhelmed, but when I do, I will lean on my Dom, my Sir."

"'It's okay to feel overwhelmed, but when I do, I will lean on my Dom, my Sir.'"

"I don't have to do everything alone. It's safe for me to surrender control."

Lindsey inhales a shaky breath and repeats, "'I don't have to do everything alone. It's safe for me to surrender control.'"

"My Sir will guide me when I feel lost."

"'My Sir will guide me when I feel lost.'"

"I am strong in my submission."

"'I am strong in my submission.'"

"I am loved, I am beautiful, I am enough."

"'I am loved, I am beautiful, I am enough,'" she echoes.

I stroke her hair and let her words sink in before I ask, "Now tell me, Lindsey: Who do you submit to?"

"You, Sir."

"And whose collar will you wear when the time is right?"

"Yours, Sir."

I pet her hair again before cupping her cheek. Lindsey savors the touch, resting her head against my hand in submission. Her eyes remain on mine, and we stay like that for a few minutes before I have her stand.

When we're face-to-face, I lean down and kiss her. "How do you feel?"

"Calm." She hums. "Centered."

"Good. I'm going to write those down for you, and you're going to add them to your daily routine. When you're feeling unsure, you're going to repeat those to yourself, and you're going to lean on me when you need me. Do you understand?"

"Yes, I understand."

"Good girl. Now, what do you want my help with first?"

She smiles. "I could use your help picking up Kas's room."

"No," I tell her easily.

"What?" she asks, confused.

"I think Kas can pick up her own room when she gets home, don't you?"

"But I told her—"

"She'll survive. If there's something you need to do that she can't do, that's one thing. But just like her mom, I think Kas needs to understand that there are some things she is responsible for, and cleaning up her own mess is one of them."

"Burn." She chuckles.

I gently tug on Lindsey's ponytail in warning. "That wasn't meant to be mean, and if I remember correctly, I've told you that you're not always going to like me or what I have to say. I'm here to push you and take care of you. Let me."

Lindsey blows out a breath and nods. "You're right."

"I always am."

She rolls her eyes, and my grip on her ponytail tightens until her head is pulled back, her neck straining slightly.

"Does my bratty slut need a lesson before we get her house in order?" I threaten, though my tone has a slight tease to it.

"I think I do," she answers, her tone near breathless and pupils now blown.

My dick jumps to life, and I pull her head to me so our lips are close. "Lesson number one: Brats don't get what they want." I pull my lips a touch away, stepping back from her.

Lindsey blinks, her body and mind taking a second to realize I'm no longer in her space and I'm not going to tell her to bend over and present her naked ass to me, something I know she wants. That "funishment" can come later after we've addressed the things making her life harder. The things she's been avoiding.

"Now, I think we should start with your finances."

Lindsey groans, and I know I've hit the jackpot.

"Okay, fine," she mutters. "But do I get something if I'm a good girl?"

"I guess you'll find out," I tease back.

37
Lindsey

I DIDN'T THINK I'D ever want someone to meddle in my personal affairs after Jeremy, but here I am, having Dane not only help me clean my house and with my bills and finances but now fold my underwear as well.

"You really don't have to—"

"I know that"—Dane grins as he pulls out a lacy bralette from my laundry basket—"but I want to."

"Well, thanks. You've helped so much already today. I owe you for folding laundry with me."

"You don't owe me anything. I told you, I'm happy to help."

His words turn my insides to goo. Accepting help isn't something that's been easy for me, but Dane, he's different. It's probably because of our dynamic, but at the same time, I believe him when he says he wants to help. He doesn't make me feel like a burden, and in the hours that we've been together, nothing has felt forced or weird. It's just been . . . good. Easy. Easier than any relationship has been in my life.

I pick up the pants from a pair of scrubs to fold them, a reminder that I have work tonight. I usually don't mind going—I like what I do—but I'd rather stay here all night with Dane.

"You know . . ." I point at the now-folded bralette he put on a pile of other underthings. "I was wearing that the day I ran into you at the games."

He looks down at it, then, before I can comprehend what he's doing, he snatches it and shoves the thin material in his pocket with a sly smile.

"What are you doing?" I laugh.

"Keeping it."

"Starting a collection?"

"You could say that," he says as he picks up the last item to fold.

When I asked him for my underwear earlier at his place, he told me no, that he was keeping them. I blushed, but secretly, I loved it. I love that he wanted to keep a piece of me, a souvenir of our first night together.

I don't know what he plans on doing with them, but it isn't my job to know. Dane is my Dom, and if he wants something, I'm learning that I give it to him without question as long as I'm comfortable with it.

Our session by the fireplace earlier only showed me even more how much he cares. Especially with the promise of building toward a training collar. It proved to me that he's not just committed to the dynamic we're building but to my life and mental health, too. He's choosing to move slowly instead of rushing the commitment like I thought I wanted.

No one's ever cared about me like that before, at least not to this extent. I still wonder what it will all mean—if the collar will come with promises like monogamy and everything that could follow—but right now, I'm too happy and content to overthink it. One thing at a time.

I place my pants in a pile before Dane starts to put everything we folded back in the basket. When he's done, he asks, "Would you like help putting them away?"

"It's fine; I can do it later."

He nods. "Alright, what next?"

"You don't have to do anything else. You've

already helped me cancel a dozen subscriptions I didn't even know I was paying for, dusted, done the dishes, and organized my fridge." I almost flush at the last one. I think he threw out something from the back that was at least two months old. It was embarrassing. "Were you a housekeeper in another life?"

He chuckles. "No, but my dad was very strict, and I did a lot of chores."

"I can relate to that. Having a strict dad, I mean. Ours was very rule oriented, the opposite of how I am with Kas. Which, now that I think about it, is probably why I'm the way I am with her."

Dane nods and leans back on the couch. "Makes sense." He studies me as if he's figured something else out about me before he continues. "I was my parents' only child. My mother didn't like to do housework, nor did she like to parent me, as I mentioned. She took on the friend role.

"My father was the opposite. He always treated me like I was an adult, so as soon as I was old enough to work, I was just an extra set of hands, a little soldier. I had lists each day he'd make me get done, even when I was in school or working long hours with him in the summers after I started learning the logging trade."

I scrunch up my nose, feeling sad for the young Dane I never knew. That's no way to grow up, but in many ways, it explains why he is the way he is. He's regimented and likes routines, which probably make him feel safe. Just as I'm learning that having boundaries and rules makes me feel safe. Given this, it's interesting that I've slipped up so much with Kas.

"Did you ever get to play and be a kid?" I ask.

Dane pauses, his hands resting on his knees, gripping the fabric. "Not often, just at school during recess. Eventually, my old man did teach me how to speed climb the poles, and I liked that. He liked it, too, because I could compete and earn extra money when I won. He loved when he'd win in the adult competition and I'd win in the kids'."

"I'm surprised you still enjoy it."

"Did you watch me compete at the games that day?" he asks.

I shake my head. "I was planning on it, but when I ran into you, I was rushing out to come home and take advantage of the empty house."

Dane nods, and I like that he doesn't question the decision I made. He knows me well enough now to understand why I chose to do that over watching the competition. Though now I wish I had seen him compete. Hopefully next year.

"What do you like about speed climbing?" I ask.

Dane's hands relax against his legs. "It challenges me, and it's something I'm naturally good at. I also like the adrenaline—all the reasons I enjoy working out and running."

I make an *ew* face. "I hate running. So does Kas."

He chuckles. "I know, she looked like I asked her to go to hell and back when we ran a bit at the course yesterday."

I smile. "Sounds like her."

"She did it, though. I was proud of her. She's also good at axe throwing." He says it with a small smile, like he's remembering an inside joke. My interest piques, not only because of the smile, but also because it made my stomach flip when he said he's proud of her. I don't know if that's a good thing, but it makes me scoot closer to him.

"Really?"

He nods. "It's with rubber axes. But when she's older, I bet she could easily take part in the games with a real axe if she wanted."

"Did you tell her that?"

He shakes his head. "She was hanging with her friends, but I will if you think she'd like hearing it."

"I do. Kas is like me; she needs reassurance about things." I pick at invisible dust on my shorts. "I don't think her dad gives her enough of it, since she only sees him once a month. I try to stay up-to-date on her life and do so where I can, but she mostly plays her games. The first thing she's shown interest in outside of them is the obstacle course, but I think that's because of a boy there. So if she's good at axe throwing, definitely encourage her."

Without thinking about it, I place my hand over the one Dane has on his knee. His fingers lace with mine, and a second later, I'm being tugged into his side.

I let out a small yelp at the sudden movement. His chest shakes with laughter, and I smile up at him before settling into his side. His body is warm and strong, and sitting here with him on my couch is something I could get used to. I should take the moment to ask him if he thinks our relationship will go beyond our D/s dynamic, if he sees more days like this together, but I keep it in.

"I'll tell her then," his deep voice rumbles. A

second later, his lips ghost against the crown of my head. I lean into the kiss and enjoy the silence and embrace of the man I'm quickly becoming more and more at ease with.

I don't know how much time passes, but before my eyes can become heavy, Dane shifts, and I look up at him.

"Can I ask you something?" he asks.

"Anything."

His arm is now around my shoulder, and his hand trails down my bare arm. "What happened between you and your ex-husband?"

"He's a cheating bastard, that's what." I blow a breath through my lips. "Among other things."

Dane stops stroking my arm and grips it. "I'm sorry, I shouldn't have asked."

"No, it's okay. Honesty, right?"

His arm resumes stroking as he nods. "Whatever you're comfortable with."

I snuggle into Dane's chest further, not caring if this is or isn't a thing I should be doing as his submissive. He doesn't seem to mind. In fact, his body relaxes when I put my head over his chest, his steady heartbeat pounding in my ear as his other hand comes to rest on the knee I've folded under me that is now on top of his thigh.

"We met in our twenties in school," I start off. "I was smitten with him. He said he loved my curves and my brain, loved that I wanted to help people and be a nurse. Eventually, we got married, then I got pregnant with Kas shortly after I started working at a local ER. Jeremy was interning at his father's agency, training to be a sports agent himself."

"Don't tell me he slept with another intern," Dane snarls.

The anger in his tone only makes me like him more. "He could've, and maybe he did, but I bring it up because that's really when our relationship started to change. He wasn't into my pregnancy and didn't show up for a lot of the doctors' appointments. Nathan or my mom came more often than he did."

Dane squeezes my arm he'd been stroking, and it gives me the strength to continue. It's been a long time since I've told my story, but it feels good to tell him.

"Jeremy didn't want to touch me, and every time I tried to initiate intimacy, he'd make up some excuse and spout asshole comments about my changing body. It only got worse after I had Kas. He started constantly asking when I was going to lose the baby weight or get a consult about my C-section scar." I pause to wet my lips. "Then he started acting like a jerk about how much I was working. He wanted me to stay home and raise Kas but also wanted me to pick up extra shifts. Looking back on it, I think it was so he could have his affairs without the risk of me finding out. Eventually, I did, though.

"I came home from a shift early. Kas was at my mom's for the night, and I walked into a candlelit dinner. I thought it was for me, maybe his way of trying to reconnect with me, until I heard the moaning."

"Jesus Christ," Dane mutters under his breath.

"Pretty sure I said something similar when I walked in on them going to town." I groan, wishing I could burn that image from my retinas forever. "Eventually, I found out her name is Ava. She's the exact opposite of me: short, thin, and blond. She's also only twenty-four. She was younger then, but they're still together."

"I know he's Kas's dad, but if you want me to put a hit out on him, I'd be happy to do it."

I snort. "Do you know a lumberjack hit man?"

"It's logger," Dane playfully corrects like Kas would. "And no, I don't know any logger hit men, but I bet I could find one on the dark web."

I smile against his chest. "I appreciate the offer, but despite him not being there during my pregnancy, he does love Kas, and she likes seeing her dad. I think she'd be upset if I had him killed."

Dane's gaze is cool, but I catch the anger in his eyes. "I'm sorry you had to go through that. You deserved better."

I don't look away even though in the past, I might've. I also would have disagreed with him, thinking that I did deserve what happened to me. But Dane…he makes me want to believe that I deserve better, that I deserve someone like him. Someone who is patient, who listens, who knows what I need to feel comfortable. Like last night, when he took care of me, when he worshiped my body and even my scar. He never pushed too much, only the right amount.

"Thank you," I whisper, "that means a lot to me."

He takes my hand on his chest and brings it to his lips, kissing my knuckles. "Can I ask you about one more thing?"

"I'm in a sharing mood, so ask away."

He plays with my fingers before speaking. "In your finances, you have a lot of legal fees. You're already divorced, but the majority of your income goes to your lawyer, and you didn't mention any child support. Why is that?"

I sigh. "That's because the asswipe isn't paying it. He's fighting the amount the courts settled on."

"Prick," Dane mutters.

I smirk into his chest. "Small prick."

Dane's chest shakes. "Noted."

I'm silent for another moment before I ask, "Any cheating exes in your past?"

"No," he answers. "No exes, period."

I sit up so quickly, I almost bonk my head on his chin. "What?"

"You thought I had a lot?"

I chew the inside of my cheek, and Dane is quick to tap the indentation I'm making, so I stop.

"Good girl," he praises. "You were saying?"

Heat creeps up my face as I go on. "I didn't know how many, but I thought you'd have at least a few."

"I had two different girlfriends in high school, but I don't count them. Young kids doing what they do. But in my adult years, there's no one I would consider an ex."

I blink at him, and I can tell he's attempting not to smile. "Not even before you moved to Starlight Haven?"

He shakes his head. "Nothing serious or long term. Like I mentioned last night, I traveled a lot when I was younger, then I moved here and have kept mostly to myself. As you know, my submissives are not intimate with me. We have our platonic online dynamics, and that's that."

"Except for me," I say.

"Except for you," he reiterates.

I'm about to ask him about the painting of the woman above the fireplace and what she is to him if not an ex, but my question is cut short by my phone going off. It's sitting on the cushion next to me, so I reach for it, checking the caller ID.

"It's Jeremy." At Dane's grumpy frown, I almost laugh. "That means it's Kas. She doesn't have a phone of her own."

His features ease slightly, and he nods. "I need to use the restroom. I'll give you some privacy."

I nod and pick up the phone, watching him walk off as I say hi to Kas. I smile when I hear her voice, and Dane looks back over his shoulder with a small grin of his own. Rightness settles in my bones, not only at the sound of my daughter's voice but also because a man I think I'm falling for is moving so easily through my home as if he belongs in it.

I don't know what the future between us holds beyond what we've discussed, but I do know one thing: I'm happy. For the first time in a long time, I can honestly say I'm happy.

Daily Check-Ins

Sunday, 12:00pm PT

Me

Sir, I finished filling out the spending tracker you gave me.

Sir

How did it feel?

Me

Scary but good. Like I have a plan to move forward.

Sir

That's what we want.

Wednesday, 10:01pm PT

Me

Can't sleep, Sir.

Sir

Why, baby? You need your rest.

Me

I'm thinking about you . . .

Sir

Anything specific?

Me

What it would feel like if you were here next to me.

Sir

Soon. Would you like me to call you and talk to you while you fall asleep?

Me

Yes, Sir. I would like that.

Friday, 8:01am

Me

Scheduled a meeting with Jeremy and his lawyer.

Sir

Yours will be there as well?

Me

Yes, Sir.

Sir

Good girl. How do you feel?

Me

Like I want to cancel.

Sir

Journal on why that is, and we'll talk about it tonight on our call.

Me

Can I skip that part, Sir?

Sir

Only if you're looking for correction instead of comfort. Decide which one you want. But I don't think you'll like the punishment.

Monday, 10:30am PT

New voice note from Lindsey:

"I promise I'll be good, Sir. Please, please, may I come?"

New voice note from Sir:

"Absolutely not. When you don't follow through on what you say you're going to do and sass back, you don't get what you want. Now be a good girl, and drink your water before you have to go back to work."

Tuesday, 4:00pm PT

Me

I packed my lunch for tomorrow.

Sir

Good girl. Did you remember extra protein? You have a twelve-hour shift tonight.

Me

I did, though I could think of a different kind of protein that I want more...

Sir

Such a cock-hungry little slut.

Me

Only for you, Sir. I hope I can show you again soon.

Sir

Keep being a good girl, and you will.

Friday, 8:00am PT

Me

Good morning, Sir. Kas is sad that today is the last obstacle course session.

Sir

Good morning, baby. I've been thinking about continuing it during the school year. I have to talk to the city about it.

Me

Really?

Sir

You know I don't say things I don't mean.

Me

I know, Sir. She would like that. I would, too.

Sir

When you drop Kas off, meet me by the bathrooms. I need to kiss you.

Me

Just a kiss?

Sir

Greedy girl. You'll take what I give you. Now tell me, did you get your full eight hours of sleep last night?

[IMAGE ALT TEXT]: Dom is standing close to the camera. Only his jaw, covered in well-trimmed salt-and-pepper facial hair, and his lips are visible.

Auto Captions:
Did you get in your full eight hours of sleep, baby?
Hmm, I'm so happy to hear that. You know I love when you take care of yourself for me.
Why? Because then I get to play with you.
What kind of play?
I guess you'll have to continue to be a good girl so you can find out.
When?
Such an eager and impatient girl. But if you stay good, I want to see you tonight.

150,151 Views
Username @DomInTheWoods
view all 151 comments
1 HOUR AGO

38
Lindsey

THE AFTERNOON SUN BEATS down on me as I sit and enjoy the warm August day. Fox, Morgan, and Nathan are playing cornhole with Kas, and I'm sitting on a folding chair drinking a can of seltzer while I smile down at my phone, replaying the new video DomInTheWoods posted earlier, reading the captions again and again.

My smile grows wider as what he said truly sinks in. When Dane posted videos similar to this one starting about two weeks ago, after our in-person scene together, I thought I was imagining it, making up something that wasn't there. But now...Now I'm sure I'm not making it up, because his recent Loopr videos have all been inspired by our interactions.

I open the messaging app we use and type out a text to him.

Me

I like your newest video.

Like it's been for a while now, his response comes through quickly.

Sir

What did you like about it?

I consider what to say. I haven't asked him point-blank if his recent videos are directed to me, because like I said, I thought maybe I was imagining it at first. But with this last one, I'm positive they are.

We just had a conversation this morning about how my sleep schedule was improving, especially since I've stopped covering my coworkers' shifts on a whim. Dane helped me see that with budgeting and enforcing a spending tracker, I could stop trying to kill myself to make ends meet and only take the occasional extra shift.

Along with that, I've been pushing Jeremy on a resolution with child support, and I think the end is in sight. Dane's been there every step of the way, not doing the work for me but checking in to make sure I follow through and don't back down on my demands for what Kas and I deserve. It was hard at first, but I forgot how nice it is to have someone constantly in your corner, cheering you on.

And Dane... he's been that for me.

Me

I liked that I knew you were talking to me, but everyone in the comments felt like you were talking to them.

Sir

What's your answer, then?

Butterflies fill my stomach at his reply, because it confirms I was right.

Me

I want to see you tonight, too.

Sir

I can't wait, baby. You've been so good; I think you deserve a reward.

The butterflies in my stomach multiply. True to Dane's insistence on slowing things down and working toward my training collar, we haven't been physically intimate in person beyond a stolen kiss at yesterday's obstacle course session. We have, however, continued to flirt and be playful in our messages and when we speak on the phone and over video.

On Monday, he had me wear the remote-controlled toy to work again after he told me to make a list of things I love about my body and I sassed back at him. He never turned it on when I was on the floor, but he edged me on my breaks until I finally gave in at lunch and texted the things I love about myself, and he let me come.

My body buzzes when I think of that moment. Not only because the orgasm was intense, but also because I nearly gave myself away when Billie showed up and sat across from me right after I came. Dane loved it when I told him what had happened, and while it was embarrassing, and Billie asked if I was sick, I loved it, too.

The more I hand over control to Dane, the freer I am. It's interesting, because had you asked me if that would be the case before I started working with him, I would have thought it a ridiculous notion.

After everything with Jeremy and the way he tried to dictate my work schedule and how I parented Kas, I thought giving up control would make me feel small or trapped. But it hasn't. I've leaned in and embraced my submissive side, the one that's been there all along. Everything is different with Dane.

Looking back on my time with Jeremy, I think I stayed with him and let him say the things he did to me because I didn't want to be alone. I liked the idea of having someone, even if being with him meant constantly shrinking to fit into the version of me he was comfortable with. His control wasn't rooted in care; it was about power, about keeping me dependent.

Dane's control doesn't strip me down; it builds me up. It doesn't silence me; it grounds me. What we're doing isn't just exciting or fun; it's changing me. I feel more confident every day, more capable. And because of that, my relationship with Kas is improving, too. I'm showing up differently in my life—for her and for myself.

She's pushed back like any kid would when given more boundaries and rules, but it turns out, it's true that kids need structure and discipline just like adults do. I'm also starting to like playing Critter Cove with her more, something Kas thinks is hilarious but that I can tell she loves by how she smiles each time I suggest we play.

I give my attention back to my phone, wondering if the reward and finally being alone together again means what I think it means. Maybe tonight he'll give me my training collar. I do think I've earned it with all the work I've put in to show my commitment to myself and to working with him, not to mention the trust we've been building together.

I type out a response to him with a small smile on my face.

Me

Thank you, Sir. I'm happy I've pleased you.

"It makes me happy, too," a low voice says from behind me.

If I wasn't sitting, I would have jumped ten feet in the air. "Jesus!" I say loud enough that the others look in my direction. I turn in my chair to find Dane grinning down at me as he slips his phone in his pocket.

He looks handsome, his hair styled perfectly

like it always is and his beard neatly trimmed. He's got on a short-sleeved red plaid shirt that reminds me of the Brawny paper towel man.

Before I can say anything, I hear Kas yell, "Logger Dane!"

My gaze shifts to follow her as she runs—actually runs—over to Dane's side and surprises me even further by hugging him around the waist. I watch the interaction in strange awe because Kas doesn't hug anyone except her family. She's more of a high five kind of kid. Maybe she was sad about the obstacle course ending not only because she was losing the free time with her friends thanks to school starting but because of Dane, too.

The idea makes my heart pound in my chest, and a question that's been itching in the back of my brain pushes to the forefront. Is what I'm building with Sir more than just a very intimate D/s dynamic? Does he want more with me like I've started to want more with him? I'm talking beyond morning check-ins and meeting up at his cabin for in-person scenes.

"Hey, Captain Kas," he greets.

Kas makes a playful gagging noise as she pulls away to look up at him. "That's another bad one, Logger Dane."

He chuckles and pats her shoulder. “I’ll keep trying.”

“You do that,” she sasses back.

I stand from my chair as Fox walks over, Nathan and Morgan behind him. I make eye contact with my brother, who’s confused, then with Morgan, who has the gleam of someone who won the lottery. Her features are lit up, and I know by the cock of her brow that she wants to pull me to the side and ask why Dane is here.

But I don’t actually know why he’s here, and I never told Morgan I contacted her friend that night nor that I’m his submissive. I know Dane wouldn’t have told her, so there’s no way she could know, anyway.

“Dane,” Fox’s deep voice resonates.

“Fox,” Dane greets back.

“This is a surprise,” Morgan adds as she hugs him.

“I didn’t mean to intrude,” he says as he pulls back, nodding at my brother.

“Did you need something?” Fox asks.

The two burly, tattooed men share a look, one that says a whole lot of nothing but also tells me they must talk more than I thought. Not that I would or could know that information. It’s not as if I've asked Dane who he talks to in his free time or if he has beers with Fox. We have plenty of other things we talk about. Like my routines and emotions, and how we're both feeling in our growing dynamic. We've even talked more about our own personal likes and dislikes. I found out the other day that Dane enjoys cognac, especially now, since my eyes remind him of the rich brown color.

"No," Dane says. "I was walking and ended up here. Sorry to intrude."

My stomach flips as my gaze connects with Dane's. There's a mischievous sparkle in them because he knew I was coming here today with Kas, which means he isn't sorry he intruded. One thing I've learned about him is there are no accidents; everything he does is intentional. That means he came here on purpose to see us. The butterflies I felt earlier come back with more force, so much so that my throat starts to tickle.

"You're not intruding," Morgan chirps. "The more the merrier. You know, I've been trying to get you to hang out with us forever."

Dane nods, his hands now in his pockets. "Still, I should've called. This is family time." His hazel eyes drift back to mine as if he's saying that last part to me.

Before anyone can respond, Kas interjects, "You can stay, Logger Dane."

"Yeah, Logger Dane," Morgan parrots.

Kas giggles at her aunt calling him by the nickname she gave him. "We're playing cornhole! You have to come see me toss!" she says as she jumps up and down. "I'm good at it like I am with throwing the rubber axes."

"I have no doubt about that; you're a natural at games," Dane praises.

Kas blushes from the compliment but pops her shoulders back with confidence. The action warms my heart because ever since I told Dane to encourage Kas, he's been doing just that. She's completely forgotten about her crush on Tyler and didn't even mention him or look at him when I dropped her off at the course.

In the last two weeks, all she talks about is Dane, how she wants to learn how to throw a real axe as soon as she can, and of course, her video games. She's spoken so much about "Logger Dane" in the past weeks that Jeremy asked me about him. It was a question I ignored because my ex doesn't need to know anything more than that he's her teacher.

I feel someone staring at the side of my head

and turn my attention from Kas, who's still smiling broadly at a man nobody knows I have a unique relationship with, to the person staring at me. Or should I say people.

Nathan is grinning like he's caught me with my hand in a cookie jar, and Morgan is still glowing. Nathan asked me a few times since he dropped off Kas from her dad's if I was seeing someone, but I denied it, because it was technically true. I'm not really "seeing" someone. I thought he believed me, but whatever I'm doing now must have given me away, because the twinkle in his eyes tells me my jig is up. The problem is: How do I explain that Dane is my Dom, not my boyfriend?

I could tell Morgan, but the way she's smiling says she already knows. It makes me think Fox knows, too, which means that maybe Nathan knows as well, and that's why he's been asking me if I'm seeing someone. The idea of them knowing feels invasive and weird, and now I have the desire to run inside and bury myself under blankets even though my skin is hot and itchy.

The excited tickle in my throat turns to a cough, and I pick up my seltzer, but it's empty. "I'm going to get another drink; does anyone need something?"

"I'll take a beer," Nathan says. "Do you want anything, Logger Dane?"

Kas giggles louder when her uncle calls him Logger Dane, but I can tell by the questioning yet playful tone of his voice that Nathan does know something is up. *What* he knows is the million-dollar question.

"Sure," Dane says.

"I'll take another beer, too," Fox says.

"Can I have one of those flavored waters, Mom?" Kas asks.

"Yeah, honey."

She cheers, and it makes everyone smile, even Fox.

"Anything for you, Morgan?"

"I'm good, thanks."

"I'll come help you," Dane adds before I can turn to leave.

I open my mouth to argue that I can do it alone, but the gaze he's leveling at me is one that I know not to argue with. If I do, I may get edged or something of that nature later instead of receiving the reward I was hoping for.

"Thanks," I say.

I head toward the cabin, catching Nathan's and Morgan's eyes as I do. They're still smirking, and Morgan even winks at me. I start to wonder how I'm going to explain my relationship with Dane if they don't already know what's going on. If they don't, would Dane even want them to know?

My early thoughts come back. Does Dane want more with me like I've started to want more with him? The training collar is one thing, and we've talked more about what that will mean for us. In my understanding, it's a commitment to structure and growth but not necessarily permanence. It could be considered a stepping stone to more, but is there more for us? Because the next step does not only include me, it includes Kas, too—and all my baggage.

I'm so lost in my thoughts that I forget Dane is next to me until we're walking up the cabin steps and he's opening the door for me. I step inside and go to the kitchen, my awareness now zeroed in on his presence behind me. The back of my neck prickles, and before I can reach for the fridge door, he's spinning me around and pressing my ass into the counter.

"Dane," I gasp.

His body molds to mine, and as if my hips have a mind of their own, I lift them so there's no space between us. The heat of his groin presses against me.

"Hey, baby," he says, the timbre of his voice lighting sparks of electricity across my skin.

My attention leaves his eyes and focuses on his lips. Lips I've missed kissing. Lips I've imagined doing so many wicked things to me since our night at his cabin. Every thought I was having before leaves my brain with him so close, his warm, sculpted body touching mine.

"What are you doing here?" My question is near breathless, and he wets his lips with his tongue.

"I needed to see you."

Not wanted. *Needed.* Like he needed a kiss from me yesterday, even though it was quick and chaste. His admission makes my pulse pound in my throat.

"Couldn't wait until tonight?" I ask.

Dane's lips get closer to mine. "I was already on my way here when I texted that, so no. I couldn't wait."

His hands move to my hips, fingers sliding into the loops of my jean shorts. He pulls me closer so I can feel his growing erection, and I almost groan embarrassingly loudly at the feel of it.

Dane tucks a strand of hair behind my ear and cups my jaw. I rest my cheek in his hand, absorbing his strength and grounding myself in him. His hips shift against mine, the heat of him reminding me that now is not the time or place to kiss him or even be in this position with him. But apparently, I have no self-restraint when he's this close to me.

I close the distance between us, bringing my hands up to his shoulders and tugging him down so that we're evenly matched. He backs me further into the counter, bringing our bodies impossibly closer. A sound akin to a whimper escapes his lips, and arousal floods my core. I never thought a man making that noise would turn me on, but he's making it because of me.

My mouth parts, and our tongues tangle together. I groan and lift my hips higher, seeking friction. He tastes so good, and his touch on my body is addictive. I lose myself in him, in the way he smells so masculine and woodsy, a smell that reminds me of home and everything that makes Dane, Dane. My hands trail down his back, and when they reach the top of his leather belt, a throat clearing stops me.

I push him away in my shock. My eyes meet a smiling Morgan's, and heat blooms in my cheeks.

"Don't stop on my account; just wanted to see if you needed help. Been in here awhile, and Kas was getting worried."

I don't know if Morgan is telling the truth because I don't think we've been in here that long, but either way, Dane and I have been had. If she didn't know anything about us before, she does now. And unless I beg, Morgan won't keep this from Fox and Nathan. They tell each other everything.

Dane's fingers brush mine, and I look up at him. I don't know what I expect to see, but an adoring smile isn't it.

The next thing he does shocks me to my core. He leans down, pressing a kiss to the crown of my head before addressing Morgan. "I'll let you two talk."

He squeezes my hand and looks in my eyes as if to say *share what you want* before he steps to the fridge and takes out the drinks we were supposed to get for everyone. With a final glance in my direction, Dane leaves me with a grinning Morgan.

When we hear the cabin door shut, she walks to the dining table, sitting in the chair facing me before gesturing to the chair across from her.

"Tell me everything."

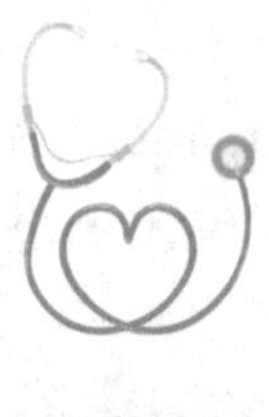

39
Lindsey

By the time I've finished giving Morgan all the juicy details, we've both finished half of our spiked lime seltzers.

Morgan's cheeks are pink as she says, "I'll admit, when I asked you to tell me everything, I didn't think you would."

I press my lips together, looking down at the table. Morgan reaches across the table and places her hand on mine.

"No, please. Don't be embarrassed. I'm glad you did. You just keep so much to yourself, I didn't think you would."

She's right. While I consider Morgan one of my closest friends—if not my only real friend in Starlight Haven—I normally don't share like this. But I guess that's something else that's changed in me since I've been with Dane. He's showing me how much I've been missing by not being honest, by keeping my life locked up and not asking for help.

Things are much easier when I don't act like everything is fine.

"I'll admit, it's nice to have someone who knows."

Morgan smiles and squeezes my hand again. "Feels good to get things off your chest sometimes."

"It does," I say honestly.

"I'll admit, when I emailed Dane to let him know you may contact him, I was ninety-nine percent sure you would, but there was the one percent that thought you wouldn't."

My eyes go wide. "You emailed him?"

She nods. "Drunk emailed. I'm lucky Dane likes me, because it was super obnoxious."

"What did you say?"

"Just that a friend of mine might be emailing for his services. I didn't give him any information or say you lived in Starlight Haven." She winces. "I hope you're not mad."

Dane offering a month of his services for free makes more sense now. I bet he and Morgan worked it out in that email chain.

I shake my head. “No, I’m not mad. Thanks for letting me use up the favor he owed you so I could work with him.”

She smiles and waves me off. “Don’t mention it.”

I smile back, flushing a little.

“What is it?”

“Honestly, I’m a little embarrassed that you saw this part of me before I did, that you knew someone like Dane was exactly what I needed. I wouldn’t have even known to look for it if you hadn’t shown me his videos.”

“I know I’m with your brother so it’s kind of awkward to talk about this kind of thing, but you’re my friend, too. I have a lot of experience as a submissive; I’ve been in the lifestyle since I was a young adult. I also have experience as a Domme.”

“You’re a switch?” I ask.

She nods. “Yes. You’ve done your research.”

I chuckle and take a drink of my seltzer. “I’ve become a bit obsessed in the last month. I like to learn.”

“You and Nathan have that in common. Among other things.”

“Okay, ew. Stop there.”

Morgan laughs. "Sorry. Sometimes I'm a bit too open."

"I know." I chuckle with her.

When our laughter subsides, Morgan reaches across the table and takes my hand. "I'm happy for you, Lindsey. You've been through a lot, and both you and Kas deserve a good man like Dane in your lives who loves you like he does."

My eyes widen, and I nearly choke on my own saliva. "Whoa, that's getting way ahead of ourselves. Dane is just my Dom." I say the last part quietly, even if nobody is around to hear us.

She cocks a brow. "If you think that, you're blind."

I pull my hand from hers and sit back. "He doesn't love me."

"Tell that to the man outside who keeps looking this way, trying to see you through the tiny kitchen window."

I turn in my chair and notice that I can see Dane with Kas from here. They probably can't see me at this distance, but I can tell that his head is looking toward the cabin as if he's attempting to see in. I turn back to Morgan and ignore her smug smile.

"Our relationship... it's not like that. Like I said, he's my Dom."

"Are you sure that's all he is?"

"We've never said otherwise."

"Well, I know this is not how Dane treats clients or hookups. He also doesn't give their kids nicknames. He doesn't even interact with their kids if they have them, since he doesn't know who his clients are. He *definitely* doesn't kiss his submissives on the forehead or send them sex toys."

I blush a deep red, but Morgan continues.

"He also doesn't help his online clients clean their homes or invite them to his cabin. I haven't been to his cabin, and we've been friends for five years."

I almost bite the inside of my cheek for the first time in a week but stop myself because I can hear Dane scolding me before I do it.

"I think you know, too, that Dane didn't walk here today simply because he found himself meandering to our cabin. He came here because he knew you and Kas would be here."

I blow out a long breath because she's right. I know she's right. "Still, love is a stretch. We've known each other for only a month. I'm his submissive, not his girlfriend."

"Lindsey."

I look up from my hands to meet Morgan's eyes.

"Has Dane told you much about his past?"

"Some," I say, thinking of what he told me about his parents and why nobody in Starlight Haven besides Fox and Morgan seems to know him. That he prefers the peace and quiet of being alone and the anonymity of his work online.

"Then you know that Dane isn't like most men around here. He doesn't go out and pick up women at Moose's or flirt with the locals. He keeps to himself; he always has. Fox and I have asked him to hang out with us on multiple occasions, and he's always busy. But you know what I've heard recently?"

I shake my head. "No, but I know you'll tell me."

Morgan laughs, muttering something about how Nathan and I are so alike before she continues. "That he goes in and picks up his food inside the diner instead of having Cheryl bring it to his car. That he talks to the parents at the obstacle course. That he was even seen at the hardware store picking out paint. Two weeks ago, he called Fox and asked about working for us again this fall and winter."

My interest piques at that. As far as I know, his Pro Dom business is going well. There'd be no reason for him to pick up work as a logger. I have no idea what the paint is about, unless it's paint for his paintings.

"And how do you know most of this? I thought you hated town gossip."

"I do. Nathan, however, loves it and tells me everything he hears."

"That tracks." Nathan has really taken to small-town life, and he loves talking to anyone about anything. Something we *don't* have in common.

"He also heard that you and Dane had an intense little run-in before the first day of the obstacle course and that Dane was seen coming out of the bathroom after you at the General Store."

My skin burns. "God, this town is way more nosy than I thought."

"The nosiest," Morgan confirms.

"So Nathan knows about Dane and me?"

"I don't know if he knows more than the gossip, but he asked me if I knew anything, and I said no, because I didn't know the details. Fox stayed silent, but Dane was at our house a few weeks back, and they talked. Not sure what about; Fox wouldn't say."

I nod, wondering when and what they talked about, but it's none of my business. I'm just glad to hear Dane talks to someone other than me and his clients. It's clear he and Fox are similar, too. Not only in the dominant quality they share but also how they move about in the world and keep to themselves.

"You should tell Nathan when you're ready. He'll be happy you found someone. I know he's been worried about you, though less so recently."

I skip over the part where she mentioned I've found someone and think of my interactions with Nathan. "Why less now?" I ask.

"He said you're confident, that over the last couple of weeks, you've been more rested and happy. That Kas seems happier, too. And I have to agree. You've also been letting us help you more with watching Kas, and I love that. We enjoy having her here with us, and I know Fox will be sad now that she's going back to school."

I smile. "Kas will be, too."

"Back to what I said before." Her tone turns a bit more serious. "You may think love is a stretch, but I know love."

"It's too soon," I interject. "It wouldn't make sense, since our relationship isn't like that."

"Lindsey," Morgan says gently. "Love rarely ever makes sense, but it doesn't need to. And take it from me, love happens when love happens."

"I think you're getting ahead of yourself," I counter. "Dane doesn't love me. I don't even know if he wants to be in a real relationship with me. And don't forget, I come with a daughter and enough baggage to fill an airplane. Not to mention, he hasn't even collared me yet."

Morgan's eyes bug out of her head. "You've spoken about collaring?"

I swallow. "I think he's going to give me a training collar tonight."

"Lindsey! What the hell?"

"What?"

"I know that collaring isn't the same for everyone in the lifestyle, but in all the research you've done, you probably know that, for some, it's a big step in a D/s dynamic. Have you talked to Dane about what that means for you both?"

"Yes. It's a commitment. To him, to our dynamic. To structure and growth."

"Yes to all those things, but have you discussed

what it means to both of you on a deeper level? What it could mean for your future?"

My stomach flips. I think about the times Dane and I have talked about it. "He said it was a commitment, but I thought he meant to him and our dynamic we were building. Not a commitment to dating him or marriage or him becoming a stepdad one day," I tell her honestly. "That's real relationship stuff."

"A Dom/sub relationship is very real. Realer than most."

"I'm not the only one he has," I argue.

"Maybe not, but yours isn't virtual. I don't think I need to reiterate what else is different between you two. Is there a reason you're hesitant to believe he wants to be more than just your Dom?"

The insecurities I've felt before come back to the surface. "I think because he does this for a living, and he hasn't expressed wanting to change his life for me. Not that I would expect him to. We're still fairly new, and like I said, it's not only me in the equation here."

"Mom!"

Morgan and I both sit up as Kas comes

barreling into the house as if she knew I was speaking of her. She has dirt on her cheek, and her hair is wild.

"Look what Logger Dane made me out of some leaves!" She holds up her wrist, and I see he's woven a bracelet for her and tied it around her wrist.

"Wow, that's cool."

"He made you one, too." She holds out her hand, and the bridge of my nose stings. I take it from her, running my fingers over the woven bracelet.

I feel Morgan's eyes on me, and I know what she's thinking without looking at her, because I'm thinking the same thing. Not only did he make Kas a bracelet, but he made me one, too. Maybe to some it wouldn't mean anything, but like I've said before, Dane always does things with intention.

I blink to keep any tears from forming. "Will you tie it on my wrist for me?"

Kas nods and ties it in a knot that Dane showed her how to do, too. Once it's secured around my wrist, Kas bounces on her feet. "Now we match!"

"We do."

"Logger Dane is sooo freaking cool, Mom. He also chopped a big log. Even Uncle Nate said he's cool. Well, he tried to say he's rizz, but that's so embarrassing."

"Did he now?" Morgan asks playfully.

I want to gag at the tone she used but smile instead. "Dane is pretty cool, huh?"

Kas nods. "He said he'd teach me how to fish, too! Can I go?"

"You want to fish?" I ask, my eyes wide in shock.

"Yeah!" she cheers. "He said we could eat what we catch."

My heart thumps in my chest at the image of Kas standing next to Dane, fishing, of all things. Then cooking a meal out of what they caught. It reminds me of something my dad used to do with Nathan, but on the ocean instead of a lake or river. It makes my heart yearn for something I haven't let myself think about or at least tried not to think about: a family. With Dane.

"Right now?" I ask.

"Yeah! Why not?"

I look at my watch and see it's after four. "You have the end-of-summer party at Moira's, so not tonight. But another day."

Kas's face goes from disappointed to happy. "Really?"

"Yeah, if that's what you want."

Kas pumps her fist and then runs out of the cabin back to the men outside. I turn to watch through the kitchen window. I can't see everything well, but I see the moment Dane's eyes fall on Kas. He gives her a high five and smiles at her before looking toward the cabin again. My chest aches to go to him, to put my arms around him and kiss him.

I glance down at my new bracelet before I look over at Morgan, who's watching me quietly. A moment later, she stands and walks over to my side of the table, placing her hand on my shoulder.

"Take it from someone who's not only in the lifestyle but in a relationship with two men, one who has a hard time sharing his feelings. It's important that you speak with Dane and make sure you're on the same page. Don't assume anything about what he does or doesn't want. From my perspective, the man is ready to marry you tomorrow, and he's been saying and doing things you haven't taken to heart because you've been afraid to let him in fully. Which is understandable, considering what you've gone through with your ex."

Her words sink into me, and I know she's right.

"Talk to Dane. Discuss your future before you accept his collar. It may be a little scary, but things will work out. I know it."

I exhale a breath, and rub my thumb over the woven leaves, the texture soft yet firm. I don't know why, but it gives me strength. Just knowing that the item around my wrist was made by him for me is like he's here without being next to me or touching me. "I'll talk to him."

Morgan squeezes my shoulder. "Good. Now let's get back outside; our men are waiting for us."

I stand and hug Morgan. "Thanks for being here for me. And for Kas."

She hugs me back tightly. "Always. We're family."

40

Dane

The last time I was this nervous was the first time I topped a submissive in my early twenties. Another Dom was watching, and the entire thing was intimate but also felt clinical. He was my mentor, there to see if I did anything that would make my partner uncomfortable. I didn't, but it was helpful either way because I've always been a perfectionist.

In this case, my nerves are not about doing a scene with Lindsey again in person—I've been craving it since the last one—but everything to do with what I plan to ask her. Her progress with me is beyond anything I could have imagined.

When I said she was born to be a submissive, I was right. She's only proven that to me the more we've worked together. She's still a brat and will keep those tendencies because it's part of who she is, but she's grown in her confidence and willingness to submit to me. I know that will only continue the deeper our relationship grows, which is why I'm going to present her with the training collar I've gotten for her tonight.

I glance at the clock on my wall as I hear the gravel crunch beneath the tires of her car. It's five minutes to seven, and with Lindsey, I know she'll give herself a pep talk before she knocks on my door exactly one minute before the clock hits the hour.

I look around my space. I would have lit candles on the table, but after she told me the story of how her asshole ex cheated on her, I don't want her to be triggered. Instead, I dimmed the lights, put a small bouquet of wildflowers that Kas picked for me earlier on the table in a vase, and left a square, velvet, black box in front of the place where Lindsey will sit.

The sound of her car door slamming makes the nerves in my stomach build, and I square my shoulders. I let her knock and pause for a few seconds, inhaling a breath before opening the door.

While I've learned how to keep my nerves from my features, I can see them clearly on Lindsey's. She's smiling, but there's a tiny furrow in her brow, and she's gripping her purse in front of her tightly. It's not unusual for her to be nervous; everything we do is new to her. Tonight, though, what I'm going to ask her is new for me, too.

"Hi," she greets.

"Hey, baby."

The grip she has on her purse relaxes a bit, and I open the door so she can come in. The smell of her floral perfume wafts past me, tickling my nose. Once the door is locked, I face her, taking her purse and hanging it on a hook near the door where I keep my keys.

We stare at each other for a moment. She's beautiful as usual. Her hair is lightly curled, and she's wearing a bit of makeup. Instead of a dress like last time, she's got on a flared black skirt that hits mid-thigh and a rust-colored V-neck shirt that brings out the chocolate notes of her eyes and hair.

I reach up and take a lock between my fingers, feeling the silky texture. "All this for me?" I ask, pulling gently on the curl, which bounces when I release it.

Her tone is cheeky and playful as she asks, "Who else would it be for?"

I put my hands in the pockets of the black

slacks I chose to wear that match the black button-down I have on. The top buttons are open, and the sleeves are rolled up to my forearms the way I know Lindsey likes. It's hard to miss when she stares at my chest and arms whenever she can, practically salivating.

I cock my head. "Already trying to get spanked?"

She almost bites the inside of her cheek, but I see her thinking better of it. Good girl.

"No." She swallows and grips her hands in front of her. "Just a little nervous."

I like that she's being honest, even if I knew the information she just shared. I step closer so I can feel the heat of her body and brush my finger down the round curve of her jaw. I could tell her to kneel, allow her submissive pose to ground her, but not yet. We need to talk first, and I don't want to get caught up in a scene. I don't want her to be influenced in any way to say yes to what I want to ask.

I stop stroking her jaw to gently cup her cheek. "Is there a particular reason that you're nervous?"

She wets her lips, and her skin flushes pink. "I—" She tries to look down, but I hold her face firm. Her jaw clenches beneath my touch, but I don't waver in my eye contact, softening my gaze so she feels safe to tell me.

"Nathan, Morgan, and Fox know about us," she says.

Of all the things she could have said, that was not what I expected. Especially when we haven't even made it to the dining table yet.

"They do," I answer simply. I was going to ask her how she felt about that before I presented her with my collar, but she seemed good earlier. I know it's a step in a new direction, one I admittedly didn't think about when I showed up at their cabin earlier—I was only thinking about seeing Lindsey and Kas, too. Not about what the others would think.

"What are we, Dane?"

The way she asks the question, uncertain and small, punches me in the gut. "You don't know?"

I hold her chin, my stomach rolling at her words. I thought I had made myself clear about what we were. I thought our discussions of the training collar and calling her mine showed her how I felt. Then there was today at the cabin, the bracelets, my growing relationship with Kas.

"We've never talked about what we are."

"We haven't?" I challenge.

"Tell me when," she says, defiant.

My lip twitches at her tone, but I don't ask her to say it again in a nicer way. We can address her brat side in our scene later.

"At your home two weeks ago, and several times since then."

"That was different; we were talking about our dynamic, not about you showing up at my brother's or offering to teach Kas how to fish. Not about you kissing my forehead like you're my boyfriend in front of Morgan."

I release her chin and trail my hand down her body. Goose bumps flare over her arms, and her breathing turns sharper.

When I reach her waist, I stop. "You're right; we didn't talk about what our relationship would look like outside of our D/s dynamic."

Her eyes soften, and I grip the soft flesh of her hip.

"I have owned up to about my failures with you before, and I'll do so again now. I've told you that my relationship with you has been different from the start. As I've said, I have not had a dynamic like this with anyone else. I know I'm a good Dom, but I am human, and when I'm with you, Lindsey, sometimes I forget myself. I believed the words I spoke and your acceptance of my actions meant we were on the same page."

She swallows. "You are a good Dom, Dane. I didn't mean for you to question yourself. I just—things are complicated in my life, and . . . Do you really want a relationship with me? Outside of what we have, I mean."

"First, it's good for me to question myself, and it's good for you to challenge me in these cases. But I need you to know that I never meant for you to doubt how I feel about you or where this relationship was heading. I wouldn't have set you on the path to earning a training collar if I didn't want you, Lindsey. Not just the submissive side of you—all of you."

I look down at the bracelet I made for her earlier, which is still on her wrist. My heart thuds in my chest. She didn't remove it.

I brush my fingers over the woven leaves, and her hand closes over the one I still have on her hip. Her fingers tighten, and I look up at her.

"You'd really want that?"

The way she sounds unsure kills me, and I know I have a lot to make up for. Looking back on the past few weeks, I realize this conversation should have come before tonight.

But like everything with Lindsey, things are different. And as I told her, I've made mistakes. We moved fast and fell hard, at least I did. And I believe she has, too. In the last two weeks, we *did* take a step back, took the time to build our relationship as a Dom and sub, and we learned more about each other outside of that dynamic. But I never told her that I already view her as more than just my submissive.

"Allow me to use my words and actions, Lindsey." I carefully lower to my knees and look up at her. I didn't expect to be in this position tonight, but I want to convey to her where our relationship is heading if she accepts it.

"What are you doing?"

I take her hands in mine and exhale a calming breath. I dip my chin and bring the tops of her hands to my forehead, resting them there in submission before I bring them to my lips.

I kiss her heated skin then speak up to make sure she hears my words clearly. "I want you, Lindsey. I've wanted you since the moment we ran into each other. I've never felt this way about anyone before. You make me want to show up better—as a man, as a Dom. You make me think about things I didn't think were for me…

a future, a family, something real. When I told you you're mine, I meant it. If you're ready to move forward, I want to be with you. I want to be yours. Fully. Honestly. Not just claim you with my collar, but with every part of me."

"Dane, please, get up."

I shake my head. "No, baby. I won't. Because I need you to hear me. I need you to understand what I feel for you, what I'm saying."

She stares down at me, and I can see her brain moving a mile a minute. When her gaze flicks behind me, I look over my shoulder and follow her line of sight. I turn back around and take her by the hips, pulling her body into mine.

She lets out a small squeak, her hands falling to my shoulders to steady herself.

"The painting is of you," I tell her.

She blinks, her fingers digging into my shoulders. "What?"

"I told you, Lindsey. You're mine, and I mean that. There's no one else but you."

"But how?" She looks at the painting then back to me. "You painted this before you saw me—" She flushes.

"Saw you naked?" I finish for her.

"Yes." She smiles back sheepishly.

"From the moment we met and started talking, I'd close my eyes and see you. I painted you after we spoke one night, and it felt right to hang it."

"It's a beautiful painting. And maybe a little creepy."

The playful smile on her lips tells me she's back to being sassy, and my pulse quickens in my throat. I pinch her hip, and she yelps. "You love it," I say.

Lindsey studies me, her gaze more intense than I'm used to. I don't blink, just wait. Eventually, one of her hands leaves my shoulder, and she threads it into my hair. Her fingers glide through the short strands, the sensation sending a shiver up my spine.

"Are you sure you want to be mine?" Her tone attempts to sound playful, but I hear and see her fear, the fear that I don't mean what I say. It makes sense given what I know about her past, and I feel like an idiot for not seeing how wrong I've gone about this with her.

"I don't say things I don't mean. Or have you forgotten?"

Her fingers slide from my hair to my jaw, playing with my beard now. "I haven't. But I'm not like the others. I'm new to this, and half the time, I don't know what I'm doing, and—"

"What others are you speaking of?" I stop her.

"Your other submissives."

"There are no others."

She tugs on my beard. "Will you please stand? I can't take you there anymore."

I give her a knowing smile, loving that she's proving how right she is for me. I stand and lead her toward the kitchen table. When she's seated, I sit at the head of the table near her. I don't miss the way her eyes stare at the spot where I had her last time, her clamped nipples pressed into the wood and her ass in the air while I spanked her.

"Lindsey." I draw her attention back to me. Her eyes are dilated again, and her breathing has changed. "I meant what I said." I take her hand on the table in mine and squeeze. "There are no others. You're the only one I want. The only one I need."

"I know you don't do what we're doing with anyone else, but your clients—"

"You're not hearing me," I stop her again. "There are no others."

"What?"

"I've spent the last two weeks since I left your

cabin helping my clients find Doms to match their needs. I'm still in the process of helping some find new Doms, but we've ended our relationships. Like I said, there are no others."

"What? Dane, no!"

Her panic confuses me. "I wouldn't lie to you about this."

"No, that's not what I mean. It's your work, your job! What are you going to do now?" Before I can reply, she asks, "Is that why Morgan said you asked about working for them again?"

"She told you about that?"

She exhales a hard breath. "You can't give up income for me, and I'm sure your submissives depend on you."

My clients were disappointed and upset, rightfully so, but I didn't leave them in the lurch. I needed to do what was right for not just me but them as well. It was unfair not to give them my full attention.

"I'm not, baby. I'm not giving up anything for you. I'm giving it up for me."

She stares at me, confused, but before I speak, I take a few calming breaths, not only to calm myself but also to calm Lindsey. When the air around us has settled, I scoot my chair closer to her so that our knees are touching and I can take both of her hands in mine.

"Hang with me, because I swear this will all have a point." I rub my thumbs over her knuckles, and she nods. "I've told you a bit about my parents, but the home they kept wasn't a nice one. They fought a lot and were cruel to each other. They weren't in a dynamic like we are, but my dad lorded over my mom and me like a king. She turned to me because she needed a friend, and I was that for her. To my dad, I was a worker, a person beneath him.

"When I left home at eighteen, I'd already battled with my own dominant tendencies. I didn't want to be like him, but I also didn't know how to be any other way. So I found kink, found a Dom who taught me a lot of what I know. I found a way to be a better man than my father and accept who I am."

I take a breath. "The life I've built since then has worked for me. I found peace in the woods and comfort in my dynamics with my submissives online. For years, I've had no desire to disrupt what I built or attempt to bring someone into my life that could be more. Until I met you, Lindsey."

Her cognac-colored eyes become glassy, and her grip on my hands is so tight, our fingers are turning white.

"It's okay," I hush. "I didn't mean to make you cry."

She shakes her head. "It's just… You've been through a lot, and I feel honored that I'm the one you chose to let in."

"You've been through a lot, too. You're an incredible woman, and I'm the one who's honored that you've trusted me the way you have."

She looks down at our hands then back into my eyes. "I still don't understand why you gave up your clients for me."

"I didn't give them up—I let go because it was time, for them and for me. But you? You're mine. You're the only partner I want in my life. And if you'll let me, I want the honor of taking care of you, of being the Dom you deserve. The kind of man you'd want not just for yourself but for Kasandra, too."

At the sound of her daughter's name, a tear drips from the corner of her eye. I release one of my hands from hers and wipe it off her cheek.

"Everything you've been saying sounds like you're proposing," she says.

I consider telling her that, in my own way, I am. The relationship we have is still building, and we're not ready for marriage yet, but our dynamic, the training collar I'm going to offer her... I hope one day it will all lead to that. Not just marriage but a permanent collar.

That thought alone would've scared me once, but not with Lindsey. With every day that passes, I see more and more that I want anything and everything that has to do with her. I hope that, after all is said and done, she does, too.

"Is marriage something you'd want?" I voice.

She blinks and nods. "There was a time when I would have said no, but that was before I met you."

I kiss her knuckle softly. "That's good to hear, because I feel the same way. I should have asked you that sooner."

"We're learning and growing together, Dane."

"We are." For a moment, I mull over what to say next. My plans for tonight got derailed a bit, but we needed to have this discussion, and I'm glad we were able to be open and honest with each other. It means what we've been building is strong.

I pull my hands from hers, and my eyes drop

to the velvet box I'd laid in front of her seat before she arrived. She follows my gaze, and her breath picks up.

"I did want to make a different kind of proposal tonight. We can discuss it if that's what we're both ready for."

"Sir?" Her voice is soft as she uses my honorific instead of my name, but I can hear the bit of excitement in it.

"Open it, baby."

Lindsey sits up straighter in her chair and pulls the box closer to her. Her fingers tremble as she lifts the latch. Her intake of breath is sharp as she stares at what's inside. "A training collar, Sir?"

"Yes," I reply. "I had it made for you."

Lindsey takes the thin black leather choker from the box. In the center of it sits a silver O-ring, one I can fasten a leash or other fun things to.

She places the box on the table and holds the collar reverently, a fresh wave of tears glistening in her eyes. "It's beautiful, Sir."

"I've also had a day collar made, a necklace for you to wear that isn't so obvious. I can show it to you later, if you choose to accept."

She wipes a tear from her cheek and looks at me. "I accept, Sir."

Her eagerness pleases me, but I need to be sure. "Before you do, I want to talk about what this will mean for our future."

I take the collar from her hands and hold the stiff yet soft leather in mine.

"If you choose to wear it, it's confirmation that you're mine, Lindsey. We will be exclusive. You'll be my submissive, and I'll be your Dominant. Outside of that agreement, you'll be my partner. 'Boyfriend' seems too average for what we'll be, but that's what the world will know me as. I will not only take care of you, but you'll also submit to me as you have been. We'll discover exactly how that works for us day-to-day, as I don't believe twenty-four seven submission is what either of us want. But the bottom line is that this collar"—I hold it up—"isn't only your commitment to me. It's a commitment to yourself, to your submission. To wherever we choose for our relationship to go in the future, marriage or otherwise."

Lindsey shifts in her chair. "You're positive you want all that with me, Sir?"

"You're the only person I want this with."

She smiles, and another tear drips down her cheek.

"It's alright if you need more time to think—there is no right or wrong answer. I know this is a lot to take in."

Lindsey leans forward. "I've been thinking about you giving me a training collar for weeks now. I want your collar, Sir. I want to explore with you, to see what our future holds together. I'll admit I was scared before, but when I think about committing to you, I'm not scared anymore."

The slight tension in my shoulders eases, and Lindsey looks down at the collar before meeting my eyes. "Will you put it on me, Sir?"

Joy I've never felt before radiates through my body. I lift my hands and hold hers so we're both grasping the collar together. "Are you accepting my training collar, baby?"

"I am, Sir."

"Do you accept me as your Dom to guide you, protect you, and take all that you are as mine?"

"Yes." She nods. "I do, Sir."

If I was the type of man to cry, my eyes would match hers. Instead, I squeeze her hands again before I sit back, keeping the collar in my own.

"Kneel for me," I command.

There's no hesitation in her body as she gets off her chair and kneels the way I've taught her. Like the good girl she is, she leaves her eyes on mine, palms up and knees spread wide. I would have preferred her naked for this, but that day will come. Hopefully when I place a permanent collar around her neck.

When she's settled, I stand and walk behind her, moving the chair so I have more space.

"Lift your hair for me." When she holds her hair back, I pause for a moment and take in the scene of her fully submitting to me, waiting for me to secure my vow to her and hers to me with this simple choker. I know the training collar is only the first step in our future together, that our relationship and dynamic will evolve, but I never thought I'd have this moment, nor did I dream of it. But now I can't imagine it any other way or with any other person.

I bring the collar around her neck, her entire body becoming lighter as I secure the snap in place. Lindsey lowers her hair, and I circle around her, pushing my own chair back so I can hold her chin in my hands.

Her cheeks are wet, but there's an ease about

her that wasn't there before. Her features are soft, her eyes now clear. I admire her, knowing this is a huge moment for us.

"Beautiful." I brush my hand down the column of her neck, my fingers lingering on the leather. "How do you feel?"

Her warm eyes lock with mine, and her easy answer hits me square in the chest like a lightning strike that shoots shocks through my body and lights every nerve and blood vessel on fire. "Like yours, Sir."

I hum in Dominant pleasure, pressing my thumb to her lower lip. "Good. Because you are. Now, it's time for you to show me."

I turn and reach under the cushion of my chair, where I stowed another special treat. I pick it up and turn back to her, her eyes widening as I snap the clip on the end of the leash to the O-ring of her collar.

I turn and gently tug. When she doesn't move, I look over my shoulder with a devilish grin. "Well, don't just kneel there, baby. Follow me."

41
Lindsey

I CRAWL BEHIND DANE like a pet on a leash. I should find it humiliating, but in fact, I find it the opposite. I feel calm, at peace, especially with the weight of Dane's—my Sir's—training collar around my neck. The gentle pressure of it along with the tug of the leash as we head toward his bedroom is a feeling I didn't know I needed.

I've read about being collared on blogs from submissives on sublife.com. Many say it was a day they'll always remember, maybe even the best day of their life, regardless of if it was a play collar, a training collar, a collar of consideration—the next step up—or a permanent collar.

Over the last two weeks, I've imagined what it would be like to receive my training collar, what it would look like and feel like around my neck. But nothing could compare to the actual thing.

And while I can't call this the best day of my life, since becoming a mother holds that spot, hearing Dane's vow, feeling him put the leather choker around my neck, is a close second. It's hard to describe how it feels other than right.

The bridge of my nose stings, and I blink back the tears, bringing my focus to the bite of the wood floor on my knees as I crawl and the gentle rustle of Dane's slacks as he walks in front of me. We pass through a doorframe, and when the edge of his bed comes into view, he stops. Like the first night I was here and he had me crawl, my skirt is short, and my sex is partially exposed. I feel the air of the room against my heated skin, the black thong I wore for tonight already soaked. I debated if I should even wear underwear, but I slid this pair on at the last minute in hopes he would like it.

Dane turns so he's facing me, the leash tugging gently on the collar around my neck. I swallow but don't move, staying in this position until he tells me otherwise. He hums to himself, the sound only serving to make me wetter.

A second later, he unclips the leather leash but doesn't give me instruction. There's a heated pause in the room until the floor vibrates with the weight of his footsteps. He walks around me, taking his time as if he's observing a piece of art.

My thighs begin to shake, not from nerves over what I believe will happen tonight but from desire. The more comfortable I get not only in my body but in my submission as well, the more I enjoy the feeling of being erotically objectified by him. I trust him completely, and there's never been a day in the last few weeks that he hasn't called me beautiful or given me praise.

Dane's hand pets my hair, his fingers tangling in the strands. I gently lean into it like a cat wanting more. His warm chuckle fills the space, and he scratches my scalp before continuing a heated path down my back. When he reaches my ass, he flips up my skirt, fully exposing my backside to him. His fingers caress the skin of my cheeks, and I nearly moan when his touch dips dangerously low, near my back entrance.

Before he can touch the tight ring, he grips the lacy fabric of my thong and tugs on it. The wet fabric pulls between the lips of my pussy, rubbing against my swollen clit. The pressure between my ass cheeks only adds to the interesting sensation, and this time, I don't hold back my loud moan.

Dane must enjoy my reaction, because he does it again. My hips naturally move forward to gain more friction, and the desire to rest my weight on my forearms so my ass is in the air for him becomes heavy in my mind.

A resounding smack echoes. The skin of my ass stings from his smack as I cry out.

"I didn't tell you to move, did I, baby?"

"No, Sir," I say through a pant.

I force myself to stay still as he starts to play again. He stands directly behind me, feet bracketing my calves. He runs his hands down my ass and grips the skin, hard then soft. I don't know what he's doing, but *playing* feels like the right word.

His finger runs between my ass cheeks, and he pulls my thong repeatedly. I bite my lower lip, and I don't doubt he can see how turned on this is making me.

But he never touches my pussy or my asshole, a place I can't stop wishing he'd touch and play with. It's a thought I never expected to have since I didn't consider myself someone who enjoyed anal play. But with Dane, I want to give him everything.

"Did you wear these for me?" Dane's rumbling voice asks as he tugs on the thong.

"Yes, Sir. I wore everything for you."

"Hmm, as you should." He pulls again on the thong, holding it tight against my clit. I whimper, expecting him to drop the fabric. Instead, he continues the pressure against my heated sex. The contact feels amazing, but the lack of movement is driving me wild.

"Sir." My voice is pleading. "Please, Sir. I need to come."

The warm, rumbling laugh that leaves his chest is dark and deep. It floods my pussy with more arousal, and my need for him only grows.

"I bet you do." He tugs harder on the thong to the point where I hear the rip of the seams. I didn't know that sound could be a turn-on, but I want to hear it again.

"Sir." I barely stop myself from moving my hips to create friction.

"Yes, baby?" he asks playfully. The bastard.

"Please."

He has mercy on me and releases the fabric. I exhale in both relief and annoyance. I wanted to come, not for him to stop. Another slap echoes, and my ass shakes from the force of his hands coming down simultaneously on each cheek.

My cry is loud, and my nipples tighten. He

does it again, then one more time before his hand gently soothes my sensitive skin. My fingers dig into the wood of the floor, my breaths short.

"You're sexy like this." Dane's voice cuts through the sensations and feelings I'm experiencing: pain, pleasure, humiliation, and desperate need.

He gently strokes the skin of my ass. "You're mine to play with, aren't you?"

"Yes, Sir."

He strokes the skin again before he says, "And mine to punish." His hand comes down once more on my ass before he hums. "And mine to do with as I wish. Isn't that right, baby?"

"Yes, Sir."

He hums again, his touch leaving my body as he steps back. His footsteps are brief as he comes to stand in front of me, and his fingers grasp and lift my chin so I can see his eyes. He's smiling down at me with a look I can only describe as adoration mixed with a hint of mischief on his handsome features.

"Did you know I could train you to stay in this position? I'd have you stay on all fours and connect the leash to the bedpost. Then I'd put a vibrator inside the pretty cunt that belongs to me—and one in that sweet ass, too. If I wanted, I'd leave the cabin and edge you for hours while I work outside or even drive into town. You'd turn into a sobbing mess until you'd be crying out for me to give you what you need. And you'd do it to please me, wouldn't you, baby?"

I swallow but answer without hesitation. "I would, Sir."

He strokes my cheek then traces the curves of my lips. "Thought so."

My lips turn up in a smile at his familiar, cocky ease, and he smiles back at me. He strokes my lips again, the tip of his finger slipping in before he abruptly pulls back and stands to his full height.

"Strip. You have fifteen seconds."

His eyebrow cocks when I don't move.

"Starting now."

42
Dane

Lindsey's hazy focus dissipates when she realizes I'm serious. I sit on the edge of the bed, arms crossed and eyes never leaving her body as she stands on wobbly legs. She needs to work on shifting from different submissive positions, but that's something we can address during her training period.

My attention shifts to my collar around her neck, to the silver O-ring glinting in the dim light of the room. It's an odd feeling to look at it, to know she only accepted it shortly before this moment, but it feels as if it's always been there, like her neck was simply waiting for the physical version of it from the second we met. I'd be a liar if I said I wasn't already imagining a permanent one, but this one suits her, and she looks beautiful. *All mine.*

I lift my gaze up her body. She's almost naked now, her clothes on the floor beside her. The last thing to go is her cute thong, the thong I nearly ripped from her body. I think she would have liked it if I had, but if I'd gone through with it, I would have rutted her into the floor like a wild animal. I have control, but that only goes so far when the woman of my dreams is presenting herself to me in such a cute little outfit, one that had me thinking of classroom fantasies where I bend her over my desk and smack her round ass with a ruler for forgetting to do her assignment.

Lindsey steps out of her thong and drops it in a pile next to her with her clothes and the heels she had on before. Later, I'll teach her how to fold them how I like, but not tonight. We'll settle official protocols outside of the ones we set during our first agreement amendment when I don't have the desire to claim her body with my cock and hear her screaming my name loud enough to wake the entire forest outside.

Her dilated eyes meet mine, and she shifts on her feet. I know she's fighting her natural desire to cover herself. Over time, that desire will be eradicated.

"Beautiful," I muse. Then I stand, commanding,

"Now crawl onto the bed. Lie flat on your back, arms above your head, and legs spread. Show me what you've freely given to me."

She scurries to the mattress and crawls on top of the waterproof blanket I had the forethought to put down. She positions herself as I asked, her body in beautiful surrender and cunt wet with her arousal. I note her chest is heaving from her short breaths, and her eyes are staring up at the ceiling.

I move so I'm standing next to her. "Lindsey, look at me."

Her head turns, and I note her jaw is clenched. I sit on the bed and caress her cheek before bending down to kiss her. She sighs against my mouth, and I deepen the kiss briefly before pulling away to look into her eyes.

"Your body is mine, and everything that's mine is perfect. Do you understand?" She exhales and nods while I stroke her cheek. "If you'd like, I can get you a blindfold, let you relax into the sensations."

She shakes her head. "No, Sir. Please, I want to see you."

I kiss her softly again. "Good, I want to see your eyes when my dick enters that sweet pussy for the first time, too. But before that..." She moans when I pull away, and I hold back a smile. "Stay in this position—don't move."

Her body stills, and I get off the bed to walk to my dresser where I have a few things waiting. I grab what I put out for tonight and go back to where my good little slut has not moved. My gaze travels down her plush body, taking in her pert nipples, wet pussy, flushed skin. Fuck, she really is perfect for me.

I lay the items near her head before I move over her, straddling her body. She looks up at me with hooded eyes, my hard cock pressing against her softness through my slacks. I smirk down at her before I reach to where I have cuffs attached to the corners of the headboard with short chains, something I installed earlier for this exact moment.

"You said you were interested in light bondage," I say as I secure one cuff to her left wrist. "Tug on it for me." She does, and I hum in satisfaction. Once I've done the other one, I sit back, making sure not to put too much weight on her.

Her arms are above her head, but now they're secured with the leather-padded cuffs. I have her tug again to see her range of motion. She can squirm and move a bit, but she won't be able to touch or grab me. Another day, I'll secure her legs, too, but this is perfect for now.

"How does it feel?" I ask her.

"Green, Sir."

I smile at her use of the traffic light system. "Good. You remember to tell me at any time if it's too much?"

"Yes, Sir."

I lean forward to reach for one of the other things I'd placed near her head. I grab one of the small white suction cups sitting there and show it to her. Her brow furrows, and I bring it to my lips, wetting it. She watches with interest as I take her right breast in my hand, squeezing it and plucking at her already hard nipple. Her hips push up against me, and I gently slap her breast.

"Oh!" she gasps.

I do it again, making sure to strike the hard bud. "Remember who's topping who, baby."

I lean forward, sucking her nipple into my mouth and getting it nice and wet. I could play with her tits for hours and not get bored, but I'm getting impatient to taste her, so I take the cylindrical suction cup and insert her nipple into it, pressing it down on her skin before I slowly start to crank the handle.

The front of my slacks gets wet with pre-cum as her nipple and areola enlarge as they're sucked into the tube. Lindsey's breath catches, and I give my attention to her face.

Her brow is pinched, and her mouth is parted, but she's pushing her breasts forward as if she's asking for more. I turn the crank again until the skin around her nipple begins to flush, blood pulling to the surface. Her cry of pain and pleasure tells me when to stop, and I pull back to admire my work. I gently flick the cup to make sure it won't fall off, which makes Lindsey buck her hips again.

I lightly smack the breast that's free from the suction cup. "Do you like that?"

She nods eagerly. "Yes, Sir."

"I like it, too." I suck her left nipple into my mouth to give it the same attention as the other. The chains attached to her handcuffs rattle, and the sound has me grinning around the heated, plush skin. I suck again before pulling back, taking the other suction cup and placing it on her breast. Her eyes are hooded as she observes the nipple expand and rise into the plastic. When I'm satisfied with its tightness, and I've made sure it won't move, I grab the last thing I got for tonight.

I slide the little pink finger vibrator over my pointer finger in front of Lindsey's gaze so she can see what I'm doing. I click the on button, and a buzzing fills the air. I hold it to Lindsey's lips.

"Kiss it." Her lips pucker, and she does it before I trail it down her cheek so she can feel the sensation. When I reach her neck, gliding over her pulse point, she wiggles.

"Ticklish?"

"Yes, Sir."

I skim the buzzing silicone down her chest. Feeling a little sadistic, I hold it against one of the section cups pulling at her nipples. She arches, chains rattling.

"Oh my god."

I press the vibrator against the other one, her eyes closing as the pleasure mixed with pain courses through her body. When I see her forehead start to shine with sweat, I gently ease myself off her and situate her so her feet are planted on the mattress and her legs are spread. I stand at the foot of the bed, realizing that the part of my pants that was connected with her pussy is soaked. I fucking love how wet she is for me.

"Eyes on me."

Her hooded gaze settles on mine as I remove my clothes, the vibrator still buzzing on my finger. My dick is heavy and straining, pre-cum leaking from the slit. I want to be inside her, but I'm not deviating from my plan, especially when my meal is spread out and waiting for me so patiently. Her cunt is literally weeping for me, begging me to taste her.

"You come when I tell you to, do you understand?"

Lindsey nods eagerly. "Yes, Sir."

I situate myself on the bed between her legs, looping my arms under her thighs and pulling her pussy toward my face. The action is abrupt, and Lindsey squeals, chains rattling until they're pulled taut and her wrists are straining against the cuffs. I seal my lips around her swollen clit, her squeal turning into a deep moan that melds with mine as her flavor bursts over my tongue.

I'd forgotten how much I enjoy the taste of cunt. But Lindsey's—it's the best I've ever tasted. She's tangy and a bit sweet. She moans and squirms under my attention, but I hold her tighter, sucking and lapping at her arousal.

"Sir!" she cries, hips lifting into my mouth.

I pull back and free one of my hands, slapping her clit. Hard. "Do not come yet."

Her thighs shake, and she groans. It sounds sassy to my ears, so I smack her clit again before I latch my mouth over the bundle of nerves and suck.

"Oh, shit," she cries.

I move my hands so that I'm pinning her thighs open, taking the finger that has the vibrator on it and running it over her skin as I flick my tongue on her clit.

Her whimpers fill my ears as I continue my torture. I hold her shaking thighs wider as I lick down to her entrance, my tongue dipping in until I feel the fluttering muscles of her inner walls. She's close to coming, but I don't want her to yet.

I grip her thighs tighter and lick downward, my tongue exploring the tight ring of muscle that I plan to thoroughly use whenever I fucking want. It is mine, after all.

"Sir!" Lindsey yells when my tongue rims her asshole. "Oh my god!"

I chuckle and continue to lick the sensitive area before swiping my tongue up to find her pussy again. I follow that path a few more times until she's a sobbing mess, begging me to let her come.

"Please, Sir. I can't—I don't know if I can stop it."

I lick back to her clit, swirling my tongue around the hard nub. "You have been such a good girl." I press the vibrator on my finger to her clit, and she jackknifes off the bed, straining harder against her cuffs.

"Sir!"

I slide two fingers into her entrance, fingers curling to find her G-spot. I begin to thrust in and out at a pace I know will make her body sing for me. I lower my lips back down to her clit and suck, alternating the suction of my mouth with the vibrator along with the thrusts of my fingers. I want to overload her body so she doesn't know what she's feeling, so when I tell her to come, she floats among the stars with my name on her lips.

Without my hands holding her open, her thighs clamp around my head, and I drown in her scent and taste.

"Dane—Sir—oh, fuck. Please, may I come? Please, may I come, Sir?"

I fuck her faster with my fingers and manage to look up at her face. She's staring down at me, skin flushed, the suction cups still on her breasts, and her body coated in a sheen of sweat. Her lower body tenses, and her thighs squeeze around me. She has been such a good girl, and I'm ready to see her fall apart.

"Do it, baby. Fucking soak me."

Her head presses back into the bed as I take her clit into my mouth and thrust my fingers hard into her cunt, adding a third one for good measure. She shakes and cries my name as her orgasm crashes through her body.

Wetness coats my fingers, and I have no doubt she squirted for me. I'd bet money I'm the first and only man who has ever make her do that. I lap at her cum, tasting it and groaning as its heady flavor covers my tongue.

I eat her out until she's a quivering mess, her thighs clamping at my head like a heartbeat. When I press her legs open with my palms, her hips shift and chains clink as she tries to get away from me. I don't let her, cleaning her sensitive cunt and swallowing every last drop of what's mine.

After I'm fully sated, I kiss her clit and turn off the vibrator, setting it on the bed. I ease up her body, still holding her thighs open and kissing the shaking skin. It's salty from sweat, but I worship every space of skin I can get to.

I trail up until I'm at her lower stomach, nipping gently at her C-section scar and the skin of her belly, over the faint lines of stretch marks and dimples. I run my tongue over her heart, which I can feel beating, then to her tits being tortured by the suction cups. I leave them for now, licking the swells and then up her sternum until I reach her face. It's wet from tears, and I devour them, kissing over her flushed cheeks until our eyes meet.

Her breathing is hard, my beard soaked like I asked her to do. Her eyes are hazy, but there's a satisfied smile on her lips.

"You did so good." I kiss her softly. I do it again and again until her breathing is more even and she's dropped back down into her body. I bump the tip of her nose with mine, and her smile widens.

"You okay to keep going?"

"Green," she says eagerly.

I nibble at her lips until she opens for me, sucking on her tongue. She moans at the action, her hips lifting so my cock drags against her wetness, making me hiss.

I reach up and flick the suction cup on her nipple. She cries out, and I swallow it with my mouth, turning her into a puddle beneath me once again before I pull back. "Does my needy slut want her Sir's dick?"

Her desperate whimper is all the answer I need, but like a good girl, she uses her words. "Yes, Sir. Please, I need your dick inside me."

I finger her collar and tug on the ring, enjoying the way she flushed a deeper red after she finished her plea, like she can't believe those words came out of her dirty little mouth.

"Well." I nip at her lower lip. "Since you asked so nicely."

43
Lindsey

My body is wrecked in the best way, and Dane's giant dick hasn't even split me in two yet. He kisses me again, the taste of my cum now on my lips. I moan into his mouth, hands still bound and nipples still in the suction cups he put on them.

I thought my orgasms couldn't get better after the last one I had on his lap a couple of weeks ago, but I was wrong. Now I'm wondering if each one will top the one before. I smile against his lips, and he pulls back.

"What?" his questions.

I shake my head. "Nothing, just—happy, Sir."

His hazel eyes are dark with need before he nips at my lips then kisses down my neck. I want to put my fingers in his hair and bring him back, but all I can do is strain against the cuffs.

He sucks on my pulse point then shifts to my breasts. My gaze follows his actions as he gently starts to unscrew one of the suction cups.

I hiss as the blood travels through the once-suctioned skin, the sensation of pins and needles spreading through my breast. Sir studies my reaction carefully, and when he sees I'm okay, he brings his lips down and runs his tongue over the suction lines before sucking my nipple into his mouth.

I moan, wrists straining again, his beard tickling my flesh as he works all the sensation back into my breast. When he's done, he does the other one, and a fresh wave of arousal wets my pussy.

I didn't know it was possible so soon, especially after I squirted—another thing I didn't think I was capable of. I've read about it online and wondered, but thought only some women could do it. But with Dane, I'm starting to see that anything is possible, especially when it comes to the things he can make my body feel and do.

With the suction cups now gone, he brushes his hand over my nipples, and I hiss. The bastard smirks before his fingers trail up my arms and over my armpits. I squirm and buck, but he only laughs, the vibration of it going straight to my overly sensitive clit.

He undoes the leather cuff on my right wrist, then my left. He checks my skin and kisses the inside of each wrist on my pulse point before he checks in with me.

"Okay?" he asks.

"Perfect," I reply, even if my arms feel a bit like noodles.

Dane shifts off me, but before I can wonder where he's going, he lies beside me on the mattress and tugs my body into him, pulling my leg over his so my center is lined up against his cock.

It's hot and long, and the wetness of his precum stains my skin. If I wasn't so desperate to feel him inside me, I'd ask if I could use my mouth to tease him. But I need him, more than I think I've needed anything in my life.

His strong palm grips my outer thigh, and he thrusts his hips up so his shaft slides over my slit. When I moan, he captures it with his mouth, his tongue sliding along mine as we start a now-familiar dance. He sucks and licks, and I grip his shoulder, allowing him to delve deeper into my mouth. By the time he pulls away, my lips are swollen, and I'm aching for him. Sir uses his fingers to grasp my chin.

"Do you want me to get a condom?" he asks.

I think he already knows the answer before I say it. I want to feel him. All of him. "No."

The word sparks something in Dane's eyes, and a growl leaves his chest. He rolls me back with only the strength a man like him can have and pins me to the mattress, the wide head of his cock prodding at my cunt. His cunt.

"Are you sure?" he asks, a brow raised. "There's no going back after this, baby. You'll be mine." He leans down and bites my lower lip, pulling back as he rolls his hips teasingly against me. "I won't be able to let you go."

I bring my hand up, my wrist red from the cuff, and touch the collar on my neck. The silver O-ring is cool beneath my touch. "I thought I already was."

He pauses, his eyes softening. For a moment, I think I said something wrong, but then his lips are back on mine in a punishing kiss. My chest arches up, sensitive nipples brushing against his hard pecs.

He moans into my mouth, his hips thrusting forward as his tongue massages mine. One of his hands brushes down my side, over my stomach, and moves between us. He positions his cock directly at my entrance, nudging the head inside.

He parts from my lips, our breathing labored. "Tell me who you belong to, Lindsey."

"You, Sir. I belong to you."

He smiles wolfishly, pressing the tip of himself just slightly inside, making me whine in need.

"And tell me who this cunt belongs to." He pushes just a tiny bit farther. "Say my name."

"You, Dane," I gasp. "Only you."

In one smooth thrust, he sheaths himself inside my pussy. My mouth parts in a silent cry as he stretches and fills me. He grunts, his body falling forward so our hips are completely flush with each other and his hands brace on either side of my head.

My fingers dig into his hips to hold him in place as his forehead drops to mine. We both still, the importance of the moment freezing us. Our breathing is the only sound in the room, and after a few moments, he lifts his head. "You feel so good, baby."

My fingers flex on his hips, and I swallow back the emotion building in my chest. I've never felt so full, so on fire from the inside out.

"You do, too," I murmur.

He brushes a lock of damp hair from my face before his hips slowly start to move back. I gasp, my fingers digging into his skin again.

"Am I hurting you?" he asks.

"No." I shake my head. "You're a lot, but I like it."

His familiar smirk tugs at his lips before he retorts, "Of course you do."

I pinch his hip, and he growls, a dangerous sound that makes my toes curl. He pulls back, and the sensation of his big dick sliding out of me, the curved tip dragging along my inner walls, has me moaning and lifting my hips up to chase him.

"Sir—" I cry, the last of the word cut off when he pistons his hips forward and thrusts back into me. My body jiggles from the force, and my hands grip his toned ass, holding him to me. "Oh my god!"

"Dane. Call me by my name."

He pulls back against my hands and thrusts again. I swear I can feel his dick in my throat, and while it hurts a bit, I like it and only want more. I dig my blunt nails into his flesh and shift my hips. He tuts, pinching one of my nipples—a warning to behave—as he pulls out and teases my entrance with the head of his cock.

"Dane," I whine. *"Please."*

"Are you going to be a good girl for me?"

I suck my lower lip into my mouth and nod. "Yes, I promise."

He grins and sinks in an inch, then another. My toes curl as he shifts so his lips can brush the crown of my hair before he's nipping at my earlobe.

"Feel that, Lindsey?" he asks as he pushes in another inch until almost half of him has slid in. "That's me inside you, where I belong. Filling you up, owning every inch."

I cry out again as he bottoms out, then sharply thrusts, his chest pressing into mine, our slick bodies hot against each other.

"Yes!" I cry.

He pulls halfway out and pistons in again. My inner walls clench around him, and he grunts. "So fucking tight. So desperate to be full of me, aren't you?"

"Yes—" He thrusts harder again. "Fuck!"

Dane kisses up my jaw, and his fingers brush my throat before he grips it. "Look at me."

My eyes snap to his, and a bead of sweat drips

down his brow. He touches my collar, taking the O-ring and tugging on it so I feel its weight around my neck.

"You're going to touch yourself."

"Y-yes, Dane."

"Show me how good I make my pretty slut come."

My pussy clenches, and I almost tell him I don't need to touch myself to come. His dick is hitting the perfect spot inside me, and he knows exactly what I need.

He ruts into me harder, his thrusts wild, and my back arches off the bed. It takes all my focus to remove my hand from his ass and slide it between us. My fingers find my swollen clit, and Dane seals his lips over mine as I cry out from my touch.

He moans into my mouth, the sound of our skin slapping and the wetness of my pussy only adding to the heat of the moment. He takes me so close to the edge that I begin to see stars forming in my vision. I hold back, my eyes watering from all the sensations.

Dane parts from my lips and tugs again on my collar. "Tell me you're mine while I'm fucking you, Lindsey."

"I'm yours."

"Who's the only one who gets to fuck you?"

"You, Sir."

"Who owns this beautiful body?"

"You!" I cry as his dick hits somewhere inside me that makes my solar plexus sing.

"Say my name, baby."

"You, Dane!"

"That's right." He thrusts. "Come. Give me what's mine."

The stars behind my eyes explode into galaxies as my second orgasm of the night takes over. Every nerve in my body ignites, and my hand between us stills, my other gripping onto Dane as he thrusts until I feel him release inside me. The warmth of him, the fullness I experience as his cum empties into me, is nearly too much. Tears slip from my closed eyes, and Dane's lips are buried against my shoulder, sucking the skin as he comes. I use the last of my strength to clench around his length, and he growls into my neck, biting my skin hard enough that I know there'll be a mark. Good.

At some point, the heat of his body and the buzzing I feel from my orgasm—along with his cock twitching in my pussy—makes me float to the same space I went the last time I was here.

My muscles are complete and utter jelly, and the hand that was holding on to Dane drops to my side. My whole body is fluttering with aftershocks as Dane kisses up my neck, over his collar, until he's lifting off me and cupping my face, wiping at my tears.

"Lindsey," he says quietly. "You still with me?"

My eyes are barely open, but I nod with a sleepy smile. "I'm here."

"Did I hurt you?"

"No, but you split me in two."

He wipes at my wet cheeks with such care that my heart flutters. "Let me put you back together."

The bed shifts, and I almost pull him back, but I have no strength. I close my eyes and float among the clouds until he returns.

It could have been hours, but I'm sure it was only a minute. I shiver when a warm cloth drags over my body, but when he gets to the space between my legs, my eyes snap open, and I grab his wrist. "Leave it."

Dane's hazel gaze is dark and simmering, and

I swear I see his softening cock twitch. "Want to say please?" he warns.

"Please, Sir. *Dane.* Leave it."

He grins and finishes wiping me off, leaving his cum to drip out of my pussy and onto the blanket. I revel in the feeling of his spend, in the aftershocks of my orgasms, and in the lightness of my body. I know I'm going to be sore tomorrow, but right now, I feel better than I ever have in my life.

After he's put the washcloth in the bathroom, Dane returns. He has me drink water then checks over my wrists and nipples before he dims the light and finally settles beside me, pulling me into his arms so my head rests in the space between his arm and his chest.

The quiet of the room and the heat of his body begin to lull me into sleep. It isn't until his lips press to the crown of my head that I look up at him.

His eyes are closed, but I know he's awake. There's a content smile on his lips as his thumb methodically brushes over the skin of my arm. I study the slope of his nose and the colors of his beard, the handsome lines of his masculine jaw and the subtle age marks on his brow. It's a beautiful face. A perfect face. And it's the face of the man I'm in love with.

"Dane," I murmur.

His eyes open, and his gaze finds mine, his brow pinching when he sees the serious look on my face. "Are you okay?" he asks.

For a moment, I hesitate, wondering if it's too soon to say what I'm thinking out loud. But then Dane lifts his other hand and gently hooks his fingers through the O-ring of my collar. The weight of it grounds me like an anchor, and the fear disappears. "I think I love you," I say.

His fingers still on my collar, and his grip on my arm tightens. The concern on his face fades as his lips tip up at the corners.

"You think you love me, or you know?"

My pulse thuds in my ears. "I know."

Dane tugs tighter on my collar then moves so our mouths are nearly touching. "Good." Our noses bump together, and the warmth of his breath ghosts over my lips. "Because I know I love you."

He seals his mouth over mine and pours the words he spoke into me. I thread my fingers into his beard, and I fall into the feeling of him, letting him pull me close so we're molded together, our bodies like one.

I don't know what our future holds. We still have a lot to figure out, obstacles we'll have to face, starting with telling Kas about us. But this is Dane. This is *us*. And I know we'll find a way.

44
Dane

"Axe marks the spot!" Kas cheers loudly as she jumps up and down.

We're in the elementary school's gymnasium for a parents' night, where I've set up some little games for the kids, one of them being the kid-friendly axe throw. I stare at the rubber axe embedded in the target next to another one—it does kind of look like the axes are making an *X* when you stare at it.

"Slay, Chaos Kas."

"OMG." She giggles. "Don't ever say that again."

"Slay or Chaos Kas?"

She rolls her eyes. "Both, Logger Dane."

"I thought you liked that nickname best?"

She sighs, but the smile on her lips tells me she likes it and she's just ribbing me, as she enjoys doing. "At least it's better than Captain Kas."

I ruffle her hair, and she groans but doesn't stop smiling.

It's been about three months since my life-changing night with Lindsey, and since then, things have been good. More than good. So good, in fact, that I'm still getting used to how good things can be. Especially since I've started integrating myself more in Lindsey and Kas's life.

It was a little awkward at first. Lindsey and I haven't had a direct conversation with Kas about how serious things are—serious as in, we're-moving-in-together serious—but she knows her mom and I are "dating." That word feels too small for what we are, but it's the simplest one to use, especially while Kas is still getting used to me.

That said, she's adjusted to me being around a lot easier than I expected. I've watched her on weekends and evenings while Lindsey's worked, and she's even taught me how to play Critter Cove. We also spend our Saturday afternoons together for obstacle course sessions, which have now moved inside, since it's November, and it's getting cold out.

When I called Levi and told him I wanted to continue the course, now on weekends since school is in session, he thought I wanted him to teach it. I told him that I would be the one to do it, and he thought I'd been taken by body snatchers. He asked if it had anything to do with the woman I was seeing, one who happened to be the mom of one of the kids, and while I was annoyed he knew, it wasn't like it was a secret.

I called him not long after I gave Lindsey her training collar. We hadn't exactly been out frolicking like most couples, but we were already the subject of small-town gossip. It's why Lindsey and I decided to tell Kas we were dating not long after that night at my cabin. She deserved to hear it from us, and we didn't want some other kid—or their parents—bringing it up before we had the chance.

"Did you get two bull's-eyes in a row, honey?"

At the sound of Lindsey's voice, the peace I feel when she's at my side returns, and a smile tugs at the corner of my lips. Both Kas and I turn our attention to her as she walks over. She's wearing tight jeans and a thin, green V-neck sweater, and while it's pretty, my eyes go immediately to the delicate necklace I placed around her neck three months ago. It's her day collar, the one she can wear out and about and not cause any heads to turn.

It's a golden choker with two strands. One has a couple of white beads in the middle, and the other has an O-ring that sits perfectly at the center of her throat. I was happy she liked it and agreed to wear it. I prefer the leather one we use when we do a scene, though, which is a rarity lately, since we have Kas and, of course, her job. Not to mention my work.

I may not be a Pro Dom anymore, but I still have my Loopr account, and it's thriving. Lindsey loves that I kept it, especially since all the videos I record are me pretending that I'm speaking to her or involve things she's told me to put online.

She likes that other people drool over what she has, and I can't say that doesn't turn me on, so I've kept up the channel and have been using a lot of the money to fix things in her home. Like staining her private dock on the lake and putting together the loft above her room as a place for Kas to game and Lindsey to read.

Along with the Loopr account, I've been working a few days a week for Fox and Morgan, helping with some reforestation projects, which means I've gotten to know Nathan better, too. I like him. Which is good, since I plan on making him my brother-in-law in the near future.

"I did!" Kas answers Lindsey's question. "I can't wait until I can try with a real axe!"

Lindsey chuckles. "Eventually. But I'd rather you keep all your body parts until you're older."

"Gross, Mom. But Logger Dane won't let me chop off anything. Will you?"

"I won't," I promise.

"See?"

Lindsey laughs again before she looks at me with a smile. I pull her into my side, her body settling against me like a missing puzzle piece. She places her hand over my chest. "I know you won't," she says to me before turning her gaze to Kas, who's smiling the way she does when she wants something, all sweet with big, wide, puppy-dog eyes. "But we've talked about this, Kas. Not until you're older."

She pouts. "How old?"

"I think ten is a good age."

"That's like two years from now!"

"Way less than that. You're going to be nine in January," Lindsey counters.

"But *Mooooooom*," Kas whines.

"But *Kaaaaaaas*," Lindsey parrots.

She huffs, crossing her arms over her chest. "I'm going to ask Dad what he thinks."

Lindsey stiffens in my arms, and I gently rub my thumb over her hip in a calming motion. I've spoken to Lindsey about how much she wants me to interject with Kas when she talks back or is misbehaving. She's said she doesn't mind me laying down the law if I need to, but it's still new territory, and I want to tread lightly. I've been very careful not to overstep so I don't upset Lindsey or Kas. Kas already has a dad, even if said dad is a complete and utter asshole.

I've had the displeasure of meeting Jeremy and his new wife once. Lindsey and I drove Kas to his place, then spent the weekend with her mom a couple of weeks back. Lindsey's mom, I loved. Jeremy is the dictionary version of a weasel.

We didn't speak for long, and thank god for that. Had I listened to him make passive-aggressive digs at Lindsey for another second, I would have knocked him out. Lindsey had to practically drag me away as it was, and I left in a bad mood, one that only Lindsey was able to get me out of later that night by reassuring me that his words didn't hurt her anymore, especially since I'd come into her life.

I'm about to tell Kas to listen to her mom, but Lindsey beats me to it. "I don't care what your dad says; he doesn't have experience with axes or axe throwing."

"No." Kas rolls her eyes like both she and her mother love to do. "Not that dad—Logger Dad."

My hand on Lindsey's hip stills, and she tenses in my arms. I have to admit, of all the funny, sassy, or unexpected things Kas has said, this one has caught me the most off guard. We'd planned to tell her tonight about the move—that I'll be officially living with them, even though I spend most of my time there already. What I haven't told Kas is that I plan to propose to her mom. I was going to ask her this week, when I have her to myself while Lindsey's at work.

I want to make sure she's okay with it, because if I wanted permission from anyone, it'd be Kas, especially given that my relationship with her mom evolved quickly. Quicker than most relationships do. It's a trait Lindsey joked must run in her family, since Nathan fell in love with Fox and Morgan over a snowed-in weekend together. But love, I'm figuring out, rarely makes sense. And trying to make sense of it or control it will drive you crazy. It's better to simply surrender to it.

"Kas," Lindsey whispers. My grip on Lindsey's waist stays firm as I look between them.

Lindsey's brown eyes are watering, and her lips are opening and closing as she tries to find more words.

"What?" Kas asks, as if what she just said wasn't a huge deal. As if I'm not fighting tears of my own.

I never thought someone would call me dad, much less a cool kid like Kas. I always thought she'd continue to call me Logger Dane, no matter the status of my relationship with Lindsey.

"You called Dane Dad."

Kas shrugs, looking between her mom and me. "Is that bad?"

Lindsey shakes her head and kneels in front of Kas so they're at eye level. "It's not bad, honey; we just haven't talked about it."

She shrugs again then looks up at me. "You're always together now, and I overheard Uncle Fox talking to Aunt Morgan. He said you and Mom are like married already or something."

Lindsey's hand moves to her neck, fingering the O-ring on her day collar. Kas doesn't think anything of it, but I know she must be thinking what I am: that Kas overheard Fox talking about Lindsey wearing my collar.

While most people wouldn't know what the

necklace around Lindsey's neck could mean, Fox and Morgan do. There's also the fact that I've recently spoken to Nathan about my desire to propose to Lindsey. That could be a discussion Kas overheard that Lindsey does not know about.

"We're not married yet," I say softly to Kas.

"Oh." Kas pauses to think. "Good, because I want to be there. I was sad I didn't get invited."

Lindsey takes Kas's hands. "Of course you'll be invited. You think I would get married without you there?"

She shrugs. "I don't know. Dad got married to Ava when I wasn't there."

Her words make me feel sick, giving me yet another reason to castrate Jeremy, or hire a "logger hitman" like Lindsey and I joke about.

"Oh, honey. No." Lindsey squeezes her hand. "We would never. If Dane and I decide to get married, you'll be the first to know."

I have the urge to butt in and say that it isn't about deciding we'll get married—simply a matter of when—but I keep my mouth shut, more eager to talk to Kas about marrying her mom now. I think she'll love it even more when I ask her "permission" after hearing all this and seeing how upset it made her. I bet she'll want to be a part of the proposal, too.

"You promise?" Kas asks Lindsey, voice unsure. It makes the anger in my chest worse, because Kas never sounds unsure about anything.

"I promise."

She looks to me, and I smile reassuringly. "I promise, too."

"Okay." She nods, pulling her hands from Lindsey's. Lindsey stands, and I tug her back into my side, ruffling Kas's hair again.

She groans and pushes my hand away, but a smile is now on her face.

"I do have to ask you one thing now, though," I direct at Kas, "if that's alright?"

She puts her hands on her hips and stares seriously at me. "What is it?"

"Yeah, what is it?" Lindsey echoes, looking up to meet my gaze with still-glassy eyes.

"Is it okay if I come live with you both?"

Lindsey's grip on my waist tightens. I know her answer, and I'm glad she doesn't look mad that I asked Kas now instead of later tonight. But this felt like the perfect time, and by the warm upturn of her lips, I know she agrees.

"Don't you live with us already anyway? I saw

Mom folding your underwear the other night." She scrunches up her nose.

Lindsey chokes out a laugh and looks around. Thankfully, there's music playing, and nobody is paying attention to us.

"Kas! You can't say things like that in public."

She rolls her eyes. "I'm just saying. You don't keep underwear at someone's house unless you live there."

"The kid has a point," I add.

Lindsey gently pinches my side, and I cock my eyebrow at her. She'll pay for that later.

She flushes before turning her attention back to Kas. "That may be true in some cases, but he isn't at our home full-time. If he moves in, it will be permanent."

My heart squeezes at her promise, and I kiss the side of Lindsey's head. Kas studies us, looking back and forth between me and her mom. Eventually, she zeros in on me with her hands on her hips, features stern. It makes me think of a cop about to interrogate someone.

"You like my mom, right?"

The conversation we had this past summer comes to mind. It's a conversation I've never forgotten, because Kas is right—if you like someone, you should keep telling them until they're sick of hearing it.

"I do, Kas. I like your mom. I like your mom a lot."

"Do you more than like her?"

My gaze drops to Lindsey, her eyes shining with love. "Yeah, I more than like her."

Lindsey blushes, because she already knew the answer to that. Because I don't tell her I like her every day; I tell her I love her.

"And you like Logger Dane, Mom?"

"Yeah, honey. I more than like him."

Kas continues to scrutinize us. She does that for a moment longer before she nods in a sharp motion. "Okay, then I'll allow it. You can move in. But you'd better not make me eat your weird omelets."

My chest shakes with laughter, and I pull Kas in by the shoulders for a half hug. "I won't."

Kas hugs me back before hugging her mom. She pulls back and puts her hands on her hips. "So can I throw a real axe now, Logger Dad?"

I'll admit, the combination of her puppy-dog eyes with her calling me her own version of dad nearly gets me, but there's no way I'm saying yes. "Like your mom said, not until you're ten."

She groans. "No fair!"

Lindsey sighs, and I kiss her head, enjoying the way we already feel like a family and have for a while now. I've even started attending family dinners alongside them with Fox, Nathan, and Morgan at least once a month. It's taken me some getting used to, being around people all the time, but like I told Lindsey, I find my peace with her. And wherever she and Kas are, I'm happy. It's also nice that I like Fox, Nathan, and Morgan.

On top of that, I'm learning to be more social with people in town. That, I don't like as much, but I'm getting used to it.

"It may not be fair," I tell Kas, "but your mom is right. We don't want you to chop something off or poke your eye out."

"Can't I poke my eye out with a rubber axe, too, if it hits my face just right?"

Lindsey snorts as I purse my lips. Leave it to me to find a family that loves to talk back. Nathan is the same way. I can't deny that I like it, though, especially when Lindsey does it when we're alone.

"Maybe, but only if you're being reckless. Which I know you won't be, since you want to keep throwing axes and practicing for the tournament next month."

She groans, but before she can say anything

back, Moira runs over. "Kas!" The brown-haired girl stops in front of her and grabs her hand. "Max dared Levi to beat his record for how many marshmallows he can fit in his mouth! You have to come see."

"But his mouth is bigger than Max's; of course he's gonna beat him."

Lindsey and I look at each other and grin at her logic. Levi's been helping with the course lately since his leg is out of his cast and he's healing well. While the guy still annoys me most of the time, he's good with kids, and I needed the extra set of hands since more kids have joined the weekend course.

One thing I've learned about him is he likes to take the kids' dares, because it makes them laugh. Last weekend, they dared him to hop like a frog for the whole two hours we were there, and he did. His leg was sore afterward, but he said it was worth it because the kids enjoyed it. So I'm not surprised that he's doing this marshmallow dare now.

"So?" Moira giggles. "It's gonna be hilarious!"

Kas smiles and nods. "Can I go, Mom?"

"Yeah, we'll find you in a few minutes."

Kas starts to run off with Moira, but before she gets too far, she lets go of Moira's hand and runs back to us. I don't know what she's going to do, but then she wraps her arms around my waist and hugs me.

"Just so you know, Logger Dad. I like you, too." She squeezes me one more time and then runs off.

"What about me?" Lindsey calls after her.

Kas stops and rolls her eyes playfully before coming back and hugging Lindsey. "I like you, too, Mom."

Then she takes off with her friend toward where Levi is standing with a bunch of kids and some parents around him. I have no idea where he got marshmallows for this dare, but I'm not going to ask.

Lindsey clears her throat to get my attention. "Well, that was..."

"...unexpected?" I answer as I pull her into me so her arms wrap behind my neck and our bodies meld together. I don't care that there are other parents around or that they're probably watching us like hawks, since we're still the hot gossip until something better comes along.

"Yeah. Are you okay?" she asks.

"Why wouldn't I be?"

"That was a lot, but you handled it well."

I take one of my hands and bring it up to finger the delicate O-ring of her choker. "You're mine, Lindsey. Kas…she may not be mine by blood, but she's…" I look over to where she's smiling and laughing with her friends. "She's mine, too. You know I'll do anything for the both of you. For our family."

Lindsey swallows, her eyes watering again. "How the hell did I find a man like you, Logger Dane?"

"It's Logger Dad now," I tease, brushing my fingers up her neck until I'm wiping away a single tear. "But you watched my videos, thought I was hot, and drunk-emailed me."

Lindsey laughs and swats my chest. I grab her hand and kiss her palm before pulling her in for a kiss. It's short and sweet, nothing beyond PG, but a kid running by yells out "Ew!" making us pull away with a laugh.

"Later," I murmur low in her ear. "After I remind you what happens when you misbehave."

"Misbehave?"

"I think I remember someone pinching me."

Mischief flashes in her eyes. "Is that a threat?"

I grip her chin and tut. "No, baby. It's a promise."

Epilogue

Lindsey

Two years later

My heart pounds in my ears—*boom, boom, boom*—matching the sound of Dane's—my Sir's—footsteps walking toward me across the wood floor.

He stops directly behind my form, which is fully nude, save my leather collar, and the hair on the back of my neck stands on end. No matter how many times I've kneeled in this position, how many times I've waited for him in our bedroom with my head down, knees spread, and palms up, it always feels the same.

Exciting. Safe. Like home.

"Someone's been a naughty wife." Sir's deep voice rumbles, sending a shiver up my spine. Not only from the devilish tease in his tone but also because I love it when he calls me his wife—almost as much as when he calls me his. It makes my insides melt and flip in a way I'll never get used to.

His fingers brush over the top of my head. My hair is down and slightly curled, as he likes best. He walks in front of me, and his strong fingers grip my chin, lifting my gaze to meet his. His hazel irises are warm and steady with a sparkle of mischief in them. It's a look I've come to know well: one that means I'm in for a night of pain and pleasure. My favorite.

He strokes my chin. "So pretty like this," he murmurs. "Too bad kneeling won't get you out of your punishment."

My pulse spikes, and I wet my dry lips.

"Tell me," he continues. "What did you do today that displeased me?"

"I talked back when you asked me if I had done my morning routine and I hadn't."

"Hmm." He traces my lower lip with his thumb. "You did. And why did you do that?"

Embarrassment burns through me, hot and heavy in my lower belly. I naturally try to look down, but his grip on my chin stops me.

"Tell me," he commands sharply.

I swallow hard. "I—I don't know, Sir."

His mouth curves into a slow, dangerous smile. It's the kind that makes my core clench and my pussy wet.

"You don't know?"

I swallow again and shake my head.

"I see." He pulls his hand back, and I keep my eyes on him since he didn't tell me to look down. He looks near menacing in his black slacks and black button-up, the attire he likes to wear when we're doing a scene.

Dane puts his hands in his pockets. "Do you want to know what I think?"

"Yes, Sir."

"I think that you wanted my attention," he says, almost amused. "That you're a needy wife who missed her husband's hand."

"Yes, Sir," I say, not denying it because... he's right. He usually is. I *do* want his attention. I've been craving his touch, his control, the grounding presence our scenes give me.

Life's been hectic lately. We still have sex, we still care for each other daily, but we haven't had time for real scenes, the kind that center us in our dynamic. The kind where I'm his and he's mine in a way only a submissive and Dominant can be.

Over the last two years, Dane and I have shaped our D/s relationship into something that truly fits us. He gave me my permanent collar on our honeymoon six months ago, and since then, our connection has only deepened.

He's my Dominant, and I'm his submissive, but not every moment of every day. We're partners first. We've created a structure that allows us to be everything else life demands: parents, professionals, and people who sometimes just need to rest.

Still, our dynamic is always present, woven into the fabric of our lives like a thread we can pull tight when we need it. Small rituals keep us grounded: our routines, the way he reminds me to drink water, how I kneel beside the bed for our Sunday check-ins. Even when we're not in a scene, that trust and structure is always between us.

To the outside world and to Kas, Dane and I look like any other married couple. And in many ways, we are. But beneath that, there's intention in how we move through our life together. Beyond the check-ins and routines that keep our dynamic alive, there are other, subtle ways I serve him, and countless ways he shows up for me. He takes care of Kas and me in every way that matters. He's renovated our home, stepped in as a steady provider—something that took me time to adjust to after so many years of doing it alone—and he's become the kind of "Logger Dad" Kas brags about at school.

With his support, I was able to cut down on hours at the hospital over the years and spend more time with Kas, something not only I needed, but she needed, too. Dane, for lack of a better word, is perfect. He doesn't like when I say that, but to me, he is. He's the man of my dreams, and I find so much joy and happiness in what we've built together.

The only downside to the life we've created is our lack of alone time. Kas has gotten very into axe throwing, and we've been entering her in some competitions for kids that take us all over the place. Then there's the fact that she loves having friends over, and we've also got her school projects and other activities. It's a lot, and by the time our heads hit our pillows at night, Dane and I are exhausted. The last time we had a good scene was weeks ago now, and I need him. So yes, now that I think about it, I did act out this morning on purpose.

Sir hums, and my mind focuses back on him along with my gaze.

"And now you're going to get it, aren't you?" he asks.

I nod quickly, my cheeks burning.

Dane takes his hand from his pocket and brings it to my lips, this time palm open. "Kiss it, and ask me nicely."

Arousal coils low in my stomach. "Please, Sir, may I have your hand?"

He toys with the silver ring of my collar, as he likes to do. This permanent collar has a heart-shaped ring instead of a circle. "Since you said please."

He snaps his fingers and points to the bed. "Get into position, hands flat on the bed."

Anticipation surges through me, and I stand with an ease that can only come from practice. Sir walks to our dresser, but I don't pay attention to him, knowing I'll take whatever he's going to give me. I reach our mattress, the one I covered with a waterproof blanket, and get into the position he taught me early on in our relationship.

I lie on my stomach, right cheek against the mattress and hands flat on the bed so my forearms bracket my head. I arch my back as best I can so my ass is up and my legs are spread, putting the pussy he owns on display for him. The cool air of the room ghosts over my heated skin, and my inner thighs are already wet from arousal.

When I'm in position, Sir walks back over. He makes sure to stand where I can see him, and my pussy gets wetter when I note what he's holding. The thrusting/vibrating butt plug, lube, and a paddle I got him for his birthday last year. It has BRAT etched in it, and it leaves the word imprinted on my skin for a brief time.

His curved smile has my muscles tensing. He doesn't say anything as he lays the paddle near my head, leaving the plug and lube in his hands.

"Safe word?" he asks.

"Red."

"Good girl." He holds up the plug so I can see it better. We've used it before, and I've taken his dick in my ass many times over in the last two years, but I know when he puts that in, it's going to make my spanking extra impactful. Not to mention, he likes to fuck me with it inside me, especially since it can thrust and vibrate at the same time.

"I'm going to put this in, and you're going to take it, do you understand?"

"Yes, Sir."

He nods and steps behind me. I exhale to relax my buzzing body, and when his warm, strong hand slides over the flesh of my ass, I sigh in relief. I needed his touch more than I needed air.

"I'm going to give you exactly what you need, baby," Sir says as he continues to stroke my skin. "I'm going to take care of you."

The bridge of my nose stings, and I nod into the mattress. I don't know if he sees it or not, but he knows those words mean everything to me.

His hand glides down my spine before he takes his touch away. A second later, cool lube is squirted between my ass cheeks, and he opens me up with one hand while the other brings the rounded silicone edge of the plug to my tight ring of muscle. Sir is quiet while he plays, dipping the tip in and out, teasing me as he always does.

My body tenses when the tip slips further in. "Breathe. You can take it. It's not even close to the size of my dick."

His very "Dane" comment has me smiling into the mattress, but it does the trick. I release a breath, and he slips the plug farther in, gently kneading my ass cheek as he does.

"That's it. I love watching your greedy hole take my plug."

I moan and push my ass back. His devious chuckle meets my ears as he adds more lube before twisting the toy around in circles, stretching me until I'm relaxed enough for him to push it all the way in. The moment it settles, the burn and stretch makes me whine. Sir praises me again and taps the broad end of the toy before playing with my ass some more.

He spreads my cheeks and kneads them, digging his nails in hard then pulling back. My pussy gets wetter the more he plays, and mixed with the burning sensation from the plug, I'm a live wire. I've been with him long enough to know he's doing it on purpose so my body is overly sensitive and I feel the impact of his coming strikes deeply and fully.

"Hmm," he says. "So pretty." His hand comes down on my ass, and I clench around the plug. It wasn't a strong hit but a promise of what's to come.

Sir rubs over where he just smacked. "You get restless when you don't feel my hand on you, don't you?"

"Yes, Sir." I moan when he plays with the plug. He hasn't turned on the vibration or the thrusting yet, but I know they're coming.

"You need my rules, my discipline," he continues. "You need the reminder of who you belong to."

"I do, Sir." I moan again as he twists the plug.

"Then let me remind you." His palm comes down on my ass, and my hips thrust toward the bed as I bite my lower lip to keep from crying out.

Dane must see it because he moves, leaning on the bed so he can run his finger over my lip, pulling it from my teeth. "No need for that. We're all alone, and I want to hear your sweet cries. If I didn't, I would have gagged you." He taps my cheek and stands up straight, moving behind me again.

"Ten spanks by my hand," he decrees. "Then we'll do five with the paddle. You'll count each one."

"Yes, Sir."

His hands rub over my ass cheeks, playing with me again, building me up by squeezing and tickling my skin. He does it over and over until I almost sass him to get on with it, but then he taps the button on the plug. At the same time the vibration and first small thrust penetrate my tight back entrance, Sir strikes.

"One!" I cry.

"Good girl." He taps the button on the plug again, and the thrusts in my ass become faster. I grip the blanket in my hands, and he spanks me a second time, this time harder and on the same spot as before.

"Two!"

He drags his hands over the flesh and toys with me, his finger gliding over the top of the plug before he reaches my pussy. He dips his finger inside me, and my eyes burn with an unsatisfied need.

"My eager slut, dripping for her husband's dick already." He spanks me a third time, and I cry out my count before he says, "Too bad you were naughty, or I'd already be balls deep inside my needy wife's cunt."

His palm strikes, this time in an upward movement. I hardly have the fifth count out before he spanks me again, then again, harder each time, alternating cheeks. By the time he finishes the tenth spank, I know my skin is red, and my eyes are burning with tears.

My husband pauses and admires his work,

fingers tracing over the areas he hit. "Fuck, baby, I love seeing you all marked up."

"Sir," I whine as he taps the butt plug so it slows down, thrusting and vibrating at random intervals.

"Yes?" he asks cheekily.

"Please, I want more."

He grips my ass cheeks, and I whimper into the mattress.

"You crave my paddle? Or do you want more of my hand?"

"Paddle, Sir. Please." My glassy eyes observe the wooden implement that's been lying by my head on purpose, the side that says BRAT facing me.

He picks it up and holds it to my lips. I kiss it without him needing to tell me to. I've learned in our years of play that it's his way of asking for consent, even if I'm asking him to do something to me in the first place.

"Fuck, baby. I like when you ask me nicely for what you want."

His praise fills my chest, and my fingers grip more firmly on the blanket in anticipation of the pain. There was a time, when I first became his submissive, when I wasn't sure if I'd like the pain from a paddle, and I don't think I would if it were administered by anyone but Dane. He always knows how to make it good for me, when I've had just enough or need more.

I've built up my tolerance and discovered that I find peace and grounding in being disciplined, which is why I'm here right now. Submitting to him and his punishment reconnects us. And like he said, it reminds me that I'm his.

"Remember, we'll do five. No more than that."

"Yes, Sir."

He drags his hand down my spine then over the heated skin of my ass. The plug is still thrusting and vibrating inside me at its sporadic pace.

"Relax, baby. You know it hurts more if you're tense."

I exhale and sink into the mattress. Not a moment later, the first strike hits my left ass cheek. Pain flares on the already sparking skin, sending pleasure to my core and tearing a cry from my lips.

"One!"

"Perfect," Sir praises. I hardly have time to register his praise before he strikes my right cheek. My cry is hoarse as I count, and a tear slips down my face. "I love seeing what you are on your skin. My brat." He paddles me lower this time, near where my ass and thigh meet.

My hips thrust forward, and I choke on the number three. His hand brushes down my back, and he soothes me with his praise, telling me how much he loves me and how well I'm taking his punishment.

When the fourth one hits, I sob into the mattress, releasing any and all of life's frustrations that have built up since our last scene.

"Hush, now; you have one left. Can you take it? Can you do one more for me?"

His hand caresses my back, then trails down to my ass, tracing the letters now imprinted on my skin. I suck in a breath and surrender to the pain, surrender to his touch.

His fingers trail to my pussy and then to my clit, circling it gently. "Tell me, Lindsey. What do you want?"

"One more, Sir. Please." My voice is soft yet somehow strong. I know I can take one more. I know I can please him.

"Such a pain slut, aren't you?"

"Yes, Sir."

His fingers dip inside my pussy, and I moan into the mattress, but as soon as they're there, they're gone. I know what's coming next—I don't have to see him to know. I exhale just as the paddle strikes me for the fifth and last time, my ass jiggling from the force, and my hips thrusting into the edge of the bed.

I expel a cry loud enough that I swear the trees shake outside, but the strike of the paddle is quickly replaced by Dane's soothing touch and his praise. I smile as I float in what I now know as subspace. In this place, I only exist for my Sir. I'm completely in submission and am no longer thinking about what I need to do or anything in the outside world, just him and the space we've created together.

His touch on my smarting skin shifts lower until he's playing with my pussy again. I'm so wet, you'd think I'd come already, but I haven't. He hums low in his chest, fingers slipping inside and curving until he hits my G-spot.

"So wet for me baby," he growls, "so tight." He punctuates his comment by gently squeezing my ass and adding a third finger, stretching me.

"Sir," I moan. "Please, Sir."

His fingers stop, and all I feel is the weight of them inside me alongside the butt plug still thrusting in my ass. "Please, what?"

"I need your dick, Sir. I need you to fuck me."

He chuckles darkly. "I know, baby." His fingers curl and rub against my G-spot again, this time in a faster and firmer motion. "But I'm playing."

I groan, and he gently pinches my sore ass, making me buck forward. "Remember who's in charge here."

Sir thrusts his fingers deeper inside, swirling them around, pulling them out and pushing them back in so I can hear the sound of my arousal.

"This body," he says, "is mine."

His fingers thrust faster, and I whimper.

"I own it, and I can do whatever I want with it. Isn't that right?"

"Yes, Sir." I moan as he clicks the thrusting plug back to the higher setting. "Tell me who gets to decide how it's used?"

"You, Sir."

"Who gets to decide when it comes?"

"You, Sir."

"When it hurts?"

"You, Sir."

"When it's fucked?"

"You, Sir."

"Good girl. Now go to the middle of the bed, and humble yourself."

I don't waste any time getting into what he taught me is the "humble" pose. My head is down, forehead on the mattress, ass in the air with knees open and arms in front of me, palms down so I can use my hands and forearms to support me.

I can't see Dane like this, but I hear the rustle of his clothes and the snap of his belt as he removes it from his slacks. I imagine him folding his shirt and his pants as he likes before standing back to admire my body, which he calls beautiful every day, often multiple times a day.

Eventually, his steps move across the wood floor, and the mattress dips from the weight of him as he gets behind me. He runs his hands up the back of my trembling thighs, opening them wider so he fits between them.

"My beautiful wife." He trails his finger through the wetness on my thigh. "My sexy fucktoy."

I groan, more arousal flooding me as he dips two fingers inside me again, and I clench around them. He laughs softly but adds a third finger, scissoring them and stretching me.

"My pretty little pain slut."

The hand not inside me scrapes over my abused

skin before he taps the butt plug to the highest setting. The sensations have my eyes watering and a whine erupting from deep in my chest.

"I can feel it thrusting and buzzing," he comments, emphasizing his point by rubbing his fingers against the barrier between my ass and pussy. "You want me to fuck you while this toy fucks your ass, baby?"

"Yes, Sir. Please."

"Hmm." He thrusts his fingers deeper. "Then that's what we'll do. I think my good wife deserves a reward for her submission."

"Please," I whimper.

Dane's fingers leave my fluttering pussy, and the bed shifts beneath me. I only have a moment to miss his touch before one of his large hands grips my waist, and I feel the broad head of his cock at my entrance. He toys with me, sliding it up and down my slit, lubricating himself with my wetness. I'm about to plead, to beg, to say I'll do anything for more when he finally has mercy on me.

In one thrust, Dane sheaths his cock inside me, the force of his hips pressing my forehead into the mattress and my chest down so my hard nipples rub against the blanket.

"Goddamn, baby." He pulls out then thrusts back in. "This cunt was made to be mine."

I lose all ability to speak at the feeling of his dick inside me along with the plug thrusting and vibrating in my ass. It's so much, almost *too* much, but it feels good, and I'm so full. And I know it feels good for Dane, too.

When I adjust, I grip the sheet and whimper, wanting more. I push my butt back against him, and he responds by gently slapping it. The combination of the new sting atop his earlier punishment makes me scream.

"That's it, let me hear how good I make you feel."

"Sir!" I cry as he thrusts harder, both of his hands gripping my hips and pulling me closer to him, giving me the deep sensation I wanted. He knows I like when he's rough, when I can feel him in my throat and I'm sore for days. He knows I need to feel him now more than ever, that I want to be reminded that I'm his.

"What do you need?"

"Harder," I moan.

He growls and leans forward, his cock penetrating even deeper. He alternates between short, hard thrusts and longer strokes, driving me crazy.

"God, the vibrations," he moans. "Feels so good."

His hips slap against my ass, and my eyes roll back into my head.

"Up on your hands," he barks.

I'm nearly too far gone to listen to his command, but somehow, I manage. Once there's space between me and the bed, Dane wraps his strong arm under me and pulls me up. I let out a noise of surprise as he holds me to his chest, forearm banded around my breasts so I'm secure. He kisses the skin of my neck above my collar, his breath short against my cheek from exertion. The new position makes my pussy tighter, and I have to clench my ass to keep the toy from falling out.

"Perfect," he mutters against my ear. He moves his hand to my throat, squeezing it just enough to cut off a bit of air but so I can still speak.

Thrust. "Who do you belong to?"

"You, Sir."

Thrust. "Are you going to be a good girl from now on?"

"Yes."

Dane laughs. "I doubt it."

I smile, because he's right. But my husband loves my bratty side, even when it annoys him.

He nips at my earlobe and punches his hips

up before he moves the hand on my waist to my clit. I cry out, and he grips my throat harder, pressing my collar into my skin.

"I'm gonna come, baby. Come with me."

He circles my clit continually. The pressure in my lower belly pulls tight like a bowstring, and my eyes prickle with tears at the intensity of all the sensations.

"Come," Sir growls.

My body submits, and I fall apart. My pussy clenches around his cock, and Dane's thrusts turn shallow, though his grip on my body remains strong and steady. I feel him coming before I register his own groans of pleasure, his cum warming my insides and filling me up like I love.

For what feels like forever, I float and fall, basking in the feeling of being held, being loved, being owned by a man like Dane. My Dom. My Sir. My husband.

When his cock is spent and my aftershocks have subsided, I realize that Dane clicked off the plug at some point. He holds me to him, catching his breath, before he kisses my cheek and gently lowers me down to the bed, making sure I'm okay.

When he tries to leave to get some water and a cloth to clean me up, I stop him, wanting him to hold me longer. He gives me what I want and holds me closer.

With his dick still inside me and the plug filling me up, I revel in the feeling of it all. Dane grips me around the waist, tangling his legs with mine until there's no telling where I end and he begins.

I lift my chin to meet his gaze. His eyes are soft with what I can only call awe, and his skin is flushed and sweaty. I don't need to ask him to kiss me; he already knows it's what I want. Our lips meet in a lazy and slow dance, one filled with all the promises we've made to each other in the time we've been together, both when he first collared me and again when we married and graduated to a permanent collar.

To guide, protect, and love.

"I love you, Lindsey," he echoes my thought as we pull apart.

"I love you, too, Dane."

He kisses the tip of my nose, his eyes reverent as he says, "Rest; I'll take care of you."

You already do.

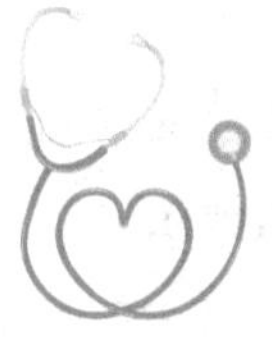

BONUS CHAPTER
Climb My Pole

Lindsey

This time last year, I was exhausted and horny, and my life was a mess. Now, I may be tired—because what mom and woman in her thirties isn't—but I'm not dead on my feet. More importantly, my life is no longer a mess. My finances are in order, my ex is paying child support, and I'm working less at the ER. That means I get time to not only spend time with my daughter, Kas, and my family, but to rest.

I look through the crowd of people at this year's annual Logger Games, recently renamed from the Lumberjack Games due to my amazing daughter having a discussion with Morgan about making it inclusive for all, and find the man responsible for the changes in my life.

Dane's in his speed pole climbing gear standing next to his friend and fellow logger Levi. He's been coaching the younger man the last few months so he doesn't break his leg again like he did last year. I trail my gaze down his tall and well-muscled body, licking my lips at how good he looks. I didn't think seeing him in long shorts and a tank top with high socks and climbing boots would do it for me, but my god, does he look like a snack. I'm glad he changed when he got here, or I don't think I would have let him out of the house—competition be damned.

"Stop drooling, you're grossing me out."

I huff a laugh and turn to glare at my brother Nathan. "This is payback for all the times you've drooled over Fox and Morgan in front of me."

He rubs his thumb and pointer finger over his beard, brown eyes that match mine amused. "Okay, fair. But I don't have my lumbersnacks to drool over right now, so it feels slightly unfair."

I laugh again. "You'll see them soon enough."

"Hopefully, they'll be back soon; I know they wanted to watch."

Fox and Morgan's company, Starlight Lumber

& Logging, run this event, which means while it's happening they're always being called somewhere to help with something. Nathan helps, since it's basically his company now, too, but since Kas is at Jeremey's this weekend, he's supporting Dane with me at the Speed Pole Climbing Competition, where we're hoping he'll win for the sixth year in a row. Nathan's going to film it on his phone so Kas can watch later.

The sound of a chime over the PA system draws my attention back to Dane. His hazel gaze, which I could stare into for hours, isn't focused on Levi anymore, but on me. We may be a good distance apart, but I feel like I'm right in front of him. The crowd fades, and I hardly hear the man over the speaker saying it's time for the competitors to take their places at their poles.

My hand automatically reaches up to touch my day collar around my neck, the golden O-ring on a double golden chain warm due to the heat of my skin on this hot July day. The corner of his mouth lifts, eyes simmering with the promise of time alone later. Time where he's my Dom, and I'm his—no responsibilities or possibilities of Kas bursting into our bedroom to disrupt us.

My heartbeat quickens, and I smile softly

back at him. We've only been together for a year, but within that year, he's become my everything. Not only my Dom, but my loving fiancé, my best friend, confidant, the man I rely on to hold me up when life gets to be too much. He's become a second dad to Kas, someone she can count on to help her with her homework and teach her how to axe throw. He's even promised to teach her how to speed climb when she's a bit older. He's also a friend to Nathan and his partners, and my mom loves him. Truly, he's the best thing that's ever happened to me, and he tells me every day that I'm the best thing to happen to him.

I mouth the words *I love you* just before he's jarred away from my field of vision, breaking the spell we were under. I blink and find Levi tugging an annoyed Dane toward his assigned pole. Dane looks over his shoulder again and mouths *I love you* back before he gives his attention to the competition.

"That was sweet." Nathan bumps my shoulder.

"I thought it was gross."

He shrugs. "Just the sexy eyes, but that was sweet. I like seeing my sister in love; it looks good on you."

"Thanks." I blush. Nathan opens his mouth

to speak again but then his eyes catch something, and it's his turn to blush. I know before I've even looked who he's spotted.

Fox and Morgan make their way through the competition area. They're easy to spot, given their tall stature and tattoos. I smile when I see their gazes locked on Nathan and elbow my brother in the arm.

"Now who's being gross?"

He laughs. "We're being sweet."

"Yeah, right." I look back to Fox, who's licking his lips, and Morgan, who's smirking. I swear, the three of them have some sort of telepathy—a throuple connection. They say dirty things to each other with just their eyes. But according to Nathan, Dane and I are no different. Yet, I don't think we're as bad as these three.

The two approach, greeting me before standing on the other side of Nathan.

"Glad you were able to make it in time," I say.

"Us, too. There was a mini fire at the funnel cake stand," Morgan laughs.

"What?!" Nathan and I both exclaim.

"It was small; all good now," Fox assures us.

"Nobody was hurt?" Nathan asks, looking his partners over.

Fox and Morgan shake their heads, amusement sparkling in their eyes.

"We're good, Wolfie. Don't worry." Morgan pecks his cheek.

I turn back to the poles, ignoring all the competitors except for Dane. The announcer gives a ninety-second warning, and my heart thuds in my ears with excitement. I've seen Dane train for this, but this is the first time I've watched him compete. I won't lie and say I'm not nervous, since Levi broke his leg last year, but I trust Dane, and he's done this many times before. I have no doubt he'll win again; it's just who he is.

Nathan bounces next to me. "Oh, this is so cool. It's fun knowing someone who is competing."

The announcer begins to count down from ten, and I grip the ring of my collar. Dane is fully focused on this task. He's already rechecked his harness, and I can see his muscles flex even at this distance. I swallow hard, my gaze traveling up his arms to his strong hands gripping the rope he uses to climb the pole. I'd be a liar if I said I'm not imagining those hands gripping my hips as he pounds into me.

I blink and bite my lip. Now is not the time to think about that. With Kas out of town until tomorrow, we'll have plenty of time for that tonight—but not right now.

"Competitors ready?" the announcer calls out. "Three—"

I hold my breath as they count down and grip my necklace tighter.

"Two—"

Nathan grips my elbow, and I think my heart stops beating.

"One—go!"

Dane explodes from the ground, and cheers around us erupt. I scream his name before I even tell my brain to do it, yelling at him to go as hard and as fast as he can. Nathan and Morgan join in while Fox makes a loud wolf whistle.

"Come on, baby, come on!" I yell louder as he gets halfway up the pole. I have no idea how the other competitors are doing or if anyone is even close to catching him, because I can't take my eyes off him.

I know his body is strong and powerful—he works hard for it—but to see him in action, climbing up a ninety-foot pole using a rope, climbing spurs, and his body is incredibly impressive. His muscles work, calves and biceps flexing, and with each foot he places on the wood, he climbs higher and higher.

"He's doing it!" Nathan shakes me while holding his phone in his other hand. "He's going to win again!"

"Of course he is," is all I say.

The moment he hits the finish line at the top of the pole, my heart bursts with joy, and I cry out in happiness with the people around me.

"He won!" Morgan cheers.

"Beat himself again by a fraction of a second," Fox adds.

Dane drops down the pole at lightning speed, and the moment his feet hit the pad around the bottom, my feet are moving.

"Linds!" Nathan calls. But I don't stop. I don't care if I look like a lunatic or if I'm breaking rules. Fox and Morgan sponsor this whole event, so people can kiss my ass.

I lift up the rope barricade and ignore someone asking me where I'm going. Dane is already unclipping all his gear when he turns and makes eye contact with me. He drops his rope and takes off his harness before he jumps down off the mat to the ground. He keeps his eyes up as he bends down, taking off his spurs. I can feel people watching me as I run to him, but I don't care.

I'm a woman possessed, and the desire to jump into his arms and kiss the hell out of him like a main character in a rom-com is too strong to ignore. He stands to his full height and opens his arms right as I jump up, wrapping my arms around his neck and my legs around his waist. He catches me with no hesitation, lips sealing over mine as his hands grip my bottom, plastering our bodies together.

A year ago, I would have never done this. Never felt comfortable enough to participate in such a public display of affection that I initiated, but with Dane—it feels right. Perfect, even. Everyone in town may know he's already mine, but now I've claimed him for all to see. Cheers and wolf whistles reach my ears, and I know it's because of our kiss, but I'm too focused on the way my man's lips feel against mine, and how he smells of woods and the saltiness of sweat, to care.

Dane's tongue licks at my lips and I let him in, the taste of him exploding across my taste buds. He's normally the one to dominate our kisses, but he lets me take control of this one. I'm gripping my legs tighter around him, trying to pull him closer into me, when the sound of a horn makes me jump. Dane chuckles against my lips and pulls away, dropping his forehead to mine.

"Now that's what I call a reward, ladies and gentlemen. Let's hear it for our winner for the sixth year in a row, Dane Woods!" the announcer calls over the speakers, more cheers and whistles exploding around us, bringing me fully back to reality.

"Oh my god," I huff out. "Did I really just do that?"

Dane nods against my forehead before lowering me to the ground. I expect him to wave to the crowd or something, but instead he takes my hand and tugs me behind him. I keep my eyes lowered as we walk past volunteers and other climbers, skin burning pink. I don't look up until the sounds of the crowd have faded and Dane pulls me into a small tent that hardly fits us both, dropping the flap behind us. It's meant for people to change in if they don't want to use the big tents with other competitors. It's dark and hot, but it's as private as we can get here.

He lifts up my chin with his fingers, my eyes meeting his. The corner of his mouth is lifted into a smirk, and his pupils are dilated, the black taking over the hazel irises.

"Don't you ever be embarrassed to love me out loud, baby. Do you understand?"

I swallow hard, not expecting his words to bring up such emotion. It's times like these that solidify that I chose the right man to be in my life after my ex. Dane loves me, all of me, and he wants the world to know he's mine just as much as I am his.

"I do," I reply, unable to respond with any other words.

He strokes my chin. "Now"—he leans in to brush his lips over mine—"I would like to claim my reward."

I clear my throat, cheeks burning again. "More than a very public kiss?"

He nods. "Think you can be quiet while I taste you, baby?"

My pussy clenches, and I nod. I don't actually know if I can be quiet, but my core is throbbing. The only reason I'm not dry humping him is because he's holding my chin.

He nips at my lower lip. "Good girl."

He drops to his knees before me, the low light

of the tent making his dark silver hair near black. His fingers curl under the waistband of my shorts and I've never been gladder I chose to wear my ones with the elastic band today. He easily pulls them down along with my underwear until they're at my ankles but doesn't remove them completely. He shoves my feet as wide as they can go and before I can blink, his hot mouth is on me.

I cry out and grip his short hair, nails digging into his scalp. I feel the hum of Dane's chuckle against my already swollen clit and know it's because I just said I'd be quiet, but his mouth feels too good to not make any noise.

He circles his tongue over the bundle of nerves several times before sucking it into his mouth. I grip his hair tighter, shoving his face further into my pussy. He doesn't try to pull back; instead, he suctions my clit harder. I bite my lower lip hard enough that I think I might break the skin, but I don't cry out again.

The sensation of pleasure builds in my body as the man I love, the man who willingly gets on his knees for me in the middle of the tiny tent after he just did something incredible, makes my legs shake and my skin burn hot.

His hands grip my ass, dragging me closer

yet. I would have fallen forward had I not been holding on to him. He moans into my sex, licking and sucking every inch of me, lapping me up until I feel myself on the brink of an orgasm.

"Dane!" I cry.

He stops his onslaught, pulling back against my hands. My release teeters on the edge, and I curse under my breath. He gently smacks my ass, looking up at me with wet lips and my arousal marking his dark beard.

"Since you can't be quiet, cover that mouth, baby."

He doesn't give me a chance to respond; instead, he dives back in like a starving man. I keep one hand gripped on his hair while I bring my other up to cover my mouth. He holds me to him so I remain standing, lips and tongue doing wicked things to my clit. The orgasm that almost happened before builds back quickly, warmth pooling in my lower stomach and electricity sparking through my veins.

I cry out against my hand, holding him on my clit as he suctions it into his mouth and his blunt fingernails dig into my ass.

He releases it a moment later and growls, "Come for me."

The tip of one of his fingers presses to my back entrance, and he sucks at my clit, the dual sensations forcing me to fall over the edge.

I scream into my hand like he knew I would, legs shaking as my release floods my body like a tidal wave. Dane holds me to him as I come, my hips riding his mouth as he slowly licks at my pulsing clit, prolonging my orgasm for as long as he can.

Minutes, or maybe it was only seconds later, Dane pulls back. He waits until my legs are steady then tugs up my underwear and shorts before standing. He brushes a lock of damp hair behind my ear and kisses me gently, the smell of me on his beard and his lips plump.

"You're beautiful," he says.

"You're not so bad yourself, six-time Speed Pole Climbing Champion."

He blushes. My giant, often serious Dom and gorgeous fiancé blushes. I love it.

"Did I tell you congratulations yet?" I ask.

"I think your public kiss said it all."

Now I'm the one who's back to blushing. Especially since now, we can add semi-public orgasm to the list of what happened today. "Think anyone heard me?"

"If they did, they're lucky."

I flush a deeper pink and shake my head at him, wiping off his beard as best I can. "Come on, let's go home and get cleaned up."

"What about Fox, Nathan, and Morgan?"

"We'll text them and let them know we need to reschedule."

"Really?" He smirks. "Someone anxious to start our alone time?"

"You bet." I nip at his lips and smirk back. "I've got my own speed pole climbing competition to take part of."

I pull back and open up the tent flap, the midday sun streaming in. My eyes meet Dane's, and he's smiling at me, his eyes warm and full of love. I know that's what mine look like, too.

"Well." I hold out my hand. "You coming?"

"Always, baby." He tugs me back into him. "But just so you know. Nothing about climbing my pole will be fast."

I cackle with laughter and tug him from the tent, ignoring anyone around us as I pull him toward the parking lot and back to our home.

Acknowledgments

I'm crying happy tears, because I love this book SOOO much, and I know many of you waited for a long time to read it. I hope you enjoyed it as much as I did writing it and that it was worth the wait!

Axe Marks the Spot is also my first book that was fully traditionally published by Forever, and for that, I'm so grateful. This was made possible because of my amazing agent, Jill Marr, my editor, Sabrina Flemming, and, of course, Hachette Publishing Group. Thanks for making a big dream come true.

Now, I want to take a moment to thank the people who made another book possible. My besties Nicole Reeves, Elliott Rose, Bailey Hannah, and M.A. Wardell—you're always in my corner, cheering me on and brainstorming with me. Truly, I can't thank you enough. LOOK AT WHAT WE DID?!

Special shoutout to Siân (@booksofaginger) for helping with the original plot of this book with me. Like always, I changed it a million times, but thank you for being my sounding board. I truly appreciate our sessions together. Love you!

Big, big thank you to my alpha, beta, and sensitivity readers who helped me with all of the kink and D/s dynamics of this book: Kasandra, Heather, Alexandra, Jennifer, Stephanie, Tamara, Allie, Rachel, and Jess. I also have to give a huge thanks to my friend and fellow author Jillian Graves—you made this book even better!

As always, I can't forget to thank my editor who did the first pass, Mason Frey, my cover artist, Brenna Jones, and of course, my Smut Obsessed and Smut VIP House of Smut members on Patreon—you know who you are. Thank you so much for your love and continued support! I'll be forever grateful to you always.

And most importantly, to my family—my mom Linda, my dad Randy, my sister Tanya, and my grandma Darlene—none of this would be possible without your support, patience, and constant encouragement. I love you so very much.

Until next time...

Xoxo,
Kayla

About the Author

KAYLA GROSSE, author of the international bestseller *Trick Shot: A Spicy Christmas Novella* and a collection of sweet and spicy plus-size romances, grew up in a suburb of Madison, Wisconsin. Though she lived near a big college town, her backyard was a cornfield, and her favorite hobby was riding her horse and imagining herself flying through the fields with a cape on her back and a sword in her hand. Her overactive imagination led to writing lots of fanfiction and scripts, and publishing several books.

When not writing, Kayla can often be found riding horses or drinking fancy espresso. She lives in California with her cockatiel, Fiyero, and Quarter Horse, Atlas.

Want more lumbersnacks?
Get bonus chapters, work in progress sneak peeks, access to NSFW artwork, and safe for work artwork at: www.patreon.com/kaylagrosse

You can find Kayla at
Website: www.kaylagrosse.com
Instagram: @kaylawriteslife
Facebook: Kaylaholics Facebook Group
TikTok: @kaylagrossewriter

Thank you for reading this book and for being a reader of books in general. We are so grateful to share being part of a community of readers with you, and we hope you will join us in passing our love of books on to the next generation of readers.

Did you know that reading for enjoyment is the single biggest predictor of a child's future happiness and success?

More than family circumstances, parents' educational background, or income, reading impacts a child's future academic performance, emotional well-being, communication skills, economic security, ambition, and happiness.

Studies show that kids reading for enjoyment in the US is in rapid decline:

- In 2012, 53% of 9-year-olds read almost every day. Just 10 years later, in 2022, the number had fallen to 39%.
- In 2012, 27% of 13-year-olds read for fun daily. By 2023, that number was just 14%.

Together, we can commit to **Raising Readers** and change this trend. How?

- Read to children in your life daily.
- Model reading as a fun activity.
- Reduce screen time.
- Start a family, school, or community book club.
- Visit bookstores and libraries regularly.
- Listen to audiobooks.
- Read the book before you see the movie.
- Encourage your child to read aloud to a pet or stuffed animal.
- Give books as gifts.
- Donate books to families and communities in need.

BOB1217

Books build bright futures, and **Raising Readers** is our shared responsibility.

For more information, visit **JoinRaisingReaders.com**

Sources: National Endowment for the Arts, National Assessment of Educational Progress, WorldBookDay.com, Nielsen BookData's 2023 "Understanding the Children's Book Consumer"

www.ingramcontent.com/pod-product-compliance
Lightning Source LLC
LaVergne TN
LVHW030017300626
842253LV00039B/564

* 9 7 8 1 5 3 8 7 8 3 0 0 9 *